COLD WARRIOR

Robert Tucker

Cold Warrior by Robert M. Tucker

Cold Warrior©2024, Robert M. Tucker

Wise Words Publishing

An Affiliate of Tell-Tale Publishing, LLC

Swartz Creek, MI 48473

Printed in the United States of America

PROLOGUE

1957

"Your mission is to have children," explained the balding Soviet bureaucrat with a benign condescending smile.

"Have children?"

"Yes, but they must be born in America so they will be naturalized citizens."

"How many children?"

"I would say no more than three. That's enough mouths to feed."

"How will we live? Who will pay us?"

"You will receive an annual stipend of ten thousand American dollars. But you both must find work. You must become citizens and assimilate into American society. We have picked a small town for you to live in. You will speak English. You will teach your children to speak both English and Russian."

"How will we know what to do when we get there?"

"Someone will meet you and provide you everything you need, beginning with documents that will establish your Canadian citizenship. From the time you get off the ship in Montreal, Quebec, he will guide and direct you every step of the way and will be your contact and adviser. Here are your passports. The two gentlemen who brought you here will assist you in purchasing suitable clothes and baggage and prepare you to travel. You may ask them any question."

"We are grateful for this wonderful opportunity, but why have we been selected to do this?"

"The purpose will be explained to you at the appropriate time. Suffice it to say what I am telling you is a secret you may not share with anyone else. To do so would place your mission at risk and," he gave them a warning stare to emphasize his quiet understatement, "it would mean the end of your lives. As of this moment, you will not return to your home in Yaroslavl. You are employed by the KGB."

The newly married couple shifted uncomfortably in their hard chairs.

"Don't be alarmed. You have nothing to be concerned about. You are going to lead normal lives, raise a family, but not in the Soviet Union, in America."

Vasily maneuvered the black Ford coupe into the growing line of trucks and cars waiting to cross the border from the Canadian to the American side. He gave his fedora a determined tug, then thought better of positioning the brim low above his eyes. The customs officer might consider him suspicious.

Although the officers didn't always ask to see identification, if one did, Vasily would have to show his driver's license. It was not unusual for Russians from Toronto to enter the United States, but his last name, Kerenski, might lead to further questions.

The ongoing investigation by Senator Joseph McCarthy had ignited a climate of fear that anyone could be accused of being a communist spy and could be deported, especially if he were Russian.

He glanced at his wife shifting her body in agitation.

"This is taking too long. The line is too slow. I have to pee very badly," she said in Russian. "The pressure." She rubbed her small hands over her enlarged abdomen that pushed at the seams of her blue cotton summer dress. "The baby could be born by the time we get through."

"As soon as we get across, we'll find a place for you to relieve yourself."

"We should have left last night when there weren't so many people."

"That's the point. When many are crossing, the guards are not so careful. They are pressed for time."

As they approached the kiosk and clustered brown brick buildings, the raised black and white striped barrier pole was lowered. The vehicles stopped moving forward.

"What is it? What's happening now?" Nadia's voice rasped in a tight wheeze.

"I don't know. I can't see far enough to the front. It looks like they might be changing guards." Vasily craned his head out the window. "That's it. That's what they're doing. The barrier is going up again. There, the line is moving." He centered himself. His knuckles stood out as his hands gripped the steering wheel. "We'll be across in no time."

Nadia sensed a clear warm liquid seeping down the insides of her thighs. "We have no more time. My water is coming."

"Hold it back! Hold it back!"

"I can't hold it back. I have no control."

"The baby cannot be born here. You cannot let it be born here. It has to be on the American side."

"You'll have to tell that to the baby. I have no control over what happens."

"Don't spread your legs. Keep them tight together."

"If the baby starts pushing, I have to give it room. I will be in pain. I will have to scream."

"That will surely get the attention of the guards. They will take you to a hospital over here and the child will be born a Canadian citizen. The child must be born in America, or the plans will be ruined."

"You should have listened to me. If we had crossed last night, we would not be having this problem."

"We're getting closer, just a few more cars."

"There is more water running down my legs."

"Squeeze, my darling. Squeeze."

Vasily removed his hat and looked up at the red-coated guard's sunburned face with a broad jovial grin. The straight broad brim of the policeman's brown hat grazed the roof of the car, as he leaned down to look inside at the couple.

"You going over for the day?"

"Ah - no, officer. We are going to visit for a short time with my wife's sister in Wisconsin."

"I see your wife is pregnant."

Vasily nodded. "We will be happy with either a son or a daughter."

"Are you Canadian citizens?"

"Yes, we live in Toronto."

"May I see your driver's license?"

Vasily struggled to remove his wallet from the seat of his trousers and removed his drivers license for the officer's inspection."

"Will you return in time for her to have the baby in Canada?"

"That is our plan. Our visit will be short."

The officer returned the license. "Mr. and Mrs. Kerenski, I hope you have a healthy baby." He waved them on.

Vasily resisted the urge to floor the accelerator and maintained a reasonable speed pulling away from the checkpoint. "How are you doing?"

"I can't squeeze any longer."

As they approached a billboard sign that said, "Welcome To The United States of America," her water bag broke and gushed over the passenger seat and the floor in an explosive wave.

A Michigan highway patrol officer spotted the tall disheveled man wildly waving his arms to flag him down at the side of the road,

Barely understanding Vasily's mix of Russian and broken English, the heavyset patrol officer, Henri Coopman, grasped the urgency of the situation as soon as he looked inside the car and saw the flushed, heavy-breathing wide-eyed woman wearing a European peasant headscarf. Her left hand clutched the steering wheel and her right the door handle. The soaked skirt of her drab dress clung to her protruding abdomen where she had pulled it above her thighs. Most importantly, she had shed her underpants exposing a thick bush of dark hair at the apex of her splayed sturdy legs.

"Follow me," Henri ordered Vasily. "We'll get her to a hospital. Follow me."

Vasily lunged back into the car, disengaged Nadia's tight grasp from the steering wheel, and followed the highway patrol car clearing the way with lights and sirens.

Kasia Kerenski entered the world as her mother was rushed screaming into the emergency room of a community hospital in a suburb of Port Huron.

Vasily never ceased to marvel at their good fortune. He had been plucked from the obscurity of working as a molder in a rubber auto tire factory in Yaroslavl, near Moscow, and his new bride removed from the repetitive monotony of assembling small gears and springs in an alarm clock factory.

They had been driven to Moscow in a black Government Mercedes by two clean-shaven stern-faced officials in equally black suits and ties. Little was told to them other than they had been selected for a special meeting at the Kremlin in Moscow.

At first, Vasily feared they were being arrested by secret police for some unknown reason. They had known of workers disappearing and being imprisoned in Gulags in Siberia during Stalin's reign of terror. But since Nikita Khrushchev had become Premier, Soviet life had changed. He had brought reconciliation and healing to the people oppressed by Stalin, released those imprisoned during the Great Purges and restored them to a liberalized society that encouraged and supported freedom of expression in the arts and literature, music and poetry, and in clothing fashions.

As an overture to peaceful coexistence with the United States, Khrushchev had attended the Geneva International Peace Summit in 1955 to promote a quest for arms agreement to reduce hostilities between the two countries. However, out of cold war fear and suspicion, he had rejected an Open Arms Policy proposed by the U.S. President, Dwight Eisenhower, that the United States and Soviet Union conduct surveillance overflights of each other's countries for reassurance that the other was not preparing a nuclear attack.

Vasily and Nadia had been among the mass migration of landless peasants who had left the countryside poor villages and moved to large Soviet cities to work in factories and live in one of the millions of cheap residential low-end flats that had been constructed all over the Soviet Union.

Despite the austerity of the government vehicle and their two escorts, Vasily and Nadia hoped for a beneficent reception. They were not disappointed.

CHAPTER ONE

The Innocent Years

At an early age, Kasia Kerenski discovered she was a contortionist. She had the ability to manipulate her body into positions that defied reality. She used contortion shapes and positions to express her emotions and entertained her younger brother and sister.

Her mother and father admonished her not to do her acrobatic tricks in public where the neighbors or anyone else would see her.

"People will think you're a freak and should be in the circus," they warned. "And we don't want to be noticed."

Kasia carried their burden with only a twinge of guilt because she so enjoyed what she could do with her body and her postures and positions made her younger brother and sister laugh, especially when they tried to imitate her and fell and rolled over consumed with screams and giggles.

Her human knot was a front bending skill, folding forward at the waist with the legs straight, then placing both legs behind her neck and shoulders with her knees bent. Back-bending, she touched her head to one of her feet, then all the way to her rear, while doing a handstand or lying on the floor

She executed splits in front-bending or back-bending positions. Lifting her arm to the side, she could dislocate her shoulder by passing her arm behind her head and across the top of the shoulders.

Nadia quickly discovered the difficult task of curbing Kasia's curiosity about the lakeshore town outside of their small white bungalow house on a quiet side street.

From first grade on, Kasia realized that school was the gateway to the world of information and ideas she could learn and experience.

On non-school days, Nadia became concerned when Kasia left the house to join her neighborhood friends without telling her. With her two-year-old daughter, Alexis, and three-year-old son, Eugene, in tow, Nadia would go looking for her.

Repeated attempts to extract her from playing with her friends ended in Kasia's threat to do an acrobatic stunt. Nadia noticed that no other mothers watched their children at a local park or in neighboring yards. Not wanting to draw unfavorable attention to herself, she discontinued monitoring Kasia and just asked that she be careful.

With the self-confidence of a six-year-old, Kasia's response was, "Mom, I'm always careful. I can take care of myself."

Being inconspicuous weighed more heavily on Nadia than on her husband, Vasily, who enjoyed socializing and drinking beer at a favorite pub with Russian friends with whom he worked at the factory. She insisted that she and her family not attend the Russian Orthodox church some distance from their home in favor of a local methodist chapel to which they could easily walk.

During summer months, other than bathroom breaks and lunch time, at the end of the day, her dirt-smudged daughter burst through the front door shouting, "I need food. I'm starving." She snatched an apple or banana from the fruit bowl her mother kept filled and wanted to know what was for supper besides *pelmeni*, a Russian dish of pastry dumplings filled with minced meat and wrapped in a thin, pasta-like dough slathered in butter and topped with sour cream in a soup broth. Kasia complained she would rather have hot dogs or hamburgers and French fries.

Nadia observed her rapid growth, long legs and big perfectly formed feet providing a foundation for her skinny body that became more supple and strong with each passing year.

During the evening bath for each laughing splashing child, Nadia was amazed that she and Vasily had created them. Shy Eugene had inherited his father's prominent nose, dark hair and brown eyes. Kasia and Alexis were blonde and blue-eyed like their mother.

Kasia observed from time to time how stressed her mother was caring for Eugene and Alexis and helped with the cooking of meals and cleaning pots and pans and dishes.

When Kasia noticed her brother and sister turning the pages of children's books, she had her mother check books out of the library so she could read to them. They loved and admired her for the attention she gave them. She was their playmate, their big sister.

She taught them board games and helped them learn words and how to read.

She made up games and stories with imaginary hero and monster characters they performed.

Together they watched Mr. Rogers, Sesame Street, and the Brady Bunch. The puppetry of Sesame Street especially fascinated Kasia. She avoided playing dolls with Alexis and was not amused by Eugene not allowing her to play with his GI Joe action figures. Regardless, she let him use her Etch-a-Sketch and Lite Brights.

Her skill at playing jacks was unmatched by any of her school friends.

When winter blanketed the city, She took her brother and sister sledding and showed them how to build a snowman.

Plagued by sunburns and mosquitoes, she went bike riding with her friends to the beach during hot humid summer months. Not intimidated by the vastness of Lake Michigan, they swam and soaked for hours in the cool waters.

Besides giving birth to and mothering her children, Nadia had no idea what their future might hold. Other than raising and protecting her eldest daughter, she and Vasily had been told a special future was promised for her. Their handler from Toronto had stopped contacting them after their first year in Racine. Along with thousands of other Eastern European emigres, their daily routines helped them adapt to a new culture that left them only with memories of their past life in Russia.

Vasily worked on an assembly line at the Modine Manufacturing Plant. Nadia managed their home life, shopping at the corner neighborhood grocery store or the Kohl's supermarket, cooking, cleaning, and doing laundry.

As a teenager, Kasia's shyness and social awkwardness distanced her from boys and their hot rods until her best friend, Vicki Smollet, convinced her to join the Horlick High School cheerleader squad.

The dedicated demanding team activity used dance and acrobatic stunts combined with shouted slogans to entertain the student and adult spectators at sporting events and to encourage louder and more enthusiastic cheering. Cheerleading gratified her by giving her an outlet for performing her acrobatic skills to the thunderous drum rhythms and inspiring brass and woodwinds of the school band.

Team dancing, stunts, and pyramid-building gave her a sense of confidence, acceptance and belonging with her scarlet and gray uniformed friends that extended beyond the classroom and football field. She did not think of herself as a Russian, but as an American Girl.

She liked dancing and would go with a few girlfriends to the Ivanhoe and the Nitty Gritty dance clubs located downtown where loud rock-n-roll music and gyrating twisting bodies limited conversation.

During the final semester of her senior year, she received a letter informing her she had been awarded a full ride scholarship to the University of California, Los Angeles. A personal check for ten thousand dollars to cover travel and initial living expenses was enclosed with the letter.

Her mother and father took the announcement as the event that would begin their daughter's special future. In the beginning, Kasia was unsure whether she wanted to live so far away from her family until she perused a curriculum catalog and discovered she could major in dance and theater. The future suddenly seemed like a fun adventure.

CHAPTER TWO

1978 - A Fixed Point

Kasia Kerenski focused on a single point in space several feet away on the rehearsal stage and quickly arranged her body in a relaxed static pose that she held unmoving for five minutes. She then established a second fixed point to create an invisible construction block, which established her mime wall. She made a stylized movement, keeping the imagined two points the same distance from each other.

As she changed her posture, she synchronized her moves to create the illusion she was dealing with an imaginary external force of climbing a nonexistent rope. After one minute, she descended the imagined rope, pretended to engage in deep thought, then discovered three imaginary balls which she picked up from the ground and pretended to juggle while staggering about the stage. As a wide smile of success spread across her blank white face, she mimed losing control of the balls and her expression changed to one of grief. She mimed dismal sadness and shed tears of frustration.

She next pulled an imaginary yoyo from her imaginary pocket, inserted her right index finger in the loop and manipulated the yoyo up and down on its invisible string as she strolled about with a self-satisfied expression on her face, humorously canting her head from side to side until suddenly the yoyo stopped on a down-stroke and remained at the end of the string.

Despite her efforts, the yoyo refused to come back home. Finally, with a look of frustration, Kasia grabbed the yoyo and rewound the string. She fed the string out from the spindle allowing the yoyo to descend. Again, it refused to climb back up the string to her hand.

Her expression changed to rage. She jerked the loop off her finger, shook her finger in disapproval at the yoyo lying on the ground, then gave it a kick that sent it several feet into the air according to the trajectory her black-rimmed eyes followed. She swiped her palms together and her blackened lips curled in a deprecating grin that she had rid herself of the nuisance.

She turned and bowed to her instructor and audience of classmates who applauded her performance.

"Well done," said her dance and mime professor, "Well, done."

Kasia nodded in appreciation, then suddenly mimed clutching a painful lower back and limped off the stage and down the side steps to the audience seats.

"Next up," called out the slender middle-aged woman with dark hair pulled back on her head in a neat taut bun.

Kasia transferred her purse and small backpack to the floor as she lightly lowered herself to her seat in the front row and watched the next performer.

Her thoughts drifted slightly from impending final exams, including her dance and mime performance classes, to an encounter with a strange man who had introduced himself as Giorgio in the Hollywood bar where she waitressed part-time. His manner had been friendly. He had ordered a beer on tap and helped himself to the free peanuts and pretzels in a small bowl on the table. She noticed he spoke with a slight accent familiar to her from hearing her parents speak Russian when she was a child. She had become fluent in spoken Russian, but could read in only a rudimentary fashion from the few books provided by her mother and father. She had later taken three years in college to fulfill her language requirement.

"We need to talk, Kasia Kerenski." He spoke in Russian, catching her up short. She responded in English.

"How do you know my name?"

He reverted to English. "I know your mother and father, Nadia and Vasily."

"From where? Are you a friend or relative?"

"A friend. They've told me all about you. I recently saw you in a stage performance at UCLA. Royce Hall. You know you're a very good actress."

"My parents never told me about you."

"I'm taking this opportunity to introduce myself and to offer you an invitation." He graciously handed her his business card.

She read it carefully, then stared at him. "Why does an owner of a Beverly Hills beauty salon have anything to do with my parents and with me?"

"Do you know who gave you your scholarship?"

"My scholarship? You?"

"Not me personally, but I do business with the company that funded it. I sent the check to your parents."

At the beginning of her high school senior year, Kasia had received a letter and scholarship to UCLA from an anonymous benefactor. She asked her ballet teacher, Antonia Mazarek, if she had some part in it. She said she had not.

Antonia had been a ballerina who escaped from Czechoslovakia just ahead of the Soviet occupation to put down the Prague Spring. When reformist Slovak Alexander Dubček came to power in 1968, he had governed a period of political liberalization in Czechoslovakia that continued until the Soviet Union and members of the Warsaw Pact invaded the country to end the reforms.

As the Soviets sent in thousands of troops and tanks, Antonia joined the large wave of immigrants escaping the occupation. She had come to America to live with relatives in a Czech community in Racine, Wisconsin.

Kasia respected the small lithe red-headed woman more than any other adult in her young life. She remembered Antonia's parting comment when she left home to go to college in California.

"We come into the world without knowledge and are unprepared for what we will encounter - the arrangements that have been made for us without our consent. We are still forced to deal with them."

Amid tearful goodbyes exchanged with her parents and brother and sister, Kasia had boarded a train to Chicago, then had traveled on a United Airlines jet (her first airplane trip) to Los Angeles, California.

Her unknown benefactor had provided her with expense money, some of which she used to stay in a hotel near the UCLA campus her first night. The next morning, she went directly to the registration office to enroll in her classes and be assigned a room in the women's dorm.

Majoring in dance and theater arts, she had lived in the dorm for her freshman and sophomore years, then shared an apartment with two other students, a pre-med major from San Diego and a business major from Fresno until a year ago when she moved in with a young musician, Herb Wilcox, who accompanied her during her street mime performances.

Kasia wished she could make Giorgio Mykola disappear as easily as an invisible object during a mime performance. By interjecting himself into her life, he had become an undesirable fixed point, an external force that was not imaginary.

"This is getting to be very strange," she said to Giorgio.

"Your benefactor can be helpful to your career, as well. We have much in common, my dear Kasia."

She stiffened and shot him a caustic look. "I don't have to listen to any more of this. I have tables to wait on."

"But I have aroused your curiosity."

"No. you're a stranger who has been suspiciously snooping in my life. I don't trust strangers, especially bald middle-aged men."

Giorgio chuckled. "You think it is incongruous to shave my head bald and operate a hair salon. My head is my trademark."

"I've had attempts to hit on me, but this is the worst."

"I'm not hitting on you. We have important business to discuss."

"I have no business with you except to bring this beer. That will be three-fifty. Here's your check." She tore a short form invoice from her tablet and dropped it on the table. "I'll be your cashier when you're ready." She turned and quickly walked away to a far section of the bar.

Giorgio watched her with narrowed eyes. Bringing her in would be more of a challenge than he had anticipated. He wasn't accustomed to dealing with young independent minded women. He noticed she had slipped his business card into her apron pocket. He had her attention and she was curious. He drained his beer, dropped a twenty-dollar bill on the table, and left the bar.

Kasia watched him go out the front door. She reached into her apron pocket and touched the card. A chill went up her spine as a nagging thought came to her of why her mother always seemed overly cautious, not wanting her to draw attention to herself. As a young girl she had never given it much thought, believing that her mother was paranoid. Her mother had never given her any details, but she suddenly realized the danger her mother hinted at existed in a very real way. She chewed her lip and wondered how she could escape the attention of the bald creep whose card now lay crumpled in her hand.

***

Gordon Frasier had been recruited by the State Department upon publication of his doctoral dissertation on causes and future implications of the Cold War for the United States. A graduate of Yale University in the fields of political science and international economics, he had studied the history and patterns of social and economic development that locked the Soviet Union and the United States in a confrontation of suspicion and distrust.

Among Gordon's observations was that the history of Russia propagated a constant fear of attack by hostile neighbors. Russia's strategy was to try to take over its neighbor states to provide a buffer zone. He advocated that the United States had a duty to confront

Soviet aggression with "unalterable counterforce" and maintain a policy of long-term containment.

After the Korean War, the federal government increased military spending that expanded the middle class. Companies that had never been involved in the military were drawn to the Department of Defense as a profitable market, in fact, their best customer. By the mid-1950s, there were over 40,000 defense contractors working for the federal government. By the 1960s, more than half of all government expenditures went to the military. By the 1970s, the Department of Defense had more economic assets than the 75 largest corporations in America. With so many people depending directly on companies supported by the Department of Defense, the United States had established a permanent wartime economy, the military-industrial complex."

Americans prospered. They made up only 6% of the world population, but produced and consumed one-third of the world's goods and services. During the 1950s, America's Gross National Product (GNP) increased 51%. Defense spending fueled the growth. Home consumption also drove economic expansion. In the 1950s, 29 million new Americans were born. To meet the consumer demands of this increasing population, American industry expanded and mass produced new cars, clothing, and thousands of consumer items.

Frasier worked in the National Clandestine Service team. He recruited and handled agents to collect human intelligence. Supported by millions of dollars in CIA funding, he had established a Los Angeles brokerage firm, Emerson, Hudson, and Williams, as a front for detecting foreign espionage in the California military industrial complex.

In the mid-1970s, the KGB tried to secretly buy three banks in northern California to gain access to high-technology secrets. Their efforts were discovered and stopped by the CIA. The banks were in Palo Alto, Sacramento, and Oakland. These banks had made numerous loans to advanced technology companies and had many of their officers and directors as clients. The KGB used a Moscow bank to finance the acquisition, and an intermediary, an international exporter, as the front man.

Now, Gordon had unearthed another elaborate scheme that prompted him to set up a sting. In the beginning, he had no predilection that the key to discovering a mole in his own organization would be a mime artist who was a courier for the Soviet KGB.

Gordon listened carefully to the agent he had assigned to keep Giorgio Mykola under surveillance.

"Mykola has a new player. I followed him into a bar where he spent a lot of time talking to one of the waitresses. She seemed agitated by something he was telling her. Then he gave her a business card which she immediately slipped into her apron pocket."

"He might have just been trying to pick her up, but we don't want to overlook any possibilities. We need to find out everything about her. Who she is. Where she came from."

"Do you want me to make the arrangements?"

"Do the research. When we're ready, I'll make the contact. If she's one of them, I want her to come in voluntarily."

As Kasia walked across the campus, Gordon worked his way through the scattered students and closed in on her from behind. Except for his short cut hair, even though he was forty, he was in excellent physical shape and looked young enough to be taken for a graduate student or a professor dressed in jogging shorts and a tight-fitting T-shirt that emphasized his biceps and pectoral muscles.

"Hello," he smiled at her and slowed to a walk keeping pace with her stride. She took one look at him and moved away.

"Kasia, it's okay. I know you."

"I don't know you."

She moved quickly on and left the sidewalk to cross a trampled grassy terrace criss-crossed with impromptu student paths. He persisted in following her.

She stopped and faced him. "If you keep following me, I'm going to the campus police."

"That won't be necessary, Kasia. I do know you. I'm Gordon Frasier."

She ignored his extended hand. "If you're a professor, I've never taken a class from you."

"I accept the compliment, but no, I'm not a professor. This has to do with that man who came into the bar where you work and gave you his business card."

Kasia's face blanched in shock. "How do you know that?"

"We keep him under surveillance. He's a Soviet spy. That's why I have to talk to you."

"If he's a Soviet spy, who are you?"

"Let's sit over here," he motioned to a nearby bench.

She ignored the gesture. "Please leave me alone."

"The Government needs your help."

"The Government? I don't know what you're talking about."

"Please hear me out. Your mother and father are part of this."

Kasia stared hard at him. "That's exactly what he said."

"I represent the government. To be quite honest, I'm recruiting you. I'm asking you to join us. We need you to learn more about Giorgio Mykola."

Kasia's anger flamed at being trapped, caught between the two men and their unknown private political agendas. "I'm an American citizen. I don't know anything about you and you're asking me to work with a Russian spy. I just want to go on with my life and forget I met either of you."

"There's something more you should know. Your mother and father came to this country as spies."

"I don't believe any of this you're telling me."

"It's true. They were monitored over the years and never did anything against the government. They've been good citizens."

A sinister chill rippled up and down her spine. "How do you know anything about my parents?"

"They emigrated from the Soviet Union and have involved you in an international plot by virtue of being their daughter."

"I don't believe a word you're telling me, mister."

"We would like you to cooperate with us."

"You said you're from the government. Who is us? Are you the F.B.I.?"

Gordon shook his head. "The other acronym."

"The other acronym? What does that mean? I still don't believe you and I don't want any part of who you are and whatever you're doing."

"As I said, we prefer you agree to join us, but we can provide other motivating factors."

"Like what, putting me in prison?"

"No, we could deport your mother and father and place your brother and sister in separate foster homes."

Terrified, Kasia turned on her heel and rushed to join a crowd of students.

Frasier looked after her for a moment, then jogged away in the opposite direction.

For two days, Kasia resisted taking the bus from the campus along the expensive homes and condos lining Wilshire Boulevard to Rodeo Drive. She didn't feel comfortable in that area of ostentatious wealth. She had grown up living in a small Midwestern town populated by conservative, hard working middle-class men and women. She despised herself for succumbing to the innuendo of the two men who had forced themselves into her life for similar, but different reasons. Out of her love and concern for her parents and brother and sister, she had decided to investigate further what was being done to them and to her.

She stepped off the bus and looked again at the business card that had invaded her life and would not go away. She walked to the salon located three blocks up the slight incline of Rodeo Drive. His name on the signage confirmed her fear that he was who he said he was. Peering in the large front display window, she walked past once slowly and continued to the next corner.

Giorgio noticed her and excused himself from cutting a client's hair. He dashed out the door and saw her looking back at him from the corner. He waved and encouraged her to come inside.

CHAPTER THREE

A Reluctant Spy

Kasia created a story about herself to tell Giorgio and dispel any suspicions he might have as to her loyalty, which was not to the KGB or the CIA. Her loyalty was to her family. She was looking for a way to extract herself from her entrapment but had to first understand what they were doing and how they were doing it.

In the seclusion of Giorgio's office behind a closed door, she explained that she remembered comments made by her father about her Russian heritage while she was growing up, but she never understood their context until Giorgio had approached her. She admitted that since she had been raised in an American culture, she didn't have as much of an appreciation for her ethnic heritage but honored what her parents had done for their country.

"My father and mother often reminded me that, although we were Americans, we were Russians first and foremost. You see, all my life for as far back as I can remember, they told me I was destined for a great mission in life that would be revealed to me at an appropriate time. I had no idea what they were talking about and wouldn't have understood it even if they explained. Obviously, that time has arrived. You would think that such a preoccupation would have unduly influenced my childhood years. I didn't really think much about it."

Giorgio lit a cigarette, then deftly offered it to her for a drag. She shook her head. "No thank you. I don't smoke."

Kasia watched his piercing blue eyes cowled by bushy black brows converging over the bridge of his straight nose. Gunmetal blue whiskers were of such an intensity that, even though she might have witnessed the act, she would have questioned that he had shaved that morning.

He flashed strong white teeth. "Please continue."

"I became interested in dance and Russian music at an early age. My ballet teacher was and still is a wonderful friend. We exchange letters. She introduced me to the great Russian composers and their works. I knew very little about Russian history until I took a course in college and studied the language."

"Your childhood intrigues me, especially considering who you have become. Someday, when we have a little more time to spend together, I will tell you about mine, which is also fascinating."

"I'm sure it is."

He grinned. "I have an assignment for you."

She watched him intently.

"An engineer, an employee of a major defense plant here in Los Angeles has approached us with an offer to sell electronics designs of new missiles being developed under a defense contract. You will be a courier on a microfilm pickup made by one of our agents. We've been promised nine more after the first, so the transfers will be made at pre-selected sites where you present your street mime performances. He will drop the microfilm into your hat, as if depositing money."

"How will I know him?"

"You have no need to know his name or the source."

Kasia hesitated a moment, then nodded.

"Good. A man we will call Janot will come to the bar where you work, The Green Machine. He will act drunk and obnoxious to you, placing his hands on your lovely ass, that sort of thing. Just be friendly. You will pass him the microfilm along with his change."

"How long is this arrangement?"

"Until Janot advises you otherwise. Our source has promised the deliveries at a very high price. If all goes well, we will continue the relationship. Part of the agreement is that we smuggle him and his wife out of the country into South America where, he says, he will continue to work for us."

"He must be bitter about something."

"Yes, very." Giorgio lifted his glass of vodka from the desktop. The liquid warmth filled his belly. "His disillusionment with the U.S. Government is our opportunity. The company stole several of his patents. He stands to profit by working with us."

"Where and when shall I expect the first drop?"

"The drop will be made in a taped rolled dollar bill. Before we leave each other today, I will give you more operating expenses. I know how lean street life can be. I have been there myself in Moscow. Perhaps someday, you will visit there."

His spacious grin twitched slightly with affected self-consciousness.

Irritability pricked her at this charade. She sipped nervously from her glass of water. She determined she would never drink alcohol at any of their meetings. That she maintain a clear head was critical to never making the wrong kind of statement that would arouse suspicion.

Since she had been approached by the two men, Giorgio and Gordon Frasier, anxiety attacks had plagued her when she was least prepared to handle them, on the street, riding the bus, during a meal, waiting on tables, lying in bed awake at 3:00 a.m. in a cold sweat, unable to breathe fearing her heart would stop.

Kasia did not fully comprehend the implications of being used in the KGB legal resident strategy to plant her as a spy in the United States. Working independently of the Soviet diplomatic and trade missions, if discovered, she would not be protected by diplomatic immunity. She had to ensure the KGB did not realize how or when she would be forced to cross over and work for the U.S. State Department, the CIA.

She was determined to find a way to escape them, though there seemed to be no way out for her.

She must be a chameleon. To survive, she had to steep her life in pretense and pretending. She felt a weakening inside, an emotional cancer rotting the reality of who she thought she was.

Entertaining an audience gave her great satisfaction. After a performance, she could resume being herself. Now, the self she had wanted to become as an adult was shattered. She had hoped to try acting in live theater for a few years, then go into teaching young people at the high school or college level.

As a loving and caring young woman, marriage and children had been part of her plans. She wanted her children to experience what she had.

She reviled what her handlers on both sides were forcing her to do as a political victim.

Kasia left the salon and rode the bus west on Wilshire Boulevard to Westwood adjoining the UCLA campus. What she hoped had been imaginary had become real. She did not know what she should do next, where to turn.

Two days later, she received a phone call at her apartment. She did not recognize the hard male voice that gave her curt instructions. There was no greeting, the spoken message, and no conclusion but the line going dead.

Taking only her purse, she left the apartment and walked to the side street in Westwood Village where she saw the black Mercedes with dark tinted windows at the location the voice had described. She looked about to see if someone was following her, then approached the vehicle with trepidation, not knowing what to expect.

The passenger back door slowly opened, pushed by an unseen occupant. She stopped. The voice she had heard on the phone now spoke to her from the darkness of the interior.

"Get in and close the door."

She risked only a glimpse at the man's threatening face. He wore a black suit. He spoke to the driver. "Go." He did not look at her again.

The vehicle took her to the Los Angeles financial district and entered an underground parking garage. When the car stopped, another agent opened the door and instructed her, "Come with me."

She got out of the car and followed him. He was younger than the first man and also wore a black suit. He did not speak to her but took her in an elevator to the fourteenth floor of the office building. They left the elevator and walked along a deserted dark carpeted hallway to an unmarked door. The escort motioned for her to enter. A few moments later, she sat facing Gordon Frasier across his large wooden desk. He did not rise to greet her and at first, said nothing, only watched her. His gaze intimidated her, but she quietly vowed not to show her nervousness.

Finally, she broke the silence. "Why am I here? Where am I?"

"We will bring you here from time to time to question you."

"I'm not doing this willingly."

"I know and we appreciate your sacrifice for your country."

"I don't feel patriotic, Mr. Frasier, if that's your real name."

"Works for me. So how did your meeting with Giorgio go?"

"You must follow me around."

"I don't, but there are others who do."

"All the time?"

"You are under surveillance."

"How creepy. Do you have hidden cameras in my apartment so you can watch me take showers and use the toilet and have sex with my boyfriend?"

"That's proprietary information."

"But you do things like that."

"We use surveillance technology."

"All right, Mister Frasier, I'm working with you only because I'm being forced to. But if I hear one thing happens to my family, it's all over."

"I promise that as long as you cooperate with us, nothing will happen to them."

"I don't believe you. I don't trust people like you."

"We aren't the bad guys."

"But you do the same things."

"We protect American interests and American lives. So, what did Giorgio tell you? Did he ask you to do anything?"

"He knows that in addition to being a student, I perform as a street mime and work in a bar. But I'm sure you know all that too."

"Yes, and by the way, that musician you live with, your boyfriend – Herb Wilcox."

"I figured you'd know about him. What about him? He's a good guy."

"I'm sure he is. Just don't tell him what you are doing, about any of this."

"If I did, you'd have to kill him. Is that it?"

"You're being overly dramatic."

"He won't know. He's a nice person. I wouldn't pull him into this cesspool."

"I know this situation makes you bitter, but you don't have a choice."

"How more and more I'm becoming aware of that."

"What did Giorgio tell you or ask you to do?"

"Take a drop from somebody during a street performance. I guess you call it that, a drop."

"You're a courier. That's your role. What comes next?"

"I'll pass whatever this dropped thing is to someone called Janot when I'm working at The Green Machine."

"The item is microfilm. The person making the drop is one of ours."

"One of yours? What do you mean?"

"For the time being, that's all you need to know."

"Will I be in some kind of danger doing this?"

"Like I said, you'll be covered."

"Is that it? Will I be asked to do anything more?"

"Yes, you are a key figure in something more. That's all I can tell you at this time."

"That makes me feel very uncomfortable."

"This is not a social arrangement. We aren't friends."

"That must make us enemies."

"Save your sarcasm. We're associates. Think of it that way."

"Associates? You make this sound like some sort of business transaction."

"A good analogy. We're in business together."

"A dirty business."

"Yes, a dirty business."

"Are we finished? I need to go home and study for finals."

"We're done. Thank you, Kasia. I look forward to working with you."

"I can't say the same."

"By the way, don't try to come here. We'll contact you when I want to talk to you."

"That's what I'm afraid of."

CHAPTER FOUR

A Dirty Business

At 3:00 pm, Gordon Frasier left the mid-Wilshire investment brokerage office of Emerson, Hudson, and Williams. He was late for the meeting. To avoid the afternoon traffic, he rushed his Bentley south along residential streets through Beverly Hills and Culver City to Venice. He saw Kasia waiting at the designated corner and pulled over.

She opened the passenger door. "Shall I get in the back?"

"No, up front."

When she was belted in, he pulled quickly away from the curb. "I'm going to tell you about Inca."

"Inca?"

"Inca is a name we've given to a mole. That's someone working for the other side in our organization. The agency doesn't tolerate a hidden enemy. But until I discover him, he has the advantage. We don't like being caught in the middle."

"That's how I feel."

"How's life with the band?"

"Since I never brought them up, I guess you know everything about them. I don't care for it, but I earn a living. What does Emerson, Hudson, and Williams do?"

"Import export – international trading company. Facilitates getting in and out of countries overseas."

"Not that I care. I'm not in this for a career, Mister Frasier. I'm looking for my way out at the first opportunity."

"You can drop the mister. Just call me Gordon."

"Okay, Gordon."

"Tri Con Pictures is a motion picture company. Don't question the logic behind what I'm going to tell you. Just go with it."

"Go with what?"

"We know that one of their movie directors, Michael Sloan, is getting ready to shoot a film that has a street mime as the lead character. I want you to interest Giorgio in the idea of you being in that film."

"What are you talking about? There's no way I'm getting into the movies. Sure, I can act, but I'm about to graduate. I don't have an agent and I don't have career plans. What does Giorgio have to do with the movies anyway?"

"Giorgio is a friend of Kurt Heinrich, the studio chief at Tri Con Pictures. Giorgio does his wife's hair every week. Tell Giorgio to think of the expanded options to gain information you would have that circulating in the film community could provide. Does he know you can act?"

"He saw me in a theater production and said he was impressed. I guess he knows I can act, at least on the stage."

"There are strings attached, but there's a reason we're talking about this. Let's go have a drink." He pulled into a hotel parking lot near Marina del Rey. "You're a pawn, like me, like all of us. A little higher up, some have more power than others, that's all. But eventually even they are brought down. So you're looking for a way out. Get rid of that notion. There isn't any way out. You don't realize it now, but you're in too deep. You know too much, and you're profiled as being emotional and idealistic, unstable. If the agency let you go, they couldn't trust you."

Kasia shivered involuntarily, but squarely faced him on the seat to cover her unease. "Is that a threat?"

"A warning."

"And we're supposed to be going for a friendly drink."

"This is not friendly. It's a business meeting. And we are not friends. We will never be friends."

They entered the hotel cocktail lounge and sat at a secluded corner booth, with a view of the marina. It was still early and only a few patrons hunched over at the bar. Kasia ordered a glass of Chablis and Frasier a Scotch on ice.

"Tell me about Herb Wilcox." Frasier studied her profile.

"You already know he's my boyfriend. He plays in the band. He cares about me."

"And you?"

"I can't say I'm in love with him. We're attracted to each other. We're good friends."

"You must be more than that. You're sleeping with him."

"What does that have to do with any of this?"

"There's someone else in that rock band you need to know about."

"Someone else?"

"Stephen Stull. We know he traffics and, from time to time, a KGB agent uses him to buy drugs. Stull knows nothing about it."

"Stephen Stull?"

He nodded. "That nightclub where you work, The Green Machine, is a convenient transfer point used by the KGB. The owner's not involved, but you are.

"Stull is a slimy creep. I don't trust him."

"It takes all kinds in this business. Stull doesn't know who we are and he never will. Being involved in illegal activity is a big turn-on for him. He was a local find for the KGB. We keep an eye on him, but we leave him alone. He's highly motivated for the wrong reasons. He spent half his teenage years in Camarillo State Hospital."

"What did he do?"

"Murdered his mother."

Kasia stared at him. "I really don't want him to know about me. I need to change the crowd I hang around with. I always thought Stull was a psycho even without dope. How did he get out?"

"When Ronald Reagan was governor, he shut down the mental hospitals and let loose all the crazies. But don't worry about Stull. We watch him closely. Back on topic.   Because we suspect Giorgio has ties to Kurt Heinrich at Tri Con Pictures, that link might take us into the larger entity, the Tri Con Corporation. We don't have any evidence. If we can plant you directly inside Tri Con, I'd have one more source of intel. Right now, I don't have anyone who can move openly in Tri Con Corporate circles. I want you to press Giorgio for an introduction to Kurt Heinrich. He likes to wheel and deal, be a man of influence. It makes him feel important."

"I'll have to ask him next week. When's the drop going to be made?"

"Five the first week, three the second week, and two the third." Frasier suddenly noticed a tiny red light flashing on the luminous dial of his digital watch. "Hotline. Have to run." He opened his wallet and dropped a twenty-dollar bill on the table. "You get back okay?"

"I can manage."

With a brief wave, he hurried out of the lounge to his car and took the call on his radio phone. "Security Bank."

"Johnson. We're clear. You'd better talk to Klein fast. Rockwell doesn't know about our operation. Security and management suspect Charley and they've contacted the F.B.I."

"I don't want the Feds in on it. They'll screw up the operation. I'll call Klein. He'll have to stage his agents so they only appear to be investigating. They can't make an arrest. It'll blow the whole mission. Call Charley and tell him to back off one day on the drop schedule. We need to buy some time. He can deal directly with his contact. I'll call you in an hour." He disconnected, then immediately dialed Captain Lambert Klein at the Los Angeles Quarter of the Federal Bureau of Investigation.

CHAPTER FIVE

Buskers

Michael Sloan had never quite grown accustomed to reading about the bizarre break-ins and robberies and sudden violent murders that lately had frequented the pages of the Los Angeles Times. He had reached a point in his life where he wanted to shut out the negative and downside of society. He no longer wanted to allow those events and sordid impressions to edge into his thoughts and contaminate his sense of growth and achievement and the recent phenomenal success in his career. So he had stopped reading the paper and now avoided listening to the news broadcasts on radio and television.

Occasionally, his stray glance was unable to miss scanning a section of the Times haphazardly left open by his girlfriend on the dining room table at breakfast. Feeling guilty at his lack of resolution, he would irresistibly be drawn to read the column under the provocative photograph or headline. Usually he would cut his perusal short and move quickly away as if to escape its reality, but on this occasion he continued to read in order to satisfy an inner impulse that he had too long denied, an acknowledgement of the strange and macabre in life.

During the past year, audiences had flocked in droves to horror movies, two of them his own, to fill their psyches with terror, blood, and gore of a make-believe kind. As he read on about the incident, he noted to himself how close to make-believe the actual murder of the woman seemed to be.

Ten minutes later, his maroon Mercedes slipped along the traffic stream of Sunset Boulevard, sharing it with other upscale cars, Jaguars, Cadillacs, and an occasional Rolls Royce. In that part of the city, conventional American made cars and small and foreign domestic models containing students zipping along to and from the local UCLA campus were outnumbered and seemed oddly out of place.

Moving past the garden setting of the university, his *alma mater*, he could see the cluster of buildings that comprised the departments of theater arts, film, and television where he had invested his undergraduate and graduate student years working toward his Bachelor's and Master of Fine Arts Degrees.

He had always imagined that should he achieve financial independence, he would move up the coast to Santa Barbara and buy an old mansion or a ranch in the foothills. Instead, he had opted to remain close to the Hollywood motion picture and television community for their all-important business contacts.

His home was an eight-million-dollar Spanish colonial on two landscaped acres in Brentwood. The house was more than he needed as a bachelor, but his ambition was to someday fill it with a family.

During his initial research and observation of sidewalk mimes, he had frequented the mall of the Los Angeles Music Center where several simultaneous acts were under way throughout any given weekend. The most impressive mimes appealed to both children and adults and usually played an instrument or had live musical accompaniment, guitar, banjo, fiddle, lute, tambourine, and drum.

Kurt Heinrich, Michael's executive producer who had come as a conditional part of the German investment package for his next three films, had told Michael of an attractive young woman whose mime act appeared each weekend at the Los Angeles County Art Museum. He had suggested that Michael go and see her, that she looked the part for the female lead in his next film and that he wanted Michael to "discover" her. Michael wondered why Heinrich had such a special interest in this particular mime performer.

At the encouragement of a friend, Giorgio Mykola, Heinrich explained he had spoken with her and was quite impressed. He had taken two of her business cards and given one to Michael, who had misplaced it. He hadn't really looked at the name on the card in a way that registered and now he could not remember it. He figured that if he became interested, he would just ask her.

Kurt Heinrich was a strange bird anyway, thought Michael. He continually insisted on the one hand that he didn't want to interfere with creative decisions for the film, but on the other that he was looking out for the investors' interest. And now, here he was telling Michael to consider casting an unknown in a lead role. Both Michael and Heinrich wanted to use an unknown and "create a new star," as Heinrich said.

Tri Con Pictures was financially backed by one large and three small private corporations in Berlin, Germany that fronted the Moscow Bank that had created the Tri Con Corporation. Michael's business manager had informed him that these companies were all affiliated with the multi-national American conglomerate the Tri Con Corporation. He did not mention the Moscow Bank, because they were invisible in the financial chain. The arrangement allowed Tri Con to launder money through the German companies and invest heavily in American companies handling defense programs. Tri Con Financing originated with the Bank in Moscow and was channeled through the International Bank of The Americas with branches in Europe, New York, and Los Angeles. As long as Tri Con funded his projects, Michael didn't know or care one way or the other from where the money was coming.

He had recently read how the corporation was investing in the new cable television market. According to the trades, Tri Con was buying up major shares in other film, publishing, and network television markets, as well.

Michael had only briefly met Helmut Bachmann, President and Chairman of The Board of the Tri Con Corporation. He also sat on the board as president of Tri Con Pictures. One of the trade articles had noted that Bachmann spent more time in the air conducting business from his fleet of private Lear jets than he did on the ground.

Michael had undergone far too many financial struggles getting his early films made to fault either Heinrich or Bachmann. In the face of their apparent generosity, he was willing to make a few creative concessions to their fiscal demands.

He cut southward from Sunset Boulevard down Rodeo Drive to Wilshire Boulevard, then cruised along its walled canyon of corporate high-rise buildings and exclusive shops, department stores and restaurants until he reached La Brea.

Leaving his car on a side street, he strolled through the green park area adjoining the La Brea tar pits where centuries old fossils were being discovered daily on the excavation site. Full life-size sculptures of mastodons and prehistoric dinosaurs appeared to have been instantly frozen in time and seemed drastically out of sync standing at the center of a metropolitan civilization.

Crowds of tourists roamed about the square, including many parents with their gawking children in tow, coming and going from the squat massive graystone county art museum. To his immediate satisfaction, Michael spotted three different performers where curious onlookers had encircled them to create an audience.

The acts and routines projected images that, set among a three-dimensional backdrop of modern architecture, struck Michael as bizarre and surreal, as if the mimes had been transplanted in time from the ghosts of Renaissance clowns and court jesters. Their white faces and eyes delineated with black pencil gave them the inhuman aspect of disembodied spirits imitating and mimicking life. Their performance left him feeling wary and uncomfortable about the unknown men and women behind the masks and, consequently, about himself.

In a way, they were modern cultural descendants of historical *buskers*, street performers, street musicians, minstrels, and troubadours. In the research for his film, Michael had learned that street performance dated back to antiquity, and occurred in all countries of the world.

Performances were about anything that people thought entertaining. Performers did acrobatics, animal tricks, balloon twisting, card tricks, caricatures, clowning, comedy, contortions and escapes.

They danced, sang, ate and breathed fire, told fortunes, juggled, created magic illusions, enacted mime and mime variations where the artist performed as a living statue. Puppeteers and storytellers recited poetry or prose as bards. Sketching and painting, street theatre, sword swallowing, and flea circuses were common.

The most intriguing performer, a young graceful blonde woman responding with interpretive dance to the accompaniment of a lute and tambourine, drew him across the courtyard near the museum entrance. He edged in among the crowd and, as the mime swung past with her precise disciplined movement, he realized this must be the person Heinrich had described with such Prussian enthusiasm.

He watched her closely through the entire performance and afterwards, waited for an opportunity to approach her, allowing her time and space to relate more intimately with the small children who gathered around her.

She differed from the other mimes he had seen. The genuine warmth of her personality and saucy aristocratic beauty sparkled through the anonymity of her whiteface mask and charged him with energy.

When the children had finally cleared and she was seated on a canvas backed deck chair near her props and accompanist, Michael walked over to her. He smiled and executed a mock bow.

"Excuse me, my name's Michael Sloan."

"Yes, Michael Sloan?" She struck a traditional mimetic pose and wide smile accentuated by the black makeup at the borders of her mouth, like a department store mannequin.

"Unless you watch horror movies, you probably don't know who I am."

She covered her eyes and peered through her fingers in mock horror. "Are you one of the evil monsters?" she croaked.

"I certainly hope not. I'm just the person who puts them up there on the screen. I write, produce and direct films."

The woman suddenly leaped up and walked around him, cranking an imaginary old fashion motion picture camera.

"Something like that," he said, craning his neck to follow her with his eyes. "Ah, listen, I guess I'm a little short on sign language. My producer sent me over here. He saw you before and was impressed. You might remember him. He said he spoke with you, Kurt Heinrich. If you're between acts, could we talk for a few minutes?"

The mime cocked her head and consulted an imaginary watch.

"I'm doing research for a film about street mimes," said Michael. "Could you tell me your name?" He suddenly grew aware of the man who provided her background music regarding him with suspicion and more than a casual warning in his penetrating stare.

"Kasia," she said. "Kasia Kerenski."

"Well, Kasia, if you wouldn't mind stepping out from behind your mask for a few minutes, I'd like to talk to you."

Although she desperately wanted to nod 'yes', she shook her head. Giorgio had told her that Michael would likely be there that morning and she knew she could not stall him for too long. There was a particular sequence of events to be played out. This was merely act one, scene one.

She fought down the impulse to say 'yes'. She resented that the choice was not hers, not her 'no', but the 'no' and disapproving gaze of her boyfriend. She hated his demeanor. In passing, she did say 'yes' and proceeded to introduce Herb Wilcox.

He resented that the accompanist maneuvered to create a physical barrier between Kasia and himself. His slender hand strangled the neck of his lute.

The two men barely acknowledged each other with a curt mutual nod, conveying tension and antagonism.

Michael looked over at Kasia. "I'd like to get acquainted when you're finished here today. May I take you to dinner?"

Kasia suddenly felt her hand grasped by the musician, leaving her no alternative but to say, "We're together."

"Sorry, I understand. It's not social. It's business." Michael backed off slightly to study his adversary. "Do you have a card?"

She reached into a side pack and handed him a business card.

"Okay," he said. "I'll be in touch." Glancing up from the card, he abruptly turned and walked away, leaving them to their emotional conflict his appearance and intervention had caused. He stopped, quickly scrawled his own home telephone number on the back of an old receipt he scrounged from his pocket, then returned to them.

"Here's my phone number."

She reflexively tucked it away in her apron pocket.

"I liked your performance," he said. "You're good. You're real good."

She curtsied and although her smile thanked him, her silence implied that he should move on, as her boyfriend's elbow poked her with a sharp nudge.

Michael raised his hand in a slight farewell gesture. He walked away, allowing her a chance to breathe, or so he thought, until the angry voice of Herb Wilcox carried to him.

Toward evening, the wind kicked up a chill prompting Kasia and Herb to pack their chairs and props in his van. Listening to the wistful rush of homebound traffic, she shivered at the hollow emptiness of the deserted square. The sun which had spotlighted her through the afternoon dropped beyond the tall buildings.

Herb slammed the van's sliding panel door with a vehemence that caused her to wince. He studiously ignored looking into her eyes. He had said nothing since his outburst following Michael Sloan's departure that morning. Finally, she said, "You can't hold it against me that he approached me out of nowhere like that."

"I don't hold it against you, but I'm not so sure he came out of nowhere. I suspect not. And you are thinking about him."

"Of course I am. Maybe there's a real opportunity for a change."

"Yeah, great opportunity for you. Not that way. I guess if you move on and are successful, I'll be happy for you. Doesn't do much for me."

Herb then broke his silent resolution not to ask the burning question that would reveal his suspicion and envy. "Do you know him from somewhere? I got the feeling you did."

"Sure, I party with movie producers and directors. You know that," she retorted. "That's why I've been in so many box office hits lately."

Herb frowned at her sarcasm. "I mean it's strange as hell that he suddenly showed up here today, like somebody had told him about you."

"Somebody obviously did. You heard him. That producer from Tri Con Pictures was here last weekend. Kurt Heinrich. He talked to me. You didn't get upset then."

"You didn't tell me that. I thought he was just a spectator, nobody special."

"All kinds of people come off the street. Maybe I just didn't believe him. This is California, the land of fruits and nuts."

"But you do believe him now."

Kasia shrugged.

"Yeah, I can tell you do now, and you're thinkin' about his big house and all that bread he's makin', right?"

"From the sound of it, you're thinking about him more than I am."

"I mean he really is the same guy who made those big bucks horror flicks, right?"

"You're really concerned about this, aren't you?"

"You're damn right. I thought we were together."

"Why are you being so uptight?"

"Jesus!" Herb continued to drive stiff with silence, then belligerently rasped, "You could have gone with him. Right then you could have gone."

"Will you stop it," she bristled, then settled back with an emotional flurry that consumed her, thrusting a hot sadness behind her intense blue eyes.

All of a sudden too many changes were assaulting her. She was forced to play at being too many characters at the same time. The pressure was unbearable. *"Why now,"* she thought. *"Why? I never used to have trouble handling the pressure."*

A roll of microfilm had been dropped into her hat during one of her acts that morning. The man was Charley MacIntosh, who was allegedly selling secrets on a major Government defense program underway at Rockwell Collins. What the KGB and Soviet engineers didn't realize was how worthless the information would be to them, since it was corrupted and outdated.

As a controller or conveyor of information in a scientific and technical espionage ring, she would provide the latest critical roll of microfilm she was holding to Janot, an agent based at the Soviet Embassy in San Francisco. This drop would be the tenth delivery in three weeks. She would pass it on that night at the bar where she hustled drinks and Herb played in the band.

Janot would carry the microfilm to a contact in East Berlin from where it would be smuggled to Moscow. In the meantime, Charley MacIntosh and his wife, Maggie, working as a double agent team for the CIA, would vanish enroute to South America with the assistance of the *Komitet gosudarstvennoy bezopasnosti, the* KGB.

Events were now moving forward at a rapid pace. Soon she would be at the center of the arrangements. She had followed Gordon Frasier's directions and had set up Kurt Heinrich through Giorgio. Frasier didn't know if Heinrich was clean, only a social contact through Heinrich's wife or else his mistress? Giorgio did both of their heads at his salon. Frasier suspected that Heinrich was part of a cell working out of a corporate group in West Berlin, but he didn't have the intel to piece anything together.

What intrigued Kasia was that, according to Frasier, Michael Sloan Productions was totally financed by Tri Con Pictures. Sloan did not put any of his money back into his own company. He invested in tax sheltered real estate, IRAs, blue chip stocks, and commercial and industrial properties. He was a successful businessman, as well as an artist.

The Tri Con Corporation was so vast that Soviet spies could be operating and recruiting within it and the fact was never discovered. Frasier also suspected that Kurt Heinrich could be associated with the KGB.

Giorgio had passed on her photo and resume to Heinrich with a letter he had drafted and signed. She wanted to question him about Heinrich, but Giorgio was too shrewd. He had a tendency to withhold and distort information, perhaps as a test, since he did not totally trust her any more than she trusted him. He didn't trust anybody, and with good reason.

"When you ask questions, then I begin to question you," he told her. "Your function is to follow orders, not to question me."

Just be observant, she told herself. *Be observant and convincing.*

"The fridge is empty," she said. "We have to pick up some groceries."

They pulled into the parking lot of a Market Basket in a depressed area adjoining the entire blocks of old motion picture studios along Santa Monica Boulevard sandwiched between a pornographic movie theater and a dark foreboding bar where always a pimp or some lethal looking character with a Doberman on a leash hung out in a pose of calculated sullenness at the entrance. The store was only two blocks from the apartment they had recently rented after Kasia's graduation. Bizarre street people frequented the local neighborhood, Kasia's mime white face makeup drew only a few stares, as she and Herb wheeled a grocery cart up and down the filthy aisles. By and large she was just thought to be a punk rocker.

Their take for the day, the meager contributions dropped in Herb's bowler hat, had been better than usual, amounting to nearly one hundred dollars.

To maintain her health and lean figure, Kasia selected and ate mostly a vegetarian diet of light foods, fruits, cheeses, grain breads, granola and yogurt, beans, and a variety of vegetables.

Herb's need to satisfy his appetite and counter his frustration at experiencing only minor successes as a musician consumed their cash with his purchases of meat, bread, rich desserts, wine, and beer.

Kasia believed he could assimilate so many carbohydrates and still remain slender because of his obsessive nervous energy and the inconsistent hours he kept whenever the band had a gig. He rarely had enough sleep and almost never slept well.

In retrospect, she believed her relationship with Herb had begun to unravel long before Michael Sloan entered her life. The timing just happened to be right, and Michael was the catalyst who strained what was left.

For the last few months, she had wondered about the abrupt changes in his personality, the suspiciousness and paranoia. He was not unkind to her and never had been during their past year living together. She was confident that he respected her, maybe even loved her in some way and that his recent antagonism rose from his sense of inadequacy. He didn't talk about his feelings. He blamed his lack of success on not fully utilizing his talent as a musician.

Michael's sudden appearance in Kasia's life became another competitive threat from Herb's point of view. To herself, Kasia secretly acknowledged and was excited at the prospect of breaking out of her web of artistic poverty and leaving Herb behind.

She had deliberately opted for a non-conventional lifestyle according to what Giorgio had ordered her to create to hide her identity. She was to assimilate into the culture of American street life and develop a relationship with someone struggling at the low end of popular music entertainment. That someone turned out to be her boyfriend, Herb Wilcox, a member of a small-time rock band, before she had been pulled into the role of a spy. They had met where Kasia worked as a cocktail waitress in a nightclub called The Green Machine.

Acting and espionage were closely linked. Since she had been forced into the role of a spy, her daily existence and the tensions with which she had to cope removed her from the common and mundane.

If she had to live the life of a spy, why not do it in relative luxury, now that it was within her grasp.

As they passed through the checkout line, the sudden fear seized her that Michael might not call. She worried that she might have scared him off by Herb's obsessive gesture and statement she'd made that she and Herb were "together."

She wondered if the day would ever come when she could dispense with transitory relationships and be "real" to another person. Even so, she still struggled with guilt at how quickly she must turn about. Her instincts were those of a survivor. She was a creature of the streets. Her code name, *Sidewalk*, also the title of Michael Sloan's film, given to her by Gordon Frasier, had been appropriately rendered.

Wheeling the cart outside to the van, she caught Herb's accusing stare, as though he read her thoughts, that her emotions were transparent. His sensitivity to her feelings was one of the qualities that had attracted her to him, at least in the beginning, that and his mellow baritone voice. He had the potential to become a recording star, but he wasn't political enough. He didn't portray the hype and flash and excessive lifestyle of a soloist or lead singer. So his career stagnated for want of being able to execute his personal ambition. He had to settle for backup in gigs with struggling rock and country & western bands in which the lead singers had less talent than his own.

She understood his bitterness and sympathized with him but did not support his stubborn insistence that he must be true to himself and to his art and not allow anything shallow and overly commercial to creep into his style. *"Maybe it's because everything I'm doing in my life right now is false,"* she thought. She felt she had compromised herself. The people who controlled her forced her to live without integrity, a character trait about Herb that she envied.

She had proposed that the whole concept of entertainment was nothing more than an act, the act of performance, just as much as any play, or mime, or film or theatrical performance. The audience wanted a singer who was dynamic, replete with passion, energy and enthusiasm.

Being low key and laid back was all right in the recording studio, which was where Herb felt most comfortable. In a night club or a stadium, a different kind of audience involvement transformed the experience from passive listening to a sweating physical chemistry. If Herb would only accept that fact and adjust his performance, he might one day step out from behind someone else's shadow.

Herb squeezed the van into one of the narrow spaces reserved for tenants along the back wall of the cracked stucco apartment building. He swore under his breath at the shattered glass that littered the faded macadam in silent random explosions. Complaining to the apartment manager did not penetrate the man's alcoholic haze enough for him to hire someone to even sweep away the shards. When counter challenged, Herb refused to do the task, preferring to risk costly damage to his tires rather than add yet another flaw to his ruffled pride.

He and Kasia each carried two bags of groceries through the urine-stained passageway and turned left up the stone aggregate stairs to the second level. Walking along the open balcony, they came to number 23. Herb balanced one of the bags against the door frame while fumbling to maneuver the correct key into the lock, then pushed his way inside.

The apartment smelled of dust and mold, an ill-lit unkept place, transient as their lives, a place they considered a temporary step to something better. They refused to acknowledge their established routines of permanency. They practiced only an occasional ineffectual pretense of housekeeping. Their unspoken agreement not to commit themselves to domestic maintenance expressed their shared feeling that to do so would be to admit failure.

While Kasia stacked and shelved canned goods and stuffed meats and produce into the refrigerator, Herb returned to the van for the remaining groceries. He waved to their Black neighbor, Dade

Thomas, backing his Ford pickup into an empty parking slot. Dade worked in construction during the day and played drums at night for their group when they had a gig.

The vibrum soles of his work boots crunched the splintered glass as he descended from the truck cab with a wave to Herb and a weary grin accentuated by a trim mustache and beautiful teeth. His shirtless sinewy body rippled with athletic grace and power. He walked over and assisted Herb with the last four sacks of groceries.

"Looks like you're puttin' on the feed bag."

"Yeah, filled the hat a few times today."

"Where'd you stake out?"

"County museum."

"You see Olivia?"

"No, we just got home ourselves."

Dade's regal features distorted in a sour grimace. "She went out on another one of those fucking casting calls today. Hell, she knows it ain't worth nothin'. It's a big rejection mill and she doesn't have the ego to handle it. I'm gettin' sick of comin' home and findin' her O-Ded. Why do I do it? Why the fuck do I keep her? I guess it's because I love the bitch."

"That's just the way you are, Dade. She's weak and you're strong. You need her kind."

"What I need is someone who's got their head straight."

Coming up the stairs along the balcony to the apartment, they heard a shriek and a Black woman's high-pitched laughter from inside.

"Dolores," said Dade, identifying her by her voice. "What's that whore doin' in there? She's a bad influence."

"On who? You?"

Dade chuckled. "You got it, baby." He followed Herb through the open door. "Hey, there she is!" Dade struck an expression of mock astonishment relating to his white girlfriend, Olivia, a pale ethereal blonde with large almond shaped eyes. She had been sharing some news with Kasia and Dolores, a prostitute who worked out of the same apartment building.   From Olivia's feverish countenance, Dade couldn't tell if she were high or if something great had happened, or both. "There she is. There's my movie star."

"Dade," she twitched with excitement. "I got a call back for the final reading. The casting director said it's a toss-up between me and one other. Can you believe it? It's finally gonna happen for me. I just know it's gonna happen. I can feel it in my bones."

"Fantastic, babe, fantastic." Dade kicked and whirled sweeping into the kitchen concluding the movement by setting the grocery bags on the counter. He absorbed Olivia's rush into his arms and lifted her off the floor. "Which one is it?"

"It's for a movie of the week that could go into a series."

"What's the part?"

"I'm a mental patient who recovers."

"Sounds dramatic. I'm glad you recover." Without releasing his hold on her, Dade grew serious. Sensing the subdued change, Olivia quickly reassured him.

"It's all right, honey. I told them I've been there myself and I know what it's really like. I can be convincing." She grinned at the others' discomfort. "Firsthand experience does count for something."

"You know how I worry about strong reminders," Dade lowered her to the floor.

"Don't be silly. That's all behind me now."

His understanding smile weakened her conviction, raised her self-doubt. In an attempt to shrug off the feeling, she moved away from him to the script lying on the kitchen table.

"That it?" he asked.

She nodded and held it out to him. He read the title aloud. "*Around The Corner*. Mmh, hey, baby, am I hollow inside or am I hollow? I gotta fill that space fast." He thumped the cords of muscle that networked his torso. "Let's feed and read. I have to give it my stamp of approval."

They all laughed as Dade herded her out the door. "See y'all later, folks."

"Good luck, Olivia," Kasia called after her.

"It better happen for her this time," Dolores chuckled grimly. "Or she take that last big snort in the sky. Acting - you and Olivia must be dumb ass crazy. Who needs all those rejections and all that fuckin' ass grief. I'll take one hundred bills for ten minutes in the sack over that any time. If you're gonna sell your body, then I say sell your body, if you can't sell your mind. At least they can't buy your soul and you never get turned down."

"You still have to deal with competition," said Kasia. "It's the same in any occupation."

"I've been meaning to talk to you about your occupation, Dolores, old girl," said Herb.

"You watch your langwidge, boy. Ain't nothin' old 'bout this girl. No sireeee." She thrust her barely concealed tits into his face. "For one hundred green ones, I'll give you a sample."

Herb grinned and shook his head. "It's not that, Dolores. I know you're the best at what you do. It's not that, at least not yet. It might come to that." His grin instantly disappeared, and he looked directly at Kasia.

Dolores licked her smooth lips and winked at Kasia.

"Will you do us a favor," said Herb, "and move your bed away from the wall we share? Whenever you bring a John in there, we can hear it all in quad sound. It was interesting at first, but through repetition, it's lost its entertainment value."

"All right, Herbie, honey pie, we don't want you to get over-educated and over-excited now, do we? I mean, baby, you're talkin' to the Ph.D. of cunt." Covering her wounded pride, Dolores sauntered out of the apartment, making her final exit with a bump and grind directed at him.

He shouted after her, "You forgot to close the door!"

"Fuck you, honey pie!"

He went to push it shut while Kasia emptied the remaining grocery bags. Returning, he said, "We have got to get out of this, living here, like this."

He had uttered the same words many times before. Her apparent lack of response and interest in what he had to say at the moment infuriated him. He popped the top on a can of Coors, sucked the spurt of foam, then with a sudden savagery hurled the can against the wall. Kasia tensed as they stared at the wet ribbons of beer streaking down the wall and permeating the room with its yeasty odor.

"But you don't give a damn, do you? You don't give a shit that you're gonna leave me to rot here."

An impulse of hate rose up in Kasia at Herb's weakness and self-pity. "Stop feeling sorry for yourself. Nothing has happened."

He slowly turned to face her. The cold rage she saw in his eyes frightened her, but she did not give any outward sign that she was intimidated. She thought of her parents and brother and sister. She did not waiver.

CHAPTER SIX

The Drop

Janot entered the bar later than the agreed time. Because of the warning that the F.B.I. suspected and was watching his source from Rockwell International, he had been almost reluctant to make the three hundred thousand cash payment. Another agent had picked up the tenth microfilm to pass along to the mime woman, as Janot called Kasia Kerenski. And now, tonight, he would receive it from her.

The complicated system of exchange was designed to confuse anyone following or suspicious of the transactions. The latest information from the first agent was that unless the KGB did not smuggle them out of the country at once, the source Charley MacIntosh, and his wife, Maggie, would have to cooperate with the F.B.I. in hopes of a reduced sentence for the conspiracy charges that would be brought against them. This news alarmed Janot, who planned to leave the country for Germany that night after taking possession of the microfilm.

On the chance that he himself was under surveillance, he had spent a considerable amount of time making it appear that he had driven to Bakersfield in California's Central Valley. An assistant had already sent Janot's baggage ahead packaged as freight on a flight to Berlin. Traveling light with only a carry-on, he could move quickly.

He touched his coat pocket, ensuring that his passport was still in place, then raised his hand to catch the attention of the blonde waitress filling a drink order next to the bar.

Balancing a tray of empty cocktail glasses and several beer bottles she collected after serving three customers at another table, Kasia maneuvered through the crowd past bodies hunched over in loud unintelligible conversations amid rising cigarette smoke that stung her eyes. Tears blurred her vision slightly, causing her to stumble into the heavyset patron seated alone in a dimly lit far corner.

"Easy there, honey," Janot's meaty hand deliberately pressed her tight ass, lingering and probing just a moment too long. Kasia's apology for her clumsiness reversed itself and spit out as a guttural expletive. Janot laughed his beery breath close to her face and she pulled away, resisting the impulse to smash her tray of glasses over his wide fat head. She thought of withholding the microfilm just to make the bastard squirm. But she had to go along with this planned charade.

Appearing to barely contain her anger, she grasped his hand as though to shove it away and transferred the tiny cylinder of microfilm she was clutching into his groping palm, which instantly closed around it. She and Janot had enacted a similar sequence with some variations nine other times during the past few months.

The disco-rock sound of the band swelled from the small raised platform serving as a stage in the close dismal club atmosphere. Kasia slapped her order pad down at the well and barked her next series of drinks to the harried bar tender, a thin anemic young man with premature hair loss that he attempted to compensate for by growing a long brown ponytail. She wiped at her tearing eyes with a clean cocktail napkin and stared across the tight composite of heads wreathed in ragged shifting smoke distortions of red and blue lights.

Her gaze came to rest on the band's lead singer, Stephen Stull, costumed in a black leather vest, leather wrist bands, skin-tight leather pants, and blue leather boots with ultra-high platform heels and soles. Shaking his skinny body in time to the rhythm, he pushed the microphone against his open mouth and whipped his long black hair like a greasy cyclone about his sallow face. Kasia didn't know whether she should believe what Gordon Frasier had told her about Stull. She felt more inclined to believe Frasier was lying. She didn't trust him.

Lynn Porat, the female vocalist, came in on the lyric dialogue of the dynamic thumping beat provided by Dade Thomas seated among his array of drums and cymbals slightly above and behind them to the left. Kasia disliked the ratty-looking redhead, not only for her shrill untrained voice, but for Lynn's projected contempt for everything and everyone, including herself.

A third member of the group, Randy Stiefel, crept in and out of the lyrics with alternate bass harmonics and light running passages in a high register on a synthesizer. Kasia admitted to being wary of Randy's sly devious manner and avoided him during breaks. She didn't trust him and was uncomfortable with his affected gay mannerisms. His gray hair was cut short, crew style, accentuating his striking effeminate features.

Out of the entire group, she felt only good about Herb, except for his stubborn lack of imagination and style, and Dade Thomas, who carried the ensemble on the strength of his talent with percussion instruments. She sometimes thought he threw them out of balance and had the misfortune of answering to Stephen Stull, who had originally formed the band known as Crystal Blue Persuasion.

Ironically, Stull's lack of ethics and morality bothered her as a manifestation of the compromises she made as a spy. She attributed his erratic behavior to incessant hits of cocaine. Everything he made went to pay for his expensive habit. He was not above cheating the other band members when the money came in. There had been two incidents when he had withheld half of Herb's and Dade's share of the above average take on high profile gigs. Since then, Herb and Dade always accompanied him at the point of collection. They would work only on a cash basis, no checks.

A sudden impulse to just disappear and escape her double agent role consumed Kasia, a dizzying sense of observing from a long distance removed from her own body, time, and place. She loathed and despised herself. She was sick of sharing their groveling rut of an existence. She wanted to erase the deadly pall of smoke, the dark claustrophobic walls pressing greenly in on the noisy drunken crowd. She wanted to leave the shabby apartment and falling exhausted and stinking of rancid smoke into a too narrow bed shared with a man she pretended to love. She wanted to dissolve the need to constantly be someone she was not and to let the essential core of her identity exist without subterfuge and fear. There was no relief and she needed relief.

She heard the clink of ice cubes and soft thud of cocktail glasses hitting the padded plastic tray which she obliviously hoisted to her shoulder. Gliding and baby-stepping to avoid stumbling over protruding knees and feet, she again waded out into the morass of chairs and tables.

Waiting for her cash, she glanced at her watch as the song ended with a roll on the cymbals. Two more hours. Her thoughts centered on Michael Sloan, his phone number now memorized and a copy secure in her wallet just in case she should forget, God help her, never. He had clearly wanted her to call him. She had studied body language long enough to read his nonverbal message. She had tuned in to him, but because of Herb, had been forced to overreact and seem to back away from the opportunity.

She would not make the same mistake. Her life was no longer a matter of sharing and friendships. It was no longer a question of choice, of street life now and something better later on. Later on had arrived. She couldn't afford to be hustling tables five or ten years from now and passing messages as a spy, not even one year from now, not if she could help it.

Michael offered her an alternative that would meet her emotional and creative needs and rescue her from obscurity and slavery to political causes and basic survival.

"Hey, what about my change?"

She stared down at the bushy headed man's demanding and demeaning beady eyes and automatically counted out his change. He returned a dollar tip. Deliberately neglecting to thank him and wish him a pleasant evening, she moved away in the direction of another beckoning hand.

Standing at the open stairway door of his private office, Sol Greene, owner and manager of his club, cleverly named The Green Machine, critically surveyed the audience response as the musicians acknowledged the anemic applause with a brief nod. Sol did not think they were half bad. For two straight weeks, the patron response had been fragmented, not consistently strong on the applause barometer, but most had stayed on for two or three sets, which meant money for the bar. That the group wasn't a headliner bothered Sol whose goal was to put his joint prominently on the Los Angeles map, like the Whiskey.

He knew he needed a larger dance floor, but he couldn't afford to drop any tables. That would mean selling fewer drinks from which the club derived its revenue along with a modest cover charge, which he wanted to raise, really hike it up. But to make that acceptable, he needed a whole string of headliners.

Although this group came off all right, the musicians just didn't have that kind of class. They hadn't even cut a record. Names were what he needed now, big names and very public faces. They wouldn't like what he was going to do, but tough shit. Besides, he anticipated with pleasure the reaction of Stephen Stull. That wangy prick acted like he was destined to become the next rock recording artist of the century. He was a punk, a fucking brat. Greene looked forward to putting him in his place.

"Thank you. Thank you. Great audience," Stull acknowledged the scattered clapping, an isolated drunken cheer, and a sharp whistle. "Great fuckin' audience. Yeah, man, wow!" He raised his guitar and motioned for the other members of the band to step forward. "Okay, man, you're our kind of people. Listen. We're takin' a short break now. Hope you'll stick around for the next set in about ten minutes. We have some real cool blue sounds coming up . . . a little crystal blue persuasion."

Dade Thomas punctuated the announcement with a drum roll and crash of cymbals. The band members each turned off their microphones and left the stage. Lynn moved to a table down in front to accept a drink offered by three businessmen out on the town. Sharing a joint, Randy and Lynn huddled backstage while Herb and Dade went to the bar for a beer. Sol Greene caught their attention and motioned them aside.

"Let's go to my office a few minutes. I wanna talk to you."

Carrying their beers, they followed him through a stock room door to his office on the second floor over the bar. When they were seated, he moved ponderously to his red leather wing-back chair behind a massive oak desk. Nervous aggressive puffs on his cigar exploded from his mouth.

Stull suddenly burst into the office and pre-empted what he was about to say.

"Hear that crowd out there tonight, Solly Baby? Did you hear that applause?"

"Yeah, sure, it's a good crowd tonight."

Stull trembled with enthusiasm. "You can hear that cash all the way to the bank, I bet, can't you?" He stared at Herb and Dade. "What's the meeting for? Make it short. We don't want to keep 'em waiting out there."

"The bar take is better than average," said Sol. "Unfortunately, it's the only real good one you've pulled in here in the last two weeks. What I need is to have it consistently high. Sorry to have to say this."

"Shit, man," Stull interrupted him. His body twitched and jived around the room. "That's fuckin' right. It's a good one, because our name is getting around out there." His long gnarled fingers nervously drummed the desktop as a defense mechanism in rebutting Greene's negative comment. "We're just gettin' started, man. We're gonna pull a crowd like that every fuckin' night from now on. I guarantee it. Did you see our review in the Times entertainment?"

"You can't guarantee shit, Stull. I have to cut you short by one week. Have a name comin' in who's hot on the charts. Real hot. You ain't even on the charts. You ain't even got a record. DJs don't know who you are. You got nothin' to play. My name had to even change his schedule. If I want him, I gotta bump you out early. If I don't take him now, I lose him, and I'd rather lose you."

Enraged, Stull grabbed a half empty can of stale beer sitting on the desk and pitched it sloshing onto the stained carpet. "You mother fuckin' son-of-a-bitch! You can't pull shit like this on us! We have a contract, a goddamn written agreement for three weeks, mother fucker!"

"So go ahead, sue me, asshole! It'll cost you everything you already made in legal fees in the long run, because you, asshole, didn't read the goddamn fine print. Did you? Read it, Stull. You might learn something about this business. I have refusal and termination rights with or without cause at any time. If I don't think you're cuttin' it, you're out. You're good, okay, I give you that. My guy comin' in is a star. He's better. It's that simple. Maybe I can bring you back in six months for a few gigs to make up for it, not as a headliner though. The Green Machine is movin' up as a club, see. You're not in the class where I want this club to be. Sorry, but this I gotta do and I gotta do it now."

"Sorry doesn't count for shit, Greene, you puke. Stick it up your faggot asshole, man. I wouldn't come back and play in your stinking shit-ass club again for any price."

"I'm glad to hear that, Stull." Crunching his cigar with two fingers, Greene rose, livid, leaning powerfully over his desk. "You just shit in the wrong toilet, and you ain't even a nigger."

Dade rose in a fury and headed for the door.

"After tonight," said Greene, "you're finished, permanently. I don't even want you to stay out the week. I'll stay dark for two days, if I have to. But not you. Oh, no, I don't want shit like you in my club."

Stull swept the full ashtray off the desk sending it crashing with an explosive gray puff against the wall. "Fuck you, Greene. There ain't gonna be the rest of the night."

"You ain't hungry enough, huh! You got enough dope to hold you the rest of the week? You rotten faggot!"

"Just pay up for the time."

"I don't have to pay you shit for tonight. If you quit on me with only half a performance, you don't get paid. That's in the contract!"

Stull grabbed the beer from Herb, now on his feet, and savagely threw it at Greene, who ducked, moving surprisingly fast for a man of his girth and weight. The rust-colored bottle burst against the wall behind him spraying glass over Greene's back. Greene jerked open a desk drawer and pulled out a handgun, a .35.

"All right, fucker, that's assault. Out, get your ass out of here. All of you, get out!"

As they left the office and returned to the stage, Herb and Dade tried to calm Stull enough so they could at least get through the next set. They stood arguing quietly in a corner, refusing to let Stull jump up on the platform and badmouth the club owner to the patrons. Greene thundered up behind them. "I'll give you one more fuckin' hour and that's it."

"Why don't you just give me the cash," said Herb. "We're not going to talk to you again."

Expecting the response, Greene counted out the bills he carried with him and slapped them into Herb's open palm. "You and Dade are all right, Wilcox. Sorry about the nigger comment. Wasn't meant for you, Dade. You can both do better."

Wanting to scratch out his eyes, Stull leaped for Greene, but the rotund man whirled and lumbered away, escaping Stull's clawing grasp while the crowd stared in amazement.

The marbled blue van bearing the name and logo of Crystal Blue Persuasion on its side panels ripped crazily along through the downtown night traffic of Los Angeles. At the wheel, Stull drove insanely, sending out erratic bursts of the amplified diesel truck horn, which exploded like blasts from a pipe organ, clearing the way ahead of its rushing onslaught. He ran two red lights and nearly sideswiped a car beginning to cross an intersection on its own green light.

Dade Thomas reached forward from the back seat and grabbed Stull by the shoulder. "Hey, cool it, man. Losin' a gig ain't worth dyin' over. Don't give Greene the satisfaction."

"Fuck you, man. Get your fuckin' Black hand off my shoulder."

"This black hand gonna take you by the throat, you don't slow down, mother fucker."

Gripping their seats, the other members of the band sat back, tense, on edge, sour with restraint, praying that Stull would not get them killed.

Along the Pacific Coast Highway, he pulled off into the small parking lot of a package liquor store. Herb accompanied him inside to prevent him from doing anything rash and Dade immediately scrambled up to occupy the driver's seat. Stull would have to fight him to get it back.

While Herb purchased a package of Reese's Peanut Butter Cups for Kasia, he noticed Stull lift a pint of Canadian Club whiskey and slip it into one of his large coat pockets. Stull then walked to the cooler for a six pack of Coors beer, for which he paid at the counter.

As soon as they stepped back outside, Herb growled at him. "That was stupid, man. You want to risk getting' busted over a pint of fuckin' booze? Hell, if he called the cops on you, they'd tear your van apart and find all your fuckin' dope and that'd be the end for all of us."

"Nobody asked you, Wilcox. So fuck off."

Dade stuck his head out the open driver's window. "What'd he do now?"

"Lifted some booze."

"Shit."

"Get out of my seat, Thomas."

"No way, Stull, baby, no way. Not 'til I'm safe at home. Not after that last ten miles. This ain't a coaster at Magic Mountain. You've got a choice. Either you get in quietly and pass out in the back or you fight me for this seat and I'll put you out cold real fast without the pleasure. Save you the trouble of drinkin' that piss."

Stull could never stand up to Dade in a fight, so he twisted a different kind of knife. "Sure blackjack, I always wanted a nigger chauffeur."

Dade flung open the door and attacked him like a pile driver, doubling him over with a groin kick. His rising knee hammered Stull's nose sending him backward in a spray of blood. Dade stood over him writhing in the gravel.

"Asshole, you're the only nigger here. Open the door," he called back to Herb. He hefted the moaning Stull to his feet and jammed his sagging body into the storage area of the van among the instrument cases. "You piece of shit, you make me wanna puke." Dade slammed the panel door, then climbed behind the wheel. The van roared out of the parking lot.

"All right, all right, Thomas," Stull's belated whimper rose from the rear compartment. "I take it back. I'm sorry."

"You don't have to take it back, shithead. I gave it back." Dade's dark angry eyes flashed in the glare of reflected headlights in the rearview mirror. "Greene paid us off tonight, Stull. I'll give you your cut. Then we're done."

"You can't fire me," Stull's voice bubbled with blood mixed saliva. "This is my group."

"You just fired yourself, asshole."

"Hey, shit, man, I said I'm sorry. We have an audition Monday at one o'clock. I'm pissed at Greene, not you."

"Yeah, you just suddenly come up with that audition?"

"It's a new club across town, The Golden Sparrow." Stull coughed at the blood trickling down his throat from his broken nose. "They'll pay twice what we made at the Machine. I was saving the news for a surprise."

"If we get the gig."

"We'll get it. You know we'll get it."

"Do I?"

"Hey, Kasia," Stull took a pull at the pint of whiskey. "Wilcox tells me you have a super rich admirer. He even gave you his phone number."

She ignored the remark.

"What would it take to get him to bankroll us?" He took another swallow. "Wilcox is okay with it if you sleep with the guy, if you can work out a deal."

Kasia continued to focus her attention outward on the passing traffic.

"Hey, Herbie, you better talk to your bitch there. Knock some fuckin' sense into her. She's goin' south on us. I can see it happenin'."

By the time they arrived at the apartment, Randy had fallen asleep. Under the combined effect of marijuana that permeated the van, cocaine, and straight booze, Stull could no longer even sit in an upright position. So Lynn took over driving the van, leaving Kasia, Herb, and Dade standing at the front of their building.

Following a brief vehement comment about dumping Stull and linking up with new talent, Dade bid his friends goodnight and went to the unit he shared with Olivia on the first-floor level.

"Why did you tell them about Sloan?" Kasia asked Herb, who preceded her up the stairs.

"We got to talking about money. I offered a realistic suggestion, not that you had to sleep with him. That was Stull's distortion of the whole thing. But maybe you could get him interested in us."

"Why don't you ask Dolores to do it for you?"

He stopped in mid-stride and turned. "Nobody's asking you to sleep with him. That's just the way Stull thinks."

A shout from Dade's apartment below cut them short. "Herb! Kasia! It's Olivia!"

"Jesus!" Herb bounded past Kasia back down the stairs.

"Not again," Kasia raced after him.

They found Dade standing at the bedroom door and peered around him. "Oh, my God," Kasia stepped back and took a deep breath to control herself, then went to the phone.

Olivia had slit her wrists and then her throat to ensure there was no possibility of turning back.

Kasia could not dispel the image of her frail nude body stretched out on the blood-soaked bed. Judging from the blue pallor of her skin, she had been dead for several hours.

Fifteen minutes later, screaming sirens faded and flashing red and blue lights of emergency vehicles filled the street. The apartment bustled with police officers and paramedics. After Olivia's body was removed, a detective questioned Herb, Dade, and Kasia and finally left them alone at four in the morning.

CHAPTER SEVEN

The Split

The next morning, Herb and Kasia discovered that Dade was gone. They decided he just needed some time alone. Herb wondered if Dade would be emotionally up to returning by that night for The Golden Sparrow audition set for Monday morning. When Herb knocked on his door again at eight o'clock, there was no response.

Kasia watched out the rear window overlooking the parking lot to be sure Herb had driven away before she dug frantically in her purse for Michael Sloan's phone number. Although she hadn't forgotten it, she wanted to double check.

Trembling with hope and anticipation, she rushed into the kitchen, snatched up the phone receiver, dialed the number and waited, shifting impatiently from one foot to the other.

At the sound of Michael's voice, she started to speak, then stopped short with an abrupt surge of disappointment upon realizing it was only a recording. She left a message, asking him to please return her call before five o'clock. Herb had said he would be back by then. She didn't want him to catch her talking to Michael.

Ten minutes later, as she lay on her unmade bed sipping hot spice tea, she tried to repress the persistent mental image of Olivia's corpse and to sort out her own life and motives. The phone rang. In her haste to answer, she spilled the tea, scalding her fingers. Cursing loudly, she set aside the ceramic mug, leaped up from the bed and dashed to the phone. She recognized his voice and blurted out, "Please, we have to talk. My apartment's just off Santa Monica Boulevard. I'll repeat the address."

"I know the street. Give me thirty minutes."

She heard the click and raced for the shower.

Michael's girlfriend, Lennis Perry, had left earlier that morning to spend the day with friends. During the past few months, her occasional forays had extended to two and three days. Since she and Michael maintained only a casual housekeeping arrangement, he didn't bother to try to find her after the first such incident.

When he finally located her, she had blasted him over the phone for attempting to interfere with her lifestyle and that he was invading her privacy. Then on her appearance at his house late the following afternoon, she had come on to him all soft and apologetic and coaxed him to have sex with her.

They had met at a Beverly Hills party less than a year ago. She was the daughter of an oil billionaire. Inconsistent in her behavior and lacking any goal orientation in her own life, Michael's steadiness and work ethic that had led him to financial, if not artistic success, as a screenwriter, director, and producer, attracted her.

She also hoped he would do something on her behalf, pave the way for her to get into films or at least assist her in her incompetent and incomplete attempt at writing a script.

At the time, he had felt protective and fatherly toward her, when she related how she had been rejected by her father at a young age. Michael had appreciated her youthful enthusiasm and her struggle for self-identity still wreathed in adolescent fantasies. She was nineteen. Her lithe willowy body had excited him in the manner of the thousands of enticing girls who frequented the beaches of Southern California.

He understood that her days and nights away from him were just another phase of her personal exploration. Although he acknowledged her need for self-actualization, he told her she was only changing from one situation to another without doing anything positive to develop and move ahead in her life.

She had fallen into a pattern of drug abuse and promiscuity from which he wanted to distance himself. He knew the time was fast approaching when, for her own good and his need to grow in another direction in a strong personal relationship, he would tell her to leave.

He was basically a conventional man, at thirty-six, sixteen years her senior and wanting very much to have a wife and family. He wanted to be involved in the traditional concerns and values with which he had grown up as a child.

Although he attended some of the more notorious industry parties, he preferred his own small circle of friends, fellow writers and directors and their girlfriends and families, cooking up a gourmet meal complimented with French wines and stimulating conversation that often lasted into the morning hours.

Lennis couldn't handle that. She had never attended college and she didn't read much but billboards on Sunset Boulevard. She had been raised on a diet of junk food and low brow commercial television. As a consequence, she did not possess the intellectual content and verbal skills and ability to think for herself and effectively express ideas, of which none were original in the first place. Her whole life had been programmed by the tube in an environment of wealth and luxury. She constantly returned to commercial television messages for reinforcement of her simplistic material values.

Michael seriously questioned what he had been trying to accomplish as her mentor. More likely she was playing the role of sex object for him. Waiting any longer to cut off the relationship would only make the event messy and difficult for both of them. He preferred clean emotional relationships, in which social reference points were understood between them. She may have cast her life in the milieu of soap opera. He did not. Now, another woman was about to enter his life.

The blow dryer frantically blasted Kasia's long blonde tresses. She barely finished brushing out the tangles as Michael's assertive knock sounded at the apartment door. She yanked out the plug, snatched up her purse, and raced to the door. She urgently ushered him away with a charming smile. "Hello."

"Hello. You don't have to explain anything." He matched her smile.

"But I do have a lot to say. First of all, thank you for coming."

To her dismay, they encountered Dolores coming up the stairs with a John. She bestowed an admonishing grin on Kasia and said, "You got the right idea," but saved her any further embarrassment by moving on quickly. Dolores had seen the maroon Mercedes parked at the curb.

Herb met Stephen Stull, Randy, and Lynn at the Golden Sparrow nightclub. Neither Stull nor the club manager took the news well about Dade Thomas. Stull tried to argue for more time until they could find a drummer.

"I'm really sorry about this. I don't know what to say. Hey, listen, man, give us a day to find him. His girl friend committed suicide. You gotta understand that. You heard our demo tape. We'll keep your customers buyin' drinks."

"Well, I'm sorry too, since we open tomorrow night and I need a band. He didn't show now and you can't guarantee you'll find him and have him here tomorrow night either. I have a backup group on tap and I guess I'll just have to bring them in. You understand my position, of course."

"Shit, man, come on. Give us a fuckin' break."

"There's nothing more I can do for you. I have a club to run. If you'll excuse me, I have an important call to make."

Stull motioned to the band members to repack their instruments. They loaded them back into the blue van. Herb locked his three guitars and lute in his own van and joined the others in a conference over what to do about their situation.

"We're just gonna have to hustle our ass," Stull snarled. "And that means your bitch too, Wilcox. You get her to turn on to that new fan of hers. Our survival is at stake here and what's between you and her doesn't count."

Herb couldn't believe what he was hearing. "She's not a whore, Stull. I did talk to her about approaching the guy. She won't do it."

"The fuck she won't."

"Where do you suppose Dade split to?" Herb abruptly changed the subject to ward off Stull's ugly ranting threats.

Stull coughed up phlegm and spat on the sidewalk. "Ah, he's probably doped out somewhere cryin' over his poor dead bitch."

Herb bristled. "Hey, Olivia meant a lot to him. Us too, she was our friend."

"Not mine. Doesn't matter a rat's ass to me."

"Maybe because you're the rat," said Herb.

"Fuck you, Wilcox."

Lynn Porat's eyes raked Stull with sudden unrestrained disgust. She moved away from all of them and climbed into the blue van at the wheel to wait for the pow-wow to end. She didn't want to hear any more ugliness.

"We've got no choice but to see if Dade shows up in a couple of days," said Herb fidgeting, anxious now to get back to Kasia. Maybe between the two of them, they could locate Dade.

"We could always get us another drummer," suggested Stull. "That god damn nigger. He could have at least waited until after the fuckin' audition."

Randy's lips snarled in a sardonic feral grin. "You're being overly sentimental today, aren't you, Stull?"

"Yeah, Stull, cut it out." Herb wanted to punch him in the nose. "We're talkin' about a friend. At least he's my friend."

"Bull shit, we're talkin' about bread, man. Don't be a white nigger. We're talkin' about life. His fuckin' bitch is fuckin' dead. He's holdin' us up. Ah, fuck you both. You don't know what counts. Fuck the whole lot of you."

Herb turned on his heel and went to his van. He drove out just ahead of the others. He had to buy new strings for his lute and wanted to talk to an acquaintance who might give him a lead for a temporary backup position with another group he knew that was consistently booked. It was too late anyway now to go back for Kasia and hit the street to perform a mime show anywhere. She wouldn't be up to it, not after last night and he didn't much feel in the mood himself. He was too worried about Dade.

He watched the blue van stream on past him. With Stull leaning on the horn, it moved along through the cross-town traffic on Santa Monica Boulevard.

Stull vented his rage at the loss of the Golden Sparrow gig, then turned it against Lynn and Randy. Lynn had grown accustomed to Stull calling her his bitch, although the three of them occasionally got it off together, provided Randy felt in a bi-sexual mood. But the way Stull had used the term "bitch" in reference to Olivia stung an emotion buried deep inside Lynn. She herself had accidentally O-Ded twice and had been close to death. Now she feared the sensation of going under, tripping out, losing control. Stull knew about her fear and used it to manipulate her.

When things were not going well for them, he would blame her singing or style or her appearance. He would threaten her with his lethal hypodermic needle, which he used to inject heroine whenever snorting coke didn't give him a big enough high. Lately, because he couldn't afford horse, he had tried injecting cocaine. Lynn knew the drugs would eventually kill him. What she feared most was that he would try to take her with him on that final trip.

Although any sense of romantic love had dried up or never existed between them, she felt a strange kind of loyalty toward him and stayed with him. She silently admitted she was not a particularly good vocalist. She would never be a recording star. Convinced that no one would hire her or even take her seriously, she shrunk from the idea of leaving Stull and trying elsewhere. She needed him because she could do no better and she wouldn't risk taking a dive and doing worse.

Lynn was twenty-eight. Ten years ago, just coming out of high school, she had been a groupie, traveling around the country and competing with other young girls to see how many rock singers she could get to fuck her. Eventually she had drifted into prostitution until she had met Stull when he was playing instrumental guitar with another band. Changing bands here and there, they had been on the road for most of their years together. During that time, she had had two abortions. Stull refused to allow her to use any form of birth control and he used none. Subjecting her to abortions was a kind of punishment. He had told her he would never let a kid be born by some bitch he'd fucked, even if he had to kill it himself.

Although she sensed that something disturbing had happened to him when he was a child, because of the way he treated her and his pervasive hate for all women, she never asked him what and he never offered to talk about his past.

Performing on stage lifted Lynn from her self-perception of being a loser tied to a man and a life from which there was no escape. Stull's ravings penetrated her meandering thoughts.

"I've had it up to my fucking eyeballs with this shit. Two gigs lost in two days, for fuckin' Christ's sake. My drummer split. And that fuckin' bitch Kasia backin' out on us when there's a bankroll in some dude's pants and all she has to do is spread her legs or at least ask for an investment. God damn but I could shit over this one."

"Then why don't you shut up and shit. It might make you feel better."

"Watch what you say to me, bitch."

"You start watchin' what you say to me, you prick."

Stull glanced darkly at her. "If Wilcox doesn't get her to go after that wad, I'll make her wish she never turned her back on us. Fuckin' cunt bitch. You bitches are all alike. Nothin' but fuckin' cunts. Only you don't fuck when it counts for your man." Stull turned off the main highway.

"Where we goin'?" asked Lynn.

"The house."

An hour later, the van lumbered ponderously up a rutted dirt track deep into the foothills and passed from sight along the bank of a dry creek bed.

CHAPTER EIGHT

A New Beginning

Kasia had not expected that Michael would take her directly to his house, but she didn't question the act or his motive. Going there was undeniably a sign of acceptance, no questions asked. When they arrived, she insisted on a tour and responded with a sincere compliment at the simple, yet tasteful luxury of the contemporary furnishings and décor.

They completed the tour on a landscaped patio overlooking a large pool shaped by sculpted natural rocks, a waterfall, and tropical foliage. Michael fired up a grill centered in an outdoor kitchen.

"How do you like your steak?"

"Medium rare with lots of garlic and pepper. Can I help you with anything?"

"Help yourself to anything you like at the bar."

He picked up a long-handled patio fork and gently flipped the ribeye steaks causing a momentary flare up from the fat drippings.

On the ride over in the car, Kasia had explained her relationship to Herb Wilcox and why it must now end. Michael had listened intently and with an outwardly sympathetic demeanor coupled with personal satisfaction that she was freeing herself for him.

Michael silently acknowledged that he was her ticket off the street, but he did not feel exploited. It didn't bother him that she was partly using him toward that end. He was comfortable with the nature of male-female relationships and that they always involved some kind of trade-off. One provided something that the other lacked.

Kasia's inner anxiety gradually subsided. Michael's unhurried manner calmed her and cloaked her with an instant sense of security, no pressure, no demands, just allowing their relationship to evolve naturally in its own way in its own time.

Over a bottle of expensive cabernet, he told her about the two films he had written and directed. She had not seen either of them. He justified their box office success to the low brow tastes of the mass audience.

"The way I understand it, people are afraid and angry about what's happening with the economy, that and the fact our country no longer has faith in our leaders. There's a lot of hostility and aggression out there. Horror films have become psychological safety valves. A lot of those people in the audience identify with the monsters and killers and forces of evil. Of course they'd never admit it."

"It's human nature that people carry something inside them, some dark force that's frightening and powerful, that we fear is uncontrollable and try to repress. During biblical times and the Middle Ages, that dark force was represented by monsters and demons. Ancient tribes created masks of their demon and devil gods that they believed existed.

"That dark force is where our fears come from. By putting them up there on the big screen, audiences can experience them, but keep them under control and come out of the theater unscathed. The problem now is that the images and film experience have come full circle and through the television medium they've programmed society for sex and violence. The media has dehumanized human relationships, which is unfortunate, since more than anything else in our lives, people are influenced by movies and television. Violent crimes have been on the rise during the past five years.

"In one of my films, a kid butchers his family with a hatchet. About six months after its release, some kid really did that, and the court ruled that he had been influenced by the act in my film. The kid had to be psychotic to begin with and maybe the scene in the film did push him over the edge. But I never made those films intending to screw up people's lives. It's easy to blame a movie. Anyway, I'm getting out of the horror business."

"You had to start somewhere. And," her glance encompassed the house and gardens, "you're successful at what you do."

"I almost never saw any profit. The studio went out of its way to rip me off.   I don't have that kind of trouble with Tri Con Pictures. They even helped me in the other situation, on the legal side, since they invested in my second film. I'm very happy with Tri Con. The rest of the industry could take a few lessons from them instead of always exploiting the independents. It's a rotten business wherever you have to deal with crooked people.   Not everybody's like that, but the industry's rife with graft and corruption. So yes, now I do have the financial freedom to make the films I really want to make."

He was enthusiastic about sharing his plans with her, animated, jumping up and pacing excitedly back and forth as he talked.

She listened intently as he told her about the films he planned to write, produce and direct from that time forward, films of social significance artistically executed with style, and expressing the universality of the human experience. He was certain that his next three films would generate political controversy which could be used to help publicize and promote them at the box office.

The first was to be about poverty in American cities and the daily struggle to survive while searching out a dream by which to rise above it. The second project would explore how the CIA infiltrated American colleges and universities. He had not yet decided about the third.

Kasia thought the mention of the CIA very ironic. In wanting to become involved with him, she had to be careful not to mention or even hint that she was a double agent or had anything to do with the Government.   Here was someone whose values and ideals were similar to her own. At least if she were in his films, she could embody those values. She could become the message and the messenger.

Panic nudged Kasia awake, siphoning off her wine induced doze. Groggily she looked at the wall clock. The time was well past seven.

By now, Herb would have figured out where she had gone. Dolores would have described the Mercedes and the man who had come to the apartment.

Kasia wanted to end her relationship with Herb cleanly and maturely, barred of excessive anger, either physical or verbal. Sure, it was painful for him, but he knew it was going to happen.

"Why don't you just call him," Michael suggested. "You really don't have to go back there. I mean, what for?"

"Yes, otherwise it seems like I don't have the guts to face him. It's important to me that he understands my decision."

"Do you really think he'll listen?"

She shrugged and pulled at her long blonde hair. "A phone call?" She shook her head. "That's not me anyway. That's just not my way. Besides, I have a few personal things to pick up."

"Can't they be replaced?"

"Not really, some of them are photographs."

"I'm concerned about what he might do to you if you go back there."

"Herb's not a violent person."

"Well, I'll be waiting outside."

When Kasia returned, Herb did not look up from where he sat drinking beer at the kitchen table. She stood framed against the door for several moments watching him, imprinting a final parting image of him while she sorted out what she wanted say. As soon as she saw him, she had discarded her original lines. He abruptly settled the matter for her.

"Did you sleep with him?" Believing she had, he just wanted to hear it from her.

"No, I did not sleep with him. We had dinner and we talked."

He nodded without looking at her and sipped his beer. She did not like nor could she quite read his quiet manner. There was something lethal about him that frightened her.

"I just came back for a few things."

He stared hard at her, a cold piercing expression that made her step back. "He waiting downstairs for you?"

"Yes."

"Don't worry. I'm not going out there and shake his hand or punch him out." He rose from the table a little too suddenly. Kasia sensed his intention and the beginning of his maneuver. She needed to move quickly, gather her personal possessions and leave him and this chapter of her life behind.

Trying not to appear rushed and unsettled, she walked into the bedroom and packed with haste. As she straightened to leave, he blocked her passage at the door.

"You don't have to try to prove anyth –"

His fist slammed into the side of her face and cut her short. The impact flung her across the bed. She remained still, absorbing and controlling the throbbing pain. Clutching her face as tears welled up, she watched through wet-slitted eyes and waited for his next move. He saw that he had hurt her and that was all he needed.

"All right, get the hell outta here."

She slid off the bed and picked up her suitcase. He barely moved aside, allowing her to pass. She raced out of the apartment, ran along the balcony and half fell down the stairs in her panic. She clutched the rail to break her momentum as her suitcase bumped and slid to the pavement.

Michael met her outside the car, took a single look at her face. "That fucking bastard."

"No, no, don't go back there. Don't make any more out of this. I'm done with him now and all the rest of them. I'm all right. Let's just go." She was trembling. "Let's go."

He helped her into the car and tossed her suitcase into the back. Moments later, the shiny maroon body of his car flicked past under the street lights, turned a corner and dissolved from view in the fluid traffic and neon distance.

CHAPTER NINE

The Anniversary

Although Roger Lakein's assignment was to solve the mystery, his own personal secret agenda was to distort the situation and the information coming from South American countries and discover that nothing was out of the ordinary.

The report he received did imply that the smuggling went beyond local activity and suggested that an international ring might be orchestrating the operation.

Roger smiled at the thought. According to the report, the disappearance of billions of barrels of crude oil, and tons of copper ore, nitrates, and thorium would have to be managed from outside the countries in question.

Roger had been advised by Gordon Frasier to keep his search open to options and combinations of groups and individuals who might be involved in an alleged ring. Other indicators nudged toward the belief that something of even greater political significance might be taking place, not just the obvious events themselves. Tri Con's financial and corporate growth had gone relatively unnoticed until the current investigation.

Despite the thickness of the report, Lakein noticed that the Security Bank had documented little concrete evidence. His orders were to find a source, find a place to begin the investigation in South America, then determine the link or links that would eventually move him into the alleged ring. For Lakein, his future and his life depended on keeping that knowledge an absolute secret from his employer, the CIA.

Roger put aside the report and rubbed his eyes. At two o'clock in the morning, he would have rather been in bed, but the significance of what he had just read would have kept him awake.

The report had been generated by the Security Bank in Los Angeles, a code name for the western CIA headquarters operation, directed by Gordon Frasier, that was conducting the Inca mission in South America to identify a mole in the organization. Information reporting sources from Germany, North Africa, India, and Southeast Asia, were corroborated through the Security Bank, and the document now lay before him on Santiago de Chile, South America. From here, Roger controlled covert operations for the mission.

Despite the fact he had been a field agent for the National Clandestine Service for fifteen years, the rapidity with which information could be communicated from one part of the world to another never ceased to amaze him.

Fluent in Spanish and Portuguese, he was a South American specialist and had worked on many undercover assignments to collect human intelligence.

What the report revealed to him was a general series of seemingly unrelated events and economic evidence that would have otherwise gone unnoticed were it not for the recent international growth of the Tri Con Corporation and its subsidiaries throughout the United States and in several foreign countries.

The CIA maintained a close watch on such multinational companies, which were often mini-governments unto themselves and largely determined the thrust of American foreign policy, especially with regard to third world nations.

Because of Tri Con's hundreds of subsidiary companies, many of them only paper corporations, even leading economists and financial analysts were not aware of the firm's actual size, scope, and impact on world industries.

Tri Con's major oil and mining operations in South America and the company's foreign markets had caught the attention of the CIA and had generated the study resulting in an incomplete analysis.

More than fifty percent of the crude oil and copper and nitrates mined from Tri Con's South American holdings was being shipped to other overseas markets and was not available to North American companies. The statistics were of special interest to the Department of Commerce, which was the Federal watchdog and provided oversight of international trade.

The department was concerned that trade embargoes against the Soviet Union and Soviet bloc countries were being violated since, as far as could be determined, the crude oil, copper ore, and nitrates, as well as thorium, a source of nuclear energy, were not being processed in Tri Con's designated overseas markets but were simply disappearing.

The report did not attempt to suggest how or why, only that it was happening. At this point, the mystery was beyond conjecture and understanding.

Roger's bleary eyes scanned his apartment, cool white adobe contrasted with an occasional bold abstract oil and several black and white prints by local artists. He appreciated and collected fine original ethnic art and sculpture. His sense of isolation intensified as he finished his cognac.

He had been alone much of his adult life. Loneliness was a condition of the job. After the planned revolution in Chile was underway, he could leave the CIA, retire to Europe with his newly acquired wealth and find a woman to live with him, someone who would tend to him and be an intelligent, loving companion. The prospect of retiring at the age of forty-two with his health, looks, and physique intact after only fifteen years of service appealed to his sensibilities.

He soured on The Company two years ago when his request for a transfer and promotion to The Security Bank was denied. CIA headquarters at Langley, Virginia had also turned down his request for a transfer to Europe, reasoning that the political climate was too hot in Central and South America. He was needed there for his expertise as a field man and for his intimate knowledge of Latin American politics and culture.

Headquarters had consented to a sixty-day R & R, which he had spent touring Europe. During his brief visit to West Berlin, KGB operatives had approached him with an offer to work as a double agent. Coming on the heels of his rejected request, Lakein thought he was just being tested by the CIA to determine whether his loyalty or attitude had wavered. He had not taken the bait.

Later, upon his return to South America, he was again approached by a man whom he readily confirmed was an agent of the Soviet KGB, Malcolm Karazississ. Lakein continued to be cautious, but after researching the offer and checking the reality of a half-million-dollar deposit in a Swiss account before he had even agreed to cooperate, he capitulated and crossed over to them.

After all, he had reasoned, Tri Con was still an American corporation. They were playing the same game for the same end, power through economic control of the world's markets, primarily energy and technology. Hurting from the rebuff, Lakein had become disillusioned with the whole process, especially the callous lack of concern for human life.

He had witnessed and been a party to oppression and wholesale slaughter. Although in the beginning, he joined the CIA for the excitement, glamour, and intrigue it offered, those enticements had never been fully realized once he encountered the realities, the drudgery, paper-pushing, politics, and lies associated with espionage. By then, he was firmly entrenched in the manipulation of regimes in Central and South America and not in a position to either protest or to resign. He would be accidentally terminated before they would allow him to resign.

He rose and went to the bathroom. Flushing the toilet, he stared at his mirror image and noticed that his once recognizable blonde boyish features had been taken over by the slow assault of stress and middle age.

I've really forgotten what it's like to live a normal life, he thought. *What is a normal life anymore? I wonder if I'll be able to discover it and then live it.*

His expression was lined from the gravity of what he knew and the events of which he had been a part. He had a sudden impulse to go back to his youth. He hadn't genuinely laughed or even smiled in a long time.

***

As a young woman, before she had ever met Charley MacIntosh, Maggie had nurtured a dream of becoming an international star of the stage and screen. She would have a villa on the Italian coast overlooking the Mediterranean where she and her lover would stay during the Cannes Film Festival.

She wondered why she had given up on that long ago ambition. Maybe it was the endless years spent waiting on tables during the day and performing as a stripper at night. There had been a few character parts here and there in which she played tough raunchy women. But that wasn't any road to stardom, especially in those days. It was all just a front anyway. She really wasn't that kind of woman. So what that she had been born and raised on a farm, the only girl among six brothers and a thorough education in profanity, especially after her mother had died and she, Maggie, had been expected to cook and clean for the lot of 'em.

In the early 50s, a sixteen-year-old girl on the road didn't have much choice if she wanted to survive. Moving in with a man was the quickest and easiest way to get a roof over your head and food on the table. That arrangement had become the pattern of her life. She had actually fallen in love with one of them, the seventh. By then, she had been eighteen years old and could legally marry. When he had tired of her and kicked her out, she had decided to have an abortion. The doctor had not been clean about the operation, and she had nearly died from an infection that had left her sterile.

She was endowed with a strong solid body, big breasts, tight ass, and long flaming hair that became her trademark as a popular stripper in a Los Angeles cabaret, until she met Charley. She noticed him in the audience. He came to watch her night after night, as if she fulfilled some fantasy in his life. Finally, she had responded to his incessant notes, flowers, and invitations to let him take her out to dinner and get acquainted.

He had been just as crusty and humorous then as now and knew what Maggie was doing to herself, a form of public adulation that was, in fact, personal psychological abuse. He was a good deal smarter than she and wanted to take her away from that sordid life, because, as he told her, "It will erode your sense of self-worth as a human being."

She didn't understand what he was talking about. What was more important, he loved her enough to ask her to marry him.

That she couldn't bear children didn't matter to him. If they had really wanted to, they could have adopted a child. But neither had come from a background that encouraged them to want to become parents.

Charley's father had been an alcoholic who had beaten and abused Charley's mother mercilessly until one day, in her defense, Charley had cracked his father's skull with a baseball bat. His father hadn't died, but did suffer brain damage that placed him in permanent convalescence and out of their lives.

What Charley couldn't understand was why his mother had married another man who also abused her, only this time with words rather than fists. So Charley had left home at eighteen, supported himself through Carnegie Tech and earned a degree in engineering. He had then joined the army and became an intelligence officer, opening a path to the CIA where he worked in covert operations for Gordon Frasier.

He was now acting as the employee from Rockwell Collins who was stealing alledged defense secrets and passing along the worthless microfilms to the street mime in Los Angeles.

Charley's and Maggie's marriage had been solid, enjoined by the mutual traumas of their childhood, which, at Charley's insistence, they exorcised through psychiatric counseling. In overcoming the emotional scars of their past, they discovered in each other a love and security they would otherwise have never known.

"You ready?"

Maggie pushed a curly lock of flaming red hair out of her eyes, scanned the room for the last time and nodded.

"Let's go." Charley dropped a loaded .45 automatic into his small suitcase, zipped it shut, then led the way out. "Get the light."

"Wait," she hesitated. "I have to piss."

"Hurry the hell up. If we don't show on time, we lose our contact." Standing at the top of the stairs, he shuffled his feet in an anxious fidget while his wife dashed back inside to the bathroom.

Returning five minutes later, she muttered, "I can't help it. This sort of thing makes me nervous and who knows where we'll end up. They might not even have a toilet."

"We're getting soft. That's what comes from too much of the good life. We start taking luxury for granted when we know it's not really our cup of tea. Think of it as a welcome change, a challenge," he said, as they clattered down the stairs.

"I hardly consider a flush toilet a measure of luxury."

"I'm sure it is where we're going."

"You didn't tell me that before. I was just joking about no toilet. You're holding out on me. You said we were going to manage a resort hotel," Maggie harangued him.

They walked quickly along the Marina del Rey waterfront in Santa Monica where they had lived for the past three years in a two-hundred-thousand-dollar condominium.

"You don't look tense enough," said Charley. "Pretend that you're paranoid that someone is watching us, only don't overdo it."

"Tense enough? You bet your ass I'm tense. This ain't no cakewalk. You deliberately held out on me on this one. I want to know in detail what the hell is going to happen to us."

"If I knew in detail, I'd tell you in detail. I'm just trying to keep our spirits up."

"Why wasn't I included in that meeting with Giorgio?"

"You're my wife. We're married, remember?"

"How could I forget."

"He figures where I go, you go, a traditional marriage, under the circumstances. The spooks are supposed to be onto us. They'll stage a bust later tonight and discover we've split.   Tomorrow, there'll be a little press about the incident and then the big stories will hit the media. Management at Rockwell will positively shit over this until they figure out nothing of permanent value was given away."

"How long did you say we were going to be down there?"

"I didn't."

"Do you know?"

"Yes, approximately."

"Well, do I have to get down on my knees and beg?"

"Five years."

"Five years?" Maggie stopped in shock.

Charley grabbed her by the arm. "Don't stop. Keep moving. One foot in front of the other. It's the only way." He propelled her along against the backdrop of masts and spars that rose like a forest of thin skeletal trees out of the harbor's viscous, yellow-lit black water. A sleek dark sloop with running lights coasted up the channel under power.

"You gave me the impression it would be only a year or two at the most," said Maggie greatly distressed.

"Giorgio said they had to change their plans."

"Change their plans? Five years! You're a shit, Charley. A real honest to God shit. Maybe I should pull out now before it's too late."

"Think of it as an extended vacation."

"Christ, how did I ever let you talk me into marrying you?"

"Come on, pet. We've been over that ground before. We're getting near the place. Help me watch for the signal."

One hundred yards further on, they stopped in a parking area, empty except for a few cars belonging to private boat owners. Charley and Maggie waited against the shadow covered stucco wall of the public restroom out of range of the tall streetlamp.

A cream-colored sedan pulled slowly into the parking lot and stopped near the concrete configuration of the restroom. The casually dressed driver lit a cigarette, got out and went into the men's side. A few minutes later, he returned to his car and drove quickly away.

"I saw the same thing you did," said Maggie.

"Okay, now look out there along the second dock."

The lights in the pilot house of a seventy-foot power yacht blinked on and off twice in even succession. Charley stepped inside the restroom and went directly to the third commode. Standing on the toilet seat, he reached up and felt along the ventilator window ledge until he felt a key card that would open the electronically controlled gate.

He and Maggie hurried through and out onto the dock to the magnificent yacht and, with the assistance of the captain, climbed aboard. A door opened and another member of the crew silently led them down into the rich dark wood paneling of the main cabin. Almost immediately, they sensed the vibration of the powerful engines. The craft churned in reverse, pulled clear of the slip, and headed up the harbor channel toward the end of the breakwater.

"There's food here," the blonde bearded sailor offered, "Beer, wine, vodka, brandy, champagne, whatever you'd like. You can sleep on those two bunks over there," he pointed. "If you feel like sleeping, I'll be up in the pilot house. If you need anything, just pick up that phone."

"Thanks, we didn't expect such hospitality," said Charley. "I'm sure we'll be fine."

After the crew member had departed, Maggie stretched luxuriously and leaned back on a side lounge. "Why don't we retire and just buy one of these babies. We can afford it in two more years. I could live on this instead of in a house. Bring me a beer."

Charley handed her a German pilsner from the refrigerator and poured himself a gin and tonic. He staggered slightly as the yacht took a heavy swell coming around the point of the breaker.

"At least we're traveling in style," said Maggie.

"For a while at least, eh?" Charley grinned, never letting his crooked teeth get in the way of a smile.

Maggie's expression questioned his comment over her raised beer bottle.

"They'll break up the trip," said Charley. "It'll be in stages and by different modes of travel so we can't be tracked."

"That's too bad. I was just getting used to the idea of a cruise to South America."

His amiable grin apologized for the unsettling circumstances. Maggie had always had a difficult time uprooting and making a major change in her life. This would be their fourth mission as a team since their marriage twelve years ago.

During his initial service with the CIA, Charley's cover had been as an engineering consultant working within three major defense companies under contract to the Federal Government. His ingenious personality and infectious sense of humor won the confidence of his peers and superiors alike. His identity was never suspected and in only one instance did he unearth a spy, a fellow engineer in extreme debt who, at the beginning of the Viet Nam War, tried to sell trade secrets to the Russians.

"When will we know what country we'll be in?" asked Maggie.

"They've withheld that information. I guess they figure the less we know, the less chance there is of someone following up and finding us. Let's eat, then try to get some sleep."

Maggie sensed a sudden tremor move up from the pit of her stomach. "God, I hope I don't get seasick."

"The toilet's through there," Charley pointed.

"What do we have to eat?"

"I'm not going to cook anything." He peered into the refrigerator. "How about ham and turkey sandwiches with tomato and avocado, lettuce, cheese, and a pickle? There are pickles in here too and caviar to go with the vodka and champagne."

"Pickles and caviar together? Why not? Okay, light on the mustard, heavy on the mayo for me."

"I know," Charley quickly slapped two large sourdough sandwiches together, then sat opposite her at the centrally located teakwood table while they ate.

"Our twelfth anniversary is in two days," she said. "Did you remember?"

A sheepish expression crossed Charley's sun mottled features. Coupled with shaggy gray hair, freckles, and lean boyish features, he had the appearance of a beach bum.

"Isn't it something how I can be a stickler for certain kinds of details and others just seem to slip away? But you know what the pressure has been like the past few months. It takes just as much sweat and energy to fake something as it does to do the real thing. I had to make my actions look credible."

"I've never yet known you to fake it in bed, and you don't sweat all that much. You don't have to offer any excuses."

"I love you, Maggie, very much. You know that."

"A girl likes to be reminded she's special once in a while."

"Shall I put out a 'do not disturb' sign and lock the door?"

Her nose wrinkled over a mischievous grin. "Wherever we happen to be on the twenty-first, let's celebrate somehow, okay?"

"You got it." Charley nodded, chewing a bite of his sandwich with energy and enthusiasm. "We will, hon, we will."

At two in the morning, the yacht cruised into Avalon harbor at Catalina Island, twenty-six miles from the Los Angeles shoreline. The sudden growling reversal of the engines woke Charley from a fitful doze. Rolling over, he peered out a porthole at the lights, then gently nudged Maggie awake.

"Where are we?" she yawned. "Acapulco?"

"Catalina." He pulled on and laced his shoes. Neither he nor Maggie had removed their clothes. A slight body odor clung to their garments.

The captain came down from the pilot house, politely knocked, then entered the cabin. "You'll transfer to a seaplane here. Hope you enjoyed the boat ride. Sorry it had to be so brief."

"Mmmh," Maggie mumbled, "I was just getting used to the rocking and rolling."

The captain carried bags that had been prepared for them up onto the deck. With the assistance of the first mate, they climbed down a ladder to a waiting rubberized Kodiak lifeboat, then were motored over to a twin-engine seaplane moored at the dock. They boarded immediately and the pilot and co-pilot prepared for take-off.

A few minutes later, the seaplane rose up over Avalon Bay and swung south paralleling the distant lights of the Los Angeles beachfront cities. The steady drone of the engines lulled Charley and Maggie to sleep once again, which remained uninterrupted until dawn when they set down in gentle swells at Puerto Vallarta, Mexico on the gulf.

As the co-pilot secured the aircraft at the dock, the pilot handed Charley and Maggie their new passports along with several thousand dollars in cash. "You have reservations at the Dolphin for the next three days. Someone will contact you tomorrow about your next departure. In the meantime, enjoy yourselves and have a happy anniversary."

Stunned, Maggie stared at Charley. "How did he know? You devil you, did you arrange this?"

"Well, I wanted to surprise you. I told Giorgio in the beginning I wanted to do something special, if possible. I'm just as surprised at this as you are. Royal treatment, huh?" He stretched his stiff legs.

Maggie leaned over from her seat and threw her arms around him. "Charley, for a scoundrel, you're pretty damn wonderful."

"Let's get off this tub and go have some fun." He patted the pilot on the shoulder as they stepped off onto the dock. "That was a nice smooth flight. Thanks."

"Have a good time."

After processing through customs, they checked in at the hotel, then spent the rest of the day kicking about in the warm surf and lying on the beach holding hands as if they were newlyweds.

At lunchtime, they strolled several yards up the beach to an open-air palm thatched cantina to eat grilled shrimp and drink exotic rum cocktails. After the third mind-blower, they staggered back to their hotel room, made love for an hour, then slept away the hot humid afternoon until four, when a phone call awakened them.

Charley grabbed the receiver. "Yes."

"Senore MacIntosh," a Spanish male voice spoke into his ear.

"Yes?"

"I'm sorry to have to cut your stay short, but due to unforeseen weather conditions, your flight will depart at ten o'clock tomorrow evening. A cab will pick you up at your hotel at nine fifteen and you will be met at the airport. Do you have any questions?"

"No, thank you. We'll be ready."

"Have a nice evening, sir."

Charley hung up. "Well, at least two days are better than one, or none, for that matter. We just got called back from vacation."

"Bastards."

"Not today, tomorrow. They shorted us a day. Said it's because of weather." Charley pulled her close to him and nuzzled her ear.

"Let's take a shower then go bar hopping, if you feel up to it. We can pick out our restaurant for later. They don't eat dinner down here until around nine or ten."

She wrapped her muscular dancer's legs around him. "Not so fast, Charley me boy. We have a long evening ahead of us. Don't rush the afternoon."

He chuckled. "But I'm hungry."

She stuffed a large red nipple into his mouth. "Here's something to chew on, hors d' oeuvres."

He laughed through his blocked lips.

***

The private Lear jet brought them into La Paz, Bolivia late at night on September 23, 1975. Only their glimpse of the terminal sign allowed them for the first time to know of their destination, although they were to be moved again.

A light rain misted the porthole windows of the jet as it taxied from the flight line to the pad where they would deplane. They struggled for breath upon inhaling the thin mountain air at that high elevation.

Another pilot immediately approached the plane from the hangar and met them at the bottom of the steps. In halting English, he explained they were to come with him. They boarded a World War Two vintage supply transport parked nearby, a twin-engine job that had been warming up on the pad when the Lear came in. No sooner had Charley and Maggie landed, then they were in the air again.

Their next stop, late the following afternoon, was on a small, deserted airstrip in Chile's central valley. Looking around at the landscape, they saw they were on a *funda*, a large agricultural plantation that stretched for miles.

A wiry built native beckoned to them as they descended mobile platform steps brought to the door. He introduced himself as Petra. When they asked where they were he explained in perfect English,

"This is the Montalva funda. I will take you to Santiago where you will stay for one night."

From luxury yacht to seaplane, resort hotel, and private Lear jet, they now descended the social ladder to a battered 1960 Ford pickup truck. Petra tossed their bags into the back. With some nudging and squirming, they crowded into the cab. Grinding ancient gears under the floorboards set them out along a dirt road through acres of cultivated fields.

Sudden fear and disorientation attacked Maggie. Charley detected her trembling. She had never been out of the United States before in her entire life. The distance, time difference, and various modes of travel overwhelmed her. She felt disconnected, unable to anchor herself to the security of a known reality, other than Charley.

He placed a protective arm around her seated in the middle. She could not help crying.

"It'll be all right," he said, attempting to soothe her. "It'll be all right."

Lightning crackled and thunder rumbled. Minutes later, a cold rushing downpour swept over the truck in blasting sheets and turned the road into a ribbon of mud. The whacking sound of the worn wiper blades did little more than create a greasy smear across the windshield. Charley wondered at the driver's ability to see adequately to even remain on the road.

"This will clear up soon," said Petra. "I know the road."

The storm passed as abruptly as it had begun. After three hours of jouncing in shoulder-to-shoulder discomfort, they came to a paved two-lane highway that, three hours later, led them into Santiago.

Petra drove a convoluted route that skirted the city and took them in the vicinity of enormous *barriadas*, shanty towns mired in abject poverty. Finally, they arrived at what appeared to be an old adobe warehouse with a corrugated iron roof. Petra parked the truck in an adjacent alley and herded them in through a side door.

He switched on a single bare light bulb that caste instant shadows of large, medium, and small stacked wooden crates and a two-and-a-half-ton military supply truck.

"This is where you'll spend the night," he said.

"Here? Where? On what?" Charley suspected these sudden harsh conditions were a portent of what lay ahead. He knew the transition would not be easy for Maggie. After the past few days, this was a real let-down.

"There are cots along the back wall," Petra explained.

"What do we do for light in here?"

Petra handed him a squat candle whose stubby base had been melted into a metal cup. "You have any matches?"

"Yeah, I've got matches. I can see I'm going to have to take up smoking again. Shit." He lit the candle and led Maggie past the truck deep into the warehouse. They discovered two cots in an area walled off with boxes to create an improvised room affording them privacy.

"Is this the way it's going to be from here on out?" Maggie stared at the filthy dust coated cots. She could already feel the bedbugs crawling all over her. "I'd rather sleep on the floor on cardboard before I climb on that. They look like they have a disease. What are they really going to do with us, Charley? I can hardly stand the suspense. Was managing a hotel just a carrot to lead us on?"

"No, this was the most effective way to penetrate. Pinochet's secret police don't know we're here. They don't know anything about what we're doing. Nothing was overlooked to ensure maximum secrecy."

"What is it that we're doing?"

"I have to make contact with Roger Lakein somehow. No way to use the code until we're in position. Can't even send a message yet. Have to watch and wait for the right opportunity. After all this, we can't chance blowing our cover. We have to be extra careful what we say and do. The wrong word heard by the wrong person can mean the end of us down here."

"That's comforting. Yeah, Charley, I had a good cry. Just don't leave me alone and I'll be fine."

"That's my girl. I'd hate to be going through this without you."

She half grinned, a sad droop at the corners of her mouth. "I can't honestly say I'd rather be here with you. I'd rather we were in a better and safer place."

"That's all right. We'll get used to it."

"Is this Roger Lakein our contact?"

"CIA contact and eventually our ticket home. He's in special operations, a floater, moves around South America as he's needed." Charley nudged one of the cots with his shoe and exposed a bucket with old, dried excrement still caked on its insides. "Shit, talk about luxury."

"Talk about shit."

They laughed. "This is no time to be funny," said Charley.

"I wasn't trying to be. I'm serious." Maggie burst out laughing again. Then they both laughed uncontrollably and had to support each other to keep from falling.

Petra wondered at their laughter as he left the warehouse and walked to his dingy flat less than a block away. Americans were strange. After bolting the door, he picked up his phone and dialed.

The sudden ring woke Roger Lakein from a light nap. He had been expecting the call. "Yes."

"Hello, is this Senore Scribe?"

"No, this is Senore Pantalone."

"Ah, Senore Scribe told me I should ask for you, Senore Pantalone."

"Go ahead."

"Petra, I have them."

"Good. Give them their coded instructions tomorrow morning before you take them to Puerto Montt. Jaime will be waiting to move them up the river. All clear?"

"Si, Senore Pantalone."

"Call me when you return from Puerto Montt." Lakein abruptly disconnected and slowly hung up the receiver. He knew that Charley and Maggie were part of Operation Inca and had been sent to South America to find the mole. So he was positioning them as far out of the way as possible while accommodating the Soviet KGB plans for their future use in Chile. As long as Charley and Maggie could not communicate with him, they would not discover him. He would isolate them as effectively as though they were imprisoned. He would have his revenge on Frasier.

CHAPTER TEN

The Public Image

When Giorgio Mykola brought him the idea of turning their courier into a film actress, Kurt Heinrich had instantly seized on the possibilities for espionage. She would be excellent cover for acquiring information, and would have unlimited access to media sources, scientists, military leaders, and Government officials at elite social functions where she would be recognized as a celebrity among other celebrities. But her critical use would be as an international courier. No one would ever suspect that an American movie star was carrying coded secret, top secret, and classified material out of one country into another.

"Your concept is a stroke of genius," he told Giorgio. He only regretted that he had not originated the idea. Heinrich decided to tell Bachmann that both he and Giorgio had come up with it together. Heinrich needed to make points with Bachmann. Hell, why not take all the credit for it himself. Giorgio would never know and wouldn't care.

Publicity for Tri Con Pictures' films was a priority uppermost with Heinrich. He realized how much the success of a project depended upon exposure through the press and media, in addition to traditional advertising.

Heinrich was also pleased to learn that Michael and Kasia were going to be married. But then he did something that neither of them cared for. For the sake of promoting their first major film project together, *Sidewalk*, Heinrich wanted their wedding to be a publicity event.

Michael and Kasia balked, since they had envisioned a small intimate outdoor wedding in the wine country of Northern California. Heinrich's will prevailed.

An array of motion picture and television personalities were invited to attend the lavish wedding and reception catered on one of the large studio sound stages.

Michael arranged to fly his parents and brothers and sisters from Chicago and Kasia's parents and brother and sister from Wisconsin.

A limousine was waiting for Vasily and Nadia Kerenski and their teenage son and daughter, Eugene and Alexis, when their plane landed at the Los Angeles International Airport. Kasia had spoken to her mother and father on the phone explaining the turn in her life. Believing her parents' line would be tapped, she had omitted the fact of her recruitment by the KGB.

Kasia recognized immediately that her luxurious home intimidated her family. Although she embraced them with joyous cries of greeting, they held back with a reticence and lack of their traditional warm affection that disturbed her. She began to suspect they believed she had outgrown them, which in many ways she had, but not the memories of their love and caring for her as their child.

Her brother and sister had little to say about their classes in high school and outside activities. Eugene had inherited his father's height, shaggy dark hair and lean pallor. He wore dark-rimmed glasses and conveyed the bespectacled delicacy of a quiet intellectual. Vasily proudly shared that Eugene was the top student of his senior class and had been accepted at Northwestern University in Chicago.

At sixteen, Alexis struggled with an incipient heaviness and softness of flesh that rounded her rustic face and noticeably pushed out her waist and thighs. She was clearly embarrassed by her body in contrast to the striking beauty of her older sister.

After spending some personal time with them and touring the house and property, Kasia proposed that they move to California to reunite as a family. She would buy them a home and help accustom them to a California lifestyle. Their lack of enthusiasm and regrettable comment that they didn't like California (despite what little of it they had seen and experienced) disappointed her. But she understood they did not want to stray from their comfort zone.

After initially meeting Michael's parents, both outwardly friendly and adaptable to the social occasion (Mr. Sloan was a tall, bald glad-handing owner of a Ford dealership and Mrs. Sloan was a conservatively coiffed and styled country clubber who dabbled in residential real estate), the Kerenski's kept to themselves other than to be photographed with their daughter and son-in-law.

During the reception dinner, however, Vasily tossed back several shots of *Stolichnaya* vodka and at Kasia's urging danced a Viennese waltz and later in the evening, a Russian *baryna*, a folk dance.

The studio publicists promoted the small town aspects of her family and her past, where she had been born and raised by her Russian parents, and also focused special interest on prepared news releases about her student years as a street mime, the exaggerated (for the story) poverty and hard times she had endured until she met and was now going to wed the motion picture writer, producer, auteur director, Michael Sloan, in what was headlined as a "Cinderella Marriage."

Among her former friends and acquaintances, Kasia decided to invite only one, Dade Thomas. He was genuinely happy for her that she had moved up into such a professional and social sphere.

The piece of important news that he had for her was that Herb Wilcox had fallen apart since she'd left him. Dade himself didn't believe their group, Crystal Blue Persuasion, was going anywhere but down the tubes without Herb. He was looking around for other opportunities. He said he was even thinking of going back home to Louisiana for a while. He wanted to return to his roots and reconsider how to handle the direction of his life and floundering career. Kasia asked him to stay in touch and told him he would always be welcome in her home, for which he was grateful.

Following the wedding, the reception went on for hours until Heinrich gave the signal for their choreographed departure. It was directed like a number from a stage musical. That was Heinrich.

Kasia and Michael were chauffeured by a studio limousine to Los Angeles International where they were photographed and interviewed for another hour while waiting to board the plane, in spite of the fact it was one of Tri Con's Lear Jets.

They honeymooned for one week on the island of Aruba in the Caribbean. They had rented a house that overlooked a secluded white sand beach and quiet emerald lagoon protected from the seas by a reef that extended outward from their bowl-shaped private cove. They saw and spoke to almost no one but each other, a relief after the wedding and reception.

They made occasional forays into Christianstad on the north shore of the island to purchase food, rum, beer, and wine and to take in some of the local sights. They walked around the lichen covered walls of two ancient forts, Christiansvaern and Louise Augusta.

Strolling along the flagstone walks where Danish arches lined the arcade store fronts, they window shopped and purchased a few personal and select gifts for family and friends back home.

Michael remarked how all the rooftops were covered with corrugated iron, since hurricanes destroyed anything less resilient. They visited the St. Croix Museum in the basement of the library and reviewed a history of the Stone Age Carib culture that existed on the island when Christopher Columbus discovered it in 1493.

Leaving the museum, they stopped for ice cream sodas at Rasmussen's Coffee Shop.

Earlier during their stay, they had explored old sugar mills that dotted the landscape and noticed that here and there the ancient stone cones had been converted into houses.

At their private cottage, they made love whenever the impulse seized them – in the water, on the flour white sand, on a swaying hammock during the warm nights drenched in the aphrodisiac scent of tropical flowers.

***

With Dade and Kasia gone, Herb Wilcox decided to accept Stull's invitation to share their apartment near Venice Beach. On the day he moved in his few personal possessions, Lynn was alone.

She knew that whenever Stull and Randy didn't want her along, they were engaged in a major drug deal. In addition to the now infrequent gigs, Stull had entered the underworld of pushing drugs in a big way to supplement their income and to support his own habit.

Lynn followed Herb into the spare bedroom he would be sharing with Randy. He turned at her quiet lilting invitation, a singsong, "Herbie," and saw that she was unbuttoning her blouse.

"Come on, Herbie honey, they'll be gone for hours. It's just the two of us. Nice, huh?" She slipped out of her tight jeans and stretched openly on the bed. He nodded and began to remove his clothes. He was one of the group now.

Stull transacted a five-thousand-dollar sale with a man known to him as his contact. He was paid well to buy dope for himself, especially cocaine, and for wealthy discreet users in the film and television industry.

At the agent's request, he had revealed the name and identified the home of his main dealer connection on Mulholland Drive. However, his contact always went through Stull. The knowledge gave the agent contact leverage and power, should it ever be necessary to use it against Stull.

Leaving the commode of a public restroom near the Santa Monica Beach, Stull and Randy cruised back up Wilshire Boulevard through Santa Monica and Westwood to Sunset Boulevard. They turned west and located the street in Brentwood and the house of film producer/director Michael Sloan. As they made two slow passes, Randy shot several 35-millimeter exposures with his Minolta. Then they departed quickly from the neighborhood.

One day, Herb came across a publicity feature in the Los Angeles Times Calendar section about the filming underway of Michael Sloan's next picture, starring his wife as a young single working woman in Los Angeles. Pondering a moment, Herb put aside the article and searched for his cigarettes. Finding none at hand, he wandered into Lynn's and Stull's empty bedroom.

Randy had gone out with them, or so they claimed. They tended to be secretive and excluded Herb from most of their activities, which suited Herb just fine. Other than an occasional joint, he did not use drugs. That they might be hiding drugs in the apartment concerned him. He could easily be arrested as an innocent fourth party if there were ever a bust.

Rummaging about, he accidentally knocked a file folder from the dresser to the floor, spilling several enlarged black and white photographs of the Sloan house in Brentwood, which he recognized at once, having driven past out of curiosity.

There were other shots, as well, of Michael and Kasia entering a limousine, their two Mercedes and a candid telephoto angle of Michael and Kasia in a crowd.

As he sifted through the file, his interest aroused, he heard the front door open and close. Stull caught him in the act of hastily replacing the photographs on the dresser.

"What the fuck you doin' in my room, Wilcox?"

"Looking for cigarettes. What's this all about?"

"I'm into photographing rich people – clients."

"Clients? You don't even own a camera."

"It's Randy's. The photos are clients I sell dope to. There's cigarettes in the top drawer."

"That was a quick trip to the store."

"I forgot my wallet." Stull snatched it off the dresser. "Don't stick your nose where you can't stand the smell, Wilcox." He slammed out of the apartment.

Returning to the van, he informed Randy and Lynn, "Wilcox was snooping around and found the pictures."

"What?"

"I shouldn't have left them sitting out. He doesn't know what they're for, but he's at least curious."

"What'd you tell him?" asked Randy.

"Potential rich clients for dope."

"He knows Kasia and Sloan don't do drugs. What was he doing in your room in the first place?"

"He said looking for cigarettes. It's time we dump him."

"For what? Finding the pictures? What harm can he do?"

"Plenty. He's not even into drugs and I don't need that attitude around me. I just don't want him around anymore. He's not one of us."

"Why did you ask him to move in with us in the first place?" asked Lynn.

"I wanted to keep the group together, alive. Since Kasia left him, he's been in a long slide down. I thought he'd come to depend on us. We're like a family, the three of us. Thought he'd join, but he's too much of a loner."

"Why don't you just tell him to move out," said Randy.

"I will."

"What about the gig tonight?"

"I have a backup. It bothers me that when we put together the blackmail on Kasia, he'll connect it with us because of those fuckin' pictures. He'll go to the cops because he's still in love with that bitch."

Using a stand-in, they finished their gig without Herb at one a.m. and left the small San Fernando Valley night club at two after they had packed their speakers, instruments, and amplifiers. Stull drove them up Coldwater Canyon to Mulholland Drive and pulled into the winding entrance of a large home overlooking Beverly Hills on one side and the Valley on the other. Except for outdoor decorator lights, the house appeared to be unoccupied.

Randy asked, "Who do you know lives here?"

Stull grinned. "Friend of mine. Said we could use his pad for the weekend."

They climbed out of the van. Stull produced a key. They entered the house and were confronted by a spectacular sweeping view through a thirty-foot picture window overlooking an enormous pool and, far below, the Christmas effect of a sea of twinkling city lights.

Lynn walked over to the window and pressed her hands and forehead against the glass. "Christ, let's take it over."

"Look at that pool." Randy began to peel off his clothes. "Just let me in that blue juice."

Obviously familiar with the house, Stull turned on the lights, went to the bar, lined up glasses and poured out drinks.

Ten minutes later, they were all nude, cavorting and lolling about in the warm water.

As they approached their apartment on the following afternoon, Stull noticed what he suspected was a police surveillance unit in a tree trimming van next to a woodchipper across the street.

"Heat?" Randy asked when Stull suddenly accelerated and quickly left the neighborhood behind.

"Shit, when they find what we've got stashed in the apartment, we'll have to alter this goddamn van. Take off the name. Go a dark green on it or something. Best we get out of the fuckin' state for a while.

"Where?"

"Vegas."

"Vegas?"

"Vegas – shit, we can push for the Mafia if we have to. Sure don't want to fuck with 'em. We'll pick up another drummer, maybe a bass, try the casinos. Just be cool and lay low for a while."

Stull decided he would not tell them that he was going to maintain his Hollywood drug connections.

They rolled on east through town, merged onto the San Bernardino Freeway and followed it to the Barstow and Las Vegas junction.

CHAPTER ELEVEN

The Protest

Overcoming a case of nervous jitters at going in front of the camera as the wife of the director, Kasia stopped thinking about herself and focused on her character.

With the support of the cast and crew, the production moved ahead quickly and stayed on the sixty-day shooting schedule. Everyone involved sensed the unusual motion picture would be of exceptional quality in contrast to the wasteland of commercial exploitation films. They worked long hard hours, tuning in to Michael Sloan's vision of the characters, scenes, and cinematic texture he wanted to achieve.

He rehearsed the entire cast in ensemble exercises using video playback to evaluate performances and to integrate them into the matrix of the production.

On the technical side, through detailed advance planning, he trimmed away much of the time lost in set-ups and moved the cast efficiently from scene to scene while he delegated responsibility to his able assistant director, who ensured the production was always one step ahead of what was being shot. The effort required doubling up on some of the technical crew. They completed principal photography in eight weeks and brought the film in under budget, a feat almost unheard of in contemporary production.

Michael established a low-key tone in the film, a simple and straight forward development without relying on visual gimmickry and using few special effects. The emphasis was on character and motivation in contrast to several extravagant productions that had recently bombed at the box office and lost millions through inflated budgets.

Michael observed that the epics and big pictures had migrated successfully to television and the small personal film had found a new audience in theatrical houses.

Everyone involved lived, ate, and slept the film. Even during postproduction, Kasia stayed with Michael as he worked with two editors and a specialist in cutting sound.

One year later when the final print was ready, they held private screenings before the film was to be premiered in Westwood. The consensus from most other producers, writers, and directors who attended the screenings was that Michael had created a cinematic masterpiece his first time out on a major studio production.

The film was released for its premiere the following spring and was well received. The audience gave Michael and Kasia a standing ovation. At the party following the screening, the press, radio, and television media besieged Michael and his star regarding the powerful emotional impact of the film.

The reviews all came in strong in praise and support of the work heralding "the advent of the most exciting film actress since Garbo and a director of impeccable taste, style, vision, talent, and artistic courage."

***

"Times have changed, Giorgio. I don't have to take orders from you anymore."

"Oh, and have you so soon forgotten who put you where you are today?"

"Kurt Heinrich. Not you. Heinrich."

"Heinrich is a turd, a pain in the ass, and a bore. He never had an original thought in his life. He takes credit for my idea. So now, suddenly, you are too good, too special to meet with Giorgio. Let me remind you of why we have our meetings. Even though you are an actress, you still answer to me. You are a courier and will continue to be whenever you are ordered."

"That's all over. What's past is past."

Giorgio sputtered into the phone. "I know you, who you are, and what makes you tick, and it's not true love, my dear. We will have a meeting. Soon, you will be going to the Cannes Film Festival. It has also been arranged that you and your husband and your film will be recognized in the Soviet Union."

"Why in the Soviet Union?"

"You will find out. After a short vacation in central Europe, you will be met in Moscow. You will carry a message. I will give you the message and the details at a later date. Make an appointment with me to have your hair done at my salon. You will then continue to have your hair done with me on a regular basis. I've detected a negative change in your attitude. That is not good. If you continue, it could prove disastrous for you and your parents and brother and sister. It does not take long for people to forget you when you are gone. Be careful what you say and do."

Kasia heard an abrupt click. She hung up her phone. Georgio's veiled threat worried her. She would comply with his order to carry the message, but once she had securely established her star status with a second film, she determined she would permanently get out of the espionage business, on both sides.

She hadn't spoken with Gordon Frasier in a long time either. She wondered why he hadn't contacted her. Soon, in the not-so-distant future, she would tell him she was done with the CIA.

Giorgio Mykola unlocked and entered the back door of his salon at 8:00 a.m. He was the first to arrive. Opening the heavy office safe, he carried two canvas bank bags containing petty cash up front to the reception counter and placed the coins and various denominations of bills into the cash register drawer.

Except for an occasional jogger and a few people window shopping while walking their poodles, Beverly Drive was relatively deserted at that hour on a Saturday morning. Through the front display window, he saw his assistant manager's Porsche flash by and knew that shortly she would be coming in at the rear employee entrance.

He glanced down at the appointment book filled with the names of Beverly Hills women, some anonymous, some renowned in local social and entertainment industry circles. He noted that he would be doing Kasia Kerenski's hair at eleven. When she had made the appointment, he had mentioned that he had something special to tell her.

Smoking a cigarette, Geraldine Huddleston, a chic young brunette with a model's figure, came up to the front. "Good morning, Giorgio. How was the party last night?"

"A blast – we all had an orgy in the pool."

"Ah, next time for sure I'll have to come."

She glanced around his shoulder at the appointment book. "Heavy day, huh?"

Giorgio nodded. "Is Pauley still out sick?"

"She said she'd call in this morning before nine."

"She's out too damn much, especially when we need her. Is she that sick or is it drugs?"

"Coke, I'm sure of it. That's all she talks about lately."

"Start looking around for someone else, clean and dependable. Tell Pauley I'm giving her one week and tell her why."

"We're low on cream rinse."

"Send Eddy over to the supply warehouse. They open at ten."

"With Pauley out, we're going to be short-handed."

"Call Merriam. See if she wants to freelance until we can find someone to replace Pauley. Tell her she can have the job."

"Mrs. Seligman wasn't happy with what Eddy did to her hair last time. She said she wanted you for this afternoon, but when she called in, you were already booked solid to six o'clock."

Giorgio thought a moment. Call her back and ask her if she can come in at twelve thirty. I'll skip lunch."

"There's kefir in the frig. You can drink it while you work."

Giorgio scanned the twenty stations that would be manned and busy by ten o'clock. The average take was between twenty-five hundred and three-thousand dollars an hour every day of the week except Sundays, when the salon was closed.

Projecting humor, sophistication, and savoir faire, Giorgio ran the exclusive salon on a tight schedule. Although customers were never rushed, the shop bustled with frenetic cutting, styling, conversational chatter and gossip and the roar of blow driers against a backdrop of taped upbeat contemporary music while beautifully coiffed heads were turned out with assembly line precision.

Having opened the salon ten years with his own money and a loan which he had long since paid off, Giorgio had built his reputation on the excellent service, his European style, and the skill of the people he hired.

The salon provided him a unique cover. He had studied in Moscow and in France as a young man before immigrating to New York where he became an American citizen. Moving from one fashionable salon to another, he had ended up in Washington D.C. The wives and girlfriends and secretaries of Senators and Congressmen loved to tell him the insider Government and social gossip, some of it creeping into areas of confidential information that a husband or a lover had let slip.

The situation had proved to be an exceptionally rich source for Giorgio until he suspected the FBI had planted a stylist in the salon and was also sending in clients working under cover.

Not daring to risk discovery, he moved to California during the late sixties where he became the middleman for Helmut Bachmann and the KGB mission in Southern California.

Giorgio enjoyed his lifestyle and never took a chance that would jeopardize it either through discovery by the FBI or by being compromised in some other way that would cause the KGB to recall him to the Soviet Union.

Although he would never admit it, he had genuinely fallen in love with the "real people" in town. His salon, *Georgio's,* had been written up in numerous women's fashion magazines without his ever having to hire a publicist. The high social visibility of the women who came to him carried more than enough impact to generate editorial interest. He was in his element, just as he recognized Bachmann considered himself untouchable, a corporate god, in effect. Bachmann enjoyed his status, as well. Neither man wanted to see what they had acquired come tumbling down around them. They had defected to the West without even having to defect. Giorgio smiled at the conceit.

"Giorgio," Geraldine interrupted his mental meanderings.

"What?"

"I just talked to Pauley."

"And – What did she have to say?"

"Go fuck yourself."

"Sounds like Pauley. What a bitch. Tell Merriam I'll pay her double for the week. Screw Pauley. Screw that bitch. Call her back and tell her she doesn't get even one week and no severance pay."

Giorgio was good to his staff. He paid them well in addition to what they earned in tips. Some of them grossed fifty and sixty thousand a year. Even though he eschewed the good life, it galled him when someone didn't pull his or her share of the workload. At least he had not lost his appreciation for the value of work. *If you do not work, you do not eat. You do not have a roof over your head.* All of his people respected and worked hard for him, with the exception of Pauley. Just how much coke did she think she could buy with an unemployment check?

He felt bad about Pauley because they had had some good times together. She had taken advantage of their relationship occasionally and had gotten away with it until now that she was heavily into drugs. He knew why she didn't show for work. He also knew that he might even see her again. He would not let her come to the salon and she would not cut and style hair, but he would look after her for as long as she needed it. He wouldn't pay for her habit, but he would help her get herself clean and find another job. He would go to her apartment that night and try to convince her she needed to be hospitalized. He had talked to a good doctor, one of the best. *Go fuck yourself.* The little bitch. She knew he'd take care of her. She was weak and he was strong. She needed him in a different way than all those other women who came into the salon and spilled their guts to him. He was a priest, a hairdresser, a father confessor, and for a good dozen or more, a safe fuck on the side.

Ah, these decadent westerner women, if only they didn't shave their armpits.

"Giorgio. . . Giorgio. . . Giorgio. . .what are you doing to my hair? Do you feel all right? You don't look like you're even here."

He snapped back to the present, forcing himself to concentrate.

"Darling, darling, trust me. Trust your Giorgio. Only I know you intimately, your innermost thoughts and desires, even more than your husband. He does not fully realize his supreme good fortune in having you, such a wonderful woman, for his wife. The angle you see in this style," he referenced her image in the mirror, "is a projection of your inner self, that self we have so wonderfully discovered together," he crooned.

Mrs. Lobel covered his hand with her own as he tenderly touched her flushed cheek. "Giorgio, forgive me. I didn't mean to be critical. Of course, you know what's best for me. The new angle is perfect. It brings out the hidden aspect you describe, my essential personality. You are a genius, Giorgio, a true genius. Forgive me. Will I see you Monday?"

"Two p.m. as usual."

"Wonderful. My husband will be in New York and I'm giving the maid the day off."

He kissed her hand. "My weekend will be an agony of excitation and expectation. I hope you will experience the same anticipation."

Mrs. Lobel slipped him a five-hundred-dollar tip and paid the one hundred fifty for the wash and style on the way out.

Giorgio checked the clock. Ten fifty-five. Kasia would walk through the front door at any moment. He escorted Mrs. Lobel out to the sidewalk, then rushed back in to clean and straighten his area.

All eyes turned at Kasia's entry and followed her as she passed each station to be greeted by a smiling Giorgio and a hearty *abrazo*. Royalty had arrived. Giorgio quickly secluded her from the other customers and personally shampooed and conditioned her luxurious blonde hair, which had become a trademark for the movie-going public.

"Does the little one move yet?" He delicately touched her visible abdominal bulge.

"I feel an occasional fist or foot. Although sometimes it's only gas or an air bubble."

"Gas? A film actress doesn't have gas like the rest of us plebians, does she?"

"Not during the movie on the screen."

He laughed. "I hope you have a nice healthy boy. You are my most valued customer, Kasia, in many ways. You don't mind if I tease you a little. There's a serious message in what I'm about to tell you. Giorgio insists you listen carefully to what he has to say. I offer only good sound advice, then I expect you to act upon it accordingly."

They moved from the sink to his special custom leather chair. When she was comfortably seated, he stood directly behind her studying her face in the long mirror.

"Each time you are in my hands, it is like having nature's perfection to create a new work of art. If I were a director, I would cast you in the title role of Eve in the Garden of Eden. You know, I'm writing a script in my spare time. Needless to say, it has not progressed very far. So little time, but I will complete it. Perhaps your illustrious husband would like to see it. The title is *Hollywood Eden*. It's very sexy."

"Knowing you, Giorgio, it would probably make a good porno film."

"There has been a great deal of attention focused on the failure of nuclear power plants lately. You should capitalize on that opportunity for publicity. Get out there and make speeches about corporate responsibility. Emphasize how the American multinational energy companies are exploiting the people at home and abroad by exposing them to dangerous radiation, especially if there is a major earthquake."

"I don't think the Tri Con Corporation would care much for me running around doing that. I'm an actress, not a politician."

"What does Tri Con know?"

"I work for them."

"So? Aren't Americans always critical of their employers? I ask again, what does Tri Con know? Actually, in the news, Tri Con has taken measures to ensure there are no accidents. They even closed down a reactor that is sitting on a major earthquake fault here in Southern California. Coming from Tri Con Pictures, you, as a spokesperson, will create a positive association. Your pregnancy is perfectly timed. When the crowds and television viewers see you and, of course, you will talk about the lives of American children, your screen symbol will be enhanced, as well."

"I'm not working while I'm pregnant and I'm not going before the cameras until six months after my baby is born."

"Ah, but the magazines and press will be filled with features and photos on what a nurturing mother you are."

"When do you suggest I begin?"

"There is an anti-nuclear rally scheduled at *San Onofre* for next Sunday. Why don't you take a leisurely afternoon drive down the coast and put in an appearance, with your husband, of course. A microdot is encoded on the dollar bill I will hand you as change when you pay me today. When you arrive in Moscow, your contact will be a charming young woman by the name of Svetlana Zharinova. She is a professor of the cinema at Moscow University. You and your husband will be her guests for the duration of your stay in the Soviet Union. At an appropriate time, she will tell you when to pass the bill to her. It is marked so that you will not confuse it with any other."

"Giorgio, there will come a time after my child is born when I'll want out, permanently. This arrangement can't go on endlessly."

His cool smile filled the mirror. "It would be a shame to waste such talent and beauty. Consider the consequences if you try to do something foolish. Don't throw away all that you have gained. As I said, you are my most valued customer." His razor-sharp scissors snapped dangerously close to her ear.

A long line of cars jammed highway 5 and no parking was available in the immediate vicinity of the gray *San Onofre* reactor domes overlooking the Pacific Ocean from a high grassy bluff. Michael decided to drop off Kasia as close to the rally as possible, then he would park the car a half mile up the road and walk back to join her.

The Federal guards at the chain-link gate topped heavily with concertina wire had doubled their security and an army of police officers and patrol car convoys roamed the area. A refreshing sea breeze buffeted the sweet-acrid scent of marijuana over the heads of the crowd.

Unnoticed, Kasia stood towards the rear, listening to the 70s rock band up on the platform singing a protest song about nuclear disaster. When Michael returned twenty minutes later, he and Kasia maneuvered forward along the edge of the gathering until they came to a clutch of television news cameras.

One of the unit directors instantly recognized Kasia and the rally manager came over to her. He had her place scheduled for two-thirds through the program after consumer advocate Ralph Nader and environmentalist Jerry Commoner had given their speeches.

When she was finally introduced and climbed the steps to the platform, the crowd's ovation and roar of approval swept up to her. She spoke of how unregulated multinational corporations neglected the public interest in their rush for profits and that nuclear power was a prime example. She advocated that it should be phased out and replaced with Government subsidized solar and wind powered energy.

"We don't want to have happen anywhere again what occurred at Three Mile Island. In unleashing nuclear chain reactions, major companies and the United States Government are endangering the planet. Through damage to our genetic foundation of life, it can destroy forever the future generations of mankind. Part of the tragedy is that those who are responsible, the scientists, technicians, and government officials are lying to the American public in an attempt to cover up the reality of the monster they have created and over which they have no control. Human beings designed and run these power plants. They are not infallible. We tolerate human imperfection in many things, but we cannot risk the future of life on this earth."

As she closed her speech amid cheers and applause, the media journalists crowded in to question her. The following day, several editorials criticized her for using her position as a popular actress to promote her political opinion. Another accused her of trying be "Everywoman", wife, mother, movie actress, and political activist.

The attacks angered her, and in future public appearances she defended her position that she was child-centered and family-centered and that her career did not interfere or conflict with those values any more than any other working woman.

She pointed out that she did her own grocery shopping and took her own clothes to the cleaners. She did have a house cleaning service but cooked her own meals. Although later, after her child was born and she returned to work, she would hire a nanny. But no matter how mundane her domestic activities, she could not escape the public image of being Kasia Kerenski, the movie actress.

Everything that she professed and that was documented in magazines or on television became a public display of domesticity, Kasia playing the role of wife and mother to be. Everything she did to convince the public she was ordinary only served to convince them she was anything but ordinary. They did not want her to be ordinary. She was a movie actress, a goddess symbol, and only became more so despite what she said to deny that perception.

"Women are not treated with dignity. They don't get paid for housework. They don't have worker's compensation, if they are ill. And if their husbands leave them, they're out on the street. Our society does not foster generosity, courage, or social responsibility. It is founded on cutthroat competition and that is what we see all around us and that is what we get. We live in a society that sets men against women."

The more she toured and spoke at rallies and appeared on television talk shows, the more her political expressions on behalf of energy, ecology and the environment, and women's rights became a monologue. She was a media event. The substance of what she said carried little impact with the vast general public, except for middle class women who viewed her as a glamorous figure who articulated their liberal sentiments. In those times of swinging sex and open marriage, she had a happy and monogamous relationship with her husband. However, he was a film director with the power to glorify her on the screen and in the psyches of millions of men and women throughout the world.

Because of her privilege and wealth, for others, her statements came across as sanctimonious. Although she had risen from the streets, she could never again be considered as an average woman. She was "Cinderella," the woman who had made it in the movies.

CHAPTER TWELVE

The Lure

Recognized with the New York Film Critics Circle Award, the motion picture, *Sidewalk*, was then submitted as the official American entry at the Cannes Film Festival, where it took top honors and was awarded the *Palm D'Or.*

Michael and Kasia had flown to Cannes for the screening. After spending a few days at the festival, they rented a Porsche for an auto tour of France.

Michael was elated. After accepting the *Palm D'Or*, he had received a call from Heinrich informing him that he would have *carte blanche* on his next two films.

Leaving the topless bikini beaches and frenetic hustling of *Cannes* behind, they traveled the Mediterranean coast, passing through *St. Tropez* and *Toulon*. At *Marseille*, they turned inland and followed the Rhone River north into eastern France.

Traveling without plan and strictly on a whim, they angled west from *Lyon* and enjoyed the chateaus and ancient gothic cathedrals that punctuated the fertile countryside between small rural villages that extended in a chain into north central France.

What impressed Michael was the atmospheric substance of air and light as they moved from one region to the next. Coming onto the *Velay Plain*, they gasped at the sensation of going back in time to medieval topography. A stark battlement rose like a monolithic sentinel atop a central plateau surrounded by a panoramic pastorale for as far as the eye could see.

They took time to stop in every village and to stroll along the brick and cobblestone streets. Other than *bonjour, merci,* and *oui*, Michael neither spoke nor understood French.

Relying on a traveler's guide for conversational French, and recalling somewhat her college French classes, Kasia was at least able to order meals and check them in and out of hotels and village inns.

The sampled generously of the regional wines and bought cases to be shipped directly from the vintner to their home in California.

The romantic sway of an occasional village held their interest more strongly than others. Each turn in the road revealed a visual feast and a shared emotional discovery.

They decided they would one day buy a second home, a chateau out in the countryside near a rural village.

Their mutual love and the slow pace of travel they chose imprisoned them in a sweet landscape of fantasy and time as together they passed through this sublime experience on the heels of their cinematic success. They wanted to stop time. To return home would be anticlimactic.

Yet, they were to receive still another honor. From Paris, they flew directly to Moscow to be handed the Soviet Union's Gold Medal Award, recognizing their motion picture as the best foreign film.

Their liaison and guide was a statuesque, attractive brunette woman of thirty-four, Svetlana Zarhinova, a professor of film history at Moscow University. She spoke perfect English, including the latest in American slang.

They had been invited by the Soviet Government to tour the country, so, as they were informed, they would gain insight and understanding of the economic parallels drawn in the film, *Sidewalk*, and the negative depiction of government control and propaganda the United States Government created about the Soviet Union and the lives of the Russian people.

They were told that what they would be seeing was a classless society. They encouraged Michael to portray this positive element of communist influence in his next films, which he had briefly discussed at the conclusion of the screening in Moscow. Each film project concerned different aspects of political power and how it controlled and influenced the masses.

After he lost his initial distrust of Svetlana as an agent of the Soviet KGB, Michael conveyed to Kasia that they should respond to her genuine graciousness and enthusiasm as their hostess.

Kasia watched and listened carefully for an opportunity to slip Svetlana the dollar bill containing the microdot code, which the CIA was working to discover and break. Kasia had met with Gordon Frasier the day after the bill was given to her by Giorgio. Frasier had photographed it for examination and analysis.

Svetlana never gave her a sign, which concerned Kasia. She worried that she had been compromised and that the KGB knew she was a double agent. Maybe the microdot was only a ruse to set her up, a way to get her behind the iron curtain where she could suddenly disappear. Giorgio had not been pleased at her threat to quit and he had warned her to think of the consequences. He must surely have passed on to higher KGB officials that she wanted to resign. She could be considered a security risk.

As Svetlana carried on about how wonderful life would be for the couple if they would choose to change their citizenship and take up residence in the Soviet Union, Kasia sensed they were on the verge of becoming public prisoners who had "defected to Soviet Russia of their own free will and their desire to support the cause of world communism."

The fact that endless publicity photos and video taping of their tour and activities were shot wherever they went reinforced her anxiety that the Soviet Government would broadcast the message to the world as propaganda and proof that she and Michael had defected.

Svetlana decided that as part of their indoctrination, she would take them to visit her new apartment. This exhibition of being treated to vintage Georgian wines and fantastic gourmet dinners gave Kasia and Michael their first hint of economic class distinction in what was purported to be a classless society.

When they called attention to the discrepancies they had observed of a Western or non-Marxist orientation, Svetlana diligently explained that in Soviet society, position and privilege were totally unrelated to a person's level of income.

"Just because someone may earn more money than others, does not mean that he or she may purchase luxurious housing or take expensive vacations to the Black Sea. What a citizen does in service to the state determines those tangible rewards. The more highly the state values the function of the citizen, the greater are the endowed privileges.

"Of course, crowding has always been a problem in Moscow just as in your large cities like New York, Chicago, and Los Angeles. So the state has provided mass housing," which accounted for the acres of apartment buildings constructed of concrete slabs. They reminded Michael of the stucco apartments and condominium complexes that populated the Los Angeles landscape.

Suspecting that their conversations were being tape recorded, Michael decided to risk his next question regardless. "Who are considered the Soviet elite then in terms of value to the state?"

"Plant directors and top industrial managers, our leading engineers and ranking military officers. And an important group that will be of great interest to you, novelists, artists, film directors, university professors such as myself, and members of The Academy of Sciences. And, of course, our Government officials. Let me show you something to illustrate. Kasia, do you have an American one-dollar bill?"

Kasia reached down to her purse on the floor beside her chair, opened her wallet and drew out the one-dollar bill containing the microdot. She handed it to Svetlana, who held it up next to a ruble she had taken from her own purse.

"Money is nothing more than a medium of exchange. The material it is made of is essentially worthless. What is important is the value we receive in exchanging these symbols." Keeping the dollar bill, she handed the ruble to Kasia. "Just as we exchange ideas and technology, are we not citizens of the world? Borders are no obstacle to the kind of people we are, you and I." She carelessly stuffed the dollar into her purse.

"If you ever wished to make an important film in the Soviet Union, I can assure you a warm welcome and unlimited financial support from the State. What is important to the Soviets is that you continue to discredit the capitalist system as you have done and, quite candidly, philosophically you will probably continue to do in your next films. *Sidewalk* could just as well be a film shot in Russia about the Russian people." Her preemptive smile left Michael feeling vulnerable.

"You are a true Marxist, Mikhal," she continued, "and a consummate artist of the cinema. You would not encounter the obstacles to creating your film statements here in the Soviet Union that I know you do in your own country. And you would be living at a social and economic level comparable to the one you have in the United States."

There it was, Kasia thought, shrinking inwardly at the tone of the proposal. They're trying to lure us in first before they close the gate.

"And, of course, our cultural offerings are unsurpassed," Svetlana added. "We have hundreds of theaters and opera houses. Our fashion designers provide the latest in Western styles. And the two of you will soon become parents. Students in Soviet education exceed your schools in academic achievement."

Kasia sat far back in her chair, physically withdrawing herself from Svetlana, wanting to protect her unborn child from the prospect of coming into the world as a Soviet citizen.

Svetlana smiled encouragingly. "Our educational system and universities are the finest in the world. It is primarily through education that one may move into positions of importance, not unlike in your own country."

Michael's attitude had noticeably changed. His suspicions were again aroused by Svetlana's not so subtle attempt to sell them on a

Soviet lifestyle. His capitulation or even speaking favorably of their system would provide an astounding coup for the Soviet Communist Party, which he had every intention of avoiding. It would also be the end of his film career as he knew it. He determined responding to her overtures in a noncommittal diplomatic manner would be best. What he could not possibly know was the sophisticated plot of which Kasia had become the central focus. The plot also controlled his career as a writer and filmmaker as effectively as the Soviet State exerted similar control over the minds and soul of its people. Only, in this case, his wife was trapped between the CIA and the KGB.

Of keen interest to Michael and Kasia was the opportunity to tour Georgia, the Soviet agricultural region renowned for its rich productivity and mountainous vistas.

The only knowledge Michael had of Soviet collective farm life was drawn from the Eisenstein films he had seen as a student at UCLA. The films had attempted to dramatize the thrust to mechanize Soviet farms and increase production by the country's peasants.

The farm dwellings stretched for several miles in a collective line. In plots behind each house, the peasants could grow crops for their own consumption while the large fields surrounding the line were communally owned.

They saw the counterpart of the American cowboy, Soviet style, driving cattle to pasture in the Caucasus Mountains. On one of the large state farms, they watched women laborers hand-picking tea leaves. Svetlana pointed out how prevalent the Soviet woman was in both professional positions in urban centers and in agricultural and industrial labor. There was virtually no unemployment and no job discrimination.

They toured several open markets and sampled the traditional Russian flat unleavened bread along with the famous rich Georgian wines.

Not again during the balance of their travels did Svetlana mention the possibility of Michael and Kasia establishing residence in the

Soviet Union. However, Kasia breathed a great sigh of relief after they had cleared customs and were in the air on the final leg of their return to the United States.

A week later in Los Angeles, they rushed into production on their next project, a suspense thriller that doubled as an expose' on CIA infiltration of American colleges and universities across the country. The film was entitled, *Mt. Angell.*

As advance publicity about the subject and nature of the production began to circulate, the CIA through its covert agent, Kasia Kerenski, began to acquire further intelligence about the people who ran Tri Con Pictures. Almost weekly, information was reviewed by Gordon Frasier at The Security Bank in an ever-growing file on Tri Con executives and staff who were suspect.

CHAPTER THIRTEEN

The Entrepreneur

Bachmann swiveled around in his high-backed black leather chair and gazed out over the city from his fortieth-floor penthouse office atop the Tri Con Tower building.

His company was in a unique position as far as its expanding overseas interests. Unlike most multinational corporations, Tri Con was unaffected by the unstable political climate that pervaded third world countries. Whether the CIA had a hand in it or the Soviet KGB, Tri Con stood to gain politically and financially.

Tri Con's third quarter profits for 1976 exceeded six billion dollars drawn from oil and mineral resources, an airline, shipping, steel, and electronics. Tri Con had also recently acquired a motion picture studio in Los Angeles that now had thirty films in production for theatrical and television markets, plus a vast library of two hundred films that would soon find a home with a new acquisition, Wright Cable, to be renamed Tri Con Cable Television.

As Helmut Bachmann completed a call to London, his secretary's voice came through on the intercom. "It's Alex Pondoev on line three. He's been on hold."

"Thank you." Helmut punched the plastic button. "Hello, Alex, what's the news?"

"I've closed the deal. Tri Con owns Wright Cable Television. It will give us forty percent of the eastern market."

"What's their net worth?"

"Three hundred million."

"How do they stack up on the West Coast?"

"Somewhere in the middle. Storer and Teleprompter hold positions of strength with Times-Mirror third. Wright comes in just under that."

"Why do they want to sell?"

"Our research shows they're weak in top management and shot through with politics and ineffectiveness all down the line."

"Sounds like an opportunity to put our own people in there. Call me back when the deal is set. How's your family?"

"Happy and healthy and adjusting to their new home."

"Bel Aire isn't too hard to get used to."

"Weather sure beats New York and Chicago."

"Everything running smoothly at the bank?"

"An additional fifty million came in from Europe this morning."

"Glad to hear it. If you need anything, let me know."

"Thanks, Bach, bye for now."

"Goodbye." Bachmann punched off the intercom and continued his perusal of the Los Angeles Times. An article caught his attention about the coup in East Africa. If the government fell, Tri Con's oil operation would be in the hands of new leaders and the Soviet KGB, which had masterminded the regime, change would be inside. On the surface, the situation would represent a loss to Tri Con of several millions.

He glanced at his watch, swung around and pressed the intercom. "Dorothy, is my ten-thirty with Heinrich confirmed?"

"Yes, sir, and you have a private luncheon meeting with Mister Karazississ at twelve aboard your yacht."

"When Heinrich arrives, just show him in, will you please?"

"Yes, sir."

"Thank you." He left his massive oak desk and crossed the four-inch pile burgundy carpet to the bathroom, equipped with weight training and exercise apparatus, a sauna and a whirlpool. After relieving himself, he washed his hands. While drying them, he carefully inspected his appearance in the mirror.

He had not aged badly for forty-two. His hair was only just beginning to gray at the temples and it was full and healthy, not a hint of baldness. His sun-tanned face was lean and taut and showed barely enough wrinkles around his bold blue eyes to enhance his credibility as the President of a fortune 500 company. A daily workout in his office gym and maintaining a careful watch on his diet and alcohol consumption kept his tall hard body in trim.

At ten-thirty, his secretary ushered in Kurt Heinrich, chief of Bachman's Tri Con Studios. Bachmann rose and greeted the plump-faced little man with a firm handshake and led him to a comfortable chair in the conference area. Dorothy immediately followed with a silver serving of coffee and light pastries. Kurt promptly wolfed down two. Bachmann graciously thanked Dorothy, who left the office and closed the door.

Sipping his coffee, he studied the intense expression of Kurt savoring, chewing, and swallowing, eating to avoid an immediate discussion with his boss.

"I haven't had a chance to read the trades this past week," said Bachmann. "How goes it?"

"We took in two-hundred thousand the first week on our latest release and as of last Thursday, we're now operating in the black."

"I'm confident of the figures, Kurt. I put you where you are because you know the business and manage it better than anyone else.""

"Danke, these are excellent. A local bakery?"

"You'll have to ask my secretary. Although I believe her mother made these."

"I'll place a standing order and have them sent to my office every morning. They are culinary delights.

"Has Gerta reconsidered the divorce?"

"Nein, nein, I've had it up to here with her. That is the one negative thing about living in California. Divorce is like a contagious disease, especially in the entertainment industry. She has now accused me of having a mistress."

"Which is true."

"That's beside the point. Her accusation is not warranted."

"Obviously, old friend, with her it is the point, and she is an important lady. You understand what I'm getting at."

"There is no need to worry about her loyalty. She understands me and accepts the way things are. She will not change politically."

"What about her needs?"

Kurt stared at him. "Has she been talking to you?"

"I talk with all my people on a regular basis. It's important that I know what they're thinking and feeling."

"Such as now?"

"Such as now."

Kurt grunted. "She claims I don't understand her needs. *Gott im Himmel*, I don't have time to be understanding.   We are at that age."

"That age?"

"Ja, that age. She can do nothing about herself, so it is for her to understand me."

"It would be a sorry thing for you to grow apart."

"She will maintain what is confidential to the three of us. Now that I think of it, separating will not be such a bad arrangement. All she wants to do lately is lecture me on the doubtful fact that she has become a liberated woman. I think she has been spending too much time watching our new actress, Kasia Kerenski. She has seen the movie *Sidewalk* nine times."

"You always said if Gerta liked a film, it was bound to be a big hit."

"Well, if Gerta leaves me, and she will, I promise, I can have Marilee move in and warm my bed."

"No, keep her in her penthouse."

"Is there a problem with security?"

"No, she checks out, but if she comes to live with you, the publicity will be too intense. You must keep the publicity to a minimum. We cannot risk her talking about you and you must be careful what you say, always, always."

"Ja, as always I am."

"It is important that you keep in touch with Gerta."

"We'll talk."

"I know you will." Bachmann realized that Kurt felt out of his element with his recent promotion to studio chief from executive vice president of worldwide distribution. Kurt had been with the KGB in West Germany and had come to Tri Con Pictures with a sizeable German investment package that was already essentially within a Tri Con subsidiary in the amount of one hundred million dollars. Because of the man's business knowledge and connections in foreign markets, and because he was willing to comply with Bachmann's vision of the studio, Bachmann had moved him to the top spot.

It was to Kurt Heinrich that Giorgio Mykola had brought the idea of "discovering" Kasia Kerenski and making her a film actress. The possibilities had appealed to Bachmann. As a courier, she would never be suspected and she would be able to move in and out of countries at will, where other communist agents under suspicion could not penetrate without being easily identified. That she was a double agent for the CIA was unknown to him, just as he was unknown to her except as a corporate name and face. He had once met her to offer his personal congratulations following the premier screening of *Sidewalk*. His cover had been so thoroughly and effectively created and secured that neither she nor the CIA were aware of his link with the Soviet KGB.

Born Boris Sergeevitch Pondoev, Helmut Bachmann had remained behind the scenes being groomed by the KGB for a period of ten years for his role as first a West German, then an American corporate executive.

As a youth of fifteen, he had been smuggled into West Berlin as Helmut Bachmann, rejoining his family from whom he had been separated since early childhood during the Second World War.

His fictitious parents, who were actually Soviet spies, had come through the Berlin Wall in 1958 as Fritz and Elka Bachmann. Fritz had established a mercantile business that had grown into a large company in which their spy son, Helmut, had cut his teeth. In addition, he had acquired degrees in business and marketing at Berlin University.

Within three years of becoming executive vice president of his father's firm, he had expanded the company into oil by first joint venturing with a small American company, then taking it over with a leveraged buyout. Following that strategic move, which provided him legitimate ties in Brazil and Venezuela, he had changed his base of operations to the United States with offices in New York and California.

His cousin, Alexander Pondoev, was already a United States citizen, born and raised in Chicago. His career had led him into banking and eventually corporate status with the International Bank of The Americas, through which Tri Con financed eighty percent of its business.

Millions in laundered Soviet money filtered through Swiss accounts, several European banks, and banks in South America and in Soviet Bloc countries to end up with the International Bank of The Americas. The Tri Con Corporation drew on this vast reservoir for investments worldwide.

Many takeovers had followed Bachmann's move to the United States, including a major American oil and cargo shipping enterprise. Using his Soviet financing, Bachmann had also created a new international passenger and cargo airline, Transcon, Inc. Transcon offices around the world were used as bases of operation for numerous KGB agents just as Aeroflot was used by the Soviet GRU, a competing spy agency.

Within a relatively short period, Tri Con had acquired under its corporate wing an electronics firm that Bachmann internationalized and a satellite and telecommunications company with broadcast capability throughout the world. Special electronic tracking stations were constructed in the Soviet Union and Soviet occupied territories.

Tri Con's high technology commodities and electronics communication systems were being exported to the Soviet Union and

Eastern Bloc countries in flagrant violation of the State Department Export Administration and Arms Export Control Act.

Despite Tri Con's sophisticated global communications network, it was not as effective for espionage technology as the KGB desired. The National Security Agency (NSA) intercepted and decoded fifty percent of exchanged messages using cryptoanalysis.

Secret or classified messages were sent in code or cipher, substituting a word, symbol, or symbol grouping for an entire word, word group, or thought. These coded messages were known as cryptograms or cryptographs. Breaking the codes or decrypting was accomplished through the use of computers and Mathematical analysis.

The omniscient eyes and ears of NSA's electronic surveillance systems forced Bachmann to rely on messages conveyed by courier. From time to time, he would check a courier's reliability by feeding false or worthless information to see if it appeared later in another context or prompted a reaction from the FBI or CIA. Thus far, there had never been a mishap.

Georgio Mykola had handpicked his local and international informants and messengers with extreme care and paid them well. The covert activity was accomplished under the guise of industrial espionage, rather than national or political spying and, in appearance, seemed to keep the "boss" informed about "internal problems."

"Kurt," Bachmann poured them each a second cup of coffee, "How far along is Michael Sloan on the *Mt. Angell* film?"

"He has a progressive production schedule and all the locations are here in Southern California, mostly in Los Angeles. Principal photography is about one-third completed. We are planning a pre-Christmas release for next year."

"I have an idea for a major epic I want him to write and direct for his Tri Con project. It's long range. It will take a couple of years to develop and perhaps another two or three to produce."

"I'm listening."

"It's to be set in South America, a contemporary story of a revolution on the scale of *War and Peace* encompassing both Central and South America. The title I have in mind is *Borders*. The film will star Kasia Kerenski as an American journalist and will involve an international cast. At the appropriate time, we will arrange to shoot on location in Chile, Brazil, and Argentina, depending on what the script calls for. But Chile, definitely. Given Tri Con's connections with Pinochet, that would be the best of political situations down there for us."

"The budget for something like that would be huge, forty – fifty million at least, maybe more, much more."

"I'm aware of that. The money is available. Pass the concept on to Michael. We can meet with him at his convenience to discuss it. Development will require a considerable amount of research and preparation. We have the people to support him. I suggest you start the story department on that."

"So you're looking at 1984 or '85 as the year of release?"

"Possibly. Through Tri Con's political and business contacts in Latin America, I've recently learned that those countries will be very much in the news at that time."

Kurt gave him a questioning look.

"Latin American governments have always been unstable. We have plans in progress. The film is only a part of it, although I'm not at liberty to discuss that with you at this time."

"So, you believe there will be a market for the film."

"At that time, definitely. In a sense, we will increase the market through world headlines. The motion picture will correspond to world news events."

"Is the film to dwell on significant social and political themes in Latin America?"

"Only to a small extent. Tell Michael to set the main story in the context of an international espionage thriller in which the CIA operatives are the villains. We want this to be a commercial film, not a study in politics and sociology like *Sidewalk* and *Mt. Angell*. When he's ready to talk about it, I have a few story angles to share with him, but clarify he won't be bound by them, totally. I don't want to dictate to him how he should create. His talent is a primary asset to Tri Con."

"There's no doubting he's our *wunderkind*."

"I'm afraid Lili and I have to pass on Saturday's screening of Fassbinder's film. We are obligated to attend a charity benefit for the American Cancer Society. Tri Con is a large contributor to their research fund. This year, we gave six million. We are truly an American company."

"I understand. Well, anything else?"

"No. . ." Bachmann hesitated. "Be sure to convey to Michael the importance of this project to me and to the company. It will be a high mark for us in every way."

"*Ja whol.*"

They rose, shook hands, and Kurt departed with a few complimentary words to Bachmann's secretary regarding her mother's pastries. Bachmann then asked her to arrange for a daily morning delivery of the pastries to Kurt Heinrich's office at the Tri Con Studios.

Malcolm Karazississ was waiting on board Bachmann's yacht, Trident, when the limousine pulled into the marina's private parking area. The yacht steward had served Malcolm Dom Perignon and Beluga caviar. Bachmann's guest was in a fine mood after his three day cruise up the coast from Acapulco on his own private yacht.

Although Bachmann knew of his reputation and had extensive information researched and provided through KGB intelligence sources, he had never before met the mercenary, who created revolutions for a price. He looked like a red-bearded sea captain wearing traditional white slacks and blue blazer with an elaborate red and gold coat of arms emblazoned on the breast pocket.

Bachmann was surprised at the imposing six foot six height of the man. Karazississ emanated a barely contained energy and power that overwhelmed even a man of Bachmann's physical stature and position of importance. Karazississ' apparent sophistication and social grace belied the lethal soldier within. Even as they greeted each other, Bachmann noted the rippling grace of his movements. He was in classic physical condition and would be the envy of most modern generals in the army.

The South American plan had been put into motion at a KGB meeting in Moscow three years ago. As a KGB front, the Tri Con Corporation engaged in industrial espionage using couriers taking hand-offs from a defense engineer, Charley MacIntosh, inside an American aerospace company in California.

The son of a Greek fisherman and a Russian mother, who returned to the Soviet Union a year after her son was born, Malcolm was raised on a communal farm. He was a big strong youth, intelligent, gifted, and recognized as such by a local teacher who encouraged his mother to send him to school in St. Petersburg. He had a unique gift for languages, became fluent in five, and graduated from Moscow University majoring in business and economics. He then joined the Soviet army, was trained and soon discovered as a special forces commando by the KGB. The agency recruited him to become a power broker, using mercenary military sources to undermine U.S. foreign economic and political interests.

Department V was responsible for "wet affairs" (*mokrie dela*) -- murders, kidnappings, and sabotage -- which involved bloodshed. Previously known as the Thirteenth Department or Line F, the Department was enlarged and redesignated in 1969 and tasked with sabotaging critical infrastructure to immobilize Western countries during future crises. The Department employed officers stationed in

Soviet embassies, illegals stationed abroad, and the services of professional mercenaries like Malcolm.

The First Chief Directorate was responsible for KGB operations abroad. It was divided into three sub-directorates, responsible respectively for deep-cover espionage agents, collection of scientific and technological intelligence, and infiltration of foreign security operations and surveillance of Soviet citizens in foreign countries. Segmented into eleven geographical regions, the First Chief Directorate placed intelligence-gathering officers in legal positions in embassies and elsewhere abroad. Such activities increased markedly after détente with the West in 1972 permitted many more Soviet officials to take positions in Western and Third World countries. In the 1970s and 1980s, as many as 50 percent of these officials were estimated to be conducting espionage.

Bachmann steeled himself under the intense scrutiny of Karazississ's unflinching blue eyes. "It's a pleasure to finally meet you, Mr. Karazississ."

"The pleasure is mine, sir. And please, let's be on a first name basis. Call me Malcolm."

"Excellent. The food is waiting. Shall we?" Bachmann escorted him to the luncheon aesthetically and appetizingly laid out by the steward. They began with a fresh shrimp and crab salad in a bed of lettuce and avocado, then followed with a beef tenderloin brochette on rice entre. Dessert was assorted fresh fruit, cheeses, and Remy Martin cognac with Columbian coffee and Havana cigars.

During the meal, Bachmann kept the conversation casual, discussing food, boating, women, entertainment, the world market and current inflation. Cognizant of the possibility they might be under electronic surveillance and that their conversation might be recorded by agents in a neighboring yacht, Bachmann slipped Malcolm a brief note designating a specific time and meeting place for that night when they would continue their conversation and close the deal. Malcolm nodded, touched the glowing tip of his cigar to the paper and they watched it turn to ashes. Together, they then rose and strolled about the deck, admiring the lines of this or that yacht and commenting on the rising cost of fuel and how it would affect recreational boating for all but the very rich.

When they departed, Malcolm returned to his own yacht and, appearing to be headed back down the coast, left the marina.

Bachmann made several business calls from the Trident and finished at three o'clock that afternoon. His chauffeur dropped him at his Beverly Hills mansion. The maid informed him that his wife had gone shopping and to have her hair done at Giorgio's and was expected to return at five. He took a relaxing swim, then settled down with paperwork for two hours until Lili arrived.

He greeted her with an affectionate kiss. "You're looking especially attractive, dear."

"I just had my hair done at Giorgio's. Do you like it?" She turned so he could see the back.

"Adore it. What's the schedule for this evening?"

"Cocktails at the Beverly Hilton at six-thirty, dinner at seven with a speaker."

"Have you heard from Nancy?"

"Yes, she's sharing an apartment just off campus with a friend."

"Male or female?"

Lili smiled at him. "You are a suspicious sort, aren't you?"

"Well, aren't you?"

"Yes, and her friend is female. I checked."

Bachmann laughed. "Good for you. We're both suspicious."

"She wants to know if we'd like to fly up for the Stanford – Oregon game. It's Stanford's homecoming."

"Depends on the date, but I imagine so. We can spend an extra couple of days in San Francisco. Maybe Fran and Ross would like to join us for an evening. We haven't seen them in months."

"I'll call Fran tomorrow morning," said Lili. "It's late. I thought I'd be home by five. We'd better get ready."

"I've showered and shaved. Had a nice swim first."

"I would really like to get there a few minutes early tonight. Agnes and I have to discuss a special tribute to the Holloways."

"I'll be ready." He watched her scurry off on small bare feet into the mammoth walk-in closet they shared. He never tired of her cheerful energy and petit dark beauty.

He had met Lili nineteen years ago while on a business trip in Vienna before he had come to the United States and established the Tri Con Corporation. She was the daughter of a wealthy Austrian manufacturer with whom Bachmann transacted a defense parts supply arrangement in support of products assembled in Berlin.

At a lavish dinner party, the infatuation between Bachmann and Lili Werner had been immediately transparent, much to her parents' delight. Bachmann had extended his visit for an additional three days, all of which he spent sightseeing with Lili. They took in the historic palaces of the Hapsburg monarchy, attended a Mozart opera at the *Hofburg Theater* on the *Ringstrasse*, sampled the city's famous coffee houses, and watched a performance of the Lippizaners at the Spanish Riding School.

Two months later, he returned, and they were married in Vienna. After a honeymoon in the south coast of France, they had gone back to West Berlin to plan for their move to the United States where Bachmann had purchased a New York Penthouse for his business trips.

He had never revealed to her his true origin and that he was the most unique agent that ever existed in the Soviet KGB. He was sworn to never disclose the secret, and unless he were somehow compromised, he would take it with him to his grave.

They arrived at the Beverly Hilton at six-fifteen and went in through the glittering lobby to the open bar area where guests were beginning to gather.   While Lili sought out Agnes, the meeting planner,

Bachmann ordered a V.O. and soda and leisurely scanned the richly dressed crowd of Los Angeles and Beverly Hills notables.

Although he recognized an occasional personal acquaintance, he did little more than wave and neither approached nor encouraged others to approach and enter into conversation. Considering who he was and his prominent successes incorporating a wide range of businesses, he was basically an extrovert but preferred his social privacy. He and Lili were always on the 'A' list for exclusive parties, many of which he did not attend on the pretext of business commitments.

He never confessed to Lili how much the parties and endless chain of social functions bored him to distraction. After interacting with people in his office and on the phone with others around the world all day every day, he preferred his solitude, a time to read a good book, see a film or a play, and contemplate over a quiet gourmet dinner and vintage wine with Lili.

Lili was different than he. She thrived on social energy, because that was all she had in the way of personal accomplishments. Although several of her oil paintings hung on the walls of their home, she was not particularly creative. She had once even attempted to write a novel, but did not possess the necessary discipline or imagination to get beyond ten pages.

Bachmann understood her frustration and occasionally asked her to accompany him on business trips that would afford her interesting locales in which to shop and sightsee.

She had been closest to their two children, Nancy and Rick, especially during their early years. The long hours his business demanded of him had so frequently brought him home after the family was in bed asleep that he had felt like a father in absentia. The situation had never improved over the years. He was unavoidably more married to his job and to the Tri Con Corporation than to his wife and children.

Now, their daughter, Nancy, was in her second year at Stanford University majoring in business with the goal of becoming an attorney. Their son, Rick, would attend UCLA as a freshman the following year and major in motion picture and theater arts. Since his father owned a studio, Rick's ambition was to become a film director.

Both of his children were thoroughly Americanized. He would have to keep his secret from them, as well. Even if he revealed it to them, he figured they would never believe him and that he was just making up a story to play a joke. KGB agents just were not presidents of major multinational corporations, a commonly held belief that made his cover so convincing and effective.

Suddenly, he saw Michael Sloan and Kasia Kerenski enter and mingle with the crowd. They noticed him and without hesitation came over to say hello. He envied them their exuberant youth, talent, and idealism.

Bachmann was intrigued by Kasia in that she had come from Russian stock. She had been born and raised outside her native country to become a Soviet spy. He wondered if she had shared her secret with Michael. He hoped not. If she had, Giorgio had not reported any problems or discrepancies, and Bachmann knew how closely Giorgio monitored her without actually putting her under surveillance. He had assured Bachmann that Kasia was a professional spy and loyal to the Soviet cause of dominating the world economy.

Although she carried a Russian-American immigrant name and was internationally recognized as an American motion picture actress, her ties were with the Soviet Union. Like himself, she was now in a key position to gather intelligence and pass it on to the Soviets in a way that would impact world events.

Information could come from an inadvertent comment dropped by a senator or a congressman over cocktails at a function such as this. He himself had been made privy to many matters of state interest because of Tri Con's presence in nearly every major foreign market. He was among the elite in the private sector whose business influenced the laws that determined foreign policy in favor of corporate America. Tri Con was essentially a mini-government unto itself both domestically and overseas and, like many corporations, operated independently of American foreign policy.

Bachmann had recently turned forty-two. He wanted to retire in ten years. His successor, already being groomed among the executive ranks of the Tri Con Corporation, would move upward into the president's position with no one the wiser. All his immediate under executives came from within the ranks of the KGB. All were American citizens, born or naturalized.

He surreptitiously glanced at his watch. Michael and Kasia moved on to chat with others. The time was six forty-five. As preplanned, he heard a woman's voice page him over the public address system. "Will Mr. Helmut Bachmann please come to the information desk. Helmut Bachmann, please come to the information desk."

He strode with quick deliberation through the lobby and received the note which had no meaning to anyone but himself, since he had planted it earlier upon his arrival. He, in turn, wrote out a brief message to Lili and asked the clerk to ensure that she received it within the next five minutes. Then, leaving, a ten-dollar tip, he went outside to wait for the valet to bring up his Mercedes. Ten minutes later, he was headed west on Wilshire Boulevard. Coming into Westwood, he turned north on Westwood Boulevard to the UCLA campus.

Even dressed as a bearded student, Malcolm Karazississ stood out in the evening crowd streaming into Westwood Village to eat in the restaurants and join the long lines in front of the local cinemas, one of which featured *Sidewalk*. Malcolm climbed into the Mercedes and the two men quickly drove away.

Fearing the possibility that his car might be wired, Bachmann shook his head, cautioning Malcolm not to speak about the matter at issue. As an added precaution, he turned on an electric shaver whose frequency would discourage any transmission of their conversation. He turned north on Veteran to Sunset, then headed west toward

Pacific Palisades. Leaving the car at the edge of the Coast Highway, they walked down to the beach where the noise of the crashing surf would cover anything they said.

"Tri Con has substantial interests in copper and nitrates exported from Chile. We work through two subsidiaries. I'm concerned about what is happening in the country since Pinochet has come into power. My German associates in Santiago and Valparaíso keep me well informed.

"The fascist *junta* supports the Fatherland and Freedom Party. Their Bureau of National Intelligence is headed up by a Walter Rauf. However, Manuel Contreras is the whip who handles torture and interrogation.

"Pinochet's military regime has violated all civil rights. There is no longer a congress. The courts have been neutralized and the constitution suspended. Freedom of the press has been obliterated. Books and publications that do not conform to the ideologies of the dictatorship and its administration have been destroyed.

"Thousands of prisoners are being held in *Tres Alamos* and remote concentration camps. No political parties except pro-dictator right wing extremist groups are allowed to exist. The American Government and the CIA have propped up and support Pinochet. The socialist and communist parties have been outlawed. Their leaders have either been murdered or forced into hiding or exile. Even nuns and priests are being arrested because they dare to speak out against the generals. The economy is shut down. The vast majority of the population is on the edge of starvation."

"The associates who provide your information, what is their personal interest in regime change?"

"Although they are members of the aristocracy and, therefore, not suspected by the *junta*, for the most part they are liberals, a political position they must keep well-hidden while they wear the mask of extreme right wing conservatives or risk arrest and possible execution."

"So you feel the time is right for at least an overthrow of the *junta*."

"No, now is not the time and replacing the *junta* with another dictator and his military regime is not the answer."

"Then you are talking about a true revolution."

"Yes." Bachmann looked squarely into the mercenary's piercing blue eyes that reflected the flashes of surf exploding and booming like artillery nearby.

"A revolution takes time, maybe years. It doesn't happen overnight. There's so much groundwork to be laid. Vietnam is an example. South Africa another. The price is high. Can you afford to go that long?"

"You have a blank check."

"So if I accept your offer and begin this revolution, where do you intend it should end?"

"Revolutions do not end, as you well know. Certainly not in Chile. It will link with actions to be taken in Central America, San Salvador, Nicaragua, and Guatemala. Then Brazil and Argentina will follow."

"Panama?"

"As well."

"I understand the junta offers considerable incentives to attract foreign investments, cheap labor, slave labor, low wages if any, no strikes, no unions."

"Pinochet is the opposite of Allende. The mines were seized from Tri Con by Allende when he was in power. He was on the right track but knew nothing about how to run the country. Unfortunately, he aborted the economy and because of his stupidity, set himself up to be deposed. Pinochet has gone too far the other way with his economic shock treatment and has done far worse for the country."

They had come to a standstill. Bachmann motioned that they should continue to walk while they talked.

"The *junta's* policies may have halted inflation," he continued, "but it also has no development. General Guzman himself, who is one of the big four, has openly criticized the social costs of the economic program. The *junta* has a negative world image and knows they are in need of popular support. Failure to develop a social base will mean their downfall.

"The Maritime Workers Union and other small pro-government unions allowed to function are clearly displeased with Pinochet's new labor code, because it suppresses all unions regardless of their political affiliation. So the economic conditions have not improved. The hardships are the same for the people as under Allende. They are restive and explosive, dangerous for the regime, favorable for our purposes.

"The world demand for copper has declined and forced back production in South America. Chile has had to increase imports of oil and food. The cost for food alone is well over five hundred million. According to my sources, the sharp increase in prices has caused resentment and discontent. The economic costs of the *junta* have also been excessive and have had a negative impact on the country. In Santiago and other large cities, as well as in the interior, the unease of the people is unmistakable."

Karazississ remained silent for several moments, assessing the information Bachmann had just provided him. "The U.S. Government supports Pinochet with financial and military assistance, as well as the CIA. Tri Con must stand to benefit from all this. I'm not playing politics, Bachmann, and I'm nobody's fool."

"We have a mole."

"In the CIA?"

"Yes, the CIA."

"I've been in the war business a long time. I just want to know who's paying the bill. If I'm actually working for the CIA, then I want to know. Beyond that, I can figure out why." Karazississ knew very well who Helmut Bachmann was. His reference to the CIA was to divert any suspicion Bachmann might have about him.

"I'm paying. That's all you need to know."

Malcolm stared at Bachmann's barely illuminated face. "This will take a considerable amount of planning, at least one, maybe two or three years to infiltrate and lay the groundwork before I move in troops. What of the other countries, Brazil, Argentina, and those in Central America.?"

"Other arrangements have been made. Your effort will eventually link up with those. South America will become a financial partner of the Soviet Union."

"I'll the need the assistance of your people and the identity and location of the mole."

"His name is Roger Lakein. His cover is as a journalist. There are others, including two American exiles, Charley and Maggie MacIntosh. They'll assist you as informers. The time and place of contact will be arranged. In Argentina, you'll recruit from the MIR, *Movimiento de Izquierda Revolucionario*. They are left wing extremists, revolutionaries hiding and training in Argentina. They are part of the International Revolutionary Coordination *Junta*, the JCR, with guerrilla organizations from Bolivia, Uruguay, Brazil, and Argentina. So you see how the rest of South America can fall. The MIR has guerilla warfare training programs in remote Argentine camps. They will become your source of manpower numbering in the thousands. They coordinate terrorist activity in the cities and rural areas."

"I'm very familiar with the MIR. My contact is in Buenos Aires. I need one million dollars American up front to cover personal expenses."

"It has already been deposited for you in a numbered Swiss account." Bachmann handed him a slip of paper. Karazississ would memorize the number and destroy it.

"You realize that a landing operation is out of the question."

"At the time of our first strike, Tri Con Pictures will be filming near Santiago and in the surrounding countryside and forests south of Concepcion where there's a naval base. The tanks and artillery will be staged and waiting for you at Puerto Montt as you move north. These will be brought in to the country under the belief they are being furnished by the United States Government through the CIA to be turned over to Pinochet at the conclusion of the filming. You and your guerillas will capture those armaments."

"I have another question," said Karazississ. "Why have you chosen to work with my mercenaries?"

Bachmann suspected Malcolm was trying to draw him into the trap of saying he was allied with the communists or Soviet Union in some way which could implicate him as a spy. Malcolm would have surmised that by now. Bachmann adroitly avoided giving him a clear answer. "You're an officer in the GRU."

Karazississ was stunned that Bachmann knew. There was only one way Bachmann could have that knowledge. That would make him an elite officer of the KGB.

"Now that we are clear as to who we are," continued Bachmann, "that is why I selected you. You've worked for us before in Southeast Asia and in North Africa, South Africa and Central America. You are only identified as a mercenary, politically neutral, a hired gun, but the CIA can only associate you with the KGB. We never had this conversation. You will not be traceable back to Tri Con or to me. The action in South America will be construed as a KGB or perhaps communist insurgent maneuver just as the interventions in the other countries I mentioned."

"What about those countries now?"

"For the time being, you have no concern or involvement."

"If I decide to accept your offer, one million will be transferred from the account by twelve hundred hours tomorrow."

"Shall I take you back to the campus?"

"No, I have a car and driver waiting. I just graduated. My days as a student are over."

Bachmann extended his hand. Malcolm avoided taking it, which concerned Bachmann only slightly. Malcolm had no choice but to accept the million and follow orders.

"I'll leave after you," said Malcolm. "Lower your hand in case someone is watching."

Bachmann dropped his hand. "No one is watching, I can assure you." He turned away and walked back across the sand out of the shadow of the cliff and up the long twisting flight of wooden steps to the highway. He had executed the first move.

CHAPTER FOURTEEN

An Overdrawn Account

Kasia finished her mild workout at the Beverly Hills Health Club at five-thirty, showered, dressed in a black leotard and skirt, and went to a private phone booth. Putting in a dime, she dialed and waited.

"Emerson, Hudson, and Williams," came an answer, a man's voice.

"Oh, excuse me, I'm trying to reach the Security Bank. I have a message to call regarding an overdrawn account."

"Are you on the street?"

"No, I'm on the sidewalk."

"Hello, Sidewalk, thank you for being so prompt, only three days since I know you received my message," said Gordon Frasier. "What gives"

"I'm an expectant mother. I get tired rather easily."

"I want you to deliver a message to Matthew Delugach."

"Delugach? He's Vice President in charge of overseas distribution for Tri Con Pictures."

"As you well know. There is no need to verify yourself by repeating the information over a public phone. We have reason to suspect he works for Inca, our suspected mole. We want to see if the message you give him is passed on to one of our agents in South America. The information will be interesting, but worthless. It's only purpose is to flush out Delugach. We know he's been talking to Giorgio Mykola. The discussion might have been social, but not likely. He probably knows you work for Giorgio."

"You have my undivided attention."

Gordon paused. "You need to temper your sarcasm. Handle the encounter casually, say in reference to the research being done for your husband's script on revolutionary activities in South America. The message is that you recently learned from a confidential source that the CIA has deciphered a coded message as to the identity of another spy in Tri Con. Got it?"

"Yes, will this take care of my personal banking problem? I'm reaching the point where I want to permanently close my account."

"That's not possible, Sidewalk. You're much too valuable an asset at the present time. The Security Bank depends on your unquestioning patronage. We do have a special interest in you. Your annuity comes up for renewal in about six months. You'll be receiving a required distribution. Let's discuss your options at that time. Any other questions?"

"None."

"Have a nice evening and congratulations on your pregnancy."

"Bye." She hung up. Brisk with anger, she slammed out of the phone booth.

When she arrived home at six-thirty, Michael called to her from the patio where he was working on his South American script. She stopped at the unexpected sight of the little half pint puppy who wiggled her tail, but immediately moved back to Michael at the sudden appearance of this other giant hovering human creature.

The pup sensed Kasia's femaleness, her smiling gentleness, and squirmed with delight at being touched and handled. Michael recounted how he had selected the puppy at the animal shelter and that she reminded him of a photograph of his mother. Kasia left the small animal, who had suddenly grown sleepy, and went back inside to begin preparing supper. Michael mentioned that he already had coals warming to make barbequed chicken.

Staring down at the snoozing pup, he resumed his perusal of a pocket Roget's Thesaurus in search of an idea for an appropriate name, something that corresponded conceptually to the sprightly energy combined with the doe-eyed demure attraction the blonde-coated puppy held for him.

"Pizzas," he said. "No, that's not right. Pizza. You're almost the color of cheese, but you don't look anything like a pizza. A yellow sausage maybe. A blonde sausage. Your tail's like a little white plume. Plume. It's close but somehow it just doesn't seem right. What else is there? I feel like it's on the tip of my tongue, but I can't get the word out." His searching glance suddenly landed on the word panache. He quickly flipped to the page bearing the definition – panache. Having flair and style. Flair and style. He looked at the runt. "That's you all right, flair and style. It isn't all in place there yet, but it will be. You have potential."

He sat upright on the sun lounge. "Panache, how do you like that for a name, huh? Panache. Panache."

The puppy's thick pink lips parted in what could be interpreted as a grin and leaped up and down with enthusiasm at having a name at last, or so Michael projected on the animal. He shouted into the house, "Hey, Kasia, she has a name."

"What is it?"

"Panache."

"What?"

"Panache."

"Panache?" She came out from the kitchen to the patio sliding door and peered at him as though he'd been drinking. "What kind of a name is that?"

"It means having flair and style."

"Flair and style? That little thing? You've got to be kidding."

"I'm not. It gives her something to grow into. Doesn't it fit her perfectly? She knows. It's her spirit. The nature of her spirit comes through her eyes and it's her tail and the way she crosses her wrists."

"Wrists? Dogs don't have wrists."

"Paws then. Well, heck she has wrists. She crossed her wrists. Look at her. Look at that. Wrists."

"You're looney. You could only be a writer and filmmaker. That's no name for a dog."

"I don't want it to be some mundane dog name. It has to match her personality. And in many ways, it does."

"Well, she's your dog. Name her whatever you like."

"She's your dog too."

Kasia patted her bulging belly. "I have baby enough here to worry about. Besides, she's attached to you." She waved a dish towel at him.

"What would you name her?"

"Fido or Alice or something like that."

"Fido, Alice? That doesn't show any imagination at all. They don't fit her either. You're an actress. Where's your imagination?"

"On vacation for the next nine to twelve months. You have more than enough for the both of us. Panache it is."

"Panache it is then. See, she already knows her name. Look at her."

"Where is she going to sleep?"

"I'll fix up a little place for her in the garage."

"It's getting pretty cold at night." Kasia glanced up at the graying sky.

Later, keeping a watchful eye on the puppy sniffing and poking around the living room, Michael hurriedly finished the last of his supper. Panache might squat at any moment and it would be necessary to move quickly. Newspapers covered the entire kitchen floor, but she cried and whined to get out when he erected a barrier from medium sized cartons to block her access. So he and Kasia adopted a plan of hit or miss. There tended to be more misses, so Kasia put Michael in charge of spot cleaning the carpet.

"I'm going to make her a cave out of those old carpet cuttings in the closet," he said. "And a blanket. She can have one of my old shoes and an undershirt with my smell on it. And I'll leave the garage light on for her."

"She's going to be an outdoor dog then, I take it."

Michael thought he detected the beginning of a move to squat. "I guess so."

"Well then, we have to stick by that."

"She can come inside sometimes though," he said with concern.

"But she's not going to sleep in."

He looked doubtful. "I guess she'll be okay in the garage."

"You're being very fatherly about her. In six or seven months, you'll have a reason to be fatherly."

Michael grinned. "I'm looking forward to it."

Later that evening, they dropped in at a party given by Kurt Heinrich and his mistress, Marilee, who suddenly felt terribly inferior in Kasia's presence. Kasia chatted easily with her for a short while before moving on to Matthew Delugach among the other studio executives in attendance.

When Kasia took him aside during a lull in the cocktail conversation and conveyed the message, he did not register any surprise or alarm. He smiled slightly and asked. "Are you helping Michael with his script while you're on hiatus?"

"No, he's perfectly capable of writing it himself. Why do you ask?"

"The two of you have been so involved in CIA spy plots on your last film and now again on your next one, it's starting to come out in your social conversation. I guess I don't follow what you just told me."

"It's nothing, Matt. Don't worry about it."

The warning not to receive the message and pass it along had come to Delugach from Roger Lakein through Bachmann three days ago, before Kasia had even been given the message. None of them had known who the messenger would be. That Kasia delivered it aroused Delugach's curiosity, but he had had a great deal to drink and her manner of bringing up the CIA getting a fix on Tri Con had been almost too ambivalent. When they had a moment of privacy, he mentioned the exchange with Kurt Heinrich and planted the first seed of suspicion against Kasia by the KGB.

Concerned about the puppy being alone, Michael persuaded Kasia that they had to leave the party early. She needed to get her sleep, as well.

"There was no point in staying any longer anyway," he mentioned, as they drove west along Sunset Boulevard.

"I was concerned that Heinrich would be offended, and you did seem to be enjoying yourself," she said.

"Kurt and I have been butting heads lately over the concept for the South American project. He insists that certain elements be included in the script for no good reason. He's nice and mildly okay to work with, but we always end up talking about the same things every time we get together. We aren't making acceptable progress. Too much shop talk and money talk and he wants to have tanks and heavy artillery in the movie. I don't need tanks and artillery. This is not a World War II epic. I did have an interesting chat with Miranda's husband though."

"What was it?"

"I didn't know he was a psychiatrist."

"He has a private practice in L.A. I knew that but there was never an occasion to tell you."

"We were talking about media influence and how he has to frequently deal with it with many of his patients. Anyhow, he used Patty Hearst as an example. She's a classic case of an impressionable young woman who made a cultural fantasy her own private reality. The media inundates the public with such a mix of news fact and fiction that they can't distinguish it half the time anymore.

"He attributes the high-jackings to that. Our film and television heroes always take the law into their own hands. We tend to portray the law as being inadequate, not caring, and corrupt, which is the case some of the time. So the heroes transcend the law and overcome the bad guys. The characters you portray in your films fit right in to that mode and audiences buy it, but the concept is easy to misinterpret. People think it gives them license to act outside the law.

"According to him, the way they think is 'if you don't see things my way, then you're a bad guy. Therefore, I'm justified in doing whatever I have to in order to protect my interests and get what I think you owe me.' He said that attitude is usually directed at some corporation or school or institution, but it could be directed at an individual who becomes a symbol of something. Interesting, isn't it?"

"Very."

Michael massaged the bridge of his nose. "I feel a headache coming on."

"Did you drink too much?"

"A glass of wine. No, it's a combination of sinuses and eye strain. It's been a long day and I feel wiped out."

"I'm tired too. Lately, I'm always feeling tired."

"Maybe you're getting too much sleep."

"I need it. Doctor Richards said the more the better."

Upon arriving home, they played for a few minutes with the puppy, then tucked her into her box house outside in the cold garage. Michael gently placed her inside the cave constructed of carpet cuttings on a nest made up of his T-shirt, a wooly towel, and a blanket. As he said goodnight, the pup's luminous brown eyes stared back at him with contentment. He caressed her tiny head, no larger than the size of a large egg. Then, as he and Kasia stepped back into the house, the pup emitted a high-pitched cry at being left alone. They expected another to follow, but she remained silent.

"She'll be all right," Michael hesitated, listening at the closed door.

"It's awful late," said Kasia. "Let's go to bed."

Several minutes later as Michael applied green stripped toothpaste to his brush, he said, "My cinematographer, Bill Livingston, had a vasectomy."

"He did? That's incredible. His wife must have had a hard time talking him into it. He wanted to have another child, try for a girl. She told him she would divorce him before she would let that happen. So she told me."

"He told me he had some qualms about it, but he got over it. He was finally the one who suggested it." Michael began to vigorously brush his teeth.

"Well, at least they can still have sex," said Kasia. "She threatened to cut him off."

"That's probably why he suggested the vasectomy. He claims their sex has improved because of it." Michael mumbled through a mouthful of foam and spit it into the sink bowl. "Myself, I just can't see it, not for me. I could never bring myself to do it. It's like severing a lifeline or something." He continued brushing.

"I'd never want you to either, and I'd never cut you off."

Michael finished, rinsed his mouth clear and placed his brush in the ceramic rack they had bought at an art festival in Santa Barbara. "Do we have any Tylenol?"

Kasia reached into the medicine cabinet and handed him the small white plastic bottle with the red cap. He tapped two into the palm of his hand, sucked them into his mouth and swallowed them washed down with a glass of water.

"Is your headache worse?" Kasia asked through her brushing.

"Not getting any better." Michael dabbed at his face with a damp washcloth.

As Kasia finished brushing and placed her toothbrush on the rack, Michael noticed she had neglected to rinse away a spot of paste that had fallen from her brush and now clung to the side of the sink bowl. He reached over, turned on a blast of cold water and washed it down the drain.

"You left a last splat," he grinned. "You shouldn't leave a last splat. Of course, we could always collect the globs when they dry out and serve them for after dinner mints."

"Yuk! Stick it in your ear." Kasia sat gingerly on the toilet seat and opened a book on pregnancy, birth, and family planning that she had been reading during moments spent sitting on the toilet.

"Look at your feet," said Michael. "Did you know you always toe in like that, like a little pigeon."

"I am a little pigeon."

"You're a little pigeon all right." He reached out with his large bare foot and gently touched each of her small bare feet. "Dave Wald went to the races this afternoon."

"Del Mar?"

"Del Mar."

"Did he win anything?"

"No, but he was telling me about this woman he saw in the crowd. She had a little girl with her. Right in the middle of one of the races, she just took off her blouse and walked around in her bra. He said most people didn't even notice her, but he forgot to watch the race, he was so busy watching her. He even forgot to go to the betting window. He said he was very interested in her walking around like that and no one paying any attention."

"I can imagine. She probably intended to interest somebody."

Michael shrugged.

"Are you waiting for me to get off here?"

He nodded. "There's no hurry. Take your time. I can use one of the other bathrooms."

"You have to give me time. I'm slow at these things."

"I know. That's okay. You shouldn't be rushed in your condition. It's important to relax."

"I agree. I should relax. You're belching. I hear you."

"Mm – mm."

"I can smell you. You have foul breath."

"It's the onion and garlic dip at Heinrichs. Bad combination and I ate quite a bit of it. I should know better. It's going to talk back to me all night."

A few minutes later, Michael lay in bed watching Kasia parading nude back and forth across the room, putting away clothing and arranging objects for the next day. Her abdomen bulged slightly.

"Here," she held up a tube of K-Y lubricant jelly they kept handy on the bedside table. "We should use a position that won't penetrate too deeply." She slipped under the covers and moved over against him. They kissed and played with each other."

"What's the best position then?" Michael asked.

"Rear entry."

"Doggy style?"

"Doggy style." Kasia rolled over and presented her rear to him as he rose to a kneeling position. "Somehow, doing it this way makes me feel kind of silly," she said.

Michael laughed.

"What are you laughing at?" She halted her pelvic gyrations.

They both laughed and continued.

CHAPTER FIFTEEN

The Surveillance

On July 7, 1978, an official CIA report bearing a top-secret seal was delivered by an armed courier to Gordon Frasier in the Los Angeles stock brokerage firm Emerson, Hudson, and Williams, a front for CIA operations on the West Coast.

Frasier broke the seal and quickly scanned the contents. "Holy Christ!" He rose from his desk and hurried into a neighboring office where Isaac Johnson, a young Black man in his mid-thirties, was just finishing a phone conversation. He had seen the courier arrive and from Frasier's expression, could tell that something hot had come in the door. He hung up the phone and gave his full attention to Frasier.

"Here it is!" Frasier rapped the report with his fingers. "We've finally got a fix on who the mole might be, Inca. Fifty million dollars deposited in a numbered Swiss account by an East Berlin industrial firm, Brunn Enterprises, was recently transferred to a second account held by the International Bank of The Americas, European Branch. Their counterpart in the United States is the International Bank of The Americas with branches in New York, Chicago, and Los Angeles. And get this. The Tri Con Corporation maintains accounts and extensive financial activity with all branches totaling in billions. More than fifty percent of its foreign and domestic trading and investments are handled through these banks. They also do business with a host of other American and foreign banks."

A low whistle escaped Johnson. "Looks like we pay a visit to whoever minds the store."

"We'll need surveillance in East Berlin, as well." Frasier stared out over the Wilshire Financial District from their suite of offices on the fortieth floor. "Who's the president of the California branch? And get the names and profiles on all executive officers in the other branches."

Johnson swiveled about in his chair and punched up a data series on a computer screen. The tiny white letters rippled across, flashed and disappeared to be replaced by others that finally came to rest like a settling flock of birds.

"Alexander Pondoev."

"Pondoev – Another Russian, coincidence?"

"Not likely. He's a U.S. citizen," said Johnson, reading from the data on the screen. "Born in New York City in 1941. Orphaned at age eight and went to live with relatives in Chicago. Graduated from Northern Illinois University with Bachelor's and Master's Degrees in Business and Economics. Worked for the Bank of America, IBM, E.F. Hutton, and United California Bank before becoming president of International in California."

"Who's on the board of directors? Can you get that?"

"We have complete and full information on every bank in the world." Johnson's long slender fingers tapped several more keys, prompting new names and data to appear on the gray video screen. He read off ten names.

"With all that Tri Con capital running through there, why isn't Helmut Bachmann on the board?" asked Frasier.

"Maybe he doesn't have time for it."

"He's CEO. Working with the board is one of his primary responsibilities." Frasier again studied the report. "And maybe that's why the bank can get away with what it's doing."

"Unless Bachmann is really someone else," Johnson suggested.

"What?"

"Just a side thought. I agree with you. If I had all that bread, you can damn well bet I'd be sitting at every board meeting."

"Check out these names and see if they all match up to actual people."

"What about Pondoev?"

"I want a twenty-four hour surveillance on him. I'll get a message to our agents in both West and East Berlin to track the financial activity of the Tri Con subsidiaries there."

"How did we come up with the Swiss account switch?" asked Johnson.

"We have an inside man in one of the banks."

"Lucky it happened to be one used by Tri Con or at least their main international bank."

"Tell Nathan we have a phone job for him. We'll wire Pondoev, house, cars, office, if possible, everything. Where does he live?"

"Bel Aire."

"Tell Nathan we want to know every move Pondoev makes, and we want to hear every word that comes out of him, all his habits, what he eats, drinks, when he shits, when and how he fucks and who he fucks besides his wife, and who his friends and business associates are. If he's not the head man, chances are he's high up in the cell, very high up. In the meantime, we'll increase our monitoring of financial traffic, trade and cash flow in Soviet bloc countries. It's still possible that this is only an isolated incident, but what the hell, we're here to gather intelligence. Where there's smoke there damn well has got to be fire."

By seven o'clock, upwards of sixty guests had arrived at the Pondoev residence in Bel Aire, among them Helmut Bachmann and his wife, Lili. The sit-down dinner was for seventy at round tables set with linen and candlelit on the spacious lawn and patio that extended from the rear of the modern white house. Bearing trays of hors d'oeuvres and poured champagne, liveried waiters shuttled about among the exquisitely attired crowd. A dance orchestra played waltzes and from a dais partially sheltered by the roof of the poolside cabana.

Working under the code name, Nathan, one of the waiters who freelanced with leading caterers in Los Angeles, filled a tray with glasses of champagne and set out to serve guests wandering about inside the house. Picking up an empty glass here and there, he ventured along the hall to the master bedroom where three women were pleasantly chatting. He looked in at the open door. "Excuse me, ladies. Dinner is about to be served outside. Would any of you care for more champagne?"

To his satisfaction, he saw two of them leave their empty glasses on the dresser. They took fresh crystals and moved off down the hall. He mentioned just loudly enough for them to catch his words, "I'll pick up in here."

He quickly closed and locked the door, then installed tiny, wire-thin microphones at strategic points around the room. Satisfied they could not be detected, he returned to the serving area to wait on tables.

For the next month, Gordon Frasier and Isaac Johnson scrutinized every aspect of Alexander Pondoev's life. Looking more like an ascetic country priest than a banker, Pondoev was conservative in taste, behavior, and appetites. Daily, his long skinny body traversed his pool with repeated laps totaling a half mile. He had perfunctory sexual intercourse with his wife once a week, collected vintage wines, and was a stern but loving father to his two young daughters who attended a local private school.

He conducted the business of his bank in a professional, knowledgeable manner and every transaction was legitimate and aboveboard. That he was somehow connected to the Soviet Union was unquestionable, as far as Frasier was concerned, but he and Johnson could not find the connection. All they had to go on was the isolated incident of the Swiss account. Nothing unusual had been discovered in the Berlin surveillance either. Finally, Frasier had to admit that Pondoev might not even be aware of the origins of much of the bank's revenue. The entire scheme could be engineered by someone higher up on the bank's international board of directors.

Late one afternoon during a session of listening to tapes provided by Nathan, Frasier looked up as Johnson entered from the neighboring office and motioned to Frasier to remove his headset.

"On the board of directors," said Johnson.

Frasier nodded, listening.

"We've matched a face and body to every name of every branch and to the international board, as well."

"Did Bachmann come up?"

"No."

"Shit, Bachmann is still conspicuous by his absence. Damn it, they've got this operation sewn up tight. Where the hell do we go from here? Soviet dollars are flowing through that bank into the U.S. and world markets, and everybody comes up clean. Someone's missing. The goddam mastermind behind this is a genius and he's got such a damn good cover and penetration he's not even there."

"Inca?"

"Yes, whoever the fuck that is. I don't think it's Pondoev. He probably doesn't know anything. In fact, I'm beginning to think he's there to throw us off the track. He's Russian and maybe he was recruited by the KGB without ever knowing who hired him. It happens all the time in government, corporations, schools, research centers, you name it. What are your findings on the board of directors, the international board?"

"The international board is three quarters American and one quarter German. On the American branches, all clean upstanding businessmen of various kinds and some professional people, physicians and attorneys. Basically, except for the few Germans, they're all American right down to the shine in their shoes."

"Well, HQ sure got our motor running for nothing. One hell of a lead that takes us nowhere and they're expecting us to come up with results."

"Did you see the morning paper?"

"No, I've been up half the night listening to tapes. If nothing else, at least I've got some hot inside information on Tri Con shares. They're acquiring and merging companies like there's no tomorrow, especially overseas."

"Your movie star, Kasia Kerenski, is out there on the stump again telling Uncle Sam to get his act together on nuclear regulation."

"Giorgio must have put her up to that. She didn't say. Her pregnancy on front line news gives her more impact. Speaking of Giorgio, has she had any contact with him lately that we know of?"

Frasier shook his head. "Not recently. Giorgio hasn't been much help to us anyway. He's too far removed to the outside. For what he does and what we know about him from Kasia and from Nathan's bugs, basically he's harmless. I imagine we get more value out of him than the KGB. We really need to get inside, penetrate. We're not even sure we know what they're doing and how. Every time I think we're about to have a breakthrough on the mission, it just doesn't happen. It doesn't exist and I bump into myself in the mirror. The whole thing's incomprehensible to me."

"What about the wives?"

"Wives?"

"The wives of the Tri Con execs. That's another way you could use Kerenski."

"Good thinking, Isaac. Wives - you can't get more inside than that. Lately, I'm not much on wives. What are your plans for tonight?"

"Alice and I are going out to dinner, then take in a movie."

"Care to join us?"

Frasier picked up the surveillance headset. "Thanks, Isaac, but you two need your own time together."

"Adjustment's hard, isn't it?"

"Yeah, but staying married would have been harder. I only feel sorry for the kids, but now they don't care much for me anyway."

"So what are you going to do?"

"The usual, might try a singles bar."

"Any luck?"

"Well when I tell the prospective wench that I'm a stockbroker, it's like a key that opens up the golden door. But I don't feel right about it."

"My invitation to join Alice and me still stands."

"I'll take you up on it another time. This case has got me too uptight. I'm not good company right now. Frustration is not something I handle well. Even if I can't find the answer, I need to see the light at the end of the tunnel." Frasier adjusted the headphones over his ears and took the tape machine off pause.

CHAPTER SIXTEEN

Daughter of Venus

Kasia had met Lili Bachmann and Erika Pondoev only briefly at a large dinner party given by the Bachmanns a few months after Kasia had joined Tri Con Pictures. Of the two, she felt most comfortable with Lili for her graciousness and sincerity. Her husband's powerful position as the President of the Tri Con Corporation did not seem to influence her basic kindness and outgoing friendly nature. It had been Lili who provided Kasia the opportunity to get them all together in one place at the same time.

Lili loved to play hostess. She also thought highly of the modest self-effacing actress and wanted to honor her with a baby shower that would be a minor social event. The matter did require extensive planning, since she intended to invite eighty women. She had solicited the aid of Erika Pondoev, who was Lili's close friend and also an admirer of Kasia.

When Gerta Heinrich learned about the luncheon meeting at the Bachmann mansion, she insisted that Lili include her. Gerta had finally separated from her husband, Kurt, and was continually seeking a captive audience to hear her latest gossip. In addition, Gerta genuinely liked Kasia Kerenski and would go out of her way for an opportunity to see and talk to the actress.

Lunch was being served poolside on the cabana patio, crab salad, croissants, and a deliciously dry Ginestet. Kasia declined even a single glass of the Italian white wine, a pinot grigio, however.

"Of course, said Lili apologetically. "How thoughtless of me. Would you like a Perrier?"

"Thank you, Lili."

"You young mothers today are so much more conscientious about what you put into your bodies than my generation."

"Now now, Lili," said Erika. "Let's not get carried away with comparisons and the generation gap. We aren't that far ahead of Kasia." Erika called attention to her wrinkle free skin and slender figure. "It's just a matter of taking good care of yourself. Am I right, Kasia?"

"Oh, I didn't mean it that way," said Lili. "My reference was to the fact there's more medical knowledge available and consequently a great deal more awareness."

"That's right," said Kasia. "Especially about nutrition."

Gerta had downed three martinis before lunch and was half lit. "With all these advantages you young women have, why is it they chase after older men who are far less exciting in bed or elsewhere, for that matter. That young trash who stole my husband can only be doing him for the money. His social skills aren't worth a damn."

"Gerta, darling," said Erika, "men like your husband are not stolen by young trash. They're enticed because they're seeking to recapture the lost passion of their youth."

"Ja, you mean I am the lost passion. And what about me, his wife? Am I not also entitled to some passion? Have I not given him his best years? My best years?"

"Of course, if he can do it, so can you. Take yourself a young lover."

"Ha!" Gerta's snort of laughter ejected a drop of clear mucous. Her expensive wine sloshed unnoticed onto her dress. "You must be kidding. I'm fifty eight years old."

"I wouldn't go around admitting it."

"Why not? Why shouldn't I be proud of my age and who I am and what I've done in my lifetime? Why should I try to hide the fact that I am growing old when age and death are inevitable? I do not fear growing old and dying. I only fear the callousness of those around me who see in me what will become of them in time. So all they want to do is shut me away as if they cannot stand a reminder. I was like you once, darling. All smooth and silky and svelt. Watch how it happens to you too one day, for it will most certainly happen."

"Gerta, how morbid and depressing," said Erika. "We're planning a celebration for a beautiful young woman who is like a daughter of Venus about to give birth."

"The truth can be morbid and depressing, depending on how you look at it. But no woman is a goddess. She might look like one for a short time, but her beauty passes quickly and is irretrievable, in spite of nips and tucks and health spas and face lifts and breast implants. Venus is only an ideal, an image painted by a man in the worship of youth and a mythological standard of womanly beauty that has come down through the ages as our inheritance. We, you and I and all women are prisoners of that myth."

"Believe me, I will never give my husband an excuse to go chasing after sweet young trash," said Erika, visibly irritated with Gerta's observation.

"I hope it is true for you," Gerta waved her empty wine glass as an accompaniment to her sloppy grin. "May your dream come true. But if it doesn't, you can always take a lover and have the delusion of being young and beautiful."

"All right, girls," Lili interrupted. "We're here to talk about Kasia's baby shower, not sexual infidelity."

"You put that so discreetly, Lili," Erika chomped at her salad with angry bites.

Kasia would have liked the conversation to continue in the direction it had been moving, talking about their husbands. Now, she didn't quite know how she would bring it around again. She hoped that Lili would quickly dispense with planning and only half-listened to her chatter about who should be invited, what would be served and how to handle the opening of the large number of gifts. There would be so many. Erika suggested it would not be necessary to open them all.

"But then some of the guests are sure to be offended," said Lili. "Kasia has to open them all."

"Wouldn't that be quite an ordeal, Kasia?" asked Erika.

"How about doing it in stages," said Kasia, in an attempt to ameliorate the tension among the other three women. "Since I am the one who will be opening them. I could open some before lunch and some after. Lili, you could make an announcement."

She wanted to get them off this absurd topic. She noticed that Gerta had grown sullen and withdrawn as the conversation progressed. *It's the booze,* thought Kasia. *That and Erika's snide comments and superior attitude of denial. I'm sure of it. Kasia wondered how two such totally different women as Lili and Erika could be Gerta's close friends, other than opposites attract.*

She did not think she would now be able to subtly interrogate them about their husbands unless she could divert the topic back to the subject of marital infidelity, which they clearly wanted to avoid.

She also considered asking about their husbands' businesses and what influence and involvement, as wives, they might have. Then she would be able to share what it was like working with Michael on a film. They would be interested in that. It occurred to her that their husbands probably didn't include them in that part of their lives, sharing privileged information. But you never knew what casual comments might pass between them in bed or at the breakfast table.

The wives wouldn't be expected to know or necessarily understand anything about corporate wheeling and dealing and their husbands were not the kind of men who were likely to confide in their wives anyway. These women did not keep secrets. They had little more worthwhile to do than try to top each other with the latest gossip or to complain about their maids and nannies. At least that was Erika's style.

Once Erika had had her children, she had turned them over to a professional nanny so she could forsake her parental responsibilities and indulge herself playing tennis and attending fashion luncheons.

Kasia promised herself that would never happen to her child. Hers and Michael's social life would have to take second place.

Sitting there listening to these women, how much she had not really changed occurred to her even now that she was married. Before then, she had never been only concerned about her goals and her survival. She had never been a kind of street level Erika Pondoev. At the moment, she felt rather mercenary and ashamed for even being there at that luncheon for the purpose of spying.

"Frasier, you're just going to have to lay off me," she thought. *"Just leave me alone."* But Kasia knew he would not. He had made that point clear during their last clandestine meeting, when he had ordered her to find out everything she could about Pondoev, Bachmann, and Heinrich through talking to their wives.   It all seemed to her so dirty, voyeuristic, peeping through the keyholes of people's lives.

Since his divorce, Frasier had grown worse in his attitude and feelings about women, all women. Kasia recognized this in his behavior and realized he was abusing and victimizing her because there was nothing he could do to get back at his wife. He had leverage and control over Kasia. *"I guess I'm a close enough substitute for revenge,"* she thought.

She wondered what Frasier would really do, would he carry through with his threat to have her parents deported if she just out and out quit on him without giving notice, without receiving her resignation and being debriefed through official channels. What if she stopped taking orders? They would probably kidnap her and spirit her off to a basement at Langley for interrogation.

His veiled warning concerned her. She was afraid to test him, especially now that she was about to have a child. Frasier was cold-blooded enough in his own way of using people when it came to getting the job done. She feared what Frasier might do to her and her child. If she confronted him, he might arrange for them both to disappear.

She had to go back to him with something after this meeting today, even if she made it up. His voice still burned in her mind from their last conversation one week ago.

"I want you to understand the magnitude of this mission," he'd said. "Breaking Inca's ring will have a global impact as to our energy and defense posture and capabilities. Somehow, the Russians are milking us, our resources and our technology. They're robbing us blind. It's my job - - it's my duty to discover how and to stop it. I'll do whatever it takes. The KGB has infiltrated our system like some god damn cancer. They're coming in from Canada to South America, Europe, Africa, Southeast Asia, and not you or anyone else is going to get in my way when it comes to stopping them.

"Your first loyalty is to the mission, not to your husband and child, not to your career," he paused. "To the mission. Everything else was arranged for you to create a better cover. They're just a means to an end. Only now, you've lost your professional detachment. You've allowed yourself to become emotionally committed and involved in your personal life. That's the worst mistake you can make as an agent. Let me make myself clear that you don't have a personal life. I own you."

"For Christ's sake, Frasier. I'm a human being first, not a robot," she'd spit back at him.

"If you refuse to cooperate, refuse to follow orders, it would be highly unfortunate if your husband were to learn of your many indiscretions."

"What indiscretions? There are no indiscretions.."

"Don't you bet on it."

"You would just make them up?"

"We do whatever we have to. And If you ever blow your cover to him or to anybody else – " he'd left the sentence hanging.

"Go on, what?"

"I'll leave that to your vivid imagination."

"You are unbelievable. A creep of the lowest order."

"Okay, just so we understand each other, when this is all over, maybe I'll release you. I say maybe, not definitely, maybe, as long as you see the mission through to the end. But if you fail me, I'll tear your life apart. And you know I can do that. Got it?"

Kasia had been stung. She knew she had to agree and act on the only realistic option he'd left open to her. She couldn't risk the other and he knew it.

Now, here she was with the key wives in Tri Con and nowhere to go with them, except for maybe Gerta, that poor bitter old woman.

Kurt Heinrich was a different kind of man than the others, boisterous, expansive. He did not conceal much about himself like Bachmann with his corporate sophistication and Pondoev with his cool banker's razor edge objectivity and reserve. Heinrich needed to unload his stress, confide in someone. Maybe that was part of the painful burden Gerta carried within her, the confidences he had shared and entrusted. She obviously still loved and cared about him.

Since she didn't drive, Gerta had come to the luncheon by cab. Kasia offered to give her a lift home.

"Oh, how wonderful, Kasia. How kind of you. Yes, thank you. I'll go with you and I promise not to be obnoxious. I feel so lonely in a taxi."

After expressing her gratitude for the luncheon and Lili's concern for the baby shower, Kasia departed with Gerta.

"You were the only redeeming person this afternoon," said Gerta, visibly relaxing as they pulled away in Kasia's Mercedes. That Erika Pondoev is nothing but a shallow posturing self-serving snob. Oh, Lili's okay by comparison. She means well but she's so ineffectual. I suppose it's terribly difficult living in the shadow of her husband, although I understand he cares very much for her and treats her well."

The magic word husband clicked in Kasia's mind. "You miss your husband, don't you." Kasia smiled and glanced at her. "I don't really believe you've stopped loving him either."

Gerta looked at her with a weary grin. "You're a sensitive young woman. How did you know?"

"By the way you said things about him and what you didn't say."

"For instance."

"You didn't say anything spiteful or hateful. You just described his behavior."

Gerta looked ahead as they skimmed along the lush foliated residential street. "I don't hate him. I understand him. Perhaps if I didn't understand him so well, I would feel differently than I do."

"How do you feel?"

"Sad, depressed – let down."

"The two of you have been through a lot together I imagine."

"We were very close. I believe in some way we still are, but he denies it."

"Then you still do see him."

"Sometimes he calls me. His --- mistress, she's only good for sexual pleasure. She's not particularly intelligent. So he calls me and we talk."

Kasia took a risk. "About personal matters?"

"Not so personal to me, but to him. I'm like his psychiatrist. I listen and, despite my display at Lili's, I'm not judgmental with him."

"He strikes me as a man who deals well with his problems."

"Oh, he handles them all right, but he's very emotional. You wouldn't think it to look at him, but he's actually quite a sensitive man. His cold manner puts off and fools most people. It's his way of hiding his sensitivity."

"Then there are things that really do bother him."

"Yes, yes, very much. They weigh on his soul."

Kasia glanced at her, expecting to hear more. Gerta noticed her interest. "Oh," she smiled slightly. "Excuse me for going on. I broke my promise. My husband's problems would be of no concern to you. Have you thought about names for your child?"

Kasia desperately held to the subject. "Gerta, if you would like to talk about it, I'm a sympathetic listener and I am interested."

"You are so kind. Your husband is lucky to have you. You are quite a special woman."

"So are you, Gerta. Tell me about your husband. Maybe I can learn something about relationships from you."

Gerta heaved a great sigh. "When Berlin was divided into east and west after the Second World War, Kurt and I were separated by the wall. He had been taken prisoner by the Russians in the eastern sector. I was pregnant and near the time of my delivery. I had very little food, no hospital, no doctor. It was difficult for me.

"As a young man, Kurt was one of the early pioneers of the German cinema, *Das Kino*. He despised Hitler with a passion, yet he was commissioned to produce propaganda films for the *Fuhrer*.

"I did not see him for five years after the war ended. Then one day, he was unexpectedly released through the wall with hundreds of others to return to their families. He told me he had spent his time in Moscow working with their cinema. He had hoped the Soviets would squash Hitler from the beginning. He had changed his allegiance and is a communist to this day, like many who came back through the wall.

"After living under Hitler, I understood his – enthusiasm, shall we call it, and I joined him in the party. However, I am no longer a communist."

"Yet he decided to remain a communist."

"Yes, a disillusioned one, but a communist, nevertheless."

"Why doesn't he change?"

"Oh, that's not possible for Kurt."

"It seems like a simple enough thing."

Gerta gave her a sad smile. "There are some commitments we make in our lives that we cannot turn our backs on. In this case, with Kurt, it's more than a German sense of duty."

"I'm sorry," said Kasia. "For him and for you. I know what it means to be trapped like that."

"You? Trapped?"

"I was there once."

They drove on in silence except for Gerta's occasional direction. After Kasia dropped her off at her condominium, she went to a pay phone and called Frasier.

"It's me."

"Who the hell's me?" He recognized her voice. "You didn't use the code."

"I don't care about the code. You want to hear what I have to say or not?"

Frasier did not respond for several moments. His silence came to her as a warning, the silence of absolute power.

"Frasier, you still there?"

"Go ahead – Sidewalk."

"Kurt Heinrich is a communist. He spent five years in Moscow after World War II."

"See what you can do when you put your mind to it."

"I don't like what I had to do to find that out."

"Since when have you been concerned about what you do and to whom you do it? You don't have to like it. You just have to do it. By the way, don't ever call me again without using the code."

A loud click sounded in her ear followed by a long irritable buzz that she was no longer connected.

***

In her dream, she was standing alone in the alien night. The headlights of a car approached and slowed. She could not see the driver through the dark-tinted windshield, but she knew he was watching her. She shook her head and silently prayed he would not stop. He drove on, tail lights receding along the dark canyon of tall buildings like extraterrestrial glowing red eyes.

Again she looked down the street. She had been waiting for what seemed like hours on the deserted corner. She wondered why the bus did not come according to the schedule. It should have arrived. She looked at her watch. It had stopped. She couldn't wait any longer and began to walk. Although she sensed that eyes were watching her, no one else was on the street at that late hour. She listened to the steady rhythmic click of her heels against the pavement. Then suddenly, the RTD bus was parked a short distance ahead of her in the next block. She had misjudged where it had come from and where it had stopped. She had not noticed, but by now, the corner where she had been standing was far behind her. The black mirrored windows of the bus reflected the harsh green lights of streetlamps. The tall rectangular doors stood open, waiting.

She looked inside. The driver wearing a black uniform and dark glasses sat staring straight ahead. He did not glance at her as she came up the stairwell. Her coins rained into the collection box with a metallic jingle out of sync with the silence around her. She heard the suction of the doors closing behind her.

As the driver put the bus in motion, there was no sound of an engine. Kasia looked down the long swaying aisle. A man dressed in a black suit and wearing dark glasses sat alone at the rear. She could not see his eyes. She took a seat directly behind the driver and stared out at the ghostly night buildings flickering past as the bus hurtled through the city.

After a short time, the man in black rose and came forward. He took a seat one row behind and just across the aisle from Kasia. The sticky wet syrup of fear spread through her. She hoped that he had only come forward in anticipation of getting off at the next stop.

He stayed, riding on and on, remaining where she could see him out of the corner of her eye. Knowing that she was a target, she could barely control her panic.

She sprang up and screamed at the driver. "That man is going to kill me!"

The driver ignored her as though she were just a late-night crazy on his line.

Crying for the unborn child in her abdomen, she peered out at the onrushing street. Corner after corner flashed by as the bus continued to pick up speed. She did not recognize where they were, not any of the names. She no longer knew where she was or where she was going, or why.

"What bus am I on?" she gasped at the driver.

He pointed to the sign listing. She stared. The screen was blank.

"But it doesn't say anything."

Both hands clutched the rail to steady herself. She could see the man in the dark glasses watching her reflected in the windshield glass. "Let me off," her voice expelled a hoarse whisper. "Let me off."

At the next corner, the bus swung smoothly over to the curb. The doors opened with a sucking sound and she stumbled down the steps. Her feet hit the pavement running. She heard the bus pull away behind her. Breathless, she stopped and looked back.

The man in black had gotten off and was walking steadily toward her only a block away on the deserted street. She turned to run again. Her feet would not move. Her legs would not lift. They were paralyzed. She screamed, but no sound came from her throat.

***

She woke, tangled among her bed sheets soaked with sweat, her stomach knotted in pain. A wave of nausea swept upward into her mouth. She staggered to the bathroom and fell to her knees. The nausea gradually subsided with the reality of the cold toilet bowel against her face.

The time was 2:00 a.m.

Her baby kicked and punched and moved about inside her.

CHAPTER SEVENTEEN

The Obfuscation

"She made the society column." Issac Johnson entered Gordon Frasier's office and dropped a section of the Los Angeles Times on his desk.

Frasier put his tape recorder on pause and removed the headset. A photo of Kasia Kerrenski and her child peered out at him from the newsprint.

"It's a girl. They named her Danielle."

"Like I care.   How's the tape going?"

"I might have something, maybe a breakthrough, but I'm still not certain about the reference. Thanks for showing me that." Frasier repositioned the headset over his ears. Frequently, time was an important factor in coming up with information. He had ordered the surveillance on Alexander Pondoev continued during the past year. He pressed a button and ran the tape back to replay a sequence that he thought might hold a clue to Inca.

He heard Pondoev's voice speaking into the bedroom telephone. Frasier could not identify the other party from the conversation, nor could he piece together the context. But the name Karazississ was mentioned twice. He stopped the tape, reversed it and listened to the sequence for a third time.

"I've already met and talked with Karazississ," said the unrecognized voice. "He'll be recruiting in Argentina."

Pondoev: "Do we flood the economy before the strike?"

Voice: "At least a year's worth or whatever it takes to maintain a high rate of inflation.   There's a lot of discontent among the populace and economic conditions are going from bad to worse."

Pondoev: "I'll release the funds then according to schedule. Will our partner be prepared to receive and distribute them?"

Voice: "Montalva is handling all the arrangements. I have to go. See you Sunday. Goodnight, Alex."

Pondoev: "Goodnight." A click.

Frasier turned off the machine and removed the headset. He had jotted the names and points of interest mentioned on a note pad and now stared at them.

Karazississ – recruiting in Argentina.

Before the strike.

High rate of inflation.

Montalva.

He would run a transcription of this sequence of the tape through cryptoanalysis in case it was some manner of code. *Shit, Pondoev can't be innocent. He just damn well can't. And who the hell is he talking to? Who is Karazississ? Who is he recruiting in Argentina?*

From the sound of the conversation, this Karaississ is going to recruit workers to avert a strike in Argentina. But what does Pondoev have to do with increasing inflation in Argentina?

That point struck an odd note with Frasier. Then another thought occurred to him, but it needed a connector. Was the fifty million that had been transferred from East Berlin going to be laundered into the Argentine economy?

And then there could be another kind of recruitment going on – mercenary and guerilla insurgents. And a strike could mean a military strike. These perceptions were just thoughts, speculation with no comprehensive connection, but intriguing, nonetheless. He had to find out who Karazississ was, if possible.

He programmed a code request to CIA headquarters at Langley, Virginia for an identification and information on Malcolm Karazississ. His name came through with a terrorist cell in the Middle East. Then several days later, a second report appeared. Malcolm Karazississ was an alias for Gavril Petrovski, an agent of the GRU, *Glavoe*

Pazvedyvatelnoe Upravlenie, Chief Intelligence Directorate of the Soviet General Staff whose cover name was Military Department 44388.

Attached to the elite *spetsna* commando units, Petrovski, alias, Karazississ, trained and supervised Third World terrorists in the sabotage of vital installations and in the assassination of political and military leaders. The current location of Petrovski/Karazississ was unknown.

Although the intelligence he had acquired tantalized Frasier, it was inconclusive and left him feeling frustrated, no closer to Inca than he had been before. Getting inside was a difficult proposition. The bits and pieces coming from his various sources were not related or cohesive enough for him to visualize or sense the whole operation. Even with the aid of new computer technology, creating the puzzle to put it together was a game of guesswork. He re-evaluated his sources.

Roger Lakein's reports to Gordon from South America on the smuggling of oil and minerals were curiously devoid of results and noncommittal in tone, almost as if he were holding back the intel. The informers Lakein professed to have working for him in Brazil, Venezuela, Chile, and Argentina operations sectors were not producing any significant information.

Lakein was a senior officer assigned to manage the South American contingent. He was also supposed to be working closely with CIA personnel in those countries. Frasier decided to run a check through several of those other agents on the extent of their involvement with Roger Lakein.

Langley Headquarters had denied Lakein his request for a direct transfer to the Security Bank in Los Angeles, because Lakein was more valued as a field operative. Frasier had been called in on that review, since the decision would have directly affected his mission as Director of The Security Bank. Lakein remained, or more accurately, was confined to South America due to Frasier's influence, recommendation, and finally specific request to Langley. His input was not shared or in any way communicated to Lakein who answered directly to Frasier on Operation Inca.

Frasier had run a search and selected a man from Mexico City, Carlos Villanova, Ph.D., to direct the Central and South American station of The Security Bank. Villanova's cover was as a professor of political science at the University of Mexico. He was an authority on Latin – American foreign policy and was a frequent adviser to the President of the United States.

The fact that Villanova's analytical abilities and political perspectives and understanding were greater than Lakein's had also been a deciding factor in Frasier's choice. That, and the fact that he did not have anyone who could replace Lakein in the field. The time had come to start grooming someone who could become the next Roger Lakein.

As yet, the current status of Charley and Maggie MacIntosh had not been established and no news provided to Frasier. According to Lakein, they were hidden "in position" in Southern Chile. The Soviet KGB had given them a hotel brothel to manage near an isolated military compound on the frontier. Frasier could not be certain of their immediate strategic value at such a remote location or even why the Russians would stick them one hundred miles upriver in the jungle wilderness. That was for Charley and Maggie to discover.

The communists in Chile and Argentina, the MIR, would have their reasons. The major problem of the arrangement was one of logistics in communications, which were channeled through Lakein. And what if Lakein were the mole?

Frasier would activate another agent in Brazil, a field man. Send him in without Lakein's knowledge and then see if their intelligence corroborated.

On the home front, he had Kasia Kerenski. The messages she had so far carried for Giorgio had not revealed any information of strategic value to Frasier. He was looking for corporate statistics of various companies, governments, technological research, and political movements. Cryptanalysts had not identified any codes in effect and doubted the significance or application of the figures.

As for Giorgio Mykola, he had become a familiar fixture in the system. However, Kasia could not get him to reveal from whom he took his orders. So far, everything came and went through the Russian Embassy in San Francisco. But ever since the embassy had opened shop on Green Street in 1973, the F.B.I. had not been able to keep up with the intense activity of KGB agents entering and departing from California, especially in the high technology market.

Kasia had determined that Giorgio had no direct contact with anyone within the Tri Con Corporation. He only knew Kurt Heinrich's wife on a client basis at his hair salon.

An investigation of Heinrich's background showed he was clean until Kasia had recently discovered he had spent five years in the Soviet Union and was an avowed communist.

Was it possible that orders came down from within the bowels of Tri Con to be delivered to Giorgio by Gerta Heinrich while he did her hair? What a thought. He would put Nathan on it at once.

Pondoev was involved somewhere without a doubt. He had known the name Karazississ, and Karazississ was an agent of the GRU. Maybe Pondoev was their man after all. He was in a central position of power and now definitely linked with Soviet activity, although he maybe didn't know of Karazississ' true identity. But how could he not know?

We have to get closer to Pondoev, thought Frasier. *Even if he's not the key man, he's working with someone who is. The F.B.I. would love to get their hands on this, but I'm not ready to turn it over to them, not yet, not until we make the South American connection and discover who our own mole is.*

He picked up the phone and dialed. "Hello, Nathan, I have another job for you."

CHAPTER EIGHTEEN

The Singer

The humid pall of the Mississippi sunrise roiled into the sleeping river town, burning the fog into a steaming vapor that made breathing difficult and slowed the reflexes and desire of human and beast alike to move.

Dade Thomas woke sweating on his cot in the spare second floor room of his parents' house. His sleep had been restive and, during the final moments just before waking, a disturbing dream had sent a sensation of fear coursing through his subconscious mind. The dream had been so intense that he now concentrated on the reality of his body, carefully locating its parts in time and space, refamiliarizing himself with the narrow configuration of the room, the crumbling old wood, and the scent of dank rot blowing in through the open window from off the sluggish backwater not more than a few hundred yards from the house.

What had terrified him in the dream was the sensation of dying and, when he woke, he realized that the swampy odor of the backwater and the confines of the room had been working on his mind and infiltrating his life for the past two years. The horrifying specter of Olivia's suicide had gradually faded from his memory. At least he had learned to control and cope with it.

In wanting to escape all evidence of his personal struggles for success which he had experienced back in California, he had returned to the torpid existence of his origins where drive and ambition were provided no social environment in which to flower. Frustration had driven Dade away from home at the restless age of sixteen. Twelve years later, frustration and an unrelenting depression that strangled his soul had brought him home again.

During that time, he had barely survived a combat tour in Viet Nam, a war internationally recognized as being founded on corruption and gilded with patriotic slogans. Upon his return, he had managed to clean the drugs out of his system, get a college education and begin carving out a potential career as a promising composer and musician.

Always he had lived with a struggle, first against the ennui perpetrated and laid into his life like thick southern molasses and then against the incredible stress of survival in the most ruthless and competitive of entertainment markets.

Now, he was thirty and once again lying in the bed of his childhood wondering what life held in store for him.

During his past two years in Mississippi, he had been working at a local lumber mill. Then, on weekend nights, he had become reacquainted with the music of his youth, the Cajun and Creole rhythms and, on occasional Sundays when he was not too hungover, the religious emotionalism of gospel choirs, the smell of sweating Black bodies crammed into a small white frame church. And these impressions impregnated in his mind slowly matured.

He began to play drums with musicians who materialized out of the swamp on Saturday nights and drifted back into the impenetrable silence of cypress and black water channels the following day.

He wrote down the Cajun and Creole music that had never been written before, the notation, tempos and dialect. After two years, he had a trunk filled with compositions, some verging on symphonies of his childhood and the social and cultural odyssey of the Black experience in America.

One he entitled *Black Odyssey*. It would make a powerful album if he could ever discover someone capable of singing it. He needed to find a voice that embodied the spirit of the swamps and southern Baptist gospel choirs, of street life in the cities of the North and cities and small towns of the South, an operatic voice capable of expressing the collective musical range of soul, gospel, Creole, classic opera, jazz and contemporary rock. He didn't know if such a voice even existed or if such vocal ability were humanly possible.

He sat up on the edge of the cot and felt about on the side table for his cigarettes where there had been none for the past two years. The reflex still prevailed. His pulled on the clean socks his Mama had laid out for him the night before, tugged on his jeans and followed with the steel-toed jackboots he wore while working at the mill as a safeguard against the crushing weight of falling objects and poisonous snakes that crawled into the woodpiles in search of rats.

Friday had arrived, the day he and his musician friends had been asked to play the next afternoon and night at a folk music festival in Jackson. They were to meet early in the morning at the local church and travel by open truck for five hours to the festival site.

He absent mindedly ingested the pork sausage, fried eggs, and grits his Mama prepared for him. She appreciated the additional income he contributed to her household since her husband had been disabled in an accident at the mill ten years ago. Of six children, Dade was their only son, his sisters all having married and moved away except for one whose husband was a local small businessman.

Unnecessary in his mother's mind, Dade had explained in some detail why he had returned home. Lonely for the companionship of her children, she would have liked him to remain there or nearby for the rest of her life, if he so desired. However, she exerted no influence and made no effort to control his comings and goings. He was his own man. She derived her greatest daily pleasure from being able to serve him in some way.

Her only attempt to reinforce his staying was to play matchmaker, a needless exercise, since nearly every young woman of marriageable age sought to attract his interest.

Not wishing either to embarrass his mother, whom he deeply loved and respected, or to have her humiliated through what would be certain gossip, Dade discouraged the amorous advances as best he could under the circumstances of such a close society in which few private acts or utterances survived in secrecy.

Among the group of musicians, he was the only owner of a vehicle sufficiently adequate to get them all to Jackson without breaking down. The festival was to take place at the fairgrounds where bands and soloists would perform outdoors on a platform stage constructed for the event.

Their set was scheduled third on the program, allowing them only the briefest opportunity to hear the groups before them. After they finished their set and were moving their instruments off the stage into the wings, Dade heard the voice. He stopped what he was doing and rushed from the backstage to down in front so that he could clearly see her as well as hear her.

Accompanying herself with an acoustic guitar, the slender barefoot Black woman sent the most incredibly pure lyrical music he had ever heard into the hearts of the rapt audience. He snatched up a fallen program and frantically searched for her name – Aimee Martin.

Hypnotized by what he was hearing, he stared up at her thin sensitive features, wide wonderous spiritual dark eyes that pierced his soul and woke the deadness in him like an exploding flower.

At the conclusion of her solo, the audience sat so stunned that they did not applaud. Then suddenly, Dade set the cadence. It rippled back across the sea of four thousand faces with the crackling of a spreading grass fire, then erupted into a volcanic roar as they all rose in a single body in honor and recognition of her talent and beauty.

She, in turn, was so stunned by their reaction that she could only stand there in her simple white cotton dress as wave upon wave of human sound crashed over her. It attained a pitch so that she could no longer even hear until her pocket of silence broke. The adulation finally dwindled after ten minutes. And then they reverently waited and called for more.

She was scheduled for only two numbers, but the audience would not let her leave the stage and brought her back for three more songs until the master of ceremonies took the microphone and insisted that the program move on.

While the next group set up amid loud boos and whistles intended for the M.C., Dade met Aimee holding her ancient backwoods guitar in one hand and lifting her skirt slightly with the other as she came down the rickety backstage wooden steps.

"Aimee."

She looked up with a questioning smile.

He gently touched her arm. Her closeness, the translucent luster of her eyes like those of a deer nearly took away his speech. "My name is Dade Thomas. My band was on just before you."

She nodded. "Yes?"

"Ah, where are you from, Aimee?"

"Live with mah folks on a farm up near Monroe."

"You have the most beautiful voice I've ever heard."

"Thank you. Those are kind words." She sensed that he had something more to say and waited politely for him to say it, offering an encouraging smile.

"Do you," he stammered, "can er, we go somewhere and talk?"

She nodded.

"Would you like a cup of coffee or some lemonade?"

"Feelin' a little parched. Ah'd love some lemonade."

"Come on." He took her by the hand. As they walked through the roving crowd and food vendor stands, her eyes flashed up at him with shy amusement.

They found an untrampled patch of grass under a tree and sat in its shade. She leaned back against the smooth trunk and smiled in friendly expectation of whatever it was this gawking handsome young man might have to say to her. They sipped their lemonade.

"Aimee, I was born and raised here in Mississippi, but I've lived and worked some years in California. I'm a musician, like you. No, wait, not like you. There's no one else like you. I play rhythm, instrumental and I compose. I'm going to make a record album. May I show you the music?"

She nodded.

"Aimee, please understand, I'm not out of my mind in what I'm saying, or maybe I am, but it's only because of who you are. You are the music. Do you understand what I'm saying?"

Her smile confirmed that she did.

"I want to take you home with me but I know I can't ask that of you. May I come to see you and bring you the score? I don't have it with me. It's at home locked in a trunk."

"I suppose we'll just have to get married then."

He rocked back shocked into silence. He wondered if she were socially backward in a backwoods sort of way until she broke into peals of laughter like clear running water at his stunned expression.

"You only asked me where I came from," she said. "You didn't ask me where I've been."

"Where have you been?"

"Julliard - on a special scholarship."

"Julliard – that explains it. I'll tell you what. Let me come home with you. I want to meet your parents and your brothers and sisters and grandparents and aunts and uncles and cousins, all your family. And – and you mean it – what you just said?"

She chuckled. "Provided I like your music."

"Aimee – Aimee – can I, may I kiss you?"

She leaned forward and wrinkled her nose at him.

***

With their worldly belongings in the back of Dade's pickup truck, they drove to California. Aimee selected the melodies and lyrics from Dade's score that she would prepare for a demo tape and added a few of her own compositions.

Dade explained to her that, although he had been out of circulation for two years, he did not feel they would encounter any obstacles they could not overcome to establish her as a major newly discovered talent.

When they arrived in Los Angeles, Dade's first move was to relocate Herb Wilcox. Without any idea where to begin his search, he went to see Herb's mother, whom he had met in Burbank on two special occasions after he and Herb had joined Stephen Stull's group, Crystal Blue Persuasion. He brought Aimee with him to the door.

"Hello, Mrs. Wilcox."

"Yes?" The semi-elderly woman viewed them with slight trepidation.

"I don't know if you remember me. We met briefly about four and a half years ago. I'm Dade Thomas, an old friend of Herb's. We played in a band together. This is my wife, Aimee."

"I'm pleased to meet you," Aimee extended her hand.

"Yes, I think I do remember you, Dade. Memories start to fade at my age," her dry lips parted in an unapologetic grin.

"I'd like to get in touch with Herb, but I'm sure he doesn't live in the old place. I've been gone for two years, back home in Mississippi. Can you tell me where I can find him?"

"Come inside, please. I'll write down his address and phone number for you."

They followed her through the living room into the kitchen where she scrawled on a notepad next to the phone.

"Can he be reached during the day?" asked Dade.

"He has an answering service."

"Thank you, Mrs. Wilcox. Now, I have another question, although I might already know the answer. Is he still in music?"

"Yes," she smiled warmly. "Very much so. Music is his life you know."

"I know. Thank you, Mrs. Wilcox. It is a pleasure meeting you again."

She waved them goodbye, watched them walk to his truck, then closed the door.

Dade left a message, and Herb returned the call two hours later to the motel room. He gave them directions to his apartment along with an invitation to dinner. Dade and Aimee brought a bottle of red wine. Before the evening had ended, they were sipping Jack Daniels and talked and sang together until long after midnight.

Herb could hardly believe Aimee's incomparable voice. He grew excited at the prospect of doing an album with her and Dade. What bothered him was Dade's intention of going to Kasia Kerenski and her movie director husband for financing.

"It's been a long time, Herb. In the run of things, what the hell does it matter? Everyone stands to profit all the way around."

"Maybe, but with me it's still a little thing called pride."

"Well, the way I see it, it's a business proposition, a partnership. Not like livin' on the street waitin' for someone to pass by and toss a few coins in your hat or hustlin' a gig. Talk about pride."

"Listen, Dade, it's your show anyhow. I'll just be one of the band, okay?"

"You'll get a cut. I promise that."

Herb smiled. "I'm glad you came back. After what Stull did to me, I'm really glad."

"I don't understand why the cops couldn't find him. He's just not that smart."

"All I know is he disappeared. That's good enough for me."

"Someday, though. Someday."

"It can be somebody else, not me."

"Guess I'd just as soon not come across him either."

"That's best."

***

Not knowing if Michael Sloan would remember him, Dade left a phone message at Michael's production office that he wished to get in touch with Kasia. To his surprise, Michael personally returned the call and invited him and Aimee to dinner.

Following a gourmet meal of, during which they brought each other up to date, they went into the living room where Dade asked if they would like to hear Aimee sing.

When she was finished, Michael wanted to know from where the music had come. Dade went out to the truck and returned with a copy of his score. Michael poured them all brandies and they talked business.

Two days later, Michael and Dade met with Michael's attorney and business manager to form a recording company that would be a subsidiary to his motion picture production company. Michael was to be president and Dade would be vice-president.

The first album to be produced on their *Sidewalk* label would be Dade's rock symphony, *Black Odyssey*. They would follow with a second album entitled *Rocking Horse*, based on emotional impressions that spanned the two worlds of adults and children. Michael's and Kasia's daughter, Danielle, would appear on the album cover photograph riding her rocking horse.

Two months after their alliance was announced in the trades, Time, Newsweek, and other magazines and periodicals, with a photograph of Aimee Martin on the cover of Rolling Stone Magazine, *Black Odyssey* shot to the top of the top ten list for singles and albums and stayed there. Six months later, Rocking Horse followed and nestled into second place until the volume sales on the first album began to subside.

In celebration of their phenomenal success, Dade and Aimee accompanied Michael and Kasia and their daughter to their chateau in France.

Dade and Aimee then went on a concert tour of Europe over a period of three months before returning to a homecoming concert at the Universal Studios Amphitheater.

From the sidewalk to the stars, they had all reached a pinnacle of success with its creative freedom and the material rewards associated with vast personal wealth.

Riding high on the euphoria of power, they tended to forget what life had been like to struggle and to carve out a place for themselves as performing artists. Having arrived provided them an elevated sense of immunity to personal tragedy and to the suffering and dreams and ambitions of others.

But there were others who had not forgotten them.

CHAPTER NINETEEN

The Location

The South American Andes were the spectacular climax of a mountain chain that originated in Alaska and extended the length of the Western Hemisphere to Cape Horn where it sank into the icy sea at the southern tip of the continent. The range spread out into separate smaller ranges or *cordilleras* bisected by occasional fertile valleys and high cold tablelands.

Between the mountains and the sea, a shelf of land flattened the terrain along most of the western coast. The extremes of climate about which Michael had read while researching the vast cultural background for his film excited him because of the cinematic visual potential. The northern coast of Chile was a desert created by the cold northbound Humboldt Current, which produced a temperate climate in tropical latitudes, but depleted the west blowing winds of moisture before they could reach the land. The Andes sucked the moisture from the eastern trade winds.

He had also read about a tropical current known as *El Nino*, the child, which flowed down from the north over the cold Humboldt Current. The torrential rains resulting from their union turned dry riverbeds into raging rivers that swept people, whole villages, and all else in their path in a mad race to the sea. The hot *El Nino* destroyed the rich marine life of the Humboldt Current and, consequently, the fishing industries. Afterwards, the desert bloomed like a tropical region for a brief period, then dried up.

Michael nudged Kasia awake to share the unfolding majestic canvas as their plane droned on a coast route that paralleled the rising blue monolith of time that formed the geological backbone of the entire continent. The sun surfaced, spraying its golden brilliance along the snow-glazed peaks of the Andes and provided Kasia and Michael their first glimpse of South America.

They could see the two highest peaks rising and creating an impenetrable wall of rock and ice between Chile and Argentina, *Ojos del Salado* at 22,550 feet, second only in height to the Himalayas, *Aconcagua,* 22,835 feet.

Michael had been living with this cinematic panorama in his head for nearly three years. Now, the reality was infinitely more stunning than in his imagination.

As the plane pulled slightly inland from the Pacific, they saw a lush green central valley that showed evidence of extensive cultivation.

With yet another two hours before their arrival in Santiago de Chile, the flight attendants served breakfast along with customs forms and instructions in both English and Spanish on how to fill them out according to the required information.

Michael checked his passport against any discrepancies they might unexpectantly encounter, since their presence in the country was a sensitive political concern for the fascist government.

An hour and a half later, the Pan American jet came in low over the sea and touched down in a perfect landing with a puff of smoke from its wheels. Engines roaring in reverse thrust, the aircraft howled toward the terminal complex and quickly decelerated.

The first hint that something was out of synch occurred during the examination of Kasia's and Michael's passports and personal effects by a uniformed scowling customs officer. They watched critically as their documents were handed along to another customs agent, not in uniform, who had obviously been awaiting their arrival. Michael's and Kasia's eyes locked in a brief look of concern, then glanced away.

"Kurt Heinrich said we're supposed to have a special government escort as part of the arrangement to make sure we are who we say we are," said Michael in a subdued voice to Kasia. "He could be it."

A few tense minutes passed. Then the plainclothes agent returned with two uniformed officials and, in English, politely asked Michael and Kasia to accompany them.

The uneasy feeling that they were being marched to an arrest rather than a meeting seized Michael and Kasia, an emotion they communicated to each other without the benefit of words. They had no alternative but to comply. Michael half-wondered if their concern were just a matter of not being accustomed to such threatening formalities.

Their escorts herded them into an austere room offering only two uncomfortable chairs at the center. Kasia instantly recognized the space as an interrogation room.

The agent's polite tone suddenly changed. He did not ask, he ordered them to sit down. "Do not attempt to leave until certain questions as to your reason for entering the country have been clarified."

"Someone from your government was supposed to meet us here and take care of all the arrangements," Michael calmly explained. "What happened to him?"

"Senor Sloan, we are doing everything we can to accommodate you under the circumstance."

"Under the circumstances? What circumstances? I would like to call the American embassy, please." Michael suddenly rose to his assertive height.

"Sit down, Senor Sloan. There is no cause for alarm. It is in your best personal interest to fully cooperate with us."

"All right, you have our undivided attention and total cooperation. How long do we have to sit here and wait and for what reason? Who are we supposed to talk to? And what is it you or anybody else wants to know about our purpose in being here that I'm sure you already know?"

Unaccustomed to being challenged, the agent momentarily turned his cipher features away from Michael, tugged at his drab gray tie knotted tightly at his throat, and re-buttoned his gray suitcoat over his slender torso. He spoke in an undertone to the two armed customs officers, then left the room and closed the door.

One of the guards, which by now was the unmistakable role of the muscled uniformed men, moved casually into a corner, took out a large toothpick and began to nonchalantly explore his teeth while leveling a cold warning stare at them. The second guard assumed a stolid stance in front of the door with his right hand resting on the handle of his holstered handgun.

"What the fuck is going on here?" Michael slurred to Kasia under his breath.

"It's just the way they operate," she said. "I think this is their idea of an official welcome."

"Aren't you scared?"

"A little, but not really. I think this charade is all bluff and show to intimidate us so we don't try to reveal anything negative about the *junta*. Remember, we're here on a preliminary scouting trip. They know we're coming back again."

"Maybe Bachmann and Heinrich made a mistake wanting to film down here. This is not a friendly place, to put it mildly. But from what Heinrich told us, we wouldn't have any problems. They were going to greet us with open arms."

"They are. Their version of arms is in their holsters."

"Hell, the revenue the production will bring into the country alone should be worth it to them."

"These goons don't know anything about the revenue and don't care," whispered Kasia. "The worst they could do is tell us they changed their minds and put us on the next flight back to the States."

"No, that's not the worst. I'd hope for that rather than what they could do to us. I guess if it comes to that, we can always shoot in Mexico or somewhere else that's friendly."

"I'd feel better about it." Kasia glanced at the ominous looking guards. "Especially if we have to live with this day in and day out."

"Let's hope we're worrying for nothing."

At that moment, the door opened and Michael and Kasia looked up expectantly as the agent re-entered the small ill-lit room. He spoke to the two guards in Spanish. They followed him out, leaving the door ajar. Michael and Kasia listened to their receding footsteps. Michael quickly rose from his chair and went to the door.

"Don't do anything that can cause more trouble," said Kasia.

"I won't. I wonder why they left the door open. Do they think we'll try to walk out of here? How stupid do they think we are?"

After what seemed an interminable wait, a serious middle-aged gentleman entered the room and in a gracious manner introduced himself. "Senor, Senora, I apologize for your inconvenience and the delay. I hope there are no misunderstandings. My name is Eduardo Alcaguaya. I will be your escort and guide and accompany you on your search for locations for your motion picture."

Considering their initial treatment at the hands of the customs officials, Michael couldn't be certain if the dark-skinned athletic man were a government agent or not. He had been briefed by Helmut Bachmann, the Tri Con Corporation CEO what to do in the way of surveillance. Nothing Michael and Kasia said or did would go unnoticed.

"Welcome to Santiago," Eduardo continued with a smile. "First, I will take you to your hotel. Please, come with me." He motioned them out through the door. Michael shot an angry glance in the direction of the guards as they departed from the interrogation center.

On their scenic drive from the airport, the spectacular view of mountain peaks that ringed the city alleviated some of their tension. They were surprised at the dingy atmosphere and absence of tall modern buildings. The drab dark clothing of the *Santiaguenos* they saw along the main street, Boulevard O'Higgins, accentuated for Michael the oppressed life of the citizens scrambling to board tightly packed small buses, *liebres*.

"You will have a few hours to relax at your hotel," said Eduardo, easing the luxurious black Mercedes past streams of traffic and bold pedestrians. "I will pick you up for lunch, then show you the city this afternoon. Early tomorrow, you will see our agricultural region. On the third day, we will take a small private plane south to *Concepcion*. That is where the forest and lake country begin. It rains much of the time there through fall and winter. For us, that is January through August. No doubt, the rains could affect your production schedule."

Eduardo checked them into their hotel and followed the bell-hop with them to a functional, but comfortable room. As the young Hispanic man set down their luggage, Eduardo mentioned, "My room is next door. If you need me, just pick up the phone and have the desk put you through."

I'm sure you'll be listening, Michael expressed silently to himself. *The place is probably bugged.* "Thank you, Eduardo. While we're in Santiago, there is someone we want to visit, Senor Claudio Montalva. He's a friend of Helmut Bachmann, President of the Tri Con Corporation and the Tri Con Industries here in Chile."

"I am familiar with the Tri Con Industries. You will be with Senor Montalva tomorrow afternoon and evening. In fact, you will spend tomorrow night at his *funda*, his plantation, and return here the following day before we tour the south."

"It sounds like you have an aggressive schedule worked out for us."

"There is much to see and the country stretches for many thousands of miles, as I'm sure you realize, Senor Sloan."

"Yes, and from what we've seen so far from the air, it is spectacular," Michael offered diplomatically.

Eduardo smiled his acknowledgement.

"We appreciate all you're doing to help us, Eduardo. When we are finished, I want to commend you in writing to your government."

Eduardo nodded. "I am with the Office of Public Affairs. I am an *aficionado* of the cinema, Senor Sloan, and I understand your need for locations. As a geographer, I am intimately acquainted with the entire country of Chile. I'm sure what you see will be inspiring. The fruit and wine basket are compliments of the hotel."

"I'll thank the manager personally."

With a polite nod, Eduardo backed away to the door. "I will call for you at eleven forty-five."

When Eduardo was gone, Michael gave Kasia a look of exasperation directed at their host and the political system behind him. "We're not going to see anything they don't want us to see. Just the inspiring sights. I'll have to try to break him out of that Cooke's tour guide attitude."

"Maybe he's just proud of his country and wants to show its best face." She raised a finger to her lips and shook her head, warning him to change the subject. Her sweeping gesture took in the bedside phone and graphic paintings hanging on the walls. He understood to keep his comments neutral and watched Kasia examine the lamps, phone, pictures, bed, and light fixtures. Finally, she turned on the water in the bathroom and the radio in the bedroom.

"Where did you learn all that?" Michael grinned.

"From spy movies."

"I guess we're playing footsie with the real thing. How do you feel?"

"Not too bad. I actually slept most of the night."

"I wish I had," said Michael. "I don't sleep well when I'm traveling, never have. I'm starting to feel the drag right now."

"Why don't you take a nap. I'm going to read some of this literature Eduardo provided on the country." Kasia kicked off her flats, pulled a chair over next to the double bed and propped up her feet. Michael dozed within minutes of his head touching the pillow.

For lunch, Eduardo took them to one of the finer restaurants and introduced them to the *pisco sour*, a local wine beaten into a froth with lemon juice, sugar, and egg white, and served as a cocktail.

Michael ordered a popular Chilean dish, *pastel de choclos*, a stew containing beef, chicken, corn, raisins and onions with a variety of herbs. Kasia ordered *empanades*, a hot turnover filled with edible seaweed and melted cheese. Eduardo ordered bass, *corvina*, and *choros*, large mussels.

Afterward, expounding like a tour guide, Eduardo shuttled Michael and Kasia about the city. The shantytowns, *poblaciones callampas*, (Eduardo called them mushroom settlements) were of great interest to Michael from the standpoint of his film story.

They saw packs of wild dogs, naked and miserably clad children sitting in pools of slime boiling with flies while they plucked refuse out of garbage heaps. Most of the huts along the wide dreary streets were constructed of cardboard and tin cans, and old newspapers covered the empty window spaces. The squalor reminded Michael of his tour in Vietnam.

"The residents here are not vagrants," Eduardo explained. "They have left the *campo*, the countryside, to find a new way of life in the cities. Many of these people have traveled hundreds of miles on foot. They build their huts on any available ground and here they squat."

They had seen most of the city by evening. Michael had copious notes and sketches and photos of locales he would use for some of the urban scenes.

An early start the next morning put them far into the countryside enroute to the Claudio Montalva *fundo* or plantation. In addition to being a landowner, the tall, slender, silver-haired gentleman was a university professor who had been overlooked by the junta during its repressive purge to "root out Marxism," as Montalva expressed the actions of the military regime. Knowing that anything negative he said about the junta would be reported to the secret police by Eduardo, Montalva chose his words carefully in describing Chile's outdated agricultural system.

"The workers you see are *rotos*, peasants," he said, as they bounced along in a jeep between sweeping fields of grain. "Many of them are sharecroppers. Because landowners and big business are tied closely together, land reform has always been blocked. The country does not have enough food to feed its people as a result. We must import much of what we consume."

Several miles on, they saw a single tractor and a harvester, the only two large pieces of agricultural machinery on the vast plain.

"As you can see," continued Montalva, "I have gone against the common practice, even in a small way. *Fundos* like this are owned and operated like medieval serfdoms. They cover hundreds of square miles and are not adequately cultivated because the political system here does not permit the application of modern agricultural science. Many of the owners will not even allow the use of machinery. My daughter, Gabriele, will join us for dinner this evening. She recently returned from your country. She is writing her doctoral thesis on the social and political systems in Chile from a historical viewpoint."

"Was she going to school in the U.S.?" Kasia asked.

"Yes, Harvard University. She's a brilliant young woman, somewhat outspoken, however. You must consider her comments strictly on a theoretical basis." He looked quickly in the rearview mirror at Eduardo's dour expression. "She has been out of the country for some time and must become reacquainted with the positive reforms of the current regime."

As brilliant and impressive as she was, the dark attractive Gabriele Montalva did not mince words in her assessment of the *junta*. During dinner, her father repeatedly attempted to signal her to temper her comments. She deliberately ignored him despite his privately cautioning her at length about Eduardo. She drank several glasses of wine and chose to not acknowledge his silent warnings. The presence of the two Americans created a false sense of security for her, since she was not that far removed from the liberal discussions in graduate political science and government seminars at Harvard.

Montalva tried pointedly to change the subject, but Gabriele insisted on recapitulating the inflammatory topics of fresh academic interest to her and dangerous in the company of Eduardo, who watched and listened with a bemused expression that masked his disapproval. Her preoccupation with radical views that encouraged dissension were not lost on him.

"These people have not come to Chile for a whitewash," she said in reference to Kasia and Michael. "They're going to make a film about revolution. They should know about the insufferable conditions of the people and the cruel repression by the *junta*."

Sensing and fully understanding Montalva's concern for his daughter's well-being, Michael tried to soften the tenor of the conversation, realizing the impact it was having on Eduardo.

"The film will not be about any particular regime and not even critical. In fact, a revolution is only the backdrop for a love story, more like the classic movie, *Casa Blanca*."

"Nevertheless, let me give you an accurate picture. One out of every one-hundred Chileans has been arrested since the coup in 1973. There are more than four thousand political prisoners being held in remote concentration camps and in the prisons. Even the Catholic clergy has felt the jackboot heel of the fascist *junta* if they dare to speak out against the generals. Anything that is said or done to help the prisoners is cut off on the charge that the action is communist inspired and part of a conspiracy to overthrow the regime. If I sound bitter, you may well believe I have good reason to be. My fiancé disappeared last year in one of those prison camps." Her defiant stare raked Eduardo.

She went on to describe how stoop labor was the only means that the villages had to produce their food. "The peasants use crude implements. The women and children fan out over the land to sow and harvest crops. The millions in so-called foreign aid from the United States Government never does trickle down to the people for whom it was intended. It is skimmed off the top by regime bureaucrats and laundered away into their private bank accounts."

Of vital interest to Kasia were Gabriele's description of how the women spent three to four times the number of hours working the village farms as the men. They shouldered the burden of providing food, water, and fuel for their families.

"In addition to the *junta's* embezzlement of funds, the next biggest problem is the migration of the men to find better paying jobs, especially working in the copper mines in the north. Children are kept out of school to contribute to the labor force. As a consequence, the literacy rate among women in Latin America and other underdeveloped countries has rapidly declined. Women are producing more and more children in order to build and maintain permanent family labor pools.

"Fuel is the most urgent need. More than half of every woman's day, every day, is spent in the search for fuel. What is really the height of stupidity is the agricultural training and demonstrations. The government provides them only for the men even though the women are the ones doing the farming. It's just another example of the rot and corruption by the regime. Even in the cities, the government believes that men go to work mainly to provide for their families. It's not true. Business is just selling out to that migrating horde of men looking for a job that pays better than what they are willing to pay. "

"I think you're generalizing on that point," said her father, casting a quick nervous glance at Eduardo, who rigidly sipped at his wine.

"Unfortunately, nothing short of revolution can change these unsufferable conditions," said Gabriele.

"You mean, of course, in an economic sense," Montalva interrupted struggling to repress a frantic note in his voice. His daughter had uttered the forbidden word that raised a red flag with government officials. "And the regime's economic policies are certainly most revolutionary to lead the country."

"No," said Gabriele, "I'm talking about the Nazis who run this country today with their raids, pulling people out of their homes in the middle of the night. It is a government that rules by fear. The military trials are a farce. But what is worse are the insidious spy networks where people are paid to inform on their neighbors. And when a poor family is desperately in need of food and money, some will prevaricate and see their neighbors go to prison over nothing."

"The goal of Pinochet has been to pull the country out of an economic tailspin, however," Montalva interjected, hoping to somehow repair the devastating negative impression his daughter had made on Eduardo. "Allende's policies brought our country to ruin. He broke up the plantations regardless of their productivity. The owners refused to plant their crops. With a drop in production, we had to increase food imports. By seizing the copper mines owned by U.S. corporations, Allende isolated us in foreign affairs. Our people were literally starving in the streets."

"Allende was an ignorant politician, a bureaucrat and a fool," Gabriele agreed. "He had an opportunity to do something great for this country, but he did not know how to manage it." She suddenly yawned. "Well, I'm sure I've said enough. I apologize if I have offended your beliefs in the government," she said directly to Eduardo. "Please don't consider what I've said all that seriously. It is only my opinion. No one is either going to listen or care anyway. After all, they are only words loosened with good wine." She rose from the table.

"Kasia, Michael, it's a pleasure to meet you." She reached across the table to shake their hands. "I look forward to seeing you again when you're in Chile making your movie and I sincerely look forward to seeing your film when it is completed. I imagine I'll have to come to the States for that."

"We both have enjoyed meeting you," said Kasia along with Michael's concurring nod.

"Your comments and information have been informative and helpful," said Michael.

Gabriele laughed, understanding the context of his reference.

"Goodnight."

"Goodnight, father." Gabriele unsteadily came around to his side of the table and placed a dutiful kiss on his head. "Don't worry. Anything I have to say isn't going to make a grain of difference. After all, I'm only a woman, and nobody in Chile listens to a woman, especially men." She winked at Kasia, who responded with a weak grin.

"Next time you're in Santiago, I'll take you skiing. We have some of the finest slopes in the world," Gabriele pantomimed pushing ski poles and rotating her hips. "Goodnight." She waved once and tottered out of the dining room.

They left the Montalva *fundo* just after breakfast the following morning for the return trip to Santiago. Eduardo drove in a cloak of grim silence. His former tour guide enthusiasm had disappeared like shed clothing. His mind dwelt on the words of Montalva's daughter, who at the very moment was arguing with her father over his insistence that she leave the country at once and either return to the United States or go to Argentina until conditions had changed. He knew Eduardo would report on her and Montalva feared for her life. Then, against his better judgment, he revealed to her the plan for the coup.

"Very clever," she responded approvingly. "Who conceived that idea?"

"Our American friend, Helmut Bachmann"

"Then he's not altogether enchanted with Pinochet either."

"Few men are unless they are one of his inner circle. However, after your comments last night, you must seriously consider leaving or you may not be around for the coup. You have placed yourself in a dangerous position."

"When is all this to happen?"

"It will coincide with the production of the film, which is only an excuse to smuggle artillery and insurgents and mercenaries into the country. This is all more than a year away. It cannot be done any faster."

"Are you directly involved?"

"Yes, with certain highly placed people."

"Some of Frei's old Christian Democrats perhaps?"

Montalva nodded.

"Then you must be equally as careful." She tenderly touched his arm.

"We must both be careful. But what you said last night has jeopardized your safety should you remain. There will be nothing I can do to save you once they have you in one of their prisons. Will you at least go to Argentina until I send for you?"

"Yes, I'll leave tomorrow."

Montalva embraced her. "You're the last of my daughters. If your mother were alive, she would be proud of the fine intelligent young woman you have become. But she would be even more cautionary than I. Besides, I am looking forward to the day you and Pablo have your first child."

Her eyes clouded. "Providing Pablo is still alive."

"We will find him. When the time comes, we will find him."

CHAPTER TWENTY

The Rendezvous

On the third day, Eduardo put them all aboard an old World War II DC-3 transport that created the sensation for Michael of stepping into a 1940's movie about Nazis and the use of such vintage aircraft.

Eduardo advised them to bring along sweaters and rain gear. "We will be entering a totally different climate."

Kasia and Michael were unprepared for the stunning visual sweep of green forests, fiords, valleys and mountain lakes that were unveiled below. Rugged islands crouched under the imposing *cordillera* of the Andes.

"Few people come this far south," explained Eduardo. "Fishermen, hikers, skiers, mountain climbers. Earthquakes have ravaged the entire region. Soon we will be landing at *Puerto Montt.* That is where the highway and the railroad end. You will probably want to film down here because the scenery is spectacular. However, the weather can be devastating. The archipelago stretches nine hundred miles to Cape Horn."

The geographical contrasts excited Michael's imagination as did the abrupt cultural change from the sophistication of metropolitan Santiago to this outland. The bulk of the small local population were Germans and Austrians. But their houses appeared to have been transplanted from the American South. Large, dilapidated porches sprung from old frame structures with steep pitched roofs.

"It looks like the frontier," observed Michael. "The beginning of the wilderness."

The eerie remoteness of the location seeped into them. People here were different than the Northerners, suspicious, withdrawn, and deceptive, bent on survival in this rugged terrain. Kasia knew that Charley and Maggie MacIntosh were out there somewhere.

That night, a howling wind and rainstorm confined them to their old hotel. Another American approached them as they sat at the bar passing the evening hours. He introduced himself as Roger Lakein, a freelance journalist who traveled and wrote about South America.

This was the first time Kasia had ever met or seen the man. Frasier had never even shown her Lakein's photograph, although he had told her to expect to be contacted. Lakein did not convey that he recognized her as an agent. For two hours, he bought rounds of drinks and told them of stories he had come across in this remote vastness.

"This area has its local color all right. There are people living out in the mountains and down along the coast who don't come into town maybe once or twice a year. They live off the land or the sea, not just native Indians either. In the spring, this place is like the old American frontier rendezvous days of the fur traders around here. Some of the Germans who live back in the woods take Indian wives and they come down the rivers with their families, spend a week in Puerto Montt buying supplies and whooping it up, then go back and won't be seen again until next spring.

"They've got their gunslingers too, outlaws, Saturday night brawls, even shootouts. The law sort of lets things take their natural course, except for the outlaws. That's because the loot isn't gold and silver. It's cocaine. The whites barter for it with the Araucanian Indians up in the mountains, then smuggle it out on fishing trawlers through the islands. The navy has a devil of a time keeping up with them or even trying to find them in that maze.

"The government can't send troops up into the mountains and order the Indians not to cultivate and harvest what grows naturally. Besides, without it, the poor natives would die off. Cocaine is the only thing that keeps them going up at those high altitudes in that freezing temperature. Any troops that went up there would have to start chewing the leaves themselves.

"As you might have guessed or even seen by now, the residents around here are suspicious of strangers. One thing they never have to worry about is some real estate developer from Santiago building a high-rise resort hotel. Not with weather like this and the earthquakes."

"Do you live down here?" Michael asked.

"No, I have a house in Santiago and spend time in other Latin American countries writing about their cultures and tourist and travel spots. I come down here once in a while just for a change, to get away. I enjoy the mountains, the ruggedness of the area and sense of isolation. And I like to fish. Great trout fishing in the streams and rivers down here. Isn't this storm something else? You could walk outside in the middle of the night and just never come back."

During a moment alone, while Michael and Eduardo went to the men's room, Lakein quickly and unexpectedly spoke in a low conspiratorial voice to Kasia. I contact Charley and Maggie MacIntosh every two or three months. They're prepared to assist the MIR guerillas coming over from Argentina in establishing a base camp in a remote wilderness area

"Charley and Maggie?"

"I've been told you're informed."

Kasia nodded.

"They'll stay hidden until the time of the strike in Santiago after the heavy artillery for the film production arrives."

The information plunged Kasia into a mental turmoil. This was the first she had ever heard about the film production being used as a front to overthrow the *junta*, but she listened with the attitude that she was aware of the plan all along.

As far as Lakein knew about her, she was a Soviet agent and had no affiliation with the CIA. Neither did he know that Charley and Maggie were part of the CIA operation to unearth the mole working out of the American embassy in Santiago. Without realizing what he was doing, in passing on the information to Kasia, Lakein had walked right into a trap, and he did not conceive at the time that she was the bait.

Gordon Frasier and the CIA suspected that Lakein was being paid off by some entity high up either in South America or else from a European source as an intermediary for the Soviet Union. The trap was designed to hopefully lead the CIA to that source on the supposition there was an active KGB cell working within the Tri Con Corporation.

Kasia had to exercise special care during her exchange of information so as not to inadvertently tip off Lakein he was being drawn in.

The news of the recruitment and movement of guerilla forces astounded her. Obviously, she was intended to report the covert activity back to Gordon Frasier. She wondered why he had never mentioned to her what was going on in South America. Also, Lakein was not passing on this information to the CIA according to what he was supposed to do.

Kasia wondered who was financing the insurgent army migrating from Argentina. To ask that question of either Lakein would give away her position. That information was clearly not intended for her to know. She was being used as a pawn somewhere in the confused middle. The likelihood occurred to her that maybe even they didn't know the monetary source. Lakein was still considered a direct channel to that source.

She would pass her message along to Frasier at the first opportunity after she and Michael returned to California. Frasier would alert CIA headquarters at Langley. Command operatives there would, in turn, alert the Chilean *junta* whose forces would intercept, capture, and execute the insurgents. The whole affair would have to be orchestrated so as not to scare off Lakein and send him underground before the CIA could discover the identity of the mole in the Tri Con cell.

Later that night, Lakein woke out of a sound sleep as though he had been stung. Pieces from his subconscious mind were suddenly coming together almost too fast for him to manage. The message he had received from Helmut Bachmann had told him to meet Kasia in Puerto Montt and bring her up to date on Charley and Maggie and the MIR situation. Lakein had questioned the logic and advisability of doing this rather than continue to use their usual code and Russian satellite communication system. But the coded message was valid.

Now, in the middle of the night, that the CIA might have broken their code and sent him the message as though it were coming from Bachmann electrified him with a warning impulse. He had no actual proof that this was the case, only a terrifying intuition. He knew that feeling had to come from somewhere. He had always been skilled at detecting what was unspoken, the hidden intent behind the mask of espionage.

Was it something Kasia had said or something in her manner? In his mind, he went back over their brief encounter at the hotel bar. Their time had been very compressed, only the duration while Michael and Eduardo had gone to the men's room. Then a cat and mouse pattern began to emerge from the distant past.

Frasier had once attempted to send him a covert message through Delugach at Tri Con Pictures that Lakein would receive had Delugach taken the bait. If Lakein received the message, he was to have reported that information to Frasier. Lakein had stopped the message cold and Delugach had not passed it on to him. Lakein had later reported that he did not receive any planted message.

Frasier had trapped him. Lakein now realized he should have reported to Frasier that the message had come through, even though it had not. Only Lakein could have warned Delugach through Giorgio Mykola to act as if he didn't know what the message was about.

Lakein knew that Kasia was a courier and informer for Mykola. Frasier had never told Lakein who was giving the message to Delugach, but it would have to be someone already inside, a double agent. Frasier had contrived the whole situation to set him up. Now he had done it again by having the double agent, Kasia Kerenski, receive information from Lakein about the pending coup.

Lakein paced his room in a cold sweat that he had been so cleverly duped by Frasier. Then a related inference set his thoughts racing in another direction. Was Frasier on the take with Tri Con and setting him up to take the rap for collusion with the KGB?

"I've got to bury Frasier," he said aloud. "I've got to get to him and come out of this clean or I'm a dead man."

Frasier had forced Lakein into a position where, to survive, he must play both sides against the middle. Now that he had divulged the secret of the coup, he had to go after Frasier while at the same time he scuttled the conspiracy, which was exactly what Frasier wanted him to do.

What Lakein had to avoid at all costs was leading Frasier to Helmut Bachmann. Frasier couldn't know that Lakein was secretly working hand in glove with Bachmann just as Lakein couldn't know if Frasier himself answered to Bachmann. The relationship between Frasier and Bachmann was only conjecture on Lakein's part at this point. For now, Lakein had to make a pretense of moving against the CIA.

Lakein would return to Santiago, then fly on immediately to Nicaragua with a message through a courier for Giorgio Mykola to receive in Mexico City. "Inca is a star in your galaxy." Kasia Kerenski would have to be terminated so that Lakein could maintain his credibility with Bachmann.

Gabriele finished packing her single suitcase, hoisted her dress carrier to her shoulder, and clattered down the tile stairs to the living room as her father pulled his Mercedes around to the front entrance of the *hacienda*. She stowed her luggage in the back seat, then slipped her lithe figure into the front passenger seat.

Bordered on each side by cultivated fields, the driveway out to the main road was several kilometers. Two military jeeps blocked their passage. With a hand casually resting on his holstered .45 magnum, a young blonde Germanic-looking captain waved them to a halt. They saw submachine guns trained on them by four other security police. In Spanish, the officer asked to see their identification, then ordered them to step out of their car.

He called to one of the sergeants, who handcuffed Claudio Montalva and roughly marched him to one of the jeeps while Gabriele watched in defiance until the captain ordered her to be handcuffed and placed in the other jeep.

The Mercedes was left where it had been stopped, its engine still running.

Montalva realized there was no way out for either his daughter or for himself. He only hoped the police would not torture them. He did not know how his daughter would endure. The thought of the sadistic devices employed by the secret police to induce pain sickened him with fear.

He was not a hero or a martyr. If necessary, he would make a deal, then talk, tell them what they wanted to hear, even if what he said were lies. So far, they were being arrested only because of Gabriele's statements criticizing the *junta*. The police did not suspect him of involvement in a conspiracy. Mere words, he thought. Provocative statements were sufficient to bring the ruthless power of the police down upon their heads. He silently cursed his daughter for not heeding his warning. Then he prayed for her. She would need divine intervention to escape what was in store for her. She could have been on her way to Argentina this very moment had she not been so stubborn. He had wanted her to leave the day before, but she had insisted on staying. He regretted not being forceful. He had always been gentle and loving in his protection of her.

He had always been a careful man. He had no choice but to exercise care both in his statements and behavior. The secret police were jackals that preyed on individuals, those who expressed discontent, even though they outwardly conformed to the fascist laws. A single man or a woman alone could do nothing against them.

The ride to Santiago in the open jeeps was made in silence. The wind whipped their faces. The captain delivered the Montalvas to his headquarters where they were separated and placed in holding cells without any explanation or regard for their comfort or personal rights, which did not exist.

An hour later, two armed guards escorted Montalva to an interrogation chamber. They ordered him to sit on a stool under a hot light, where he remained for another hour. He could barely see their faces, since the rest of the room was in partial darkness.

The door opened suddenly, startling him and admitting a shaft of light that stopped just beyond his circle. The officer who came in to question him, Manuel Contreras, was only a few years younger than Montalva and treated him with respect.

"You're highly regarded by highly placed officials in the government, Senor Montalva. You're a landowner, a professor of economics, a counselor to the administration. It is indeed unfortunate that your daughter has returned to her homeland politically contaminated. It is not our intention to harm you."

Montalva's weary eyes meekly followed the rigid lines of the man's uniform. A rush of relief weakened him so that he was unprepared to handle the next statement.

"We only ask that you tell us truthfully the extent of your daughter's intentions to conspire against the regime."

"Sir, if I may explain, Gabriele had consumed far too much wine and was parroting propaganda learned from her American university. Conspiracy does not even enter the question."

"I want you to step over to this window for a moment." Contreras guided him gently but firmly by the arm.

Somewhere, a special light was turned on to illuminate the adjoining room. Through a one way mirror, Montalva saw his daughter totally nude, strapped down spread-eagled on her back on a shining steel examining table. An electrode had been inserted into her uterus with the thin cable trailing off the table to an encased electronic device on a counter nearby.

"The charge she will be given is very high. The voltage will cause her to become sterile. Only you can save her by providing us full information in answer to my question." He led a trembling Montalva back to the chair.

No matter what he said, Montalva knew he would implicate himself, as well. The police would hold him responsible for not immediately informing on his own daughter.

"She has been home to visit for only a few days. She was going to visit her sister in Argentina. Granted her views sound radical to the regime and its objectives, but I can assure you they were mere mouthings of a new college graduate who lacks political acumen and sophistication. She was exposed, unfortunately, to Marxist literature, which, as you know, is widely read in American universities."

"Think of your potential grandchildren by this young woman, your daughter, Senor Montalva."

Montalva studied the now unbelievably cool deadly eyes. He had only heard of Manual Contreras and the inner empire of fear and torture he ruled. The reality of his inhumane acts unnerved Montalva. He decided to attempt a ploy. "Then you yourself have not yet heard the rumor," he said.

"I am always interested in rumors. There is usually a reason for them. I hold any rumor suspect."

"I would have thought your investigators would have discovered that information."

"Tell me the information, Senor Montalva. What is the information."

"What I'm about to tell you I have also shared with my daughter. She knows no more than what I am about to say, which is all I know, as well."

"You are keeping me in suspense, Senor Montalva. If you cooperate fully and openly with me, your daughter will not be harmed. So, the rumor – the information."

"Several communist agents have infiltrated the country and are establishing a base to launch a coup."

"Their names?"

"As I said, it is only a rumor. I am not involved and do not personally know any of their names."

"Where did you hear this rumor?"

"From a clerk at the American embassy."

"His name."

"I don't know his name but I can identify him."

"If I showed you a photo, you could identify him."

"Yes, or I can point him out."

"What were the circumstances that he told you this rumor?"

"I happened to be at the embassy on an errand for a business associate. I overheard the comment while waiting in the outer office. Apparently they were in the process of an investigation. That is why I thought you already knew of it."

Carefully weighing the information, Contreras studied him for a long time. "An American film director and his wife, a movie star, came to visit you. What is your association with them?"

"They are employed by the Tri Con Corporation in California."

"Yes, we know."

"Then you must also know that Helmut Bachmann, the president of the Tri Con Corporation, and I are good friends. Mr. Bachmann conducts extensive business in Chile and is a supporter of the regime. The film director and his wife visited me at his request so that I could show them my plantation. They have come to Chile to scout locations for the director's next film."

"I know why they are here. Your answers are satisfactory. I'm going to release you, Senor Montalva, but you will be under surveillance. You may not leave the country for any reason. Should you attempt to do so, your daughter will be tortured until death. She will be held as my prisoner to ensure your cooperation in this very important matter to the regime."

"But – you said," Montalva rose, indignant with rage.

"Control yourself, Senor. Your daughter cannot be trusted. You yourself said she has Marxist leanings. She cannot be allowed to go free to blatantly tout her irresponsible radical philosophy. Our session is ended. You will be returned to your home." Contreras signaled to the guards to take Montalva away.

"Let me speak to her, please. Allow me to speak to her."

Contreras' back disappeared through another door that led into a small control room from which he could privately view Gabriele Montalva. Reaching for the control panel, he pulled the lever slightly forward and experienced a surge of excitation as Gabriele thrashed and screamed at the mild voltage. He pushed back the lever and stared at the spasmodic trembling of her vulva.

Desperate with anguish, Montalva had attempted to see his daughter through the one-way glass as the guards herded him out into the hall. Then through the walls he heard Gabriele's horrifying screams that went on and on and on.

CHAPTER TWENTY-ONE

The Tour

Inca is a star in your galaxy.

Helmut Bachmann stared at the coded message which had come from Roger Lakein in Santiago, Chile. Bachmann was fully aware of operation Inca, the CIA mission to find the mole in Tri Con's South American enterprises and the suspected KGB cell within the Tri Con Corporation which would lead to him.

The message indicated that the CIA had now infiltrated the cell and that an agent was dangerously close to him. That Kasia Kerenski, film actress, was the agent astounded him.

The CIA investigation of his South American to Europe shipping operations was unquestionably evident. Bachmann realized he could no longer risk coded letters, wires, telexes, satellite communications and private phone conversations with his ten different operations directors in Chile, Argentina, Bolivia, and Brazil.

So far the CIA has had no channel to trace the disappearance of oil and mineral resources back to the parent company. Lakein had effectively neutralized that effort. And even if, by chance, the information was discovered, there were those individuals farther down the corporate food chain who could be held responsible.

Until this latest unsettling news from Roger Lakein, Bachmann had not considered it necessary to vary his precise schedule of loads and deliveries to the Soviet Union. Now he would have to change or risk certain discovery. Discovery of one such element in the corporation would logically lead to another in a chain reaction and result in a not so covert investigation of Tri Con and all its subsidiaries, of which most existed only on paper.

The IRS and the State Department would tear them apart. Accustomed to taking calculated risks, Bachmann acutely realized this was one he could not afford.

The tanker loading operations had recently been changed. The multiple buoy systems with their submarine pipelines had been installed sixty miles offshore in international waters. Both Tri Con oil tankers and those of foreign registry could be simultaneously loaded and fueled through the submarine pipelines that carried the oil out to the ships without them having to come into port. The buoys also saved cargo transfer time and required no operating personnel, eliminating the possibility of investigation from air, shore, or by sea.

Lighting the first cigarette he had smoked in the past six months; he stared out over the city of Los Angeles from his penthouse office. Operation Inca presented him with a major problem.

His secretary called to remind him of his dinner engagement with Michael Sloan and Kasia Kerenski that evening at seven to hear about their trip to Chile. He checked his watch. The time was five fifteen.

He called the studio and left a message for Heinrich to come to the house thirty minutes early. When Heinrich arrived, Bachmann led him into the library and closed the door.

"Are you ready for this? Your suspicions about Kasia Kerenski have been fully realized. She's a double agent. The message came through Roger Lakein in Chile."

"Do you really trust Lakein? This could be a maneuver of a different kind."

"I don't have any reason not to trust him, unless you know something I don't."

"I'm always suspicious of field agents and their hidden agendas."

"What would he be hiding?"

"I don't know. It's just a feeling I have about him."

"This isn't about him. It's about Kasia Kerenski."

"How much do you think she knows?"

"At this point, it doesn't really matter, but we must put her out of the picture, permanently."

Heinrich sipped at his scotch. "If she were to be murdered, the FBI will crawl all over us."

"Murder is out of the question. But if we remove her from the United States and she's on foreign soil, a terrorist's bullet would not likely be questioned, even by the CIA. A public assassination by someone posing as a third world fanatic, perhaps a Muslim, would never be traceable to Tri Con."

"Her second film, *Mt. Angell*, is scheduled for release in Europe this month," said Heinrich.

"Send her with it on a promotional tour. I'll talk to Werfel in Berlin later tonight. He can go through channels in Libya to plant an assassin. The most important factor is that her death must occur in the presence of the media to create the illusion of a radical third world political statement. After all, she's a movie star, a symbol of Western depravity."

"Shall I bring up the tour at dinner this evening?"

"Yes," said Bachmann. "Stress how important it is that she go. I'll get them talking about Chile and tell Michael how much I like the script."

"What if he wants to do the tour with her?"

"Tell him no. You need him at the studio. The South American production demands it. Kasia can handle the tour with assistants very well on her own."

"What a shame. What a waste. She's good. She's very good. *Gott im himmel*, she fooled us all. What a cover, eh? I wonder if Michael even knows."

"If he does, that's all for the better. It will add credence to her assassination on the tour." Bachmann glanced at the grandfather clock against the far wall. "They'll be here in ten minutes."

"What will become of the South American project? She's supposed to star in that film, as well."

"It will go forward as planned with a new star. There are plenty to choose from."

Heinrich puzzled a moment. "I suppose there are others around if the price is right, but maybe no one else acceptable to Michael. He might not be up to handling the film with the death of his wife."

"Then you hire another director. It doesn't matter who does the film as long as the production is in South America so we can legitimately move in artillery and supplies."

"Did Lakein tell her that the film was to be used as a front for the coup?"

Bachmann studied Heinrich for a moment. "He didn't say, and I don't know. I doubt it. If he did, it's not likely he would admit to it."

"This could be the hidden agenda I talked about. If he did tell her, then the CIA knows, and Pinochet's army and secret police will be waiting. The guerillas will be walking into a trap."

Bachmann crossed the room and stared out the window overlooking an acre of manicured gardens. Suddenly turning, he said, "She doesn't know. She can't possibly know and the CIA doesn't know."

"How can you be sure?"

"Because the FBI has not come after us."

"They could be watching and waiting."

"Lakein is too careful. He would not have made that kind of slip. He no more knew she was a double agent than we did and he had no reason to even discuss the coup with her. He discovered her by some other means."

"I would feel better knowing how," Heinrich rose from his chair.

"Have Giorgio investigate it. Wait. Wait a minute. As of this moment, Giorgio can no longer be of use to us. Of course he has been compromised by Kasia long ago. I'll take care of Giorgio."

"What if the assassination attempt should fail?"

"I have a contingency plan. If she survives, we let her go to South America with the film production. Arrangements will be made so that she and her husband will never come back." Bachmann moved to the door.

Heinrich set his empty cocktail glass on the table and followed him out.

***

When Michael kissed Kasia goodbye at the Los Angeles International Airport, he held her an extra moment, knowing that he would not have the opportunity again for the next four weeks.

He personally did not agree that the promotional tour was necessary for the European market, but Heinrich had insisted on it, stating that Kasia's public appearances would definitely influence audience attendance and box office receipts for the film, Mt. Angell, during its initial foreign release.

Following her European tour, Kasia would stop off in London, then travel on to Brazil.

As she settled into her seat in the first-class compartment of the Boeing 747, she was aware of the male eyes that tracked her. She wore Calvin Klein tans, a light blue silk blouse and a tan suede jacket. Normally, she liked to remove her shoes, but decided to sacrifice the comfort out of precaution, since the hollowed heel of her right shoe contained a tiny roll of microfilm given her by Giorgio.

Bachmann had not yet informed Giorgio that he had been compromised. For reasons of his own, he wanted to wait until after the assassination of Kasia Kerenski. Knowing that Kasia would reveal the microfilm coded message to the CIA, the message, once it was decoded, was designed to distort the information assumed known by the CIA and throw the investigation completely off the track. Kasia was not told who would receive the message, only that she would be contacted at some point during the tour.

Among the eyes that casually, and some not so casually, watched her, she wondered if she were being shadowed. The sensation lingered somewhere at the nape of her neck.

She reflected on how shocked Giorgio had been when she reported her contact with Roger Lakein in Chile and information about the MIR military buildup for a coup. He had questioned her at length about the meeting with Lakein, how it had been arranged, who else she had talked to, the times and locations. His face had turned white when she told him that Lakein had come to her.

After that, Giorgio had grown evasive, constantly avoiding her. He stopped coming to the salon when he knew she had a reservation and delegated a talented young woman to do her hair. Geraldine kept remarking on the sudden change in her boss and the fact he had not shown up for days on end and would not answer his phone.

Kasia sensed that she had been plunged into the heart of the Inca investigation, but without knowing how or why or understanding her function and position in the process. These thoughts pushed her to the edge of her nerves and she worried that she was being set up for what she might discover.

A heightened sense of paranoia suddenly overwhelmed her, but she controlled the urge to leap out of her seat and rush off the plane before it left the gate. But it was too late. The doors were closing.

As a major celebrity, she was accustomed to people watching her and the eyes and cameras following her about. It piqued her knowing what she carried in the heel of her shoe could so completely alter her sensitivity and perception of onlookers.

She accepted the champagne offered by the smiling flight attendant, hoping that it would calm her nerves. She opened one of several magazines taken from the refreshment cart. Lately, almost every major fashion and news magazine featured her photograph on the cover or else an article or story on her phenomenal rise to prominence as a motion picture star.

She had tired of reading them as just so much publicity manufactured and encouraged by the studio to assist in the promotion and marketing of her films. Most of the features exploited feminist and inspirational success story angles. Another featured an interview with the winner of a Kasia Kerenski look-a-like contest, Melinda Jakes, who lived in the San Fernando Valley.

A few men's magazines addressed the erotic challenge of her film image and occasionally, provocative photos of her appeared that she wondered how and where and when they had been taken, probably in studio dressing rooms and on sets where publicity photographers cranked out the film. A few she recognized as stills from nude scene out-takes.

The sensational headline of the article she had just opened sufficiently startled her enough to cause her to read beyond the teaser copy.

IS KASIA KERENSKI A RUSSIAN SPY?

She wondered if someone there in the cabin had planted the magazine and was observing her reaction or anyone else in the first-class cabin who might chance to read it, knowing she was on the flight.

A late middle-age corporate executive shedding his suitcoat across the aisle caught her surreptitious glance and gave her a warm smile. Anxious to not encourage his approach, Kasia nodded briefly and once again devoted her attention to the article.

The magazine's editorial position was ultra right-wing conservative, which explained, in part, the attack on her and her liberal husband which comprised most of the copy. The editorial derided his film statements against United States war hawks, corporate corruption, and exploitive consumerism.

The article questioned her political allegiance. That her parents had been Russian émigrés from Canada was mentioned. The journalist would have had to conduct investigative research to learn that.

By the conclusion of the article, she expelled a small sigh of relief that the whole matter had been structured around several suppositions by a right-wing editor who had created a hot topic to sell his magazine.

She would have liked to attribute no further credence to the piece or to the magazine itself, but she noted its several million distribution. Even negative messages registered in the minds of the public. She could not help but to feel unsettled.

Possessing so much at this point in her life, she occasionally experienced the fear of loss, that her fantastic film career would come crashing down around her, that her daughter would have leukemia, that Michael would have a heart attack from the stress he must endure as a director.

She had carried messages and been a courier long enough. Now, as a motion picture actress, wife, and mother, she had become the message.

Hans Frederick Werfel met her in West Berlin. He was the president of a chemical manufacturing company that was a major subsidiary of the Tri Con Corporation. Werfel also directed an energy research program funded by the West German government. The main project was associated with oil drilling operations in the North Sea, a perfect opportunity to channel oil from American Tri Con tankers into Soviet pipelines.

As they drove through the streets of Berlin, Werfel maintained a light conversational chatter, complimenting Kasia on her cinematic achievements. He had already attended a private screening of *Mt. Angell.*

He informed her she would be attending a champagne reception in her honor that evening to be followed by a private dinner party with thirty guests. He assured her she would not be bothered by the press. However, the following day, a publicist would assist her at the post screening press conference.

The long Mercedes limousine merged with traffic on the Autobahn and soon left the city behind. Werfel's home was a large country mansion secluded at the center of a one-hundred-acre wooded estate patrolled by a small army of special security guards and Dobermans.

A valet carried in Kasia's luggage, and a maid showed her to a spacious bedroom overlooking a manicured garden and a glass enclosed swimming pool and spa. A brownstone stable and paddocks extended from the gardener's cottage and a second house where the trainer of Werfel's Trykhaner breeding mares and stallions lived.

In her room, Kasia bathed, then took a brief nap. A light knock at the door awakened her. The maid looked in and advised her of the time of the reception and inquired if she might assist Kasia in her preparations. Kasia thanked her but said it wouldn't be necessary.

Since she spoke and understood only a limited amount of German, Kasia was at a conversational disadvantage during dinner. With Frederick acting as intermediary and playing the gracious host to men who imagined what Kasia was like in bed, to their wives who took mental notes of how she was dressed, made personal comparisons, and envied her status and beauty, she managed to endure a boring evening. She felt as though she were an interloper rather than an international star attraction.

The elaborate ten course dinner ended at eleven. At twelve, Werfel visited her room, expecting to have sex with her. He accepted her turndown with his usual amiable remarks and hoped that she would join him for a ride before breakfast early the next morning.

Although she enjoyed the misty cross-country canter and Werfel's lecture on the rising international popularity of the Trykhaner breed, Kasia could not call up any enthusiasm for her press conference that afternoon.

Her negativism required a great deal of control and intensified beginning with the dinner party and the smooth-talking Werfel's proposition. She decided that following the screening, she would arrange for a special flight back to the United States. The message in the heel of her shoe be damned.

As the closing credits of the film rolled up the screen, the lights were raised. Kasia walked forward down the theater aisle to grand applause. She moved quickly to the steps at the side of the stage apron that would bring her up to where the M.C. was adjusting the standing microphone.

The applause nearly drowned out the high-powered rifle shot that missed her head as she leaned down for a greeting hug from the M.C., who was a foot shorter than she. The bullet ripped through the screen. Kasia fell, pushed by the M.C. "Stay down," he shouted into her ear. Together they hugged the stage floor and belly crawled behind the curtain into the wings. Instantly, the auditorium erupted with a pandemonium of screams and bodies trampling over each other in a rush to escape the would-be assassin.

Untouched and unhurt because of the reflexive action of the M.C. to save her, Kasia scrambled to her feet and rushed further backstage in search of a door out and discovered the exit. She pushed open the door and ran frantically along the side street a few yards until she realized she must remove her shoes. Pulling them off in mid-stride, she continued stocking-footed until a line of heavy traffic halted her flight.

Looking back to see if she were being pursued, she moved to the side of the building and pressed herself against it for support until she regained her breath. The multiple back-firing of a truck caused her to whirl in fear.

A passerby from the evacuated theater audience recognized her and assisted her in finding a police officer. The limousine was contacted via car radio. Thirty minutes later, she was rolling out of Berlin back to Werfel's mansion.

CHAPTER TWENTY-TWO

The Unexpected Visit

Frasier had never met Roger Lakein but could identify him from a photograph. He instantly recognized him studying the building directory in the foyer. Frasier wondered what had brought him to The Security Bank unannounced when he was supposed to be in South America. What was he doing in California?

Obviously, Lakein had come to see him. Frasier did not intercept him. He needed time to think and he needed to make a phone call to Langley before he talked to Lakein.

In the reflective glass encasing the directory, Lakein saw Frasier hesitate several feet behind him. He did not move or indicate he had noticed the evasive action as Frasier walked quickly to an open elevator to avoid an encounter.

At the top floor, Frasier rushed from the elevator to his private office and closed the door. He picked up the red phone, his hot line to Langley, and dialed the coded number.

"Security Bank. . . Lakein' has just made an unexpected appearance in the lobby." He listened to the response. "Right." He hung up and waited for Lakein's arrival on the elevator.

Although he knew of The Security Bank, this was Lakein's first visit to Emerson, Hudson, and Williams. His move was handled with professional decorum as Frasier met and introduced him to a few other key support personnel.

When they were alone drinking coffee, Lakein wanted immediately to bring up the subject of the agent who had been murdered in Brazil. The mere mention of the incident would be to challenge Frasier, who directed the Inca mission. Lakein was not supposed to have known about that CIA plant, a further implication that Frasier was playing him.

"You must have an urgent reason for leaving your post with no advance communication," said Frasier. "Coffee okay?"

"Yes, nice flavor, Columbian."

"Well, why are you here?"

Lakein put down his cup. "I'm here to do a little research."

"Research? Isn't that our bailiwick?"

"It's intended to move the mission forward a little more quickly than the original plan so that you don't have to wait for information from the field."

"What kind of research?" Frasier snapped out the question.

If Lakein were in league with the Tri Con mole, he certainly had balls to walk right in on the operations center. Frasier would have to closely monitor him while he remained.

"I see an opportunity to get a fix on our mole, but first I need to know who else you've put in the field."

"Meaning?"

"Meaning you didn't notify me you had an informer in Brazil."

"Couldn't you have just called and asked me about it?" Frasier expertly covered his shock. "How did you find out?"

"I depend on my own personal network of spies and informers throughout the country. Not quite by accident, your man was murdered."

"Cigarette?" Frasier extended a hand carved wooden box sitting on the coffee table.

"No thanks. I gave up smoking five years ago."

"So did I, several times." Frasier selected one. A concise flame leapt from his gold plated lighter. He concentrated on the flame dancing off the wick.

"I want to know how many more you have and where they are located," said Lakein. "I can't run my operation down there and be kept in the dark as to what you're doing with covert operations. We might be working at cross purposes."

"Tell me about your opportunity," Frasier fenced.

"I believe I can lure the mole into a trap, but as I said, I need to know what you're about."

"Impossible."

"Are you willing to listen?"

Frasier nodded.

"We leak the word in South America that we have a fix on the mole and are waiting and watching for him to lead us to the cell, to the top in Tri Con. That should spook him enough to cut off diversionary tactics. Through my informer or yours, we monitor where the activity suddenly stops and trace the origin of the order to cease."

"So you think our mole answers to someone high up in Tri Con, such as in Europe. A novel perception, one that I had not entertained before. Please go on."

Lakein was opening himself up to Frasier, who encouraged him very carefully. Frasier suspected more than ever that his man sat before him.

"We have no way of knowing the extent of his autonomy to act on his own," said Lakein, "or from whom he takes orders, until we test him."

"Who do you suspect?"

"There are any one of a dozen possibilities in at least four different countries, Argentina, Brazil, Venezuela, and Chile."

"That many. I notice you left Europe out of the list."

"In my opinion, Tri Con is financially entrenched in all of them."

"I know. I have a key operative in each country."

Lakein stared at him. "You mean we all have the same orders regarding Inca?" He could not possibly know that Frasier was lying to him. "Is the duplication necessary? Four separate investigations?"

"South America is a large continent."

"But four of us each believing we're directing the field operation – we're working at cross purposes, unless that's your intention." Lakein could sense Frasier's sudden electric silence as if he had been struck. He had tested the waters and found them hot.

As for Frasier, he marveled at the implied accusation that he himself was the mole and Lakein's attempt to manipulate the circumstances to make it appear that way. "On the contrary, it's a perfect system of checks and balances," Frasier paused. "Suppose one of you is the mole?"

"And you think one of the big four is it?"

"I don't think anything yet. I'm not the sort to make rash judgments and jump to conclusions. I'm still seeking evidence."

"And what about my plan? You can implement it with the big four, or is that already part of your checks and balances?"

"Another plan is currently in effect."

"I'm listening."

Frasier did not take the bait. "It's confidential. It doesn't interfere with your operation. It runs parallel to it. In fact, it will assist you in extracting the mole and bringing him to the surface."

"And it's in effect?"

"At this very moment."

Lakein suddenly shed his antagonism and suspicion and become conciliatory. "It would help me to know so that I don't inadvertently commit an error. My function is to coordinate, not counter the investigation."

"You're performing your function admirably. I've already commended you to Langley."

"Tri Con Pictures is planning to shoot a film in Chile."

"I'm fully aware of that." Frasier tapped his cigarette into a spotless ashtray.

"It's hard to believe Pinochet is so willing to cooperate. Normally he doesn't allow foreign media of any kind into the country."

"Tri Con has big business in Chile. I imagine Pinochet is willing to grant a favor for the revenue."

"The production will be monitored, of course. Contreras and his secret police are very thorough."

"Tell me about your proposed research," Frasier's antennae were out. The yellow light warned Lakein to proceed with caution.

"I want to do a run on several key Tri Con personnel both in the states and in South America."

"Their names?"

"I'll provide you with a list. It's likely to grow depending on the relationships I discover."

"You could have just sent me the names and saved yourself a trip. Being here is not the most effective use of your time."

Lakein's cold stare bore into Frasier. "I'm here because I'm doing my job. Why are you running interference on me?"

Frasier held his steady gaze for a fraction of a second too long, then smiled, but not with his eyes. "Are you telling me you would like some assistance?"

"Thank you, no. But I don't want interference."

"I'll have one of the programmers explain the coded recall system to you."

"I know the system."

"It's been changed since your early days at Langley. We're open here around the clock." Frasier rose. "I'll introduce you to the boys and girls in The Security Bank."

Lakein followed his aggressive stride out of the office and down the hallway. The Security Bank was a large open space office system with several terminal stations around a massive computer center. Messages and data were fed into this *security bank* from the decoding center in Langley, Virginia and from other sources throughout the world via satellite and direct computer input.

Authorities in political and corporate espionage manned individual stations with massive video screens similar to a war room or space command center. Each agent had been hand-picked according to his or her field of expertise. Some worked in teams electronically processing and programming the volume of information pouring in from all parts of the world, including the Soviet Union and Soviet Bloc countries and mainland China.

The coded data encompassed every social, cultural, political, and economic development in every country and in each region or sector. Weather reports and agricultural reports and analyses mingled with the recorded movements of military forces and placement of heavy artillery, missiles, aircraft, and ships.

Out of the vast matrix of acquired data, the analysts could reconstruct an entire picture of the conditions in each sector and predict how they would impact local politics and, in turn, United States interests at home and abroad. Much of American foreign policy was determined on the basis of the information. In the world of espionage, knowledge was power.

Lakein and Frasier arrived last at the South American station where a team of two men and one woman were running a program on El Salvador. Lakein watched with envy as the data flowed out in snappy precision on five video screens.

Four years ago, his request for a transfer to The Security Bank had been denied, despite his intimate knowledge and expertise on Central and South America. Officials at Langley had considered his value to the CIA far greater as a field operative. That was where they expected him to remain until retirement.

His appeal through the chain of command to reevaluate the ruling had come back to him, mission confirmed as stands. Do not pursue further.

He had, however, ignored the dictum and voiced his discontent at ambassadorial social gatherings to his associates in Chile and Argentina and Brazil. A few months later, a covert KGB recruiter had approached him.

Lakein knew the man but had never suspected he was a Soviet spy. His name was Carlos Berg, an executive administrator with Tri Con Oil in Brazil and Venezuela.

The KGB had been watching Lakein for some time. Berg's discreet offer appealed to the disgruntled Lakein's bruised pride at the price tag of one million dollars U.S. in a numbered Swiss account.

At the time of the offer, Lakein considered two significant options, both of which he kept to himself. He could cooperate and work with the KGB and retire to France a wealthy man in five to seven years, the CIA never being the wiser, or he could become a double agent and uncover the entire plot being channeled through Tri Con.

He suspected that the diversion of Tri Con's South American oil and mineral resources to the Soviet Union was only the tip of the iceberg.

He did not share this observation with Frasier, his case officer, that he had been approached, nor his theory with Langley or The Security Bank. He wanted to blow the entire operation wide open on his own and show those bastards at Langley what a mistake they'd made in denying him the well-deserved transfer and promotion. By then, the KGB operatives who were using positions within Tri Con as their cover would be cleaned out like a nest of termites and he would surreptitiously move his million to his own numbered Swiss account.

The KGB would never know he had compromised their operation. To hell with them all. They were corrupt as the day was long. He was smarter than both sides and would play them off against each other. He would come out clean and rich.

"I'm just up from South America," Lakein shook hands with Bruce Villanova, the senior officer at the station. "One of your field men was accidentally murdered at a storage site. Murder is not usually considered an accident. There was an explosion. The report states the cause was a gas leak. Someone sent him a going away present."

"That report came across my desk last week from Elias Kotter. He didn't know you were in Brazil."

"I don't publish my itinerary."

Catching the note of antagonism, Villanova glanced quickly at Frasier who was standing off to one side. Frasier didn't bat an eye.

"Roger's up here to research Tri Con."

Villanova gave Lakein a questioning look.

"He has a theory he wants to introduce into the program."

"Fine, we'll be glad to help."

"I work alone," said Lakein bluntly. "Your staff assistance is not necessary."

Villanova stared at him, then back at Frasier wondering if this encounter were some sort of power play.

"I'll explain later," said Frasier.

"Does he know the system?"

"You can ask me directly," said Lakein. "I know it as well as you."

Frasier raised his chin with a placating thrust. "Have Marlene get him started. We'll go out for lunch, 11:30." Frasier left the station and walked back through The Security Bank to his office.

For five days straight, Lakein ran decoded informational data by him on the computer. Among others, Kasia Kerenski's entire history was reviewed. Roger learned that her parents were Russian émigrés who had come to the United States just after the Second World War.

Lakein familiarized himself with her entire dossier. Among her contacts of the past ten years, he came across Giorgio Mykola, a known KGB agent working at a Beverly Hills hair salon as a front.

A second local California individual that caught his attention was Stephen Stull, a drug addict and rock musician.

A microfilm file of incredible letters received from Stull begging to work for the CIA related to his background in a mental institution, Camarillo State Hospital in Southern California. The details revealed he had suffered a severe psychopathology culminating in the grisly murder of his mother.

Thereafter, he exhibited pseudo-sexual tendencies while undergoing psychiatric treatment. He was not indicted by reason of insanity. When the California Governor, Ronald Reagan, curtailed funding for state mental hospitals, Stull was released back into society along with all the other inmates.

His last listing located him as a contact for illegal drugs. He was known to be hiding out in Las Vegas. An address and phone number were provided. Lakein had found his man.

***

Lakein drove from the Hotel Bonaventure at five during peak evening traffic. Certain he was being followed and watched by Frasier's men, he changed from one clogged freeway to another and chased along surface streets through the garment district, then cut back to the Civic Center at Grand Avenue and Hill Street. At the Arco Plaza, he dodged down into the subterranean parking lot and left his car.

Walking toward the elevator, he suddenly stepped aside and slipped into a deserted Mercedes with the key left in the ignition. He drove quickly up to the street, took a direct route to Olympic Boulevard and headed west to Beverly Hills.

Checking in at the Beverly Hilton Hotel, he declined the services of a bellhop and carried his single suitcase up to a mid-level prepaid suite. He hung a 'Do Not Disturb' sign on the exterior door handle and locked the deadbolt. He went to the door that connected his room with the next. His knuckles rapped a series of three – two – one on the door.

He listened to the metallic click and roll of the lock. The door opened. Helmut Bachmann motioned for him to enter. Lakein stepped through with his suitcase. Bachmann closed and relocked the door.

"Bothersome, isn't it, all this?" said Lakein.

"But necessary. Care for a drink?" Bachmann moved in the direction of a stocked bar.

"Glenfiddich."

"Soda?"

"Straight."

Bachmann brought him the fine Scotch. "Sir down. You've come a long way," he grinned. "We have a little less than one hour. What did you learn?"

"Frasier has a dragnet in South America with key agents spying on each other, some kind of overlapping checks and balances. He doesn't trust his own people. He's also recruited informers I don't know anything about. One of them was discovered and murdered by your people in Brazil, a staged accident."

Bachmann nodded. "The situation is growing hot."

"Too hot. That's one of the reasons I came north for a visit. It has never been healthy in the tropics, too many insects. Your Berlin man fucked up terminating your movie star. The attempted assassination made the front page in Rio. What the hell happened in Berlin? Did you change your mind?"

"Wrong time and place. The purpose was to establish an intent. The gunman is a professional. He did what he was ordered to do, create chaos. When the time is right, he'll finish the job. Kasia Kerenski was supposed to get away. It must not appear that we are behind her assassination."

"That's right. This time, I'm going to take care of it myself."

"You can't take that chance, not personally."

"No, not personally. I don't operate that way. I've found someone." Lakein finished his drink. An edge of froth clung to the rim of the glass. "You're not drinking."

"I have a cocktail party to attend at seven." Bachmann poured him a second Scotch. "Who is he?"

"Stephen Stull, a drug dealer and rock musician wanted by the FBI for trafficking. Kasia used to hang around with his band as part of her cover before she became an actress. He has a history of psychosis. Murdered his mother when he was a child and underwent rehabilitation. I use that term advisedly, since he was released from a mental institution when they were all shut down in California."

"Do you know where to find him?"

"Yes."

"Why is the CIA holding out on the FBI?"

"Frasier considers him a valuable source for drugs, kinky sex, blood work, anything dirty. Stull's file is crammed with sicko letters begging the Company to hire him."

"What do you have in mind?"

"I'll go talk to Stull, give him money and an unofficial critical assignment from the CIA. Play up that Kasia is a Soviet spy and needs to be terminated in a specific manner. First, he has to kidnap her and her child. Hold them for ransom to make it credible, then terminate them."

"Why the child?"

"Innocence — If he takes only Kasia, the FBI will suspect and go after the KGB. It would give them an excuse to investigate Tri Con. Because Stull grabbed the child, the motive will be ransom and a cash transaction. Has to be."

"Taking the child bothers me."

"Would you rather be bothered by Uncle Sam?"

"Go ahead, if it's really necessary."

"It is, and don't worry, it won't be on your conscience."

"Where is Stull?"

"Las Vegas." Lakein nursed his drink.

"When are you leaving?"

"In fifteen minutes."

"By car?"

"Only to the airport."

"Do you have your ticket?"

Lakein nodded and patted his inside coat pocket.

"Don't show," said Bachmann. "Charter a private plane from Van Nuys."

"Good thought."

"Anything else?"

Lakein deliberately hesitated as if giving serious consideration to a thought uppermost in his mind. "Yes," he looked directly at Bachmann. "Frasier is with us."

Bachmann froze, staring at him, weighing Lakein and his statement.

"He's on the take," Lakein further tested the waters and began to sense they were cold.

"How? If he were with us, I would know. Did you recruit him? If so, I'm delighted to hear it, but who's involved? Who paid him off?"

"It isn't me. I thought maybe one of your people got to him."

"Then it was done without my knowledge. And if so, he's setting us up on a chance that the operation will lead him directly to the source, me. Where did you get your information and what proof exists that he has in fact come over to us?"

Lakein did not respond for a moment. "Then, it's as I suspected, a set up. I got it through his double agent," he lied. "Your movie actress, Kasia Kerenski. It's not true then?"

Bachmann shook his head.

"This is just one more reason to have her terminated. The way Frasier uses her to set us up is throwing us off."

"Did you really think I have an inside deal with Frasier?"

"Only because of what she told me," Lakein lied again.

"Frasier must never get any further into Tri Con than he has already penetrated."

Lakein nodded in agreement.

"Are there any other questions?"

"No," Lakein finished his drink and rose.

They shook hands. "I'll leave first," said Bachmann. "Wait ten minutes, then exit by the fire stairs. Good luck."

Lakein said nothing in return. Bachmann walked out into the hall. The door closed.

***

Stephen Stull left his van parked near a tourist charter bus and followed the meandering group out onto the bridge of the monolithic Hoover Dam which spanned the granite abyss and held back the Colorado River.

His preconception about the CIA agent who had arranged the meeting was shattered when a male tourist wearing a Vegas T-shirt, tan shorts and sandals lowered his Nikon camera and spoke to him. Stull could not see his eyes because of the man's reflective mirrored sunglasses.

"Will you just look at that long drop," Lakein pointed down into the canyon. "They say it's the highest dam in the world, 727 feet high and 1,180 feet long. Just be casual. We're talking about the canyon."

"Sure, sure thing," Stull immediately grew tense.

"Don't ask questions. Listen carefully because I'm going to tell you only one time. Would you care for a stick of gum?" He offered from a pack of Juicy Fruit. "Your code name is Gumdrop."

"Got it. Thanks."

"We've discovered that Kasia Kerenski is a Soviet spy."

"What? No shit."

"She works for the KGB. Don't stand there gawking. Take your gum out of the wrapper and chew it vigorously."

Stull did as ordered.

"You have been selected to terminate her."

Stull ceased chewing. "What?"

"Once you have accomplished your mission, we'll pull the FBI off your back. It must be done in a certain way."

Stull resumed chewing. "I'm listening."

"You are to kidnap Kasia and her child."

"Both of them?"

"Both of them. Then request a ransom from her husband for two million dollars. No more, no less. Terminate her just before you are to receive the ransom money."

"What about the kid?"

"Place her in a situation where she'll die of exposure or natural causes."

"Got it."

"Inject Kerenski with an overdose."

"Horse?"

Lakein nodded.

"From this moment, you're on your own. I don't know you and you don't know me. We never had this meeting. Don't ever contact the CIA in any way or you will be turned over to the FBI. And if you fail in your mission, you yourself will be terminated. Got it?"

Stull had ceased to chew. He spat out the wad of gum, exhausted of its flavor, and watched it fall through a thousand feet of space. When he looked up, the tourist had rejoined the group now clustered around their guide at the center of the dam.

"Gum drop. Shit."

CHAPTER TWENTY-THREE

The Abduction

Lynn Porat hunched her shoulders against the bone-cutting chill of the high desert wind sweeping unchecked across the flat. Slamming the van door, she dashed in open-toed sandals to the shabby stucco duplex in which she, Stephen Stull, and Randy Stiefel had been living for the past four years since they had fled California. Following her late Sunday morning routine, she had driven into town for pastries and donuts for them all.

Randy staggered up out of bed from the previous night's binge and shuffled out to the kitchen to discover Lynn munching on donuts while intently scanning the Calendar section of the Los Angeles Times.

"Look at this," she referred to the full page news feature by the entertainment journalist Suzanne Kirkeby on Dade Thomas, Aimee Martin, and their business association with Kasia Kerenski and Michael Sloan.

Randy squinted at the headline. "Shit! I'm gettin' sick and tired of readin' and hearin' about them."

"You're sick and tired. Let me tell you what I'm sick and tired of. It's livin' out in the middle of nowhere in this shit-pile oasis and not gettin' shit but crazy from hearin' those fuckin' slot machines every goddamn day."

"Well, don't tell me about it. At least you help pay the rent. I'm not your fuckin' old man."

"I'm a god damn singer, not a step-n-fetch-it barmaid."

"Then why don't you sing something?"

"Fuck you, Jack, and fuck him too."

"I already did," Randy barked a laugh.

"You two are disgusting."

"We fucked you too, remember?

 "You were in the middle."

"I'm tired of being in the middle. You hear me? Tired."

"I hear you."

Their attention was drawn to Stull standing in the bedroom doorway. His shaking fingers clutched a smoking cigarette. Lynn stared at his skinny legs jammed rigidly into a pair of oversized shorts. Except for his hard expressionless face, he could have been mistaken for a clown.

"And I don't want to hear you anymore."

Lynn leaped up smashing her chair back against the wall. "You're ridiculous. Look at the two of you. You're both ridiculous. I've never seen two more miserable excuses for human beings. You're an insult to society. You make me wanna puke. You're not men. You're both shit. Sick - both of you – sick. And I'm sick of you. What the hell am I even still doing with you?"

"Lookin' for the needle, little lady, sounds like to me."

"Stick your needle up your fuckin' ass and leave it there."

"I told you I don't want to hear you talk that way to me and Randy anymore. Your language is foul and offensive and what you say hurts our feelings. Why do you want to hurt our feelings?"

"Jesus Christ, you don't have to hear me anymore. I'm God damn leaving."

Stull stared at her with the lidded grin of a lizard. "How many times we heard that, Randy? Can't even count or begin to remember."

Sucking the custard out of a chocolate éclair, Randy sadly shook his head. "She sure buys nice pastry."

Stull expelled a wreath of smoke. "Where do you think you'd go?"

"Dade Thomas never had anything against me."

"Except that he has a real songbird and you're wanted by the law. Besides that you don't sing worth a damn, and you don't have a black ass."

"I can sing," the scream in her throat contracted to a hiss of indignation.

"Not any better than you can fart." Stull watched the remark slice into her worse than any knife. "Face it. You don't have talent. You're one of us. You're a loser. Don't ever forget it. There's nowhere for you to go. Nobody gives a shit about you, and nobody'd have a piece of dried-up ass like you. You're a space cadet and there ain't no way out for you but the big highway in the sky."

"No, no, you're just saying that to get to me."

"You're goddamn right I'm just saying that because it's goddamn true. You think you're so miserable. You call us shit. Look at yourself. You're nothing. You're nothing." Stull took a leisurely drag of his cigarette.

Lynn vehemently shook her head. "No, I know who I am, and I want to forget who I was. I need to get away from you. You are what's holding me back. I need to forget all that-that- "Her hand pushed away the past. "More than anything else, I need to forget it – and I really need to forget you."

"We've been out of circulation for a long time. I mean real circulation. I've been counting and I know to the day how long we've been gone. What do you say, Randy? Shall we give her the surprise package? You think she's ripe to hear the plan?"

"What plan," Lynn snorted with derision. "Your two-million-dollar ransom? I heard you talkin' the other night when you thought I was asleep. You're both out of your minds."

"How would you like to be out of yours?"

Lynn stared back at him in defiance. "I could just leave you two and go back alone and nobody in California would know the difference. You're the ones draggin' me down."

"That's right and nobody would know the difference if you suddenly disappeared out there in the desert either." Stull paused to let his warning sink in. "We don't really need you. We only keep you around to fuck. We especially don't need your mouth. How's that saying go? Loose lips sink ships."

"So, what about your little plan?"

"We've decided to pack up and leave tonight."

"It was gonna be without me, right?" Lynn's dull angry eyes raked them. "I heard you. Tonight, I work the graveyard at the casino."

"You and a graveyard could have a lot in common real soon." Stull grinned for the second time. "Loosen up." His tension at her attack had dissipated. "Our time is coming. Despite what you call us, you've been a real good girl to have around. You're patient and kind. We've all been patient, not so kind. And now what I hear from you is the voice of impatience. Our time is coming."

At ten p.m., they passed through the Vegas strip and left the neon mirage pumping its garish tubed light into the desert night.

Lynn had grown nearly immune to Stull's veiled threats and the former anxiety she experienced at much of his bizarre behavior. Her life was a testimonial to her will to prevail while adjusting to the abnormal. But after four years of living in the sordid squalor of empty souls gone up like smoke in the Vegas lights and emptier pocketbooks that drifted through the casino where she had pushed drinks and occasionally her body, a long-buried impulse to pull herself up and out and change the direction of her life had begun to ping softly. Then, after an incubation period, insistently like the peck peck of a chick's beak breaking through its embryonic shell, she had emerged gasping.

She admitted to herself that she lacked a good commercial singing voice, that she really couldn't even sing like the great ones, but she had been able to delude herself for many years to the contrary.

She didn't have the mental discipline to go back to school, to do anything constructive with her life. She had seen and lived too much in the underbelly and her brain was spaced out to the point of no return. She felt literally soft in her mind, unable to hold a concentrated thought for more than a few minutes without having to grope to recapture it as it faded.

She hesitated in her speech with occasional erratic bursts of profanity like an elderly Alzheimer victim, repeating words most used around her and the easiest to recall.

She would lose the drift in a conversation. Working in the casino had exonerated her from the obligation to communicate with anybody at length. Taking a drink order and counting out small change were within her mental grasp. For the most part, she blended with the smoke and noise, the metallic cranking of handles and occasional ring of coins accompanied by whoops and cheers as she wandered up and down the aisles in a daze. But she knew that she was something more than a receptacle for Stull and Randy's sperm. What she didn't have was a life plan or the intelligence to create one.

She didn't place much stock in Stull's wild promise of their deliverance through extortion. She had hardened realistically from her observation day after day of thousands of zombie-eyed people gambling away their lives in pursuit of an instant fortune.

She no longer believed in material fortune or was even certain she cared to have it anymore. But what she did believe in was that recent impulse, that newborn chick pecking through its shell with the desire and instinct to survive and grow.

She had been dying for some years. Now, with the chick, a feeling of peace and calm slowly began to spread and reside within her. From time to time, Stull and Randy had noticed her staring off with a fixed vacuous smile and they would look at each other and point to their heads in ridicule and recognition of what they would also one day become.

Lynn's perception of hiding as a fugitive in Las Vegas was that she existed in a graveyard of the barely living, a graveyard marked by flashing pink, red, purple, green, and gold neon sepulchers and slot machine tombstones. Now, in leaving that open asylum, the drifting and babbling behind, she believed in her resurgent growth.

She did not understand its psychological origin, its implication or how to express what she felt, only that a strange psychic metamorphosis was occurring, a euphoria of religious holiness. But an edge of fear tempered her burgeoning spirit. As she slouched in the rear of the van, unrecognizable from its many repaintings, she stared at the source of her fear.

More and more, Stull had come to personify and take on the apparition of death for her. He looked like the picture of death that so often frequented her dreams, before the warm golden light appeared and dissolved him in molten joy. He was death and Randy was death's lieutenant. She heard the little chick inside pecking, pecking to get out.

Taking shifts at the wheel, they drove straight through to Los Angeles and up across the San Fernando Valley on the 101 Ventura Freeway. At dawn, their drab olive-green van bumped along over an ancient dirt fire road deep into the Santa Monica Mountains and arrived at the deserted house where they had partied from time to time.

Stull and Randy slept in the van. They were exhausted from the all-night drive. She settled in a patch of soft grass in the warm sun and slept until she was awakened at mid-morning by the men's voices. They had gone inside the house to check its condition. Moments later, she heard them whoop and shout and come running back out into the front yard.

"Snakes! There's a nest of rattlesnakes in the cellar!"

Randy fashioned a special jig arranged with a wire noose at the end of a long pole. Using extreme caution, he and Stull reentered the house and went down into the cellar. Stull shined a torch light while Randy attempted unsuccessfully to snag one of the darting heads from the writhing coils. The intensity of the unnerving buzzing rattle increased.

"This isn't going to work. We'll have to burn them out."

"Need to be real careful about that," said Stull. "Don't want the forest service comin' up here."

"There's an old blanket upstairs. We can douse it with gasoline and throw it on the snakes."

"Okay, but we need to have the extinguisher from the van if it starts to spread."

"The blanket should contain the flames."

"All right. Let's do it."

Lynn remained outside and clear of the whole process. She heard the explosive whoosh of the flames that obliterated the reptiles leaving only charred ashen skeletons.

***

The *Rive Gauche* Boutique in Beverly Hills presented an exclusive pre-retail showing for three hours on a Wednesday afternoon. Kasia viewed original creations of Gucci, St. Laurent, Adolfo, Von Furstenberg, and Blackwell. She departed with her wardrobe increased by twenty-thousand dollars worth of dresses and shoes which would be delivered to her residence.

A pair of large dark sunglasses and a wide brimmed leather hat prevented her being recognized on the street. She always disguised her appearance since the attempted assassination and declined to have hovering body guards who would only draw attention to her.

She walked directly to her car parked in a nearby underground lot. Since her daughter was being chauffered to and from the Montessori nursery school that day unaccompanied by her sitter, the limousine was not available. Kasia preferred not to use the limousine, since it also drew the attention of the curious.

Her need for privacy conflicted with the freedom to go out into the public without fear and without being accosted by autograph seekers, onlookers, personal admirers, and the paparazzi. Someone might be waiting out there in a crowd waiting for her with a gun.

Her imprint had recently appeared on a line of women's clothing and cosmetics. A major children's toy manufacturer had paid her one million dollars in advance on the rights to create and market a Kasia Kerenski doll. Another entrepreneur had paid her two million for her endorsement of a line of cookware, despite her refusal to pitch the line in a television commercial.

As she approached her white Mercedes sports car, her thoughts were on the special birthday party she was giving for Michael at The Bistro that coming weekend. The studio executives, including Heinrich and Bachmann, had strangely not responded to her written invitation, nor to her follow-up calls during the past three days.

Following a script conference with Heinrich, Michael had come home in a sour mood the night before. They had gone out to a party and he had been reluctant to discuss plans for the production. He had avoided shop talk altogether and had dwelt on the country's crisis in political leadership, the economy, and problems of parenting for working couples.

A slight scuff and rustle of clothing gave her only a momentary warning of someone closing in on her from behind. She whirled with an adrenalin shot of fear. Her legs were kicked out from her as a black cloth sack enclosed her head and a man's weight pinioned her to the pavement. Acid fumes of amil nitrate scalded her throat and nasal passages and cut off her muffled scream. The chemical dropped into her lungs and plunged her into deep unconsciousness.

Wearing nylon stockings over their heads and faces, Stull and Randy quickly transferred Kasia into their green van parked directly next to her Mercedes. Stull slammed the side panel door shut and scrambled after Randy into the van where they peeled off their masks.

"You grab her purse?" Stull pumped the accelerator and turned the ignition.

"Yeah," Randy fished among the contents and pulled out Kasia's wallet. "Not much in cash, mostly credit cards."

"Figures. We can't use 'em. Traceable. We'll send a credit card with the ransom note." Stull drove rapidly along the parking aisle, tires squealing as they rounded the corner and headed for the exit. "How we doin' on time?"

Randy snapped the purse shut and checked his watch. "One hour."

They left the underground parking lot and headed west on Wilshire Boulevard toward Brentwood.

At four o'clock, Mrs. Clements, Danielle's Montessori instructor, told the child it was time to go home and that her ride was waiting out in front. Danielle returned the blocks and puzzles with which she had been playing to their designated shelves, then walked with Mrs. Clements through the front door where they were met by Robertson, the Sloan's Black chauffeur.

"Hi, Robertson," Danielle chirped. "I'm ready to go home."

Robertson smiled at Mrs. Clements, then hurried stiffly after the two and a half year old skip-running and jigging to the open passenger door of the limousine.

"Watch yourself and don't trip there, girl."

The nimble youngster glanced back with saucy laughing blue eyes and climbed into the passenger section. Robertson buckled her into her car seat, then gently but firmly closed the door, stepped in at the wheel and immediately pressed the button to automatically lock all the doors.

"I want to talk on the telephone," Danielle picked up the receiver. "Call Mildred."

Robertson punched the call through from his private extension. Danielle waited a moment for the matronly woman to pick up the phone at the house.

"Hi, Mildred, this is Danielle. I'm coming home now with Robertson. I want to have some milk and cookies when I get there. Okay? Okay. And some balloons. I just need some fresh balloons too. I want to talk to Mommy."

Her sitter explained, "Your Mommy isn't home from shopping yet. She'll probably get home just after you do. I'll have your milk and cookies ready for you when you arrive."

"And my balloons. Fresh balloons."

"And your balloons. Heaven help us if we forget to have fresh balloons."

"Balloons are wonderful. I like balloons, clean ones, not old ones."

"I know," Mildred chuckled. "Clean ones. Not old ones."

"Do you have some in the cupboard?"

"I have a bag of fresh ones waiting for you in the cupboard."

"When I get home, I want to see them and take them out."

"Okay, dear, they'll be waiting for you."

"Thank you, Mildred. Bye."

"Bye, dear."

Danielle hung up and began playing with the radio dials on the panel next to her. "Robertson, I want to watch Sesame Street."

"It's not five o'clock yet, sweetheart. Mildred will turn it on for you to watch when you get home."

"Okay, play some music."

Robertson turned on KJOI from the front seat. "How's that?"

"Thank you."

"You're welcome, child."

In his rearview mirror, Robertson glimpsed a drab green van rushing alongside a little too quickly from behind. He slowed and pulled to the right, allowing the van maneuvering room to swerve to the left. But instead of going around, the van moved over on him. Blaring the horn, he slammed on the brakes, catching a flash of Danielle's blonde head jerking back and forth.

The van careened back into the right lane, narrowly shaved the limousine's front bumper and rocked to a halt blocking the path of the long black car.

Quickly shifting into reverse, Robertson hesitated upon seeing a man wearing whiteface makeup and a stocking cap leap out of the van brandishing a lead pipe that descended with enough force to shatter the windshield and drivers side window in two powerful blows.

As Robertson grabbed for the phone, a squirt of mace immobilized him. The assailant reached through the broken glass and unlocked the door, jerked it open and swung the pipe. It struck Robertson across the front of his head and he fell back unconscious onto the seat.

Danielle saw a second white-faced man run from the van, fling open the passenger door and plunge in to grab her like a living nightmare.

"Daddy!" she shrieked. "Daddy, Daddy, come and help me, Daddy." She doubled up in horror as the man unbuckled the car seat straps. "Daddy, where are you?"

Randy clutched her, his hands crushing her arms. She bellowed herself hoarse with hysteria until Stull clamped an evil-smelling cloth over her mouth and nose and she fainted.

When Mildred called Michael's office, she was informed by his secretary that he was in a meeting and would return the call. The distraught sobbing woman screamed into the mouthpiece, "Please, this is an emergency. Her little girl was kidnapped."

"Oh, my God, I'll get him right away."

Michael was enduring his twenty-first script conference over a section of *Borders* and barely held his frustration in check at the demands Heinrich was making regarding scenes to be shot in and around Puerto Montt.

The door to the conference room suddenly swung open. His secretary burst in and announced in an alarmed voice, "Mr. Sloan, your child's sitter is on the phone. Your daughter has been kidnapped!"

"What? No! No!" His voice echoed the cold slug of horror in the pit of his stomach. He leaped up and ran out of the office leaving pages of the disassembled script scattered over the top of the conference table. "Call the police. Tell them I'm on my way and to meet me at the house."

He raced out of the office, bounced and careened off the opposite wall in the hallway from his mad momentum. Too impatient to wait for the arrival of an elevator, he slammed through the nearest fire exit door and catapulted entire half floors down the stairs.

Heinrich rose and closed the conference room door. Returning to the phone, he dialed Bachmann. "They've got the child."

"What about Kasia?"

"Haven't heard yet."

"Call me."

Michael cursed and leaned on the horn, pushing and bullying his Mercedes through the tangle of traffic, recklessly running red lights and executing frantic dodges and lane changes.

He arrived at the house blaring the horn as though the act and the noise would banish the specter of fear. Shouting at the black wrought iron gates to hurry and open, he roared into the driveway and shocked the car to a standstill, riding the tires into the asphalt. He plunged through the front door and shouted, "Where the hell are the police? Mildred, did you call the police?"

"No, sir, your secretary said you told her –"

He cut her off by picking up the nearest phone. "Operator, get me the police. This is an emergency. And hurry, god damn it, hurry." He looked at Mildred. "Where the hell is my wife?"

"I'm sorry, sir, I don't know. She went shopping. She said she'd be back between four and five. She didn't call."

Michael responded to the perceived slow response of the operator with exasperation. "This is Michael Sloan. My daughter has been kidnapped." He curtly rattled off his address and phone number, then hung up, trying to control his body from trembling.

"Where the hell is Kasia?" He poured himself a straight brandy and gulped it to steady his flickering nerves, but immediately regretted taking in the acrid alcoholic fumes rising back up from his stomach searing his nasal passages. The instant sensation, odor, and after taste reminded him of hospitals, embalming fluid, morgues, and death. He cursed his weakness that he had taken the brandy, as if it were an act expected of him under the circumstances. He went to the bathroom and gargled a small cup of mint scented mouth wash.

He raced back downstairs and for the first time it occurred to him that he must get control of his emotional reaction and start seeking answers himself, regardless of what the police might ask when they arrived. "Where did it happen? When did it happen? Where was Robertson? She was with him, wasn't she? She gets out of Montessori at four – thirty."

Mildred intercepted him. "Robertson is in the library, Mr. Sloan."

Michael dashed back to the room just off the front entrance. In his own panic and anxiety, he hadn't even noticed the distraught chauffeur sitting in there holding a cold towel to his forehead.

Robertson explained quickly what had happened and was just finishing his narrative when two approaching sirens abruptly cut to silence out in front.

Michael had the door open and met the three uniformed officers and one plainclothes detective running up the steps from their cars. The detective sergeant, a tall heavyset man who did not carry his weight well, introduced himself and began asking questions concerning the time and location of the abduction, information which Robertson repeated without variation from what he had described to Michael a few minutes earlier.

The sergeant immediately dispatched two of the officers to the site in search of clues and possible witnesses. The third officer remained close by with a transceiver and recording unit.

Michael described Danielle and handed over a recent photograph. He could offer no idea as to who the kidnappers might possibly be.

When the sergeant asked to speak to Michael's wife, he responded, "I don't know where she is. She was at a fashion show at the *Rive Gauche* boutique. At least I think that's where she was. Is that right, Mildred?" he asked her aside.

"Yes, sir. That's where she said was going when she left this morning."

"Where's it located?" the sergeant asked.

"Beverly Hills. When I called a while ago to see if she was there, she'd already gone. The sales manager said she'd left around three o'clock. That was two and a half hours ago."

"Tell dispatch to send three cars to that area," he spoke to the second officer. He asked Michael to describe Kasia's car and to recite the license number if he remembered, which was easy. Her personalized plate spelled her name, KASIA.

"It might be a coincidence she hasn't come home," said the detective, "but they could have taken her too. We'll be looking for her car."

"Oh, God, not both of them."

"We can't determine that yet, but obviously whoever did this has been watching all of you and knows your schedule. You're a target. They'll be after all the leverage they can get. You understand what I'm saying?"

Michael's expression conveyed he understood only too well.

"We're going to tap your phone and set up a recording unit here with two agents monitoring it twenty-four hours. We already have a description out on the van based on what your chauffeur gave us. Of course, the media has picked up on our frequency and there'll be a lot of publicity. I would advise you not to talk to the press at this time. Is your phone unlisted?"

Michael nodded.

"The kidnappers will get the number from your wife, if they picked her up too. We'll contact all news media services to relay in if any messages or information come to them anonymously or otherwise.

We'll follow-up immediately on all leads," he assured Michael. "I'm sure you realize that in a case as sensational as this, it will attract the sickies and weirdos out there claiming they're responsible. We should be able to sort them out for you. So don't overreact to everything you hear or that might arrive in the mail."

Numb with the shock of sudden despair thrust into his life, Michael could only shrug enshrouded in a rapidly encircling cloak of helplessness. As a producer and director, he was accustomed to handling stress and tensions of all kinds, but then he was always in control of the situations. Now he was in the grip of a force he could not touch, see, or with which he could not even communicate in a small way. His life was coming down around him and he still hadn't found a place to grasp and hang on.

Not more than an hour after the sergeant left, he called back and confirmed Michael's fear. Kasia's car had been discovered empty in a public parking structure near the Rive Gauche boutique. The attendant had reported a green van matching the description provided by Michael's chauffeur entering and leaving during the period in question.

The sergeant also informed Michael that because of the gravity of the situation and the distinct possibility of interstate transport, the case had been turned over to Detective Captain Lambert Klein of the FBI, who was an authority on investigations involving extortion. Klein would be coming to the house to talk to him within the hour. It was now 6:15 p.m.

Michael hung up in tears.

CHAPTER TWENTY-FOUR

The Investigation

The last thing Lambert Klein expected and the least thing he desired in his career, other than taking a fatal bullet, was to be assigned to the Kasia Kerenski kidnapping case.

He hated her. He hated her films, her statements against the U.S. Government and the power companies, and he hated what he termed her "hypocrisy of the rich and famous."

As an ex-marine captain who had risked his life for his country in twenty World War II campaigns, he could not condone or accept how she and her movie director husband talked out of one side of their mouths through the medium of their films criticizing the system of American free enterprise, at least from his point of awareness, while they amassed a fortune doing it.

He had been in police work for nearly forty years and viewed unkindly the prospect of a lonely widower's retirement at the conclusion of an active and distinguished career.

He had maintained his health through reasonable dieting, never smoking, drinking only on rare special or social occasions, and a daily exercise regimen of weight training, karate, swimming, and relaxation through meditation, a fact he never shared nor revealed to anyone, especially his fellow officers.

He personally did not feel that meditation was incompatible with the physical and mental discipline of police work and was essential in the martial arts. If others in the department discovered his practice, however, they might think he was losing it. Medication was for hippies and freaky new age fringe types.

He was a laconic individual, hard and compact in speech, as well as stature, feared by lawbreakers who knew of his reputation and respected by colleagues for his keenness of mind and body and total professionalism. His retirement from the force would leave an irreplaceable gap. Few others who stood to be promoted could measure up to his level of commitment, dedication, and personal sacrifice. If the decision were his to make, he conjectured, he would overlook them all and conduct an outside search for a younger version of himself.

He poured a cup of Japanese green tea that had been brewing in the electric pot on his desk for the past twenty minutes. Pulling the plug cord, he set the pot aside. He liked his tea strong and hot.

He had anticipated going to supper at the Midori, a small family-owned and operated Japanese restaurant where he ate on the average of three times a week. He was partial to Japanese cuisine, especially well-prepared sushi followed by donburi or beef or chicken sukiyaki.

He had seen the photograph of the kidnapped child, Danielle Sloan, on full page ads in magazines, the Los Angeles Times, and on an enormous billboard on Sunset Boulevard promoting the record album entitled *Rocking Horse*. The nature and demeanor of the child aroused his curiosity and was the single element in the case that even remotely interested him.

The little girl reminded him of his own six grandchildren, all of whom he loved dearly and profoundly. He believed that children became who they were according to the adults who influenced their lives.

He condemned the use of a child as a vehicle for commercial advertising, turning her into an object, a public image by which adults would profit. The thought and practice disgusted him. He viewed Danielle Sloan as much a victim of her own parents and their way of life as she was an innocent victim of the kidnappers.

He had little hope of the kidnappers returning the mother and her child. The risk of being identified was too great, considering the intensity of the investigation and the growing publicity. Then again, the outcome depended on the amount of control the gang (He knew there were at least two.) had or thought they had over the situation. Their manner and channels of communication when it came to stating the ransom would have considerable bearing on their capture. Reinforcing their sense of security would be necessary so they would not panic and do anything sudden or drastic. He would have to massage the situation, so to speak.

Unhurried, he left his office and walked outside to his car. There was no reason to hurry. In cases like this, there was always a lot of waiting, endless waiting when the relatives of the victims wanted immediate results.

The concept of relief played an important role in a kidnapping. The psychology of waiting as practiced by extortionists drove up the stress factor one thousand percent, finally making the victims eager to pay off quickly and end the ordeal. You could stretch a rubber band only so far before it broke.

When he arrived at the Sloan mansion, police officers had cordoned off the area and were monitoring entrances and exits through the gate across the driveway. Press, radio, and television media were barred from entry. They were another aspect of society that Klein would like to categorically reject, at least regulate and control.

Every one of them wired in to the police radio wave frequency and siphoned off the most sensational information with which to titillate and taunt the gullible public. He considered the television media an electronic bloodsucker or mind-sucker that turned what should be informative reporting and programming into a form of shallow entertainment populated by pundits who spewed narrow sound bite commentary.

He avoided watching television altogether, preferring to read his news, not hear it read to him by some anchorman or anchorwoman, and arrive at his own conclusions, rather than relying on someone else's limited rendering from a programmed teleprompter.

He showed his badge and passed through the gate and moved quickly along the winding asphalt driveway to the house. He admired the sylvan appearance of the wooded landscaped grounds. By most standards, the estate was small, not even really an estate, more like an urban park, a beautiful yard in which a child could play.

He would have to exercise self-control and a sense of objectivity. Going in on this investigation, he hated Michael Sloan's guts. He held him responsible for dangling his child out there before the public like some variety of attractive bait to tempt fate by giving some crazies the means to a get rich quick scheme.

He parked his car, went up the low Spanish tile steps to the front door and rapped the brass door-head knocker twice. A maid admitted him upon recognition of his badge and terse self-introduction. Then she went away to inform Michael of Klein's arrival.

Klein slowly scanned the living room, taking in the tasteful expensive French furniture, lamps, wood and glass sculptures, some of which featured an oriental aesthetic, and a large number of graphics and several oil paintings.

He'd be damned if Sloan's first impression of him would be to discover him ensconced in one of those comfortable looking chairs. He determined to meet Sloan on his feet, take charge of the situation and dominate the son-of-a-bitch from the beginning. But when Michael came into the room, to Klein's surprise, he recognized the puffy redness around the man's eyes as a sign he was greatly distressed and had been crying.

"Captain Klein," Michael tried to suppress the sniffle in his voice as he extended his hand. "I'm Michael Sloan. Thank you for coming."

"Mr. Sloan, shall we sit down."

"Would you like some coffee?"

Klein looked at him strangely, as if offering coffee or any other social amenity was an absurd gesture out of sync with the investigative protocol and gravity of the situation. He shook his head, waited until Michael was first seated on the couch, then took a single chair opposite him across the glass coffee table. He would not permit Sloan to play the gracious host with him.

"I take it you haven't heard anything yet from the kidnappers."

Michael shook his head with a sad quick motion.

"It's not likely you will for some time. That's how they operate."

Michael brought Klein into focus, a sudden sharpness clearing away his meandering visual and visceral withdrawal, wondering if Klein already knew of something he did not.

"They're going to make us wait. They'll try to wear you down, play cat and mouse games with the police and media and with your imagination. Keep you guessing what they're finally going to do with your wife and child."

He allowed Michael a few moments to absorb his comment. "Do you have any idea at all who they are?"

"None."

"While we're waiting, I'd like to ask you some questions."

"Anything you want."

"I'm not going to reinvent the wheel and cover the same ground the local police already have. These are questions of a different nature. Hopefully, your answers will lead me to other sources and maybe we can focus on one or two likely suspects. This process will also assist us in screening out the weirdos. You will have your share of them."

"Weirdos?"

"There are a lot of sick people out there, Mr. Sloan. You're bound to get a few call-ins claiming they've got your wife and daughter. We refer to them as deficient personalities. It gives them an illusion of power and importance just to say they did it. Obviously this was planned for a while. It went off like clockwork. Whoever did it knew something about your family's routine. Your office phone at the studio has already been tapped with a twenty-four monitor on all calls which will be channeled through our communications center. That's in addition to our watch station set up here in your house."

Klein considered leaving Sloan with a few words of encouragement, since Michael looked so miserable, but deep down he wanted the man to suffer, an impulse that caused him to momentarily question his objectivity and sense of professionalism. He was thinking perhaps someone else should be covering this case. He didn't yet have enough information to even consider the prospect of hope. What was hope anyway? A wish, a dream, an illusion that finally became disillusion.

His entire life embodied a confrontation with realities of various kinds. During his hundreds of investigations throughout his career, the victims had almost always been hopers and dreamers and, occasionally, out and out losers. He couldn't remember a realist or a pragmatist who acknowledged the savage truth of what was happening to the abducted woman or child or, in some cases a man.

Now, ironically, here was a man whose career involved creating illusions and he had become a victim of his own creation. Hope? Klein could not offer hope.

He did intuitively feel that Michael Sloan trusted him. Klein understood that he himself possessed a forceful personality that induced confidence merely by the strength of his character. He cautioned himself not to allow an air of superiority to gleam through in his words or manner. In this first of many meetings, he had probably shown less sympathy and sensitivity than he normally would. Tolerance, yes, but then over the years, mustering any greater perspective than tolerance for the human frailties he had witnessed had grown increasingly difficult.

Except in the isolation of his personal strength and integrity, he no longer could say he really knew what constituted a whole person. Perhaps that was why he felt particularly sympathetic to the abducted child, and was drawn to children in general. He was nearing the end of a cycle. He believed in the renewal and affirmation of life through children, providing they could survive and come through clean into adult life. Maybe that was his hope.

He told Michael he would be reviewing and analyzing the existing information, meager as it was, derived thus far from his own outlying investigation. Before he left, he asked Michael and Mildred, the sitter, to give him a verbal listing of the child's habits. Was she potty trained? What were her favorite foods? Stories? Songs and records? Her level of language proficiency?

His reasoning, he explained, was that certain needs of the victims might force the abductors into the open to make specific kinds of purchases, if, in fact, they were looking after his wife and child in a compassionate way.

He then asked Michael if Kasia had any unusual personal requirements, especially medically related, which she did not, nor did the child. Klein believed the kidnappers would at least maintain their victims in some form of minimum comfort, since this was likely to be a long ordeal, unless they were highly deviant personalities, a critical matter which he hoped to determine soon.

Enroute to his office, he received a call over his car radio advising him of an informant who had responded to a television news program announcement concerning the kidnapping. The officer in charge had dispatched a car to bring the individual to headquarters to be interrogated.

Klein was surprised and interested to discover not one, but two subjects, waiting for him. They introduced themselves as Herb Wilcox and Dade Thomas and explained their relationship to the Sloan family and filled him in on their past with Stephen Stull, Randy Stiefle, and Lynn Porat.

While Klein conducted the interview, detailing the lives of the three suspects according to Herb's and Dade's observations and last known information about them, he ordered a records search for criminal files he knew must exist.

The record showed that the trio were fugitives from the State of California, had pushed illegal drugs, and had been missing for at least four years.

As he scanned the file on Stull, his attention came to rest on a disturbing item of factual information. Stull had been an inmate under psychiatric detention at Camarillo State Hospital between the ages of ten and fourteen for the homicide of his mother.

***

Surfacing from a strange painful unconsciousness inhabited by impulses of fear and terror, Kasia's first awareness was of a humid darkness, although not as intense as the moment she had inhaled the searing chemical vapor and fallen into blackness.

Without moving, she located her hands, arms, legs, and feet by sensation and discovered they were bound with an abrasive hemp rope.

The mossy odor of old dank stone and concrete told her she was lying on her back somewhere underground. The smell reminded her of a cave, until the hollow sound of footsteps and the squeak of a warped wooden floor overhead placed her in a cellar.

As she rose with difficulty to a sitting position, a cramping pain bolted through her bladder, doubling her over onto her side. To relieve herself became her most urgent and critical biological need.

Her eyes adjusted to the sense of dark space and were drawn to a small source of illumination. A weak drifting diffusion of pale light filtered through cobwebs and dust.

Through sheer muscular agility, she balanced herself upright. Her high-heeled shoes had been removed, affording her the advantage of a flat-footed stance. By shuffling each foot forward, she progressed toward the light without stumbling or falling. The wall stopped her.

She blew upward at the cobweb blockage a full two feet above her head and discovered the passage of light was a partial crack and small irregular hole in the foundation masonry at the ground level.

The door at the top of the cellar stairs suddenly opened. She laboriously pivoted against the strain on her bound ankles to see who was coming down. She caught only a glimpse of a black hooded figure, as a piercing high-powered beam from a battery lantern blinded her.

She could not place the location of the person until she heard the dull impact of a plate against the floor near the moldy old mattress where she had been lying down.

"Please," she said. "I have to go to the bathroom."

She heard the clank of a small bucket, then suddenly grew aware of a second person she could not see, who untied the rope around her ankles and led her back to the mattress. She sensed that the man was thin, not much taller than herself, and he gave off a distinctly sweet body odor that reminded her of fresh cut hay.

First one, then the second one, holding the lantern, moved away from her to the steps. She caught a glimpse of the first going up to the door. As it opened, the scream of an outraged child, followed by the heart-rending cry, "I want my Daddy! I want my Mommy!" sounded from elsewhere in the house.

Kasia instantly recognized the voice of her daughter.

"Wait," she shouted.

A bare bulb protruding its garish yellow snout from a wall socket flicked on near the stairs as the two figures vanished through the open door.

Kasia worked down her panties, squatted over the bucket and urinated for what seemed an eternity. She listened numbly to the metallic gurgle as though she were a cow being milked into a pail. To her relief, she noticed they had left her a half roll of toilet paper.

Hearing her child's muffled screams of hysteria coming from an upper room of the house, she moved purposefully to the stairs and crept up to the door. It gave slightly under her touch, but a hook and eye latch brought her up short.

The screams abruptly stopped as if someone had suddenly gagged Danielle or dropped a sack over her head. Kasia knew she had to convince her abductors to bring Danielle to her so the little girl would be able to cope with this trauma without becoming completely emotionally disturbed.

She returned to the mattress and ate the vegetable and noodle stew with her fingers, since her kidnappers had not given her any utensils. Under the circumstances she felt grateful that her ankles were no longer bound. She needed mobility, but more than that, she needed to get at least one of the kidnappers talking. Her survival and that of her child were all that mattered.

***

FBI Agent Klein determined he must learn more about Stephen Stull as quickly as possible in order to understand his distorted way of thinking and perception of life and to predict what Stull might do to his victims under particular circumstances.

The following morning, he drove up the Pacific coast on highway 101 to Camarillo State Hospital to talk with the psychiatrist, Dr. Lars Knudsen, who had treated and released Stull.

Upon meeting Knudsen, Klein immediately sensed an evasiveness and underlying embarrassment that he might in some way be held accountable for Stull being out there in society running around loose pushing drugs and kidnapping people. He had been subjected to the budget cuts of the Reagan governorship and did not feel his professional integrity should be challenged by the media and so asked that their interview remain a confidential matter.

Klein agreed, since he was wanted to gain information and didn't want to chance causing the psychiatrist to withhold any insights into Stull's behavior.

As the situation stood, Dr. Knudsen's primary concern at the moment was to cover his professional ass, so a certain objectivity was likely to be sacrificed. Of this, Klein was aware. He listened for contextual implications in the flow of clinical jargon and tactfully probed for a precise focus whenever Knudsen seemed to soft pedal or circumvent an important factor that would motivate Stull to engage in criminal acts.

Referring to the open case history file on his desk, the psychiatrist restructured Stull's life for Klein.

"When he was first committed for treatment, Stephen had been characterized by his family and relatives as a meek and submissive child, filled with the goodness of God, their phrase. He avoided active and healthy participation with other children his age. He was overly serious, extremely self-conscious, had very low self-esteem and generally preferred to be alone.

"His parents had been recently divorced at the time he was committed, and his mother was sleeping with several different men. Stephen would watch their sexual activity through a small hole he had drilled in their common bedroom wall. Of course, he could hear them, as well.

"His mother was exceptionally neurotic. She dominated and over-protected Stephen. The one night she discovered him masturbating while watching her naked in bed, she herself in the act of masturbation, she severely whipped him to the point of drawing blood.

"She always spoke abusively of the boy's father, whom he never saw again following the divorce. In my one interview with his father, I noted he was passive and detached regarding his relationship with his former wife and son and I classified him as being mildly disturbed, which, of course, was a contributing factor to his son's pathological family environment.

"Stephen was admitted to Camarillo following his arrest for the murder of his mother and attempted murder of one of her lovers with a carving knife. He was ten years old at the time, but had already undergone counseling here since the age of eight for exhibiting various disturbed behaviors while in public schools.

"I treated him with drugs, both tranquilizers and energizers, but, of course, drugs treat only symptoms and Stephen remained schizophrenic in his basic personality structure.

"Psychotherapy was employed to assist him in correcting distorted attitudes and to become integrated. Two additional years of group counseling and therapy encouraged his limited development in social relationships. He was released at the age of fifteen to a licensed foster home.

"Follow-up diagnostic evaluations continued to be made until he turned eighteen and no longer revealed any overt or latent psychopathology. However, at that time, he read heavily of spy novels, thrillers, and hard core pornography and wrote many delusional letters to the CIA expressing a desire to become an operations agent or an informer for the agency.

"Of course, they didn't respond, to my knowledge, or take him seriously, especially when he started imagining he was in fact a spy and an informer and started sending them reports on his delusional operations and activities.

"According to his foster parents, his behavior and preoccupation with the CIA intensified during the next six years. He stayed with the foster family until the age of twenty-one. By that time, he had become proficient as a self-taught musician. He possessed a natural talent for popular music."

Knudsen looked up from the case file to meet Klein's thoughtful gaze. Klein asked, "Can you predict what he might do to the woman and her child?"

"No, definitely not. However, it is significant that he abducted both the woman and child and that they are both prominent in the public media. Certainly he is severely emotionally disturbed, psychotic, but I can't predict what he might do any more than you."

Klein thanked Knudsen for sharing the information, which he had recorded on tape, then drove back to Los Angeles. That Stull's motives in the kidnapping of the mother and daughter mixed with his distorted perception of a role with the CIA could extend beyond the transaction of ransom money worried him. He feared the resurgence of some impulse in Stull that would cause him to either defile or take the life of one or of both.

What if the ransom were only incidental to the actual purpose of the abduction? Klein did not want to answer that one yet, even to himself. Only, so far there had not been a ransom request.

When he returned to the office, he found a message waiting on his desk to call Gordon Frasier as soon as possible. He had debunked Frasier's theory that the KGB had discovered Kasia Kerenski was a double agent for the CIA and had removed her. Klein did not agree because no logical reason existed for the KGB to seize the child as well. Frasier had countered that taking the child could be a maneuver to throw them off.

"Klein here."

"What did you learn?"

"I'm certain it's Stull."

"That creates a new wrinkle." Frasier hesitated.

"In what way?"

"Stull may have been put up to this by the KGB."

"I still don't believe the KGB even knows about him or put him up to this or is otherwise involved. They had no way of knowing about him," said Klein. "He's been out of circulation for a long time. Do you know where he's been for the past four years?"

"No, we lost track of him," Frasier lied.

Klein pondered the disbelieved statement. He suspected Frasier was withholding information, lying, but withheld comment. "We figured he was hiding out of state, possibly Nevada or Utah or Idaho. We also suspect he may have crossed state lines with the victims. I think he saw this as an opportunity to return and receive ransom money and get personal revenge, if you follow me."

"You're referring to his former association, his relationship?"

"Yes – another question, did Stull ever know that Kerenski is an agent?"

"No," said Frasier. "That's what's strange about the situation. We were getting close to something and now suddenly, Kerenski is kidnapped. I wouldn't rule out the KGB. Stull worries me. He's a freak, a psychopath. You must get to them Klein, and fast."

"What about her husband? He was very depressed when I talked to him. Does he know his wife is a double agent?"

"No, and it's mandatory that he doesn't find out. Don't bring up the subject with him."

"I'll keep you informed." Klein hung up the phone and tossed the crumpled message into the waste basket. *Fucking CIA*, he thought. *They even peddled drugs to our own American troops in Viet Nam.*

Klein didn't trust the CIA. They had too much unregulated power and too many personal deals going on the side.

CHAPTER TWENTY-FIVE

The Vigil

Michael's head throbbed, a slow steady constant pain that exhausted him and dulled his senses and he had not been drinking. After the first series of straight shots, he had become sick to his stomach and disgusted with himself that he sought a release for his stress in alcohol. The only release would be the safe return of his wife and daughter. His personal emotional suffering was not relevant.

His sense of helplessness infuriated him and caused him the most anxiety. He wanted desperately to leave the house, to follow some clue, to act, to track them down. But there was little he could do but sit and wait or walk and wait or stand and wait. His life had suddenly become a treadmill of waiting.

His watch told him it was eleven o'clock. His body in a state of extreme nervous exhaustion told him he needed lost hours of sleep. His mind, swarming with terrifying images of what might be happening to his wife and child resisted all thoughts of sleep.

A nervous hunger crept up on him. He scavenged the cupboards and refrigerator and settled on having a bowl of vegetable soup and a fried cheese sandwich stuffed with Vlasic pickles.

What were his wife and child eating? Were the kidnappers even feeding them? They must be feeding them. They had to feed them. They couldn't let them starve to death. He had a sudden impulse to go on the public radio and television air waves and tell the kidnappers to feed them. Surely they would be listening to news reports. They would want to know the status of the investigation.

From time to time, he looked with mixed hope and scorn at the two detectives assigned to monitor and tape all phone conversations coming to the house. Both men were dozing in fitful discomfort near their recording equipment. Even the ringing phone did not catapault them from their chairs, as it did Michael, who sprang up and dashed out of the kitchen to the study in mid-bite.

Disappointment consumed him. The voice was not one of the kidnappers.

"Hello, Michael, this is Suzanne Kirkeby," her usual businesslike tone was tinged with sympathy.

"Hi, Suzanne, what is it? Why are you calling here?"

"Would you have any personal objection to my staying at your house and documenting the events of the kidnapping? Kasia and Danielle are very dear to me and to my entertainment readers and if there's any opportunity I can use the press to reach the kidnappers or ease the situation, I want to help. I'm not just after a story."

Michael knew that Klein would not approve and, at first, he himself did not want anyone else around to distract his focus. Suzanne had become Kasia's and his friend during their rise to media prominence over the past few years. She had followed and written extensively about Kasia's career as an actress. But he knew she had an ulterior motive. He didn't believe for a minute she was "not just after a story." Reporters were always just after a story.

Sensing what he was thinking, she said, "You have my word I will not release any confidential information that would jeopardize the investigation. I understand how delicate the situation is. Nothing will get out unless you or the police authorize it. The FBI has already issued a gag order."

Michael's second impulse on the matter was that maybe having someone to talk to who was a friend of the family, in whom he could confide, would be acceptable.

"Okay, I'll leave your name at the gate."

"Thanks, Michael, I'll see you in about an hour."

He called and left her name with the guard to grant her admittance.

Suzanne had wanted to contact Michael earlier, when the news of the kidnapping had been picked up on a police radio frequency, but she had realized that in his shock and trauma he would not be receptive to her request and would have considered it an exploitation of their personal relationship. She was even a little surprised that he so readily granted her permission to come to the house now. She had detected his tone of indecision.

A few members of the media and press camped at the entrance recognized her upon her arrival and called out to her as the guard admitted her through the gate. Cursing, a few got on their radio phones back to their editors and producers protesting the blatant preferential treatment being given the Times when the standing order from the FBI was no information, no print, and no broadcast until further notice.

She drove her Porsche to the front door, parked, and carried a small suitcase with her, a portable tape recorder and her attaché case.

A subdued Michael answered her knock. "Hi, Suzanne." He stared out past her down the driveway as if hoping to glimpse some approaching messenger bearing good tidings.

For a moment, he imagined he heard the laughing voice of Danielle running and playing about the yard, which was his last remembered impression of her on a Sunday afternoon. He realized that he was overly taxed and would have to rest soon. During the past hour, his perceptions had been vacillating between lingering memories, imagination, and a reality that was so terrifying, he found believing it difficult.

Through sheer psychic energy, he hoped to project a protective aura around his wife and child. The illusion was not much in the way of an effective action, but it was all that was left to him and made him feel somewhat better. For his own well-being, he had to believe his mental effort was something more than an exercise in futility.

He glanced down at Suzanne's suitcase. "You can have one of the guest rooms."

"Thanks, Michael. I'm so sorry. I'm not just here because of my job. We're friends and you know that. I want to be sure you understand that. Please don't think badly of me or that we're anything less than friends."

"I understand. I don't," he gave her the benefit of the doubt.

"I'm not just writing about Kasia and Danielle. There are issues I have to sort out in my own life and they relate to who Kasia is, what she represents. Do you know what I'm saying?"

Michael nodded.

Suzanne had been an entertainment writer with the Los Angeles Times for ten years and was also a frequent contributor to various prominent women's magazines. She had taken considerable interest in the career partnership of Kasia and Michael, especially on the issues of feminism. Seemingly overnight, Kasia had become an international symbol of female self-actualization through her first film and the accompanying publicity of her invented past and private life. Her being a spy was unknown.

Michael's scripts never resorted to the stereotypic treatment of women meted out in so many Hollywood films. His first two films and the carefully constructed publicity campaigns surrounding Kasia succeeded in establishing a unique dual image. She became a sex symbol as well as the symbol and role model for the total woman.

Michael's films thematically explored the social and economic inequities of the haves and have-nots in society as focused through the characters Kasia portrayed. The power and subconscious impact of Kasia's image caused an upheaval in Madison Avenue advertising. No longer could they appeal to housewives whose apparent major decision of the day was to chose between one floor cleaner, detergent, deodorizer, toothpaste, tampon, or dog and cat food and another. Within the past four years, Kasia's image on screen, in print, and in the television media through numerous talk show appearances, and as a news event during her speeches at the anti-nuclear rallies came to symbolize the modern woman of the late 70s and early 80s.

Suzanne Kirkeby had chronicled the phenomenon of Kasia Kerenski, not only in respect to her influence on women's issues, but also in how her film characters triumphed over exploitation by the advertising media and the corporate sector.

Returning from the guest room, she asked Michael, "Can I help you in some way? Do you feel like talking or would you rather I just leave you alone?"

His eyes blurred staring at her tumble of brown curls and brown eyes creased slightly downward at the corners giving her an engaging expression of sympathy. "Why don't we sit down for a while. God, I'm so tired I can hardly think straight. I can't remember being so tired. Do you want anything? Coffee? Tea? A real drink?"

"Let me fix you a drink."

He shook his head. "No, not for me. I can't."

"I'll make some tea." Leaving her tape recorder and attaché case in the living room, she went to the kitchen.

Michael leaned back on the sofa and closed his eyes. Suzanne returned a few minutes later with a pot of hot tea, cups, and assorted crackers, cookies, and cheeses on a tray. She placed them on the coffee table and sat near Michael while she poured and served.

She leaned forward slightly, balancing a cup and saucer on her slender knees. "Waiting is the worst kind of torture."

"It's not even waiting so much as not knowing what's happening to them, or what's going to happen. In some way, I feel responsible."

"How?"

"For putting them out there on display, serving them up for public consumption. I turned my own wife and daughter into objects that are commercially marketable. I came full circle and did to them what I've criticized about our society. Whoever kidnapped them doesn't even see or consider them as human beings. How could they?"

"But they must know how much you personally value Kasia and Danielle."

"Do they? I'm not so sure they know or would even care, for that matter." Michael yawned. "Excuse me."

"That's all right. Fall asleep if you can."

"Not yet, maybe in a while. Klein from the FBI called me this afternoon. He says he has a suspect he's looking for, two, maybe three of them Kasia used to know when she was a street mime and worked as a waitress. Herb Wilcox and Dade Thomas occasionally played in a nightclub combo with them. One of them, Stephen Stull, was treated as a schizophrenic at Camarillo State Hospital when he was a teenager."

With an intense sidewise glance through the rising steam from her tea, Suzanne studied him as he continued to talk with his eyes closed.

He tried to ease the tension from his voice. "Sometimes, I look back and wonder how it came to this. Maybe I wasn't doing something right. I thought I had everything I ever wanted, but all this now . . ." His gesture encompassed the material wealth of the house and whatever extended beyond. "This is nothing. It's empty. Without them, my life is empty."

"What about your writing, your films?"

"Sure, that's another side of me, but Kasia and Danielle are more important to me than my work."

"Obviously."

"If I did it only for the money, I wouldn't have been able to make my last two films the way I made them, without studio interference. I just want my wife and child back unharmed." His eyes blinked open adjusting to the brightness of the room. He leaned forward and took his cup and saucer. "Thanks for making the tea. Earlier, when you came to the door, you said something about sorting out your own life in relation to Kasia."

"It's because I know her personally, as well as her being an actress. My whole adult life has been a process of breaking free of the mold of tradition. I got married right out of high school at nineteen, the same guy I'd been going with for three years. We both worked and went on to the same college. My husband was a very conservative person. He kept everything inside, felt inadequate and was afraid to express himself. I tried to draw that out of him, unsuccessfully, however."

Suzanne put down her tea. She needed her hands to express herself. "Everything had to be rational and functional with him. Maybe that's why he became a computer programmer. But my whole childhood was like that. I was never particularly pretty, but I had brains. Still, I was pushed to conform to a certain feminine protocol, look, and behavior. You know what I mean. I had to break away, but I never had the chance, or I should say, I never sought or took the chance. I just wished and dreamed and thought about it."

Michael watched her as she spoke. He had never realized that as a media person she had been that affected by the media image and statement represented by Kasia. Suzanne had plain, but interesting features, a face lined with character and eyes that exuded humor, sympathy, and warmth. In many ways her job required that she be rugged and practical. She confronted the realities behind the headlines. She used to wear her hair cut short. As a reporter on the go, she frequently didn't have time to wash and blow dry it. She had only recently let the luxurious brown curls emerge, softening her appearance.

"Coming out of high school, I was overly concerned," she continued. "I guess about security. My parents were the sheltering kind. Not until I finished college and turned twenty-one did I see myself differently and that I wasn't getting the things out of life I needed. I knew I couldn't get them by remaining married. It bothered me enough to send me to a counselor. That provided some focus and understanding about my own perspective.

"Personal growth and self-awareness are just too vital to ignore, especially when it starts pushing through of its own accord. My psychologist explained the origins of these forces within us and that's why I have a special interest in Kasia, how she reconciles functioning on one level as a wife and mother while managing a highly successful public career. Besides all that, figuratively speaking, she's transcended being mortal by her screen persona. She's become a personification of success for the contemporary woman, a kind of cultural goddess, a modern goddess, a daughter of Venus. Men are either drawn to her or else they're threatened by her. But her power causes women to want to emulate her.

"On the big screen, Kasia represents a part of our human psyche. She's a projection of some aspect of ourselves and we identify with her. She becomes an embodiment, a part of who we are and what we're made of, what makes us tick. She's a heroine. When and where we're weak, she is strong.

"Just before my divorce, I went through a period of terrible depression. I just felt like my life was drying up before I'd even lived it. I was still able to function all right, go to school and work, but inside I felt a deadly kind of boredom that made everything seem meaningless and empty.

"I felt like I was looking for something that was impossible to find and I didn't know anything about. I got plenty of advice from my husband, my parents, well-meaning friends. They told me to take a vacation, stop working so hard, forget about my career that I was just beginning to explore. My analyst helped me acknowledge the dark feeling inside me and find out what was hidden there and what it wanted from me.

"I discovered things about myself I didn't really like. I was egotistical. I had ridiculous fantasies and I was always plotting and scheming to get ahead. I even cheated on two final exams and plagiarized nearly an entire term paper to get an 'A' in the class, one of my journalism courses."

Michael was not cognizant of the fact he had drifted off to sleep. Suzanne covered him with a blanket from his bedroom, then quietly departed to the guest room.

Out of the necessity to relieve his bladder, Michael woke at five thirty in the morning. Staring bleary-eyed across the sleek shadows of the long living room, his attention came to rest on the small circle of light cast over the telephone and tape recording unit in the adjoining study. Both of the attending officers lay draped asleep on a smaller couch and a large stuffed chair.

His perceptions still flitted along the ragged surreal borders of sleep and required considerable effort for him to reconcile the image and to bring into painful focus again the reality of the circumstances that had him lying there alone in cold discomfort. He hoped that maybe he had just come home late from a screening or an editing session and perhaps he was not awake at all, but had entered and become part of an uncharted cinematic sequence in his own imagination. What he felt and saw were only an impression that would one day might appear in a film he would make.

Wrapping the blanket snugly around his shivering body, he rose stiffly and went upstairs to his bedroom, stood for what seemed an unreasonable length of time waiting for his urinary tract to open, then fell into a somnambulistic state, desiring only to escape once again in sleep.

He woke later in the morning to the life-enticing aromas of coffee, toast, eggs, and frying bacon. Knowing that he would have been summoned had a call or a message come through regarding the ransom and his wife and child, he showered and shaved without tension or haste.

An inertia webbed his soul to the extent that he could make only limited flailing motions against the sticky threads of fate while waiting for the spider to come high stepping rapidly down the interwoven strands.

At the breakfast table, Michael indicated he was not amenable to conversation. After eating the bacon, eggs, coffee, and toast Suzanne had prepared, he abruptly thanked her, as if resenting her being there in place of his wife. He then went into the study, seated himself apart from the attending officers, and worked on his script to constructively channel the stress of waiting.

Klein stopped by at mid-afternoon and immediately criticized Michael for his decision to allow Suzanne Kirkeby to be in the house and privy to the investigation. He had received calls from several television news producers at the studios and many news editors questioning his fairness and credibility with regard to the gag order. Klein accused Michael of corrupting his position with the news media and they would no longer keep silent if they gleaned information about the status of the kidnapping.

Suzanne claimed she would preserve journalistic silence until such time as authorized by the FBI and police to go to press with her story. Klein suspected that Michael intended to capitalize on the publicity surrounding the kidnapping to promote his films and Kasia's career and that he was in collusion with Suzanne.

He affirmed that he would have her arrested if she wrote and released any information on or about the investigation.

Resenting Klein's attitude toward her, Suzanne informed him of her professional position and that she would honor his request.

"It's not a request. It's an order," he said.

Beyond that exchange, he would say nothing to her and spoke only with Michael out of earshot of Suzanne.

He took Michael aside and explained how he had planned to plant a story in major newspapers that the kidnappers had sent in a ransom note and that payment of one million dollars was being arranged for the safe return of Kasia and her daughter. He hoped the ploy would lure Stull into the open by his making a second request for the ransom.

The article was scheduled to appear the following day, and he didn't want Michael to see it and become alarmed and he did not want Suzanne to know about it. She would try to stick her nose into it anyway when the announcement came out the next morning.

Klein's glance of disgust at Suzanne as he departed left her feeling low, exploitive, and insignificant, despite her anger, all conditions she had tried to avoid.

CHAPTER TWENTY-SIX

The Choice

Giorgio's salon buzzed with sensational gossip about the abduction of Kasia Kerenski and her daughter, especially since Kasia was a regular with Giorgio. Her autographed ten by twelve glossy photo was prominently displayed at his station and he exhibited a stainless steel framed full size poster of her near the salon entrance.

Geraldine had seen him come in tight-lipped and apprehensive. She attributed his mood to a hangover and genuine personal concern for the salon's famous client. He had taken several aspirin, splashed cold water on his face and stalked out onto the floor.

"Oh, Giorgio, isn't it terrible? Have you heard the news?" Waving a newspaper, a woman in hair curlers rattled up to him.

"Yes, yes, a tragedy." His brusque manner did not go unnoticed by the other hair dressers. He had come in over an hour late and, in the meantime, Geraldine had taken care of his first two clients of the day. The two women were less angry at his not being there than the fact he did not apologize later.

"You'll have to excuse him," Geraldine attempted to mollify them as the women departed in indignation.

Halfway through the cut on his third client, Giorgio grew increasingly aware of Kasia's photograph smiling at him, mocking him. He muttered under his breath in Russian, cursing her for ruining his life, cursing himself for not resigning her long ago.

He had received a phone call at home from Helmut Bachmann just after news of the kidnapping had hit the stands. Bachmann informed him that the CIA had penetrated Giorgio's cover through Kasia acting as a double agent. In fact, the CIA had obviously known about Giorgio ever since he had begun using Kasia as a courier. Fortunately, she knew nothing about Charley and Maggie MacIntosh, or she would also have informed the CIA. Since Giorgio had never revealed Kurt Heinrich and Bachmann in his communications with Kasia, they were still secure.

"Within twenty-four hours, you must be in Canada," Bachmann had spoken in Russian so as not to be identified in the event Giorgio's phone was tapped. In code, his actual escape destination was Mexico City and thence to Cuba, from where he would return to the Soviet Union for a debriefing.

Giorgio asked for time to liquidate his assets.

"Impossible," Bachmann's voice came through the receiver cold and hard as steel. "You must leave at once. If you delay, you will be terminated. The FBI must not pull you in for an interrogation. You are being watched by the KGB as of this minute. Follow my orders and you will live."

"Live?" thought Giorgio to himself. "Never like this again."

He gazed around the expensively furnished living room of his luxurious Malibu home. He had made a critical error that could lead to Bachmann and the Tri Con cell should the FBI move in on Giorgio. He wondered why they hadn't before. He knew he would break under prolonged psychological and physical torture. And if he followed orders and returned to the Soviet Union, the KGB would retire him to Siberia.

What he had feared had finally come to pass. There was no reprieve, nowhere to turn. If he defected or went openly to the FBI and sought protection and asylum, the KGB would soon get him anyway. He could not hide for long.

Without explanation, he put down his comb and scissors and left by the rear door of the salon. Sensing that something very unusual was wrong, Geraldine followed and saw him get into his blue Rolls Royce. He saw her watching him as he drove out of the lot.

His time was running out. If he were not on a plane to Mexico City within the next twelve hours, he would be murdered by KGB hit men.

His depression intensified as he drove west on Wilshire Boulevard to the Coast Highway in Santa Monica, then north to Malibu. What point would there be in returning to Soviet Russia anyway? He had become a capitalist and was a communist only because of his origin.

"Christos, must I pay so dearly for a single error, really nothing more than an indiscretion? Have they forgotten the successes of all my years in this country? I gave them more than ten agents put together," he rambled on incoherently in Russian.

Unaware of a black Mercedes bearing two dark-suited men following him, he continued along the ocean front. They parked outside his house and waited. He could see them below in his driveway from his second story bedroom window. He knew they figured that since he had not acted immediately on his orders and that he vacillated with indecision, that he must be contemplating some other plan. They were staying close, playing it safe so as not to lose him.

The thought of a violent death terrified Giorgio. If he let them do it, it might be chemical and quick, perhaps a cyanide capsule, as long as he didn't resist, otherwise torture and a bullet. With cyanide an investigation would officially rule his death a suicide.

He wondered if he could possibly bargain with them, pay them off to say they had terminated him and dumped him in the sea. Then he could disappear and change his identity.

The more he thought about the prospect, the more the idea appealed to him. But when he stared down at the black Mercedes and the men, who would sit there waiting for six hours, twelve hours, he knew he would never convince them. They would take the payment, then kill him.

They were a different breed of agent than himself, professional killers, assassins. Sure, they would agreeably thank him for his money, but they would not waiver from their mission to murder him.

They rather hoped he would not fly to Mexico City. They were selected for their intensity of purpose, their cold inhumanity, and their training and skill and sociopathic enjoyment of terminating human life.

Georgio knew he was down to his final two choices. Either they would deliver his death, or he must take his own life.

He did not want to die painfully, nor too quickly. Life had been too sweet to leave it with a rush. He wanted to savor the final moments, then blissfully fall into a deep sleep from which he would never awaken.

He stripped off his clothes and padded barefoot down the lush, carpeted stairs into the kitchen. Opening a jar of Russian caviar, he spread it in mounds on thin slices of rye bread, then popped the cork on a chilled bottle of Dom Perignon.

Returning to his bedroom with the caviar and vintage champagne, he ran a scalding hot bubble bath in the tiled Roman tub where he had spent many a memorable night with more women than he cared to remember.

The champagne lifted his spirits and gave him courage, at least dulled his fear of his final act. "I've lived a good life," he addressed himself in Russian in the mirror on the opposite wall. "I have no regrets."

How empty he suddenly felt, as if he were trying to justify what he was about to do. Justify? Or work up enough nerve?

"Hell, the only nerve I've got lives in this bottle." He raised the champagne to his lips.

"What a fool," he suddenly uttered. "I should have thought to bring a woman home with me. I could have told her everything. She would have been my priestess, my confessor. We could have made love in every possible way. I need a woman to be able to die. Ah, Giorgio, if only you had a woman."

He stared at his penis now erect at the very thought of a nude woman there in the tub with him, her skin smooth and moist from the rising steam. Mentally visualizing a sexual fantasy, he then masturbated into the hot sudsy water.

He felt empty. In the final analysis, he had no true friends, no lovers, no children, no relations to whom he could turn for solace. "I am alone," he said. "My life is empty. It is empty, so I feel no remorse in ending it. Holy Mother, Lord Jesus Christos, have mercy on my soul."

Without further hesitation, he slit his wrists with a strop razor and held them deep in the hot bath to diminish the sensation of stinging pain. He watched the murky clouds of blood stream out of him like ink staining the white soap bubbles red.

The bite of pain slowly left him. Drowsy, he lay back and closed his eyes, lost consciousness, then slipped under the soothing water. He heard his mother calling to him from across her vegetable garden in the old country.

CHAPTER TWENTY-SEVEN

The Resurrection

Melinda Jakes walked home from the grocery store in time to catch the six o'clock news. Ever since the first public announcement of Kasia Kerenski's kidnapping, she had wheeled her portable television set into her bedroom where she would watch the morning newscasts while eating breakfast and preparing for work, and again throughout the evening while eating supper and preparing for bed.

The walls of her bedroom were plastered with magazine photographs of Kasia Kerenski.

She had seen Kasia's first two motion pictures twenty times each and, now, the ritual of feeding on the suspense created by the news cycles prompted her to flip from station to station to hear again and again what had been repeated by other commentators.

From all indications, Kasia Kerenski and her daughter might never be seen nor heard from again. Because the FBI had capped the investigation in secrecy, details about the kidnapping were sparse. So a major news program producer had sent journalists and mobile camera crews to various locations around the country to conduct spot interviews with people on the street regarding their reaction.

The answers to the standard question asking how the particular man or woman felt about Kasia Kerenski and her child in their present circumstances revealed a general national concern. However, several people interviewed responded that they believed the entire incident was nothing more than a publicity stunt.

Melinda bore a striking physical likeness to Kasia Kerenski. Thinking she was Kasia, people had sometimes stopped her on the street and had approached her in restaurants for her autograph.

At first, when she had denied she was the renown movie star, people would not believe her and thought she was just putting them off. They would grow angry and offended.

Frustrated by her dilemma and not wanting anybody to hate her idol, she thought that if enough fans believed she was Kasia Kerenski, then she might as well go all the way with the charade. She gave in and crossed over the line to become the Kasia Kerenski persona.

She started signing requested autographs and appeared strategically at public functions where photographers would be waiting for the appearance of celebrities and would mistake her for Kasia Kerenski.

She studied and practiced the manner in which Kasia walked, impersonated her voice, wore her hair styles and imitative clothes of the same design, at considerably less cost She had even taken first place in a Kasia Kerenski look-a-like contest sponsored by a leading tobacco manufacturer.

In 1975, Melinda had been head cheerleader at Van Nuys High School in the San Fernando Valley. She had circulated with the most popular crowd of academic achievers, social, and sports heroes.

During her high school years, the Farah Fawcett look had been in vogue, emphasizing soft long blonde hair feathered at the sides. Melinda had excelled in recreating herself as a Farrah-Fawcett look-a-like. Friends had even paid her the compliment that, at a distance, she could be mistaken for the real Farah Fawcett.

From the time she had been a small child taking her cues from her mother as to how she should dress, behave, talk, move, and generally relate to others, she had observed the time and energy her mother devoted to imitating photographs of fashion models in women's magazines.

By the time Melinda became a teenager, her concept of who she was did not grow out of personal achievement or a significant sense of self. Like her mother, who lacked character and took her female identity from the prevailing media, Melinda gained the attention and envy of her peers by looking most like their female heroes.

Her barely passing grades prevented the likelihood of her going on to college, either by design or personal inclination. At the high school graduation assembly, the valedictorian announced that Melinda had been voted by her class as the girl most likely to look like someone else. This public tribute and local observation had brought both laughs and applause. Although Melinda had good-naturedly shared the humorous barb, the underlying emotional hurt she experienced did not leave her. The feeling and realization that she was somehow a shallow empty person invaded her.

On the seventh night following the abduction of Kasia Kerenski and her daughter, Melinda woke at a rustling sound in her bedroom. She stared blurry-eyed at the snowy video pattern on the television screen she had neglected to turn off before falling asleep. She felt cold and exposed. A presence seemed to emerge from the screen and move slowly across the bed to lie on top of her, totally enveloping her.

A sudden piercing burning sensation at the back of her brain seeped down throughout her body, leaving her with a strange tingling glow. No longer cold, she rose from the bed and stepped naked before the full-length mirror on her bedroom door. Her image, the image of Kasia Kerenski spoke to her in a soft familiar voice. It told her that she, Kasia Kerenski, could never die and that Melinda's purpose in life was to provide a body for the wandering soul of the murdered movie star. In her own mind, she, Melinda Jakes, was now transformed into Kasia Kerenski, who had returned to take her place among the living.

Melinda slowly approached the mirror and with arms outstretched pressed her flesh against the smooth cool glass and tempered the burning sensation.

Wearing only a robe, she took her car keys from her purse and left her apartment at three o'clock in the morning. An impulse lead her to drive from the city into the mountains north of the San Fernando Valley.

An hour later, she left the main highway and followed the tortuous twists and turns of a narrow winding road that snaked up the rotund slopes through dense chaparral and scrub pine. A drizzling gray dawn pelted and beaded in pin-needle droplets on her car windshield. Upon reaching the crestline, she had to make a conscious effort to look beyond the hypnotic "click-swish" of the wiper blades that streaked her vision.

Kasia Kerenski had played a character kidnapped by a rejected former lover who had taken her up into these very mountains where he had tortured and raped her mercilessly for days. Melinda believed it only fitting that she, the resurrected Kasia, be discovered in this setting, a location used in the film *Sidewalk*.

She turned abruptly onto a mud-slick fire road rutted by rivulets draining from a tributary run-off further along the track. She gunned the skidding weaving car with spine-jolting snaps over the rocks and potholes up the gradual incline until her right rear tire foundered with a screaming whine of resistance.

Leaving the engine idling, Melinda stepped delicately out of the car, her cold pink bare feet sliding in fits and starts on the thin layer of chilling mud. She balanced herself against the side of the car to keep from falling and made her way to the rear to assess the situation. The sunken wheel had lurched miserably into a chuckhole where the glutinous mud sucked and dripped over the hubcap from the earlier violent disturbance.

She looked back down the road and re-evaluated her plan to get rid of the car or try to destroy it in some manner. She had intended to send it crashing into the abyss that dropped away sharply to the right. The vehicle would have finally settled far below, unable to be detected deep among the dense brush and would render the telltale vestige of her former identity, Melinda Jakes, extinct.

She decided that even if the abandoned car were eventually discovered, a probability that might be months into the future, a connection might not necessarily be made between her disappearance and the subsequent reappearance of Kasia Kerenski.

Melinda criticized herself that despite the fact in her mind she had been recently reincarnated as the soul of Kasia Kerenski in her body, she was still reasoning and perceiving from the perspective of Melinda Jakes.

She rationalized she must begin living Kasia's life to erase any element of Melinda, or her actual self would continue to linger, editing her thoughts and words and feelings.

She anticipated the moment, the first time, when she would sleep with Kasia's, now her own, husband. For the things about them as man and wife and the particulars of Kasia's career, her acting ability, Melinda would pretend she had suffered amnesia from a blow on the head. She could not possibly know the names of Kasia's friends nor how she related to them. Doctors might examine her and even X-ray her skull. That meant she had to show visible evidence of the injury.

She returned to the front seat and killed the engine. Leaving the key in the ignition, she walked back downhill along the road. She winced at sharp pebbles cutting into the bottoms of her feet.

The main road was a good five miles from where the car had stopped. Between where she stood and the time she reached the traveled road, she had to prepare herself physically and mentally for the role she had inherited.

She removed her robe, weighted it with rocks, and heaved it far out over the abyss. It ballooned slightly as it plummeted like a crimson sail lost from its mast and settled in the catching thorny branches of a mesquite clinging to the side of the slope. A sharp wind blasted and tugged at the robe, shifting it slightly but unable to dislodge it from the shrub's grasp.

To Melinda's dismay, she realized the robe could be easily seen from above. That she herself might have been taken and murdered could account for both the abandoned car and the robe like a splash of blood nesting among the brush. And still, it might be a long time before anyone actually came up that road. The fire season had faded. Even a ranger would be unlikely to pass that way.

Naked, with the rocks and gravel bruising her sensitive feet at each tentative slipping step, she made slow but steady progress. Her body trembled from the damp and cold. She regretted having sacrificed the robe. After a mile, she sat leaning against the base of a lichen encrusted ledge. She hugged her knees to her chest and rested her head so that she stared down into the crevasse created by the fold of her abdomen against her thighs.

The sudden severe drop in temperature combined with the creeping chill squeezed the natural warmth from her body. She crouched blue and shivering for five minutes. The frigid air knifed into her, striking deep and reminding her of the sobering reality of who she really was and of what she was doing. She was unable to rise and move on for fear of losing that small cup of warmth she generated doubled against herself.

She considered walking the single mile back to her stranded car and waiting sheltered for a break in the weather, or at least for the incipient warmth of sunrise, before going on. But she was Kasia Kerenski now and had no alternative but to go on, to suffer as Kasia would have suffered in the movie.

Supporting herself against the ledge, she thrust her trembling body up and began a stumbling jog, weaving through the rocks and ruts. Freezing pain jolted from her feet at each jarring step and finally forced her to stop without having gone more than a few hundred yards. The soles of her feet split and bled in a network of tiny cracks. Even walking was unbearable.

She panicked that she would not make it to the road. Someone would one day discover her decaying body curled up having died from exposure, her whole attempt a wasted effort.

She thought again of returning to the car, then realized that these adverse conditions would perhaps injure her body enough to provide the physical credibility of Kasia Kerenski's ordeal. Her feet would be bloody. She would be delirious with pain and wracked with mental agony, unable to speak.

She doggedly trudged on and overcame her threshold of endurance against the cold and suffering with the gradual return of the burning sensation she had experienced standing before her bedroom mirror. Electric shock impulses shattered her mind with feverish bursts.

Five hours later, she came to the road. Although the sun had risen, it only sporadically penetrated the gray shifting cloud cover that ensconced the surrounding granite peaks. She stood alone at the center of the cold asphalt, all sensation having fled her feet where she had walked on soles of mangled flesh and blood.

She heard the high keening whistle of a hunting hawk but could not see it for the trees that blocked her view of the sky. She had no sense of falling and did not feel the impact as the side of her head struck the hard pavement and she slipped into an even deeper unconsciousness than her trance.

***

Klein received the call from the Los Padres National Forest station at Crestline within minutes after he arrived at his office that morning. The head ranger explained how he had discovered the half-frozen mangled nude body of Kasia Kerenski sprawled across the mountain road three miles from his station while he was driving to work.

Although she had suffered from severe cold, shock, and exposure, as well as bodily injuries, she was beginning to regain consciousness. She was not coherent and occasionally babbled in delirium. She was running a one hundred four degree fever and likely had pneumonia.

Klein ordered that she be transported at once by the Crestline paramedic squad to the UCLA Hospital in Westwood where he would meet them in emergency. He hung up, then immediately called Michael to inform him that his wife had been found, but that their child was still missing. He asked Michael to be at UCLA Hospital Emergency in forty-five minutes.

Klein next ordered a dispatch of two police helicopters to comb the Crestline area and the approaching slopes while a radio patrol worked the ground. Crestline Highway was to be cordoned off at either end. A building by building or cabin by cabin search would be made and intensified in the area where Kasia had been discovered. He himself would join the search as soon as he had met Kasia at the hospital and talked with her.

Michael's shaking hand lowered the phone receiver to its cradle. What had happened to the ransom request? It had never materialized, never come through. What was the physical condition of his wife that she had to be rushed to the UCLA Hospital? Why was Kasia separated from Danielle? And what had become of their child?

A chilling fear gripped him rendering him unable to move. He wanted to project his soul and send it flying in search of their little girl to comfort her until he himself could reach her and enfold her in his arms.

After he and Klein talked with Kasia at the hospital, he would accompany Klein on the search that would be underway at Crestline.

"What is it?"

He turned at the unexpected intrusion of Suzanne's voice. His thoughts had already rushed to the mountain slopes. "They found Kasia at Crestline. She's being taken to the UCLA Hospital."

"What about Danielle?"

Michael shook his head.

"Oh, my God, that poor child."

Michael grabbed the keys to his Mercedes and lunged through the rooms and out of his house with Suzanne thrashing after him in the wake of his charge and momentum.

They arrived at the hospital and parked in the subterranean section adjacent to the emergency entrance. Racing to the door through the yellowish-green cast of underground neon lighting, Michael suddenly stopped and Suzanne collided into him from the rear.

"It will take a while for them to bring her here," Michael stood blinking sternly at the moving flashing red light of an ambulance that slipped quickly and smoothly down the ramp to the door where white-coated interns and attendants efficiently transferred a heart attack victim to a gurney and wheeled him away.

"Do you want to wait inside?"

"I guess so."

They crossed the alleyway from the pedestrian safety island and entered the waiting room near the admission desk. Michael had once filmed documentary footage in this same emergency waiting room. Sitting there now restored to him the weakening sensation of watching on the threshold of death the ravaged bodies and accompanying emotions that were carried through the doors. Some were given a reprieve. Many continued their longest journey deep into the bowels of the hospital to be later transplanted in the earth.

When Klein suddenly appeared in the doorway, Michael recoiled inwardly at the sight of the stolid, aging, yet ageless little man. He no longer knew whether to consider Klein as a bearer of good news or a middleman of death and the hidden monstrous under-life of a society, someone who negotiated with the Devil.

Klein did not come over to them immediately, although his glance caught them sitting there. He went to the admissions and medical records counter, spoke briefly with the Hispanic female clerk in attendance, then strode purposefully to Michael and Suzanne.

"The ambulance will be here in a few minutes. I've established a search at Crestline in the air and on the ground. As soon as I've had a chance to talk with your wife, I'll be going up there."

"I'll be with you. No need to stay by the phone anymore, is there? They didn't ask for a ransom."

Klein's eyes narrowed at the insinuation that he was not effectively handling the situation. "Don't attempt anything rash, please, Mr. Sloan.

They've still got your daughter and will use her to gain leverage in the negotiations. Your wife was lucky to escape alive, although I don't know how she managed it. The kidnappers will still want cash and free access to somewhere. Maybe they deliberately put your wife out there to make it appear she escaped. It will be better for everyone involved, especially your daughter, if you don't come in on the search. We need trained people and cool heads and objectivity, not emotions."

Michael shot up from his chair and towered over Klein whose hard unyielding eyes confirmed what he had just described regarding Michael's behavior and reactions. Michael silently admitted to himself that under the circumstances, he would probably not listen to orders. He was accustomed to being the one in charge.

The arrival of the Crestline paramedic ambulance broke their temporary silent deadlock. Michael pushed past Klein and ran to the door, nearly interfering with the medics as they wheeled Melinda Jakes in on a stretcher.

He stared with apprehension at the closed blue lids of her eyes and caught her hoarse breath rasping through the oxygen mask cupped over her nose and mouth. As he tried to follow them into the treatment area, a tall male intern ordered him to wait until he was called.

Klein and Suzanne came up on either side of him. He avoided looking at Klein and resented the hell out of Suzanne holding onto his arm, as if she had any business in the world restraining him. He twisted free of her grasp. Her features drooped with chagrin.

Fifteen minutes later, the same tall intern motioned for him to come forward. As Suzanne and Klein attempted to follow, he told them to wait. With undisguised irritation, Klein snapped open the leather wallet containing his badge. The intern promptly motioned him to join Michael behind the green curtained partition.

Melinda's eyes fluttered open like the wings of a baby bird attempting flight. She stared with a dull glazed expression up into the faces of the two men. The intern, who had by now been informed by the admissions clerk as to the public identity of his patient, stepped in to remove the oxygen mask.

Michael leaned in close to her ear. "Kasia, can you hear me? It's Michael. Can you talk, honey?"

Melinda moved her head in a barely perceptible nod. Michael took her hand. "This man is Captain Klein. He needs to ask you some questions. The police are searching for Danielle now. What – "

Klein grabbed his arm, cutting him short. "Mrs. Sloan, I have only a few questions. Where did they keep you and your daughter hidden?"

"I – I don't know for sure," she whispered. "They moved us around a lot."

"What did they move you in?"

"A van."

"How many of them are there?"

"At least three. I didn't get to see them all."

"Mrs. Sloan, did they keep you and your daughter separated?"

Melinda nodded.

Klein turned to the doctor. "I need a full medical report. A special courier will be standing by to receive it." He left as abruptly as he had entered.

Leaning down again to plant a gentle kiss on his wife's forehead, Michael's fingers brushed over the swollen lump at the side of her head. "Kasia, Kasia, we'll get her back. We're going to get Danielle back."

Melinda nodded, briefly half-opened her eyes, then closed them. The doctor advised Michael that he must leave for the moment until he had completed the examination and had written out the medical report for the waiting police officer.

Upon returning to the emergency lobby, Michael saw Suzanne talking on one of the pay phones and rushed across the room to stop her. "Not yet! You can't call in the story yet! Not while they've still got Danielle!"

Covering the mouthpiece, she turned and faced him. "With the police searching all over Crestline, they're going to know long before it makes the headlines. Other journalists have probably already picked up on the police calls."

Michael hesitated and released his grip on her hand and the phone receiver. "I'm sorry. I guess you're right. Klein's gone on already."

"Yes, I saw him leave."

"I'm going to stay and see if the doctor will let me talk to Kasia again. It may be a while."

"I'll stay here. I'd like to go in with you next time. I won't ask questions. I just want to see her and give her my condolences and moral support. What's her condition?"

"Not critical. At least I don't think so. The doctor must finish his examination and write the medical report for Klein. I'd better go up to the main admission desk and get her registered."

"I'll wait here." Suzanne reinserted her dime in the phone box.

Michael walked to the emergency desk for directions to the main admissions office. Then, without a backward glance, he left the waiting room.

The staccato whump of helicopter rotor blades churned the canyon air as the choppers skimmed back and forth like silver dragonflies paralleling the north and south slopes leading up to Crestline.

On the ground, using geological survey and local residential maps, the cars, trucks, and jeeps of the mobile search team moved in a slow spaced progression along the Crestline Road. They maintained constant radio contact with the helicopter crews for orders to deploy onto side roads if a cabin or group movement were spotted.

Coming over a rise, one of the choppers swooped in low for a close look at Melinda Jakes' crimson robe hung up in the chaparral brush halfway down a drop from the fire road. The pilot also saw her car mired a short distance further up the mountainside. Continuing to execute repeated inspection passes, he radioed the location of the vehicle to the nearest ground crew which proceeded at once to the site.

Klein listened to the exchange on a patrol car radio as the steps taken and information discovered about the car were transmitted back to him. The number three helicopter search pilot relayed Klein's order to run a check on the California license number and make of the car.

Within several minutes, he received the message that the vehicle belonged to a Melinda Jakes with a San Fernando Valley address. A police unit was dispatched to the apartment building. The apartment manager admitted the investigating officers, who, by the exhibit of photographs and a single one of Melinda Jakes, became aware of her physical resemblance to Kasia Kerenski. The apartment manager confirmed the similarity and told how he sometimes had pointed her out at the poolside as being Kasia Kerenski, living there part of the time as a hideaway.

He also informed the police that Melinda had a string of boyfriends, but he had never suspected she was working out of the building as a hooker. The officers took one of the photographs as evidence of the likeness and ignored the manager's comments and nosey questions.

Returning to their patrol car, they established a radio relay contact through the headquarters frequency. Klein was advised of the startling discovery.

Ordering his driver to take him quickly to a nearby windswept plateau designated as a helicopter pick-up point, he boarded a waiting chopper that immediately lifted off, cleared the trees and made an arcing long gradual dive out over the slopes and downward into the San Fernando Valley.

The chopper hovered in over the Van Nuys Airport and made a controlled descent to the landing pad. Klein saw two officers waiting for him next to their patrol car out on the tarmac. He was already mentally negotiating the emotional embarrassment of feeling foolish, but then he justified to himself he should have anticipated some bizarre occurrence of this kind. Somewhere in this case an actual person and an imaginary personality had merged. Illusion was beginning to blend with reality, even in his own clean logical mind.

He worried that this freak incident was only the beginning. The decoy feature story he had planted in the Los Angeles Times and various other papers to appear that very morning had been read by millions and picked up by the Associated Press and relayed by broadcast media throughout the country.

On the heels of the false news that a ransom demand had been received would follow that Kasia Kerenski had escaped her abductors and was now hospitalized in the critical care unit at UCLA Hospital.

To have the woman turn out to be a Kasia Kerenski look-a-like would totally undermine the investigator's credibility with the actual kidnappers, provided they were following the newscasts, which was most certain. In the reigning confusion, they would take the opportunity to create greater confusion, establishing false leads that Klein would have to sort out from among the other twisted personalities who had been calling in to radio and television stations in a personal quest for notoriety.

Klein knew from experience that once these events got out of hand, his efforts would be like trying to single-handedly contain a California forest fire. He could not deploy the entire police force to check out every story and investigate every lead, since ninety-nine percent of them lead to nowhere. He needed that one percent.

While in flight to the airport, he had spoken with headquarters and arranged for a screening code to be applied to all claims and calls in order to save time and manpower.

He waited for the skids to lightly touch the ground. He found himself struggling against an unexpected surge of reluctance to leave the security of the Bell helicopter's glass cockpit bubble. Floating high up there on wind currents in the sky felt so much better looking down at the sprawling megalopolis. His previous vantage point made the city appear diminutive and benign until he descended. Then it gradually transformed into a seething hell of chaotic needs and bizarre lives through which he had to wade and pull his own life in after him.

He thought Michael Sloan would still be brooding about the hospital corridors in his own personal limbo of impotence. Klein thought it a supreme irony that the cinematic illusions Michael had created in the past had taken root in the collective psychic mirror of society and, through several distortions, now haunted him with a terrifying reality that rivaled the fantasy of his early horror films.

In spite of the Melinda Jakes photograph, Klein wanted to be certain about her identity. The physical likeness was so exact he would not have ruled out the possibility that Kasia Kerenski possessed a double identity.

An attending nurse in recovery told Klein that the patient had been sedated and was sleeping. He learned that Michael had gone home. Klein called him and asked him to return to the hospital to verify new evidence discovered during the search at Crestline. He did not share his suspicion as to Melinda Jakes identity. Accompanied by Suzanne Kirkeby, Michael rushed back to the hospital.

Klein did not offer an explanation. He showed Michael and Suzanne the photograph of Melinda Jakes and asked him if he recognized the woman. Michael bristled, thinking that Klein was pulling some sordid manipulation to once again put him in his place.

"Okay," said Klein, "we're going to take another look at that woman in there. A very close look. She's the same woman you see in this photograph, but she's not your wife. Her name is Melinda Jakes."

"What the fuck is this, Klein? That's my wife."

"I'm asking you to inspect her entire body. You should be familiar with it. If you discover anything different about her than you know exists, any identifying marks, a beauty mark perhaps, or a mole, birth mark, whatever, you tell me."

A nurse assisted Michael in his careful visual examination of the sleeping woman he believed to be Kasia. The nurse rolled her onto her side at Michael's request.

He recognized at a glance that this person was not his wife. She did not possess the two dimples on the small of her back that so appealed to Michael whenever he gave Kasia a massage. In addition, this woman had a small scar remaining from a birth mark that Kasia did not. He straightened and shook his head with an expression of bitterness.

"She is not my wife. Kasia has two small dimples on her back right about here." His forefinger touched the spot. He then pointed to the birth scar. Kasia doesn't have any birth marks."   He and Suzanne followed Klein out into the ward. "What are you going to do now?"

"Wait again. We're going to have to wait again for the next development."

One week later, Melinda Jakes was transferred to the county general hospital and placed under psychiatric care and observation.

Michael considered paying for radio and television spot messages to the kidnappers that he was willing to offer three million dollars in cash for the safe return of his wife and daughter.

Klein advised him against the move, reasoning that it would undermine their position of strength in any future negotiations. He hastened to stress that he wasn't referring to the money either, but to the lives of Kasia and their daughter. He then told Michael about the psychotic tendencies and history of Stephen Stull.

CHAPTER TWENTY-EIGHT

The Scar

Under the cover of night, Randy Stiefel left the remote hideout and drove carefully back over the ten mile dirt road that followed the dry creek bed. Yet a mile from the glowing beams of moving car lights in the distance that marked the narrow ribbon of highway, he cut his own headlights and relied on the diminished orange jack-o-lantern illumination of the parking lights as the van trundled forward.

One hundred yards from the highway, he waited until there was no sign of an approaching vehicle from either direction. He increased his speed, switched to low beams and turned onto the asphalt, then accelerated moving out along the winding route toward the Ventura Freeway, Highway 101.

He did not want to chance drawing attention or suspicion by pulling into the small general store where the highway intersected the freeway. He continued to drive north on 101 to the Moorpark turnoff where a crowded local supermarket parking lot provided the anonymity he desired.

Entering the store, he tried to block out the feeling, whether real or imagined, that other people instantly recognized him and were staring at him in open accusation for his part in the crime. He concentrated intently on pushing the metal grocery cart along the well-stocked aisles to ward off his unease. He quickly filled the basket with fresh produce, several kinds of meat and cheeses, milk, two cases of beer, and mostly canned goods.

Except for a large picnic cooler and a gas-powered generator, he and Stull did not have a means of refrigerating their food. They depended on battery and kerosene lanterns for illumination after dark.

Their stark living conditions and the ever-present fear of being either purposely or accidentally discovered played on their nerves. The two weeks that had passed since they had kidnapped Kasia Kerenski, and her child, seemed more like two months.

Stull had been acting strange and withdrawn about requesting the ransom. His behavior had caused Randy to suspect Stull might still have plans that did not include him and Lynn Porat. The perception was not based on anything Stull had said, it was what he didn't say and persisted in not saying. And the sex between them had stopped altogether by silent mutual consent. They were dealing with too much tension and now, suspicion of each other.

As for Lynn, ever since she had come across that old dust-coated *Bible* in the house, she believed the discovery was a sign that God had given her in the house of Satan. She spent hours on end reading and spacing out on Holy scripture instead of dope. Randy was never sure anymore if Lynn were mentally with them or gone only part of the time. He suspected that when they once got the money, Stull would dump her as too great a risk and personal liability. Randy determined that if the relationship should come to that, he would have no hand in how she was treated.

He sensed his own steady deterioration from the incessant use of drugs and a perception of his life as being a total failure. He had been deeply depressed for the past five years. The drugs had only made his condition worse.

He decided he had better make a few plans for himself. Stull was not above murdering them all and ripping off the whole ransom payment.

He figured he had been with Stull as a partner long enough, hell, too long for his own well-being. He would just take his share and split, hide out somewhere for a year, maybe even two. He had a good place in mind. An old Victorian country house in a secluded valley north of Sacramento where his first lover had invited him years ago. That was when Randy had great ambitions as a musician. Even if the old friend were still there, which was unlikely, he would have a new lover or would have moved on.

What Randy had in mind was to turn the house into a small gourmet restaurant out in the sticks, provide a little musical entertainment, light rock, bluegrass, folk, and jazz. Finding a companion to live with him would pose no problem. The city of Sacramento offered up an abundance of homeless gays.

He began to sweat and tremble nervously as he approached the checkout counter. Only one person stood in front of him, an elderly lady. Her groceries had already been bagged and were packed on the cart to be wheeled out.

He watched the eyes of the grocery clerk, a laconic young woman with dark hair pulled back in a tight ponytail. When she suddenly pressed her microphone speaker button to call for a price check, he nearly panicked and bolted thinking she was calling for help because she had identified him.

Finally, pushing his full cart out the door, his glance caught the news headline on the front page of the Los Angeles Times in a vending machine. He fed it the required coinage and snatched three copies of the paper.

He continued to the van, quickly loaded the groceries, climbed inside and read the news article explaining how the abductors of Kasia Kerenski and her child, Danielle, had offered a ransom note and that arrangements were now underway for immediate payment and for the recovery of the woman and child.

As far as Randy was concerned, the news story was positive proof that Stull had double-crossed him and had already sent the ransom message and established the sequence for exchange of the victims. That explained Stull's reluctance to discuss any further plans, whenever Randy had raised the subject and had pressured him to act.

At that very moment, Randy was of a mind to just not return to the hideout. Maybe even place an anonymous call to the police. Leaving the supermarket parking lot, he switched on the radio to listen for more news and heard a general commentary about the discovery of Melinda Jakes, a Kasia Kerenski look-a-like who had unsuccessfully attempted to impersonate the movie star as a kidnap victim.

"The world's full of crazies," Randy snapped off the radio.

***

Kasia knew that at least one of the three kidnappers had left the house. She had heard the van depart some time ago.

Hearing Danielle crying for hour after hour locked away in one of the upper rooms of that dilapidated house impinged on her mind. The tone of the cry greatly disturbed her. It sounded flat and dull and repetitive, almost like a chant, a withdrawal from the reality of emotional and physical abuse, loneliness, and disorientation.

Kasia wanted to slip away from the reality of what had happened to them. She was bound hand and foot, a prisoner in a dark cellar odorous with rot and mold and decay. She heard numerous rustlings and scurrying about whose source she could not detect but could well imagine. She was certain that at one point she had localized and identified the long slow dry glide of a large snake hunting the mice that infested the crumbling walls.

Since she could see very little but shadows by the light filtering through hairline cracks along the top of the foundation, she closed her eyes and tried to sleep as much as possible. Her most difficult and unbearable stress was that she had no means or access to comfort Danielle.

For herself, she could endure and survive the physical discomfort, the dirt and sweat and smell of her unwashed hair and body. She had to by necessity. Although after lying for two weeks in a single cramped position on her back or on one side or the other, she could not help crying out and moaning from the electric pain of muscle spasms and unceasing numbness in her legs and feet. Her captors had pulled the ropes severely tight, but not enough to completely cut off her circulation. The cramp attacks resulted from not being able to stretch and move about.

Waiting .   .   . the endless horror of waiting, as though she had been buried alive in a tomb. She tried to call up and envision some grain of hope, but a despair as black as the cellar consumed her. The end of the ordeal was an unknown. Time passed far too slowly while she waited and hoped for some salvation, some form of deliverance. She could have better endured the incarceration had she been alone. So much of her thoughts and physical energy and emotional extension went out to her unseen child. She kept wondering what their captors were doing to her. She worried that if they got out of this alive, how the trauma would affect her daughter for the rest of her life.

She prayed – please let there be no murder, no dying, no death. The premonition she had experienced at the time of Danielle's birth had come to pass.

Scenes of home and love played through her mind, the security of memories that she wanted to relive again and again with Danielle and Michael. To live to live to live .   .   . That was all she wanted. She wanted to hear again each morning the approaching scuff of Danielle's pajamaed feet on the thick hall carpet, waking her out of a sound sleep with the expectant chirrup and giggle of her voice. Kasia placed herself there again in a memory from two years ago filled with light and love.

She raised her head slightly from the pillow and watched the child's curly towhead and cherubic rosy-cheeked features materialize out of the morning shadows. Now, shadows and darkness were gone. Scuff, scuff, scuff, Danielle trudged around the foot of the bed to her daddy and stood there at eye level staring at him.

"Get up, Daddy," her tiny lyrical voice piped like a chirping bird. "Get out of bed." She pulled away the sheet and blankets from his chest and tugged at his exposed arm while Kasia watched. "Put on your shirt."

"Hi, Punkin," Michael suppressed a groan with a smile and a greeting. "Did you have a nice sleep?"

"Yes, it's morning. Get up now. Let's dance. I just want to dance with you."

"Okay," trying to clear the soporific cobwebs from his brain, Michael swung his legs over the side and rose to a sitting position.

"Put on your shirt. I have to go potty first," said Danielle.

Grinning broadly, Kasia remained snugged down in her blankets to observe this sweet daily morning ritual between father and daughter.

Danielle picked up a maroon velour pullover from a chair in the corner and handed it to Michael as he rubbed the sleep from his eyes. "Here's your shirt. Put this on and let's dance."

He took the velour. "Thank you."

"Let me help you. Bend down so I can help."

He lowered himself to his knees so she could slip the velour on over his head. "Now pull it down in front," she said. She followed through with the action just as he and Mommy had been teaching her. "And in back." She stepped around his legs and pulled down the back side.

"Thank you, Honey. That was nice helping."

"You're welcome."

Supporting himself on the edge of the bed, Michael again stood and continued to the bathroom.

Danielle toddled after him and watched closely as he urinated into the toilet bowl. Kasia recalled what a special phenomenon the toilet was to their child. "It makes bubbles," said Danielle.

"Mm-mm, it makes bubbles."

"What's that?"

"That's Daddy's penis. That's how I go to the bathroom."

"Why don't I have one?"

"You and Mommy have vaginas. Daddy has a penis."

Danielle held her belly button. "I have one too."

Kasia smothered her laughter in her pillow.

"Are you done?" asked the little girl.

"Yes."

"I'll flush it." Danielle shuffled around behind him to reach the handle on the toilet tank and pulled it down. "There it goes," she said with accomplishment and delight as she watched the water swirl down and disappear with a gulp and a gurgle. Then she turned to him. "It's my turn to go potty." She pushed down her pajama bottoms. Michael lifted her up onto the toilet seat.

"Do you hear the tinkle?"

"I hear the tinkle." He handed her a folded pad of toilet paper with which to wipe herself. "All done." She dropped it into the toilet bowl. "I'll flush." She squirmed about and pulled down the handle. "Okay, now let's dance."

He picked her up and held her so that she rode easily on his left hip, her favorite and most comfortable position to be carried. She planted her sturdy little arms around his neck and rested her head on his shoulder. "Let's go dance."

Michael glanced over at Kasia, who beamed a sleepy happy smile at him. "We're going to dance."

"Hi, Punkin," Kasia waved. "Have fun."

Danielle lifted her head to gaze down at her Mommy. "Hi, Mom."

"Did you have a nice sleep?"

"I had a nice sleep."

"And you stayed in your bed all night. That was very good."

Lately, their daughter had been leaving her room and tumbling into bed with them at two and three o'clock in the morning, which frequently wreaked havoc on their own rest.

"Get Pooh Bear," commanded the little girl, whose yellow, blue-shirted bear had fallen to the floor.

In stooping to retrieve Danielle's favorite stuffed animal, Michael had to disentangle one hand from Kasia's pink floral designed slip that their daughter continually wore around her neck. Where most other two year olds carried a security blanket, Danielle had adopted a security slip from which she refused to be separated, except when she took a bath.

He carried her out into the hall and down the stairs to the family room. Standing before the Sansui turntable, he asked, "Which record do you want?"

Ever since she had been fourteen months old, Danielle had selected the records she wanted to play. At first, her selections had been on the basis of recognizing the record label by color and graphic design. Her language development had come surprisingly fast and now, at the age of two, she possessed the ability to express herself and understand at a five to six-year-old level.

Her imagination was also unusually advanced, with considerable encouragement through reading and music, play and interaction with Kasia and Michael and Danielle's sitter, Mildred, who stayed with her during the week.

The child assumed the characters of Peter Pan, Tinkerbell, and the Billy goats from the Three Billy Goats Gruff. Michael moved in and out of the roles of Captain Hook, the troll under the bridge, and Farmer Brown, a fictitious character he had created for one of her bedtime songs, bedtime being a long struggle before surrendering to sleep. Michael had composed a refrain to which he could attach innumerable verses.

Hey, hey, Farmer Brown
When you comin' back from town
Hey, hey Farmer Brown
Bring some oats and hay

Danielle would always say, "Sing about the little girl."

He would create verses that told of her day's activities relative to Farmer Brown, his farm, his cows, and buying milk from a local drive-in dairy several blocks from their home.

"I want Peter Pan," she said.

"Okay, Peter Pan it is." He put on the Disney record album, pressed the amplifier button to turn on the power and placed the needle on the spinning glossy black disc. Holding her in his arms, they danced around the living room to *You Can Fly* and *Following The Leader* and *Indians and Pirates*.

At the conclusion of certain songs, she said, "Again," with a warm glow in her voice. "I want that again," and he would replay the track.

When the record ended, he said, "Let's have some breakfast."

"No," she said, "I don't want breakfast. Let's dance some more. I just want to dance." She tugged at him to return to the record.

"Well, I need some for energy. How about some orange juice?"

"Okay."

He took a pitcher from the refrigerator and poured a small glass, which they shared.

"I'm going to make some coffee." He started to lower her to the kitchen floor, but she resisted and clung to him.

"Don't put me down. Don't put me down. I hold you, Daddy. I hold you."

"I'll hold you again, but I need two hands to fix the coffee."

"Don't make coffee."

"Oh, I need a little to wake me up."

He eventually managed to brew the coffee without putting her down. They then shared a container of raspberry yogurt, a banana, and an English muffin spread with orange marmalade.

"Let's get your mom up," he said. "Then we'll get dressed and go for a walk."

"Let's go for a walk," her voice rose with enthusiasm.

"We have to get dressed first. Let's go in and see Mom."

They returned to the bedroom where he gently dumped her onto the king size bed with Kasia.

"Get up, Mommy, get up." Danielle gave her a hug and rubbed noses. "Let's read a story."

"Bring a book and I'll read you a story. Did you have some breakfast with Daddy?"

"I ate some breakfast with Daddy."   She trotted off down the hall to her room.

"She drank some orange juice, ate some yogurt and part of a muffin with me," Michael's voice reached her from the bathroom where he was rinsing his face. "We're going for a walk as soon as we get ready."

"She should eat something more when you get back."

"Boil her an egg."

Danielle's finickiness and resistance to eating as a means of gaining their attention continually aggravated them out of concern that she wasn't getting adequate nutrition. Mildred, their sitter, claimed not to have such a problem.

Danielle returned with a children's picture book of *The Three Little Pigs* and climbed back up onto the bed to read it with Kasia. The child narrated nearly the entire story by completing the lines under each scene. She provided the wolf's "huffs and puffs" and "Little pig, little pig, let me come in. Not by the hair on my chinny chin chin."

She always described the picture where "the wolf lost his pants" from huffing and puffing too hard when he was unable to blow down the house made of bricks.

After he had finished dressing and put on his "walking shoes," Michael carried Danielle back to her bedroom to change her diaper panties and get her dressed. She stood on her bed and, as he bent over, held him around the neck to maintain her balance while he maneuvered her feet and legs into her bright yellow pants. Then they sat in a heap on the floor with the little girl leaning back against his chest while he fumbled on her socks and shoes.

He buttoned a yellow sweater on her and arranged a yellow knit ski cap over her tousled blonde curls and pronounced, "All set."

"All set." She extended her arms for him to pick her up. "Let's go for a walk."

As he lifted her, she looked back down at the bed. "I want to bring that boon," she referred to a deflated red balloon that she had habitually carried along with her Charley Dog and Pooh Bear.

She had a balloon fetish. A few dozen inflated balloons hovered just above the floor throughout the house. Danielle would poke one or two up at Michael and say, "Blow dis one. Blow dis one." In addition, he had to keep one of the kitchen cupboards stockpiled with plastic packages of "fresh ones."

"I'll tell you what," he said gently, "let's leave that one here because it will fall in the dirt at the playground and get all dirty."

"Okay, I want to take my sip though. I want to take my sip." She had not yet developed her 'L's' and consequently slip came out sip and lamb came out namb.

Wearing her robe and furry blue slippers, Kasia looked in at the bedroom door just as Michael and Danielle were about to leave.

Danielle pointed to the bed. "Get my Pooh Bear. Mommy, go to the kitchen. You stay home." She had established the walk routine as a special private time and activity exclusive to her and her Daddy. Mommy was not allowed to accompany them on their walks and Kasia respected this convention.

"Bye-bye, Mommy. Bye-bye."

"Bye-bye. You and Daddy have a good time."

"Bye-bye, bye-bye, bye-bye."

Carrying her, Michael set out at a brisk comfortable pace up the street in the direction of the local elementary school, which they visited daily on their walks. Enroute, they commented on things they saw, the colors of cars parked in neighboring driveways, cats crouched on front porch stoops, a jet plane passing high overhead, large decorative stones bordering a front terrace, birds sitting on telephone wires, decorative rose plants and blooming shrubs, older children racing down the street on bicycles.

They reached the school in ten minutes and Danielle announced, "Der's da school grounds."

Several girls soccer teams were warming up prior to their weekend match. Michael and Danielle walked around the playing field and across a black-topped area to a log climbing platform with a metal slide. He lifted her onto the slide with her armload of Charley Dog and Pooh Bear and caught her as she arrived at the bottom. Then they went into the "house" created by the structure and sat on one of the logs.

Before long, Danielle, ran over to the steps and walkway that paralleled one of the outlying classroom buildings. She derived great enjoyment from the simple act of going up and down the steps. Finally, she invited Michael with her inevitable, "Let's play hide and seek, Daddy. Let's play hide and seek."

"Okay, you count to ten and I'll hide." He dodged around the side of the building while she counted, peeking all the while through her fingers so as not to lose track of where he had gone. When she reached, "fourteen, fifteen, eleventeen," she called out, "Here I come, ready or not," and quickly discovered him hugging the wall just around the corner.

He asked, "Shall we get a drink at the drinking fountain?"

"Let's get a drink." She led the way on the run. He pushed the button to release an arc of cold clear water into which she thrust her mouth. Then looking up, she said, "You drink too, Daddy," to which he complied.

They migrated across the grass over to the jungle gyms and he supported her in climbing up on the first rung of a ladder. Then they ran to a tennis backboard they had dubbed "Mary Poppins' wall."

She stood on one side and he on the other and each knocked on their side of the wall. Michael crept around to sneak up on her and they played cat and mouse going from one end of the wall to the other.

Danielle suddenly grabbed her cap from her head and handed it to him. "You wear it."

"Oh, okay, all right." He perched the undersized yellow cap on his head and continued to follow her about. After another twenty minutes, he stuck the cap in the pocket of his tan brushed denim jeans and suggested it was time to head on back home.

"Where's your hat?" she demanded.

"In my pocket."

"Wear it. Put it on your head."

He recapped his head, picked up Danielle and set off across the playground to the gate with her kicking and fussing. "No, no, no."

"Yes, yes, yes, it's time to walk back."

"Let me walk. I want to walk."

"How about a horsey ride?"

"I don't want a horsey ride. I just want to walk."

Michael went along with her meandering stall tactic, set her astride his broad shoulders when they reached the gate and crossed the street. They stopped at pine trees growing at evenly spaced intervals along the sidewalk. These they called the tickly trees, by nature of the long tickly pine needle fingers that brushed them as they passed underneath the lower branches.

Upon reaching their house, he put her down in the front yard and they raced to the door. She doubled up her tiny fist and knocked. "Here we are. Open the door. Trick or treat."

A few moments later, Kasia admitted them. "There you are. Did you have a nice walk?"

"We sure did," Michael answered, despite the question being directed to Danielle.

"Did you have a good time?"

"We sure did," said Danielle. "I need some boons. I need some fresh boons. I need some boons. Boons boons boons."

"Give her some fresh boons," said Michael.

Kasia took a package from the cupboard and handed it to Danielle who carried it into the living room and promptly scattered the contents on the floor.

"Hi," Michael gave Kasia a quick light kiss. "Did you have breakfast yet?"

"Yes."

"Let's get something more for her to eat."

"Let's dance, Daddy." Danielle called to him from the living room. "Come on and dance."

"Okay. Make a soft-boiled egg. Two minutes, and some cottage cheese and apple sauce." Michael left Kasia with the preparation and went to dance with his daughter.

***

Kasia heard a noise overhead, someone walking across the kitchen floor, then a thump as a heavy object was dropped. The light and feelings of warmth and love, the escape into memories of her husband and child vanished. She was once again in the cold dark cellar, a prisoner.

Because of the incessant darkness, she had been sleeping a great deal more than usual. A desperate need to see something pushed at the back of her eyes, but she had only her imagination to draw on, her background training and experience as an actress and mime artist. She imagined she was a hibernating bear and allowed the sluggish sensation of lethargy to seep through her flesh and bones. She would sleep on through the cold and dark and her body would feed off the accumulated fat of luxurious living.

The more she thought about the image, she was just like a she bear .   .   . a trapped bear who hears her cub in trouble, being threatened not too far away. Given the first opportunity, she would go berserk and kill and maim to protect her cub. She would ravage her tormentors and tear out their hearts and entrails with her claws and teeth. She would crunch their skulls in her jaws and they would never again be a threat to her and to her little one. She would hang their raw bleeding hearts on a tree in the sun as a warning and a reminder to others to never tamper with her child, her cub. Ants and maggots and scavenger birds would come to feed on them.

Her mind drifted in and out of this realm of imagination, the fantasy world of vengeance. She enacted an entire film in her mind, scene by scene, line by line of the abduction, and provided a suitably satisfying ending, a goal toward which she would move in any conceivable way during her captivity.

At other times, for hours, she projected her imagination out beyond the claustrophobic darkness into the hills and fields where brilliant yellow and orange wildflowers dazzled her sight and brought her to the ground in a swoon with their intoxicating perfumed sweetness. Some of these impressions recurred to her as memories from childhood, when her parents would take her and her brother and sister out into the countryside.

Her parents had been quiet provincial people who lived by strong God-fearing ethics, a devotion to Mother Russia and her world and destiny. They owned a personal strength and sense of morality drawn from the Bible.

She had always found it difficult to reconcile her parents' reliance on traditional religious dogma.

She saw only herself changing and her parents would never change and could not. They lacked the intelligence and the emotional understanding. Their lives were too locked into an uninformed value system. That, in and of it itself, was a kind of religious enactment not unlike an Indian crop planting culture, worshipping weather gods and doing their best to live in harmony with nature.

Her personal drive and ambition had always confused and sometimes angered her parents, because of the plans Mother Russia already had for her, and because they themselves had never done anything to foster or encourage such a vivid creative imagination they recognized in her.

When she had begun school, it was the stories the teacher read aloud that interested her the most. That had been her pattern and focus all through elementary and secondary school. In high school, her English teacher, Adele McLaughlin, and her ballet teacher, Antonia

Mazarek, had inevitably moved her into the world of the performing arts.

Adele McLaughlin had recognized at once the nature of Kasia's mental gifts and creative personality by the perception with which the young girl analyzed the meanings of the various stories and books assigned to the class, in addition to the unrequired copious outside reading and book reports she submitted. It seemed as if her star student were making up in quantity of literature, much of it in advance of her class level, what she had missed as a child. As a junior, Kasia was already doing the critical reading and corresponding analysis in written and verbal essays expected of a bright college sophomore.

So during Kasia's senior year, Adele assisted her in applying for and being awarded a full undergraduate scholarship to Iowa State University. Then, following her graduation from high school, Kasia had received a four year scholarship from an unknown benefactor to attend UCLA.

Kasia let her mind drift far from the absolute darkness of the dank cellar, far into her imagination and beyond to visions in which she swam in warm blue seas with porpoises or floated among soft clouds with beautiful singing birds for her companions. Then, moments of lucidity would suddenly intervene placing her exactly where she was in time and space, cognizant of the hard floor, the ropes that bound her hands and feet, the darkness again and the pervading odor of rot.

Had she risen too high as a mortal and in emulating a kind of goddess, offended the gods? Had she been playing in a hero myth that she was now, in reality, living out?

Through her studies in high school and more intensively in college, and through her various stage roles in several university productions of Greek and Roman dramas, she had come to realize that the myth of the hero, which was the most common and best known throughout the world, was not only the basis for religions and dramatic stories, it was the structure of human psychological development. Its origins provided the foundation for the classical mythology of the Greeks and

Romans, the religious ritual of the Middle Ages and the Far Eastern cultures, Christianity, as well as among the societies of primitive tribes.

The hero myths varied, but all were similar in their structure. Although Kasia had not had a miraculous birth, hers was at least a recognizably humble one.

The mythological hero's struggle with the forces of evil and his sin of pride culminated with his death through heroic sacrifice. Kasia had no desire or impulse to become a hero or martyr or sacrifice herself for the sake of a celluloid market that fed the fantasies of millions of men and women. But in spite of herself, she had become a godlike figure, a modern goddess who was, in fact, a symbolic representation of a collective cultural psyche. She projected in heroic mythical proportion what people, especially women, lacked in terms of their own ego, their sense of self-actualization.

In mythology, the death of the hero ended a cycle out of which rebirth, growth and change occurred in both a ritualistic and religious sense. For real people, the hero's symbolic death became the realization and achievement of personal maturity. This facet of development was the movement from one age or point in a life to the next, a passage.

Kasia had become a creature of the dark who relied on her senses of hearing and smell and touch to read her enclosed world. She clocked each day by the morning and the evening visits from one of her captors who brought her food and water and untied her feet so that she could squat over the metal bucket they provided for her to relieve herself while they blinded her with light.

Always they destroyed her vision by aiming the strong lantern beam directly at her eyes, causing her to close them from the physical shock and stabbing pain of stark sudden illumination. They never said anything to her and they would not verbally respond to her questions or requests on the chance she would recognize them by their voices. She always asked them to please bring her child.

The door swung open and someone came slowly down the wooden stairs. The light was not beamed directly at her as usual, but at the floor. She realized through her senses that it was a man, as the light glanced off his naked chest. His bare feet slapped toward her across the concrete floor.

"Stull." Her voice stopped him momentarily, breaking his former confidence in his anonymity.

"Have you asked them for the money?" She waited, but received no answer and realized he must be dealing with the fact that she had identified him and would probably know of Randy and Lynn. She had made a mistake and should not have revealed her suspicion. She fought to control her rising panic, as he removed his black hood, to reveal his macabre underlit features. Then he turned away and went back up the stairs.

The sudden coolness of a damp washcloth against her hot face startled Kasia. A small flashlight with a substantially weaker beam than Stull's lantern shone in Lynn's hand. She gently cleaned Kasia's face.

"Lynn, thank you. How is my daughter? Are you taking care of her? Is she getting enough food and milk?"

"She's afraid and lonely. She cries for you and her daddy. I bring food to her, but she doesn't eat well."

"Do you talk to her? Are you kind to her?"

"Yes, I am kind to her."

"Will you bring her to me after the others are asleep?"

"If Stull catches me doing that, he will torture me. He might even kill me. He's insane. I don't know."

"Have they demanded a ransom yet? Do you know? Has any money been paid?"

"I don't know what they're doing. They don't include me. I am no longer one of them. I follow the path of the Lord."

"Lynn, please, will you help us? You say you follow the path of the Lord. In the name of God, will you please help us? I'll see to it that nothing happens to you, and my husband and I will take care of you. You will be granted immunity from prosecution. We will protect you. I promise."

"The Lord is my shepherd."

"Lynn, are you with me? Do you understand what I'm saying? This is your chance to break away from those two forever."

"My life is in His hands, for I follow the path of righteousness." Lynn rose, and taking her flashlight, walked back up the stairs.

"You're insane," said Kasia. "All of you, crazy, psychotic." Sobs ballooned out of her until, finally, her energy spent, exhaustion carried her mercifully again into the escape of sleep.

When Randy returned, the sound of the van entering the yard woke Stull, but he did not bother to rise from his sleeping bag on the floor of the front room to offer any assistance.

Randy guessed that Stull would wake at the noise, but that he just wouldn't be bothered. What was happening in the news media was too important to let wait until morning. He stepped noisily through the front door.

"Stull, you awake?"

"If I wasn't, I am now."

"They already paid off someone else."

"What the fuck are you talkin' about?"

"The ransom money – look at this." Randy held the newspaper down low in front of the light. "Crazies are comin' out of the woodwork tryin' to cash in. Half the ransom, one million, was paid to someone else. Now when it comes time we ask for the bread, we've gonna have to prove we've got 'em alive and well."

"Shit, what are you worried about? Use your fuckin' head. That'll be easy enough. I'll have the bitch write and sign the ransom note herself. Her old man can identify her handwriting. Hell, the cops'll do everything to test it short of wiping their ass with it. It's nothin' to worry about. It's to be expected. You bring any cold beer or just in the cases?"

"Yeah, I grabbed a cold pack."

"Bring me in a couple, will ya? You sure nobody followed you back here?"

"I was real careful. I didn't see anybody tail me."

"What about at the store? Do you think anyone recognized the van. It was described in the news."

"No one recognized the van. Just don't ask me to go to the damn store again. It's too risky."

"What? Why not?" Stull sat up. "Something happened, didn't it? What happened?"

"Nothing happened. I was just nervous. That's all. I felt like everybody was watching me and they were gonna call the cops. Next time, you go." Randy straightened from his kneeling position and went back outside to carry in the groceries. The realization that the dream of his future might slip away bothered him, given Stull's casualness and lack of concern about the matter of the ransom. That was to be his freedom money. What the hell was Stull thinking?

Someone shaking her arm woke Kasia. Fearing that Stull had returned, she reflexively kept her face turned away to avoid the direct light. She had grown accustomed to and now preferred the darkness. She did not know how much more physical abuse she could endure. The sensation of her wrists being freed shocked her. She realized the shaking motion had come from another pair of hands untying and tugging at the rope.

The next sensation that overwhelmed her was her sleeping child being thrust into her arms. A few minutes later, the rope binding her ankles was pulled clear.

Lynn assisted her to a standing position while holding Danielle, who sleepily murmured, "Mommy, Mommy."

Lynn slowly guided them across the dark floor and with caution up the creaking stairs. Avoiding the sleeping forms of Stull and Randy on the living room floor, they escaped out the back way through the kitchen door, taking great care not to let it fall shut behind them.

Although Kasia tried, her muscles were still far too stiff and cramped to flex and move allowing her to run. Lynn continued to support her, forcing her along at a fast, excruciating walk. Kasia suppressed the cry of pain in her throat and willed herself to endure the spasms coursing up and down her legs like electric currents.

Lynn did not use the light. They crossed a wide expanse of open space between the house and the nearest cover of dense chaparral brush and a few oak trees and boulders near the creek bank.

She intended for them to drop down into the dry creek bed, follow it for a mile or more, then climb the hills on the opposite side to return to the highway by some other cross country route than the fire road. They would hide out and wait until the following night to even approach the highway, knowing that Stull and Randy would be combing the surrounding hills in search of them.

They heard a shout back at the house. Lynn's quick glance saw the lantern torch light bobbing erratically past the kitchen window. Stull had risen to go out and relieve himself from the impact of drinking five beers before falling asleep. Discovering the cellar door ajar, he had shined the powerful lantern down the steps and the breadth of its beam showed him that Kasia had escaped.

Believing she would not have gone without her child, he doubly panicked. He snatched a paring knife form the kitchen counter, shouted to Randy to wake up and follow him. "She's gone! She and the kid are gone!"

Aroused by the shouting, Randy staggered up out of his sleeping bag and stumbled after him.

The rapid sweep of Stull's lantern caught the brief shadowed movement of the two women as they dropped over the edge of the creek bed one hundred yards away.

"Lynn's with 'em! The bitch let 'em go!" Stull sprinted madly, lifting his naked legs and feet high, pumping. He cursed as he bruised his right instep on a sharp stone.

Scrambling down the ledge onto the gravel and coarse sand of the dry creek bed, Stull paused to listen in what direction the women and child had gone, but he could hear nothing over his coughing, labored breathing and the blood pounding in his head. Moments later, Randy came sliding down the embankment behind him, dislodging small rocks and pebbles that spat hard against Stull's legs and feet causing him to jump away with a sharp curse.

"Which way?" asked Randy.

"I don't know. I can't hear 'em. Shut up!"

"Why don't you try one way and I'll go the other." Randy set off to the right with his lantern beam angled downward a few feet ahead in search of footprints. Stull took the left, almost immediately located two sets of impressions for a brief stretch of soft sand and whistled back to Randy, who came running from the opposite direction.

Three hundred yards down the creek bed, Lynn and Kasia heard Stull shouting. "We know where you are! We're comin' after you! We're gonna get you!"

"We can't move fast enough," Kasia gasped. "We've got to climb up out of here and hide."

"The sides are too steep here," said Lynn. "We can't climb yet. Keep going."

They ran on, stumbling over granite rocks and boulders they could not see bruising and tearing at their feet. Lynn did not dare turn on her light and give away their position.

Kasia's arms ached with Danielle's leaden weight. She would soon have to stop and rest before she dropped her child, but fear locked her muscles in their supporting cradle as Danielle's head bobbed against her left shoulder. Kasia was surprised that her little girl did not protest other than an occasional grunt from the shared impact of a hard step.

Instead of becoming lower, the side of the creek bank grew steadily higher as a rocky cliff rose from the stream bed narrowing through a long cut between two bluffs. Kasia could see the ledges towering above them against the night sky.

"Lynn, it's getting worse. We must find a place to hide."

"Not here. Not here," Lynn's gasping words hissed back. "If we stop now, they'll catch up to us. Keep going. Keep going."

They knew that Stull and Randy would be gaining since they were using their lanterns and were not hampered by the weight of a child.

After another quarter mile, the high walls abruptly dropped to a flat. They crawled and scrambled their way up through the slippery rocks, smoothed by years of rushing flood waters during the California rainy season.

By now, even Lynn had to stop. She pushed off into the brush praying she would not step on a rattlesnake. With the thorny branches whipping back into her face and dragging at her clothes, Kasia tried to protect Danielle's head and arms. She followed closely so as not to lose track of Lynn, who finally stopped.

Danielle whimpered at the pain caused by a spikey thorn that had broken off in the cloth of her dress and was pricking her thigh.

"Hush, dear, hush, shhh," Kasia caressed the child's forehead, pushing back her hair. "It's Mommy. It's okay now. Mommy's with you. It's okay."

"Mommy, something hurts me. Something's biting me."

"Shhh, please don't make any noise."

They heard Stull and Randy shouting at each other somewhere off behind them as they made a sweep of the area where she and Lynn had left the creek bed.

Kasia lowered Danielle to the ground and collapsed near Lynn among the enclosure of boulders she had selected to go to earth. They felt like foxes being hunted by dogs who were closing in on the scent with cries of excitement and confusion. Then suddenly their voices were silent.

Kasia wondered if they had discovered at what point she and Lynn had changed direction. Their fears were confirmed by the sporadic beam of Stull's and Randy's lights probing the nearly impenetrable brush like lethal eyes. Stull and Randy swore loudly as they encountered the thorny branches.

"Shit, they couldn't have gone in there. You can't even get through this shit. Look for tracks, god damn it. Look for tracks," Stull's voice rose to a manic pitch.

"The ground's too hard here. There's rocks all over the place. There aren't any fuckin' tracks."

Then Stull's lantern picked out a ribbon of cloth torn from Kasia's dress as she had plunged through the brush. "Wait. Here, look. Jesus fuckin' Christ, they did go in there."

Flinching and writhing against the pricking maze of brush, Stull wormed his way through with Randy reluctantly following. "Shit, they could be out the other side by now."

"Shut the fuck up and keep looking."

"Look where? There's nothin' to look for."

"Shut up. They're in here somewhere. I can feel it. They couldn't go through here any faster than we are. Stop. Listen." They heard nothing. Stull had hoped to catch the sound of their progress as they pushed along. "They've stopped," Stull now spoke quietly. "They're hiding somewhere around in here."

A small sharp cry away to the right was immediately cut off as though silenced by a hand. Stull and Randy moved unswervingly in the direction of the sound until they came to the cluster of boulders. Their lantern beams fished around the outer edge and corners of the enclosure. Then Lynn panicked and leaped and scrambled away like a spooked bear.

With a triumphant cry, Stull and Randy closed in. Stull leaped around blocking Kasia. The flash of the lantern beam stopped her cold. Sheltering Danielle, she lunged sideways and fell to her knees. Randy went after Lynn. After a brief grunting chase, he caught her and threw her to the ground by grabbing her hair and bulldogging her down twisting her neck. "I've got her," he called back.

"Hold her there," Stull's icy voice cut through the darkness, alien tone that seemed to come from the eye of his lantern. "We've got them now. These two aren't going anywhere."

Stull came over to Lynn and nudged Randy out of the way with his bloodied bare foot. Putting his lantern down, he grabbed Lynn by the hair and tipped her head back to expose her throat. A high-pitched scream like a rabbit flew from her as she saw the blade. The knife bit deep just under her left ear and slashed across. An explosion of blood ripped clear to her right ear and her scream drowned in a choking gurgle.

Stooped over her like a savage, he quickly returned to Kasia and her child. Randy joined him aiming the lantern in a pool of light over their victims. Stull jerked Kasia's head back by the hair in the same manner he had Lynn, exposing her throat while he held the blood-dripping knife before her eyes.

"Take the fuckin' kid."

Randy pulled the screaming child away from Kasia.

"Hold the fuckin' brat. Hold her," Stull ordered. "Hold her real steady. All right, bitch," he said to Kasia. "I want you to see this."

Kasia watched with a soul disintegrating scream of horror as Stull made a slow shallow cut from the outside corner of Danielle's right eye to her lip. A skein of blood trickled across her cheek and from the neck down. The child thrashed and squirmed as her body became the scream. Then she fainted from shock, pain, and terror. Her child's scream became her own as Kasia erupted upward from the ground. Stull tripped her and shouted, don't run out on us again." He tried to control his sudden choking fit. "You do, bitch, and I'll shoot your fuckin' kid full of dope. You got that, cunt?"

Hot tears washed down, coursing in dirty rivulets through the grit on her face. She wished that the blood of her child was her own and that Stull had cut her instead. "Just let her stay with me. Please, let her stay with me."

"Not on your fuckin' life. You're not gonna see her again 'til this is all over, if you're lucky."

"Then do something. Ask for the money."

"Somebody else already did and got paid off," said Randy.

"On your feet," ordered Stull. "Super bitch." Stull pulled her up by her hair. "Next time, I'll slit you and your kid from your cunt to your eyeballs."

"Let me take care of her face. At least let me take care of her face."

"How about I take her head off at the neck and then you can look after that?"

"Randy," Kasia appealed to him. "Please, we're human. She's only a small child."

After they returned to the house an hour later, Kasia called out to Danielle, "I love you, sweetheart. I'll be with you soon."

Danielle was again locked alone in a room upstairs. Unknown to Stull, Randy cleaned the little girl's wound.

Kasia lay tied hand and foot on her mat in the pitch-dark cellar.

CHAPTER TWENTY-NINE

The Separation

The warm glow of the late afternoon sunbathed Stull as he dozed on his sleeping bag outside the house in the front yard. The distant buzz of small motors startled him awake.

His first impression was that someone was cutting firewood somewhere using power chainsaws. As the sound approached nearer and nearer, he recognized what it was – dirt bikes, like the buzz of angry wasps amplified hundreds of times.

Although they were still out of sight, they were coming along at a rapid clip following the dirt road in the direction of the house. Stull cursed himself that he had not done a better job of hiding the van which hugged one side of the old dwelling. Anyone who passed on the fire road would easily be able to spot it.

Not wanting to be seen, he leaped up with the sleeping bag bundled in his arms and ran inside. He waited at a front window, watching the curve that nearly encircled the base of the hill a half mile down the winding dirt road.

Moments later, the riders appeared at the top, resting their sputtering bikes. They looked with surprise down at the house and the serpentine valley formed by the dry creek channel. Stull saw one of them point in the direction of the house. He wasn't certain they could see the van from their high angle. The hill rose considerably above the house by about one hundred feet, but was still too distant for a clear view. Suddenly, to his dismay, the riders started coming down the near side of the hill straight toward the house.

Stull kept well out of sight behind the edge of the window and motioned to Randy, who entered from the kitchen at the sound of the dirt bikes.

"Stay low," Stull warned. "Don't let them see you through the window."

The bikes bucked and careened down the slope. When they reached the bottom, the lead rider roared out ahead of his partner kicking up dust and gravel.

They swung past the house in a quick arc. Stull saw the helmeted head of the leader snap a sidewise glance at the van. The bikers stopped fifty yards up the road. Straddling their bikes in tandem, they lifted their dust-coated visors so they could more clearly discern everything, the van and surrounding area while they conferred. Then, revving up, they shot past at top speed back down the road in the direction from which they had come, but without making the climb over the hill.

Stull could not know if they had recognized the van or not from descriptions in the media, but from the behavior of the two bikers, he sensed that they at least suspected the place was a hideout. He turned and shouted to Randy.

"Get the fuckin' kid! I'll get her. We gotta get the fuck outta here now! Grab whatever you can carry!"

Clutching the black hood, he rushed down into the cellar. Randy floundered erratically up the stairs to the second-floor bedroom where Danielle was locked in.

Kasia recoiled as Stull came leaping down the cellar stairs brandishing a lantern in one hand and the fearsome black hood in the other. For her, being hooded was the ritual step taken before an execution.

Without a word, he pulled her up into a sitting position, then plunged the hood down hard over her head and with a savage twist tightened the drawstring around her neck.

"On your feet, bitch!" He heaved her up by one arm, then bent to untie the rope around her ankles so she could walk.

He herded her up the stairs and out to the van. She heard him roll back the side panel. Danielle's thin reedy cry came from inside. "Mommy, Mommy."

Kasia tumbled in on her knees and with bound outstretched hands, sought her trembling child who clutched her with her hands, arms, body, bare legs, and feet.

"Baby, Baby, Baby, can you hear me, Baby," Kasia choked on her own tears. "Hold on to Mommy. Just hold on to Mommy," she shouted through the muffling hood. She slipped her arms over Danielle's head so that they encircled her and rested her hooded face against the exposed nape of her vulnerable neck. Even through the cloth of the mask, she could sense and feel the small vertebrae.

They fell to the side with a sudden lurch as the van got underway.

Danielle buried her face in her Mommy's shoulder and was oblivious to the bump. Within moments, she fell asleep, escaping into the security she thought had been torn from her forever.

Kasia leaned back against the side panel and hummed a low barely intelligible chant to Danielle, protecting her as the van bounced violently from time to time along the dirt road leading the ten miles out to the highway. Her humming blended with the smooth humming of the tires. She forced herself not to succumb to the hypnotic motion of moving evenly and quickly through dark space, a sensation that prompted an occasional bout of queasiness anytime the van swerved or made a sudden turn.

She focused on the reality of holding her child, the feeling of her small pulsing weight against her own exhausted stinking body, the ammoniac odor of urine rising from Danielle's unwashed underpants.

Having been confined in darkness for so long, and now hurtling through darkness, but experiencing no awareness of either direction or progress, she discovered it was becoming increasingly difficult to determine the crossover between her conscious and unconscious mind. She believed she might be losing her sanity. For the moment, only her daughter in her arms kept her in that present reality.

Stull watched his speed so as not to draw attention to the van. He drove conservatively in the stream of freeway traffic headed south from Westlake and Calabasas into the San Fernando Valley. Although his inclination was to push hard, change lanes, and weave in and out among cars that were moving too slowly to suit him, in order to gain time and distance, he did not dare risk notice by the two California Highway Patrol units he saw one lane over as he checked his rearview mirror.

At the complex intersect of the San Diego and Ventura Freeways, he followed the loop bringing him around headed north in the direction of Bakersfield in California's Central Valley.

Forty minutes later, the van's engine started pulling hard making the long slow climb up the grapevine highway. Its green form gained momentum rushing downhill on the other side into a valley, then a slight swinging turn carried it off to the right on a narrow highway leading into the high desert, a desolation of exposed rough granite faults encrusted with scrubby cacti like faded green barnacles barely camouflaged the evidence of violent upheavals by ancient earthquakes.

Stull eventually pulled off onto a side road and once again Kasia experienced the sensation of being bounced and jolted over rocks and washouts.

When they were well out of sight and sound of the main road, Stull slowed and stopped the van in a hidden barren rock canyon. Randy watched him take a spoon, catheter, matches, and a packet of heroine from a metal container.

"Hold the kid," Stull ordered. "I'll take care of the bitch alone."

These were the last words Kasia heard before she felt her child being forcibly plucked away from her. Danielle woke and her pitiful cries wailed and echoed from the canyon walls like a desert creature, then were silenced by the sliding thump of the van door severing the sound and separating mother and daughter again.

Kasia sensed from the hot dry air that they were somewhere in the desert. Stull's hand shoved her high at the center of her back. She stumbled forward unable to see and wondered if she would ever see again. She smelled approaching death in the surrounding silence.

After they had walked for about one hundred yards from the van, Stull ordered her to lie down. She stiffly obeyed, dropping awkwardly to her knees and then sprawled on her side, feeling the rough gravel and sand pressing into her skin. She raised her head slightly, tense, listening for Stull, trying to interpret what his next move would be.

She heard the strike of a match, then another, then two more filling the air with sulfurous fumes. Stull suddenly grabbed her right arm. She felt the pinching constricting squeeze of the rubber catheter followed by the jabbing pin – prick of a dull hypodermic needle that made her draw back with a sharp cry. The needle was pulled out simultaneously as the catheter was released and an icy burning sensation traveled rapidly up her arm to her chest. An explosion inside her heart sent her flipping and writhing over the ground into an endless darkness.

When she finally lay quiet, Stull removed the hood exposing Kasia's face to the sun, turned away and walked back to the van.

Kasia existed in a deep coma of blackness without sensation, a bare impulse away from crossing over the invisible line forever. She did not hear the van pull away. She did not smell nor see nor feel life either within or outside her body. She was and she was not.

***

Returning to the freeway, Stull drove north, making a brief stop in Bakersfield for gas, then again in Fresno as he, Randy and the sleeping child, trembling and clutching for her absent mother, continued up through the Central Valley of California.

Shortly after leaving Fresno behind, Stull followed a directional sign that placed them on a two lane highway leading into the foothills of the

Sierra Nevada Mountain Range rising in significant purple peaks and untouchable granite spires separating California from the state of Nevada.

Snaking up a narrow road through rock outcroppings and pine forests, Stull finally settled on a turnout and parked near a rushing mountain stream. He ensured they could not be detected from the road by making a quick hike back to it to check visibility.

Randy had automatically assumed responsibility for the child, washing her clothes in the mountain stream, seeing to it that she ate the food he offered her and that she drank her milk. After several days, he sensed an attachment for her welling up from somewhere deep inside. He tried to cap and sublimate the emotion, but it persisted and finally he allowed the expression to come through.

He intended to fully care for her and protect her, since Stull had no feeling for or about her, other than as an object to be ransomed.

Danielle responded to Randy's kindness, trusting him because she had no one else to whom she could turn and sensed Randy's affinity for her even without the expression of words. He played games with her, even got her to smile. He held her and took her for walks along the creek bank and into the piney woods and told her stories. He didn't have any books with interesting and colorful pictures, but he drew sketches on notebook paper and shared objects with her like magic pinecones.

He detected something growing in him in the way of a genuine tenderness and affection that he had never experienced in his life, at least as far back as he could remember. The emotion seemed to bubble up as if from a quiet dark spring. Walking with Danielle high in the mountains removed from the depression of an urban environment, he became acquainted with another aspect of himself as a person among the scent of wildflowers and a primeval forest.

Pity and remorse flooded him whenever he stared at the child's healing diagonal scar across the entire left side of her small face. She asked him from time to time when she would be going home to her mommy and daddy. He always told her, soon.

Perceptive now of her position, she sensed that her well-being lay in the hands of this young man. She told him that she thought he was a nice man to take care of her. The unexpected words and her vulnerable innocence made him cry. He seriously questioned following through on the ransom with Stull, but he was already too deeply committed. Even should he cut and run and turn himself in with the little girl, it was not likely he would be granted immunity from prosecution. He now had to exercise caution in order not to convey his change of heart to Stull. If Stull suspected anything at all, he would kill them both without hesitation.

At night, Randy slept in the van with the child to comfort her while Stull chose to sleep away from them out on the ground next to the hot coals remaining from the supper fire. The soft curly head nestled against him nearly undid Randy and he again considered deserting Stull. He vowed to return Danielle without any further harm coming to her. He regretted that he had not intervened to prevent Stull from murdering Kasia. No longer trusting Stull, he slept guardedly, with a knife under his pillow.

As the moon rose bathing the desert a ghostly pale, Winston Mallory noted the buildup of the coyote howls, their yipping and wailing increasing in intensity. They were either on the trail of a jackrabbit or else something dead or dying was drawing them in.

He washed down the last bite of his chicken stew and homemade bread with a swallow of bitter black coffee laced with bourbon, then rose and carried his dishes and utensils to the second hand aluminum sink he had salvaged from a dump.

The range and volume of the coyote chorus intrigued him and he paused again to listen as a deep growl rumbled up from his dog's throat.

Living for many years alone on the desert, his perception of the sounds and silences were more acute than someone just coming out from the city. He read and understood the language of the desert creatures, could interpret their thoughts and intentions by the way they moved.

He had just returned late that day from visiting his aged mother over the Grapevine in the San Fernando Valley and spending a night on the town with two young women friends upon whom he had lavished food, wine, and entertainment and expensive gifts.

Other than this ritual monthly foray, he made an occasional stop at a tavern in Blythe, fifteen miles away, where he was known as something of a local character.

Twelve years ago when he had worked as a civil engineer at Edwards Air Force Base, he had occasionally frequented the tavern during off hours. The desert had drawn him out on weekends. He would drive his pickup truck deep into its vastness and then hike alone for miles exploring the canyons.

He had begun to build a hermitage for himself, an island of solace hidden away behind a meandering maze of boulders up a blind canyon at the source of a natural spring. He had constructed it of surrounding materials and had brought in furnishings to transform his rock cave into a dwelling.

Following his retirement over the years, he continued to add on sections, constructing tunnels and walls until he had a network of covered paths and runs similar to an underground mine. The enormous main living area occupied two thousand square feet, a cavern which housed an array of metal sculptures he had created.

The single antenna that poked high above the roof and connected to a strange metallic network on the rocky ridge above was the sole indicator of human habitation. Although he isolated himself from the world, Mallory enjoyed communicating with other ham radio operators. He tuned in on radio waves and frequencies that carried information privy to only a select few.

He could hear the coyotes now down near the mouth of the canyon. Their nervous yapping and howling sounded to have tripled in number, a considerable hunting pack. His curiosity fully aroused, he grabbed a flashlight and, accompanied by his black Labrador retriever, jogged along one of the winding corridors leading to the outside world.

His snarling dog heaved and strained at the leash wanting to get at the coyotes. Mallory held him in tight. The coyotes would tear the domestic animal apart, given the chance, and devour him while Mallory watched.

The man's presence, the flashlight, and a few well-aimed sharp stones sent the pack "Ki-Yi-ing" off a short distance where they barked and growled antagonizing the lab. A few gave up on the promising scent and went loping back down the canyon out onto the open desert flats.

The moonlight painted deceptive shapes and shadows and distorted actual distance. At first, Mallory could not see what had attracted the coyotes. Walking further along the tire tracks imprinted in the sand by his truck, he nearly stumbled over Kasia Kerenski's inert body before realizing she was lying there.

He dropped to his knees and illuminated her sun-blistered face. At first glance, he thought she was dead. His further examination detected a barely discernible pulse, and a heartbeat so faint he wondered if she could survive the shock of being moved.

He untied her wrists, lifted her over one shoulder, and carried her back to his cavern. He covered her with a blanket, then radioed for a helicopter ambulance from the nearby Air Force base. His next message went directly to the county police department.

The ringing phone routed Klein from his bed. He listened to the briefing from the headquarters communication center and a playback of the tape recorded conversation with Vincent Mallory.

His first impulse was to write off the old geezer as just another crackpot who had been out in the desert sun too long, but what he heard changed his mind. Three hours later, he was at Kasia's bedside in the emergency ward of the hospital at Edwards Air Force Base.

The attending physician informed him that Kasia was in a coma from an overdose of heroin and verged on death. Her chances for survival were seventy percent.

Klein got on the phone to Michael at his home, quickly explained the situation and told him that a police helicopter would be standing by at the Van Nuys airport to transport him to the Edwards Air Force Base hospital.

In answer to Michael's question, the man who had found Kasia had not seen any sign of a child or indication of a second body.

Michael arrived at three in the morning, listened to the doctor, saw his wife hooked up to the many tubes of a life support system, and openly wept.

CHAPTER THIRTY

The Ransom

Stull composed the ransom note on a warm dry summer afternoon two months after the abduction. The note contained specific instructions to Michael Sloan as to the amount, the denominations, the drop site, and time, and the manner of delivery.

He had thought carefully about the plan for weeks until it was foolproof in his own mind. He had it worked out so the transaction could take place right under the surveillance of the police and they would never realize the pick-up had been made.

That night, he got drunk on beer and tequila and wanted Randy to have sex with him. His former partner firmly but quietly denied him. Stull smiled at Randy cradling the little girl in sleep and warned him, "Don't fall in love with that baby cunt. In five more days, you're gonna give her up." Stull brandished the sealed envelope containing the note.

"Are you gonna tell me about it?"

"Not yet. It's too early. I might change the plan."

"All right, when?"

"After we get to San Francisco. We have to go through this carefully, rehearse it step by step at the place where it goes down."

"That complicated."

"No, it's deceptively simple, but it's taken a lot of thought and planning on my part. Disguise and smoke and mirrors are what're gonna make this mother fucker work like a charm."

"How are we going to handle her?" Randy referred to Danielle.

"I'll tell you after we get to San Francisco."

Seeing that his charge had fallen into a deep slumber, Randy carefully rose from his log seat by the campfire and carried her to the van. He gently placed her inside on the blanketed mattress and covered her with a warm quilt. He passed his fingers once lightly through her golden curls.

As he turned to walk back, he noticed Stull staring at him strangely from beyond the firelight. He hesitated at the expression and felt a shiver of fear at Stull's Satanic smile.

Michael's hands shook uncontrollably as he read the neat careful printing describing step by step what he must do if he expected to see his wife and daughter alive again. He feared that what had been done to Kasia would also be the fate of their child at the hands of this madman. He tried to push the thought and image from his mind.

Klein had made certain to prevent any news of Kasia being found and her condition from getting into the press so that Stull and Randy would not know she was alive and had identified them. The ransom note's author did not know she had survived.

Kasia had been transferred to the UCLA hospital intensive care unit and was closely monitored. Her doctor had assured Michael that she would live, barring any unforeseen development precipitated as a side effect of the drug. Her most critical problem was in overcoming withdrawal from the massive dosage of heroine that had been injected into her system.

She had responded to treatment to stabilize her and had awakened from her coma. She could now hear and understand what was being said to her, but her speech was still weak and her voice barely coherent.

Each time Michael went to the hospital to see her, Kasia asked about Danielle. She feared that Stull would murder their child. She described what had happened, what had been done to her on a day-to-day basis.

When she recounted the incident where Stull had cut their little girl's face, Michael had to leave the room to contain his fury.

He wondered if he held the key to their child's life in his own hands or was this ransom note a death certificate, his final memory of her. He called Klein, who requested he read the note slowly and carefully word by word, while it was taped.

Klein then asked from where it had been postmarked and the meter cancellation date. The moment he had been waiting for had finally arrived. The time had come to make his move.

His first call was to the San Francisco police. He spoke at some length to the head of the detective division, paving the way for mutual cooperation on the case toward the objective of arresting the kidnappers and recovering the child, hopefully unharmed.

Klein listened five times to the playback of the tape recording made as Michael had read the details of the ransom note. He could not be sure that they would recover the child or if they would find her body. The demands and manner of delivery and the unknown way the abductors would make their pick-up smacked too much of a cat and mouse ploy. However, he had no choice but to follow through according to the instructions and watch for an opportunity to close in.

The one positive element about the drop situation was that his agents could go in undercover without being recognized. The logistical problems were complex and the pick-up would be difficult to detect.

Just as there was a possibility the child might already be dead, there was an equal chance the kidnappers might pull the whole thing off. Never in his career had Klein encountered such an unusual and devious plan.

With an armed escort, Klein accompanied Michael to the bank and supervised the arrangement of the ransom package according to explicit directions outlined in the ransom letter. Then they prepared for the trip north to San Francisco on a special flight out of the Los Angeles International Airport.

Klein flatly denied Susanne Kirkeby's request to go with them.

***

Early on the morning of the drop, Stull drove the van south from the Mount Tamalpais area where they had camped for the past three days and nights. The highway hugged the picturesque coastline where centuries of crashing surf had cut away great gashes in the tall sandstone cliffs overlooking the cold wild sea.

He pulled the van over onto a windswept plateau, climbed out, walked to the edge of the cliff and looked down.

Randy had not been at all happy with what Stull had described they would do with the child. He would have preferred to leave her in a bus terminal or, better yet, a church somewhere in the heart of San Francisco where someone would find and take care of her, but not this.

Weathered boulders and Monterey pines leaning away from the wind screened them from the road. Randy watched from the van Stull walking back and forth along the cliff.

After several minutes, he stopped at a wide cut where a section of the plateau had eroded and washed out creating an access to the rocks and narrow strand of beach one hundred feet below. Occasional hikers had stamped out a rough path that appeared precarious, but passable. He turned and walked back to the van.

He opened the driver's door and climbed inside. "Okay, I found a place that will work." He fiddled with the metal strong box that contained his supply of drugs.

As Stull brought out the needle, Randy shouted, "No, you're not gonna do that. Not to her."

"I told you not to fall in love with her, bitch."

"I'm not your fuckin' bitch, Stull. When this is all over, you're not gonna see me again, ever."

"I know that. I've known that for a long time, bitch. In fact, I've been counting on it."

Randy held Stull's casual gaze, reading his intent, wondering if Stull were, in the end, setting him up to be caught while Stull made off with the ransom. Stull did need him to pull off the pick-up, but after that was accomplished, who knew what he might do.

"I'll take her down," Randy slid open the side panel door, stepped outside, then reached back in for Danielle whose sad trusting eyes never left his face. She sensed that something was about to happen to her and that Randy was protecting her.

"It's okay," he said. "Pretty soon you'll see your mommy and daddy again."

"Where is Mommy and Daddy? Are they here?" She craned her neck to look around the area. "I want to see them now."

"They aren't here, but they'll. . . You will see them again pretty soon."

"Pretty soon?"

"Pretty soon. . . Christ, Stull, we can't just leave her down there alone on that fuckin' beach."

"Will you stay with me until they come?" Danielle asked.

"You want to stay down there with her, bitch?" Stull snarled. "Let 'em find the two of you holdin' hands together? They'll put your ass away for the rest of your fuckin' ass life. If you want to give up all that bread for a fuckin' brat cunt, all right. It's your choice."

"I think we should leave her where someone will find her right away and take care of her. Hell, that's open beach down there. Sure, it's low tide now, but when it comes in, it'll take her away."

So then, no one will ever know the difference, will they?"

"I will."

"No one gives a flying fuck about what you know or don't know. They don't and I don't. Only you. And as of right now, your life ain't worth shit to nobody."

"She doesn't have to be down there."

"We're runnin' out of time. You gonna take her down or do I leave the both of you standin' here."

"There was a gas station about five miles back. Why can't we just put her in the restroom?"

"Because, asshole, someone will see the van and remember it. They'll remember us – what the hell we look like."

"What's the goddam difference? By now, the police probably know who we are."

"Not likely. Who would tell 'em? Nobody."

Randy pondered his choices, then spoke gently to Danielle, who clung tightly to him. "We're going for a walk. I'll carry you."

As they crossed the plateau, then started down the steep path, Danielle hid her face against Randy's neck upon seeing the dizzying height and the pounding surf below. "Be careful. Be careful," she warned. "I hold you. I hold you."

"That's right. You hold me. I need as much holding as you do. Just hold on tight, little one. We're going down to the beach."

"I hold you."

"You hold me."

"Where's Daddy? Where's Mommy? I don't see them."

"You'll see them." Randy hesitated. "You'll see them pretty soon, just like I said, pretty soon."

"Don't fall. It's a long way."

Randy caught himself as his boots slid on a patch of loose gravel.

At the bottom of the path, a four-foot ledge dropped abruptly to the beach. Holding Danielle under her arms, he lifted her down, then handed her the quilt he had carried partially wrapped around her bare legs and torso.

"I'm so sorry to have to do this to you. I'm sorry I have to leave you."

Danielle looked out at the roaring surf, then back up at his face. "Don't leave me here." Her face puckered into a tearful mask of accusation and betrayal.

"I'm sorry, little girl. I'm sorry. I wish it could be different." Randy began to sob as the scar on Danielle's face enflamed and reddened. "Stay wrapped in your blanket so you don't catch a cold. Okay?"

"Don't leave me here alone. Please don't leave me here alone." Her voice rose to a wailing pleading pitch. "I don't want to stay here by myself. I want you to stay with me. Where's Mommy and Daddy? You take me to Mommy and Daddy."

"I wish I could." His body shook and trembled. "I wish I could, but I can't."

Unable to any longer bear the contorted agony expressed through Danielle's eyes and face, Randy turned and scrambled back up the steep trail. Near the top, he paused to catch his breath and looked back down again.

The last view he had of her tiny figure, she was dragging her quilt, walking away along the stretch of sand and pebbles in search of her mommy and daddy, as the ominous swells began to build and the tide heaved and floundered grasping and sweeping out to sea whatever it could seize in its powerful unrelenting grip.

***

At twelve noon, Michael and Klein maneuvered their unmarked car through the mile-long line of traffic seeking access to an enormous flat farm field doubling as a parking lot. Heat waves shimmered in a vaporous haze from the acres of parked cars that proliferated in an orderly fashion, as more and more vehicles continuously funneled through the gate and were waved on by orange-vested attendants coughing and sneezing from the rising dust.

Klein showed his badge to gain them entry. Carrying a plain burlap sack containing the ransom money, Michael slung it over his shoulder and passed through the high arched gate bearing a reddish sign rendered in old English script, Renaissance Faire. Far behind him beyond the parked cars, he heard the descending chatter and soft thunk-thunk of a helicopter landing in a nearby field.

He passed a fire truck and crew in attendance along the one-hundred-yard path leading into the fair. Nestled in a narrow valley between rolling dry grassy hills studded with California live oaks, the Renaissance Faire Village extended like the open dusty main street of a rural community straight out of the Middle Ages. The ambiance gave Michael the sensation of walking onto a movie set, as he joined the surging throng of costumed entertainers mingling with the five thousand people who had come to buy food and wares at the open booths and see the white-faced mimes, jesters, jugglers, musicians, and players on the Renaissance stage set with its balconies and draped alcoves.

At the inspirational clarion call of trumpets approaching from up ahead, the roving crowd split to allow the passage of a royal entourage bearing an actress costumed like Queen Elizabeth on a large wooden chair transport shouldered by four strong yeomen of the guard and trailed by members of her court, knights with colorful banners flapping in the wind, counselors, musicians, and ladies in waiting.

Somewhere among the many masked figures, thirty special undercover agents circulated through the crowd, watching for who would pick up the drop. And somewhere out there were the men who had abducted and attempted to murder Kasia Kerenski and still had their child.

Even after the pick-up was made, the agents could not move in. They could only shadow the pick-up just as Michael himself was being shadowed by a wrestler in white face.

Sputtering juices from roast beef, chicken, and turkey meat struck the sizzling charcoal of open fires and white-gray smoke rolled out in clouds on the hot dry wind, blending tantalizing smells with shrill cries of craftsmen and women strolling about hawking their wares. Further on he noticed an actor dressed like Robin Hood napping on an unusually thick branch of an oak adjacent to the theater stage where a production of *Gammer Gurton's Needle*, a slapstick style comedy, was in progress performed in medieval garb.

As he shouldered his way through the crowd, Michael suddenly felt someone touch him on the left arm. He turned to see but could not determine from among the various costumed characters standing and meandering about nearest him who it might have been.

Then he felt a tap on his other arm, the one holding the sack. He whirled just in time to catch the single beckoning gesture of a man in whiteface with black makeup around his eyes, wearing the shabby clothes of a medieval peasant with a dagger at his belt.

Michael followed him through the crowd through a series of closed tent-like booths until he lost sight of him and stood looking eagerly and awkwardly about for some indication of the next action he must take.

He saw a movement behind the purple tent wall in front of him. A high-pitched voice called softly from inside, "Daddy . . . Daddy," raising the hair on the back of his neck.

He stepped guardedly to the closed entrance, parted the opening and peered into the gloom. After the bright daylight outside, it took several moments for his eyes to grow accustomed to the murky darkness.

Sensing that someone was quietly moving about in there, he entered slowly. A tall undefined shape came toward him from the right. He looked directly into the white mask of a black-robed, black-cowled figure, a personification of death from a medieval passion play.

The sudden horrible image so startled him that he jumped back. A metal pipe struck his head sharply from behind and he went down unconscious.

Moments later, a deliberately set fire broke out and consumed a neighboring tent, caught the dry leaves of a low overhanging oak, then rippled out into the yellow-brown wheat grass and crept like a spreading orange liquid stain up the surrounding hills.

Immediately, a second arsonist caused fire exploded the gasoline-soaked walls of a tent on the opposite side of the main. The crowd erupted in a pandemonium of screams and careened in a mad stampede for the gate, falling and trampling over each other like fear-crazed sheep.

Nudged by the strong wind, the flames roared along consuming the booths and false fronts of the set, creating a corridor of fire which the engine and fire crew could not reach in the onslaught of rampaging people trying to escape.

The agent who had been shadowing Michael dragged and carried him out of the burning tent just before it torched off. Then he went back in for the other man who was consumed by fire with strips of flaming cloth falling all over him. The agent rolled him over the ground and grabbed a nearby blanket to wrap the man's body and smother the flames.

He barely caught the hoarse words gasping from Randy Stiefel's scorched face. "At beach - - Half Moon Bay - - Get girl before drowns." His head fell back limp, and he slipped into the death he had just played.

Randy's skull had been split and the flowing blood blackened by the intense heat of the fire. Hearing a groan, the agent turned back to Michael, who was attempting to stand up with a wild expression of fear at the sight of the surrounding flames. The agent pulled him to his feet.

"This way? Can you run? We must run to get out of this."

He assisted Michael in a lunging lope around behind the burning stage set and up a section of black charred hill. Over the crackle of the inferno, they could hear the roaring clatter of the helicopter making rapid search passes back and forth over the Renaissance village.

From the top of the short hill, Michael and the agent sighted a lone green van moving quickly off into the distance of a neighboring valley a mile ahead of the advancing fire.

The agent waved to the hovering police helicopter to come down for them. It descended quickly and he and Michael scrambled aboard. As they lifted off, the agent directed the pilot to go after the escaping van and they whirled in pursuit like a bird of prey in a spinning tilt over the burning hills and down into the valley.

The agent radioed the chase to Klein and relayed the terse message concerning the missing child, her approximate location, and that a coast guard chopper should be dispatched immediately to find her.

Within a few minutes, they came in low over the green van, slowed by rocks and potholes along the rutted dirt track. The vehicle suddenly lurched and flipped over onto its side. The door popped open and Stull clambered out carrying the sack of ransom money.

The chopper tracked him running for a line of trees. He disappeared among a wild tangle of brush and boulders that dropped sharply into a narrow canyon where the helicopter couldn't follow and the pilot could no longer see him.

"Put us down," Michael bellowed. "I'm going after him."

The chopper hovered but the pilot could not locate a level spot to land.

"That's close as I can get. You must jump. Use the skids."

While the pilot relayed the action by radio to Klein, Michael and the agent hung from the skids and dropped to the ground. They plunged down the gulley washout through the thorns and brush tearing at their clothes.

Discovering Stull's footprints in the dry mud at the bottom where a small trickle pooled up and swamped the ground, they cautiously tracked him up the canyon. With gun drawn, the agent took the lead.

Stull suddenly hurtled down from a boulder above and behind them and stunned the agent with a single blow using a handheld rock. Then, crouched like an animal, he turned to confront Michael.

Stull's sallow sweating face was streaked with dirt and whiteface makeup, smeared black around the savage fearful eyes.

Breathing hard, he drew the hypodermic needle from its leather sheath and brandished it like a knife. They squared off, warily stalking each other. Stull suddenly swung the mail sack to divert Michael's guard and simultaneously lunged, striking at his face.

Michael danced back as the tip of the needle grazed his cheek. Grabbing Stull's arm in a karate lock, he broke it at the elbow with a loud crack like the snap of a dry branch. Stull screamed and fell, rolling away. Michael leaped and landed hard on Stull's chest, breaking several ribs and puncturing one of his lungs.

Eyes rolling in agony, choking on his own blood bubbling up from his collapsed lung, Stull lay immobilized with pain. Michael went back to pick up the fallen needle.

He returned to Stull, straddled him on his knees and plunged the needle up to the hilt deep into Stull's heart. Stull thrashed under him. His eyes widened in surprise and horror. Then he stiffened and died staring without sight from his frozen mask of death.

Not satisfied with his revenge, Michael raised a heavy rock with both hands high over his head and, uttering a savage cry brought it down on Stull's face. He raised it and smashed the face again and again until it was an unrecognizable pulp of blood-spattered flesh and bits and pieces of splintered cartilage and bone.

He staggered to his feet, his emotion spent, and went to assist the agent, who was beginning to move and regain consciousness.

Unable to find a low section or any way up to the path, Danielle finally tired of wandering along the beach. Hunger came and went and left her weakened clutching her quilt and lying in the beating sun.

She had been asleep for three hours when the roar of the surf and the cold froth swirled around her soaking her clothes and body and dragging away the sodden quilt.

Crawling frantically to escape the tugging force of the advancing tide, she lurched to her feet in a stumbling stubby-legged run along the baseline of the cliff as another wave snaked around her ankles.

She stopped and screamed at the towering onrushing walls of water that rose and crashed only yards away, following one upon the other like the curling gulping maws of foaming gray-green monsters. With the force of freight trains, the waves hurled their threatening doom at her, inch by inch, foot by foot, yard by yard.

She stood frozen, hypnotized in the face of a watery death. This was not like walking the plank with Peter Pan and Mr. Smee and Captain Hook or reading about fish swimming under the sea. These were not like the benign waves that went "smacko" where her Mommy and Daddy had taken her to the beach, and they had held hands together and they had lifted her high and laughing above the creeping bubbling surf.

She dreaded each flat of foam that licked and curled around her bare legs and feet as if tasting her before the final swallow in which she would be gulped by the mindless powerful undertow and swept away forever deep into the belly of the sea.

Pulling herself hand over hand along the base of the cliff, she reached a cluster of boulders and climbed, slipping and sliding at each step until she clung crying in despair at the top.

She could not hear the roar of rotor blades from the coast guard helicopter passing overhead once, then returning to land at the top of the cliff.

As each successive wave exploded around her rock, threatening to sweep her off her temporary refuge, she could not see or hear the man rapidly rappelling down the face of the cliff.

Just as he reached out to grab her, a large wave broke over the top of the rock and took them both. Clutching the coughing, cold limp child to him, the guardsman floundered in the boiling surf until moments later, the helicopter lifted them free, rising, rising, carefully hoisting them straight up the face of the cliff, then settling them gently on the plateau above.

CHAPTER THIRTY-ONE

The Chance

Major Yuri Metkin was one of the new breed of Soviet KGB agents, an 'S' and 'T' man, a specialist in science and technology. He was also Helmut Bachmann's chief corporate executive in the field of high technology for the Tri Con Corporation.

According to his passport, Metkin was William Blaine, a Canadian citizen who had transferred from Tri Con's Toronto office to oversee Tri Con's California operations, although the bulk of technical research was centered in San Francisco's Silicon Valley.

Bachmann had chosen to headquarter this function in Los Angeles from where Metkin deployed his sophisticated 'S' and 'T' men to Silicon Valley to infiltrate major companies and bring the materials and information home.

Metkin purchased millions of dollars in microprocessors that were then shipped to Tri Con shell corporations as legitimate exports. These receiving companies existed only on paper in various European countries and select third world nations. The plan used was similar to the smuggling of oil and mineral resources from South America to the Soviet Union. The chips, boards, and design information reached plants in Zelenograd, the Soviet Union's center of high technology where silicon chips based on U.S. designs were manufactured.

Metkin's covert agents invaded trade shows and scientific conferences and conventions, arranged junkets and meetings between American and Soviet scientists, and negotiated contracts with computer firms as a means of acquiring results of the latest research.

Forty miles south of San Francisco, high technology firms in Santa Clara's Silicon Valley had developed and refined the microprocessor, sliver of silicon the size of a fingernail. The device had revolutionized electronic warfare and communications, including bombs, missiles, laser weapons, omniscient radar and jamming devices. The military application of this tiny piece of technology would be devastating.

As an American company, Tri Con established friendships and business alliances with leading scientists and high-tech marketing executives, who became unwitting collaborators in Bachmann's master scheme to siphon off industry knowledge and circumvent the United States Department of Commerce embargo forbidding high technology trade with the Soviet Union and Soviet bloc countries.

Metkin had come up through the KGB ranks the hard way, as a military field officer in Cuba and in South Africa.

Although Bachmann's global economic mission fronted by the Tri Con Corporation had thus far proven successful, the consensus at Center in the Soviet Union was that Bachmann himself had grown power hungry and, on occasion, had refused to either obey or answer to Moscow.

He frequently countered that he possessed a more accurate political and economic perspective of U.S. industries and policy than the senior officers at Center, which infuriated them, and that he was far in advance of them regarding intelligence and information systems. He claimed to have brought Soviet high technology out of the Stone Age into the twenty-first century.

Bachmann's arrogance did not endear him to the brass at Center. They had fired several written reprimands and warnings to him during the past three years advising him of his duty and commitment, to which he had replied he had exceeded expectations long ago.

The KGB senior officers feared that in his position of prominence, Helmut Bachmann ran an extraordinary risk of being compromised. They worried at his laxity in matters of correspondence, his daring lavish Western life style.

In reality, Bachmann knew they were watching him closely for some slip-up so they could document and recall him to Moscow. So he had surrounded himself with a counterspy system to extend his knowledge and power base and be made aware of who was watching him, where, when, and in what manner.

He had no intention of being cited for error and was planning for an early retirement in Santa Barbara at the age of fifty-five.

He had suspected Metkin soon after the man had moved into the Los Angeles office, because the flow of orders and demands from Moscow nearly coincided with that appointment. He was stuck with Metkin, however. Metkin was the cream of the KGB crop in high technology espionage.

Bachmann was careful around the sly sturdy little man, who Bachmann knew disapproved of him. Metkin came from the old Spartan communist influences and looked upon Bachmann's personal wealth with suspicion.

Center had, in fact, secretly ordered him to spy on Bachmann, who pointedly excluded him from all but the primary social and business communications with his executive management team. As far as Bachmann was concerned, Metkin had outlived his usefulness to him and to Tri Con.

He did not want to terminate Metkin, even accidentally. Such an act would draw unwanted attention. Center considered Metkin of value and would immediately suspect Bachmann and come down on him hard.

On the other hand, if he set up Metkin to be arrested for industrial espionage by the FBI, the ensuing interrogation would reveal Tri Con's activity. For the present, the United States Federal Government had no reason to suspect that Tri Con was something other than a multinational corporation that owned a high technology subsidiary division in Los Angeles. Metkin was human. Just as he was looking for Bachmann to err, so was Bachmann looking for Metkin's Achilles heal.

The process proved to be difficult. Metkin was single minded in his devotion to duty and the Soviet cause, overly so, in Bachmann's opinion. Such behavior usually hid some secret vice or weakness. Bachmann went hunting for it.

Metkin lived in a North Hollywood apartment. He left early each morning for the office, returned late, and never remained at his residence on the weekends. Through one of his spies, Bachmann discovered where Metkin spent those weekends. The situation provided the opportunity Bachmann needed to have him recalled.

Metkin had unlimited access to company funds for the purpose of paying substantial consultant fees, bribes, six figure contracts, and to cover his personal business, travel, and entertainment expenses. He was an inveterate gambler who could not resist the lure of Tahoe, Reno, and Las Vegas.

On one such trip, Bachmann's spy witnessed Metkin drop ten thousand dollars at the craps tables at Harrah's. He spent on the average of three to five thousand per trip.

Bachmann's controller monitored the unaccounted-for expenditures over a two month period. Metkin never recovered his losses. Figuring he could write off the cash as operating expenses with no one the wiser, he continued his weekend junkets.

The stout balding little man with intense dark eyes was a regular at Ron Formio's craps table. Formio had been in the casino business for sixteen years and could read the behavioral signs of the addictive gambler who had no control, the compulsive gambler.

Metkin considered himself a man who took only calculated risks. Contrary to his apparent Spartan minimal lifestyle, he craved excitement and action. Espionage provided that stimulation to a certain extent and a level of emotional and psychological satisfaction. But over the past three years, his work had become routine and office bound, dull from his point of view. Gambling had compensated his ennui.

Arriving in Vegas caused a transformation in Metkin, almost the equivalent of a personality change, as if the brief flight from the Burbank airport were a passage through a time warp that removed him from reality to a fantasy world where the odds did not apply to him and where he was always on top.

He drank heavily while he gambled, straight vodka, Stoli, tossing off one double after another, bringing a ruddy glow and laughter to his sallow features. He dropped his American accent. His Russian accent calling out the placement of chips and instructions to the dice he rolled and curses drew bystanders and other players.

Eventually, Mr. Blaine would lose track of where he was and he would shout and mutter in Russian, which always aroused Formio's curiosity. He engaged the feverish man in snatches of conversation and learned that he was a software engineer and an executive with the Tri Con Corporation. Formio's interest sharpened with no apparent expression and be asked Blaine/Metkin about Tri Con, since he considered buying some stock.

"Tri Con is big in oil and computer technology, as I recall, isn't it?"

"Tri Con is big in everything," said Metkin.

"Mr. Blaine, we at Harrah's consider you one of our important VIP's. On behalf of the management, we're happy to extend our hospitality to you. Your room and meals will be comped. In addition, we're giving you ten-thousand dollars to play at the tables."

Metkin's milky blue eyes brightened. "You're giving it to me, not as credit?"

"Not as credit, as a gift." Formio had convinced his boss, the casino manager, that Blaine would drop thirty to fifty thousand of his own money to the ten 'K' gift. A great return on the investment. Of course, the room, booze, and meals were negligible. Hereafter, Blaine would have a comped plane ticket and a standing reservation. Metkin/Blaine was delighted and impressed with the arrangement.

"We're more than happy to accommodate you.," said Formio. "It would be our pleasure to offer similar hospitality to any of your high level executive associates who might be interested, as well."

The smile that wreathed Metkin's taut features instantly vanished. "No – No, I gamble alone. If you want me to continue to come here, then do not contact them."

Formio understood immediately. "Of course not, Mr. Blaine, never without your consent. We always respect your privacy and remain discreet. It was never our intent to contact them. I was only inquiring. We thought you might be sharing your experiences with them when you went back. That's all."

Metkin's head snapped in a single short vehement shake.

Formio signaled the roving bar girl to supply his guest with another Stoli to smooth his slightly ruffled feathers. Metkin drank it off in two swallows.

"Now, enough talk. I am grateful for your gift. I will enjoy it and take advantage of it. Let's play on the ten thousand you are giving me."

Formio handed him the dice.

Later, in the manager's office, Formio related the information he had surmised from Blaine's reaction. "He's playing with corporate funds. I'm sure of it."

"Did you send a girl to his room?"

"Ali just went up with him."

"Good, keep him happy and keep him coming back for as long as he can manage it."

"He'll keep coming until they find out about him. He's hooked."

"Until they catch him."

Up in Metkin's room, Ali, a tall well-endowed brunette, helped the stumbling boisterous Metkin out of his clothes and together they fell laughing onto the king size bed. Chortling obscenities and endearments to her in Russian, he roughly clutched her ample breasts and rubbed his face between them."

The quantity of alcohol he had consumed caused him difficulty in maintaining an erection despite Ali's expert tonguing of his flaccid penis. Finally Metkin protested, "Wait, wait. I have had too much to drink. First we take a little sleep. Then we can fuck."

"Whatever you say, Honey."

Metkin was snoring within minutes. Ali went through his wallet and personal belongings, but did not discover the secret compartment in his attaché case where he hid his bankroll.

She left the room for an hour, reported to Formio that she had not found anything unusual, then returned to be with Metkin when he woke from his recuperative nap. Although suffering from a slight headache, he was ravenous and refreshed. They ordered a meal through room service.

While they waited, Metkin worried about what he might have said to her in his inebriated state. He explained away his knowledge of Russian by telling her he was born and raised in a Russian speaking community in Canada where he had lived all his life until recently moving to California.

The food arrived. Metkin consumed several cups of coffee with his steak and baked potato while Ali barely picked at her fruit salad.

"I feel much better," he said when he was finished. Then with a lascivious leer, "Let's try again, eh?"

Smiling, Ali disrobed and settled next to him on the bed. His cock rose immediately at her touch. "See what a little food will do for you?" They laughed.

"Ah – This is the best weekend of my life," he said. "I wish I could stay forever."

"Like Mr. Formio told you, you're one of the family."

Grasping her by the buttocks, he pulled her over on top of him and entered with a sudden rush.

"Woowweee!" She gasped and grinned, dangling her lobes at either side of his face. "Blew your cork just like champagne there, Honey."

He grew suddenly listless and tired.

"Haven't been with a woman in a long time, have you, Honey?"

Metkin shook his head and frowned, wanting to escape from under her. "You are a good lay."

"With a compliment like that, any time you want me, all you have to do is call the desk and ask for Ali."

His eyes glazed and he yawned. "I feel like sleeping again."

"All that coffee's going to keep you awake. Remember, you've only got the weekend and the tables downstairs are waiting. Hey, I have a great idea. Why don't you stay over a couple of extra days. You work hard. You deserve it. And we'll have lots more time together. Then you won't feel so rushed. You know what I mean. We can take things nice and slow and easy. I hate to rush a good thing."

"I'll call and tell my secretary I'm visiting a relative."

"Sure, that's the spirit. What's a couple of days. The world's not gonna stop. Life isn't all work. It's meant to be enjoyed. And I want to enjoy it with you."

"Ahh, it's coming up. I think we can enjoy it again."

"See. Here, take it slow this time. She squeezed and released his cock with her sphincter muscle causing a spasm of pleasure to shudder through his entire body.

Thereafter, he could not get enough of Ali and gambling and Ali. His gambling addiction merged with the sexual pleasure Ali provided as every weekend he made his holy pilgrimage to his Vegas Eden.

At the end of six months, he had played and lost three hundred thousand dollars of Tri Con funds plus two hundred and forty thousand in house money. The house had made an appreciable short-term return on its investment.

By that time, Metkin had lost track of the figures and no longer cared. He was hooked, like Formio said. He needed Ali and the gambling tables like high quality heroine.

Late one Friday night in January, Ali met him at the airport as usual in the hotel limousine. Enroute to Harrah's, she poured him Russian vodka while he laughed and joked about the tremendous deal he pulled off with a major computer firm. Only this time he had moved the funds into a private personal account.

"One million," he wheezed. "One million."

"And you brought it all with you?"

"Not all." Metkin's head bobbed, and his eyes sparkled like a gleeful child. "Only three hundred thousand."

"Oh, William, you're so clever. Show me when we get to the hotel. I want to see it. We'll spend it together and have us a real all-out blast."

"I used a little of it to buy you a special gift," he said. "You are a special person to me, *boublischka*." He pulled out a long slender box from his inside suit coat pocket. "Here, open it."

Ali recognized at once the value of the diamond necklace at about one hundred thousand dollars. Formio didn't have to know about this little gift. She had earned it. A nice tip.

"When we go down to the casino tonight, I want you to wear it. I want everyone to see you are Bill Blaine's girl," said Metkin.

"It's so beautiful, Bill. Thank you so very much. And yes, I am your girl. You're so generous, the kindest and nicest man I've ever known. I – I just don't know what to say."

She kissed him long and passionately, then pretended to wipe tears from her eyes. "But I don't dare wear this in the casino. If someone sees it, some crook, they'll try to get it. I'll wear it when we make love. It's the only thing I'll wear. How about that? Only the necklace."

The erotic image thoroughly aroused Metkin. His trousers bulged. He could hardly wait until they got to the hotel.

At one o'clock in the morning, Metkin hit a winning streak that went on and on for a good forty minutes. Ali helped bag the chips as he handed over the dice to Formio.

Looking about the table at the exuberant faces of others who had taken a ride on his lucky throws, Metkin's eyes suddenly jerked back to a face he recognized. Helmut Bachmann's cold solemn gaze in the midst of the flushed shouting onlookers held him paralyzed.

Metkin involuntarily backed away from the gaming table. He tried to turn and slip off through the dense crowd shuffling along the walkway and conceal himself among the rows of jangling slot machines. Ali shouted, then chased after him with his winnings.

She suddenly stopped as she saw two goons wearing black suits close in on Metkin from either side and quickly escort him out of the casino. The quiet watchful man wearing a gray silk suit and blue tie who had been standing across the table from them followed close behind.

Ali hurried to the front door and peered out just in time to see Metkin strong-armed into a black limousine which pulled away in a rush with the four men.

She gazed down at the bag of chips worth one hundred and fifty thousand dollars. Her diamond necklace was secure in the hotel vault. She walked back through the noise and smoke-filled casino to the window and cashed in Metkin's chips.

"Poor Bill Blaine," she thought with a smile. "We won't be seeing him again."

Formio had been too preoccupied at the table to notice what had happened to Metkin. Later, during his relief break, Ali told him that Blaine had been arrested by the FBI for embezzlement of corporate funds. Formio just shrugged. "Easy come. Easy go." He lit a cigarette. "There's another regular I want you to take care of."

Enroute to the airport, Bachmann did not offer Metkin any explanation. None was necessary. Sitting stiffly between the two KGB hitmen with a .45 magnum jammed up into his ribs, he fully expected to be terminated out there on the desert and tossed into some isolated canyon where his corpse would be ravaged beyond recognition by coyotes and vultures.

But when they reached the airport, the KGB agents took him on board one of Bachmann's private Lear jets. Metkin then knew he was being taken back to the Soviet Union. He would have preferred a quick execution out there on the desert compared to what would be done to him in Moscow.

Bachmann himself made sure the cabin door was sealed before walking across the pad to where his own jet waited to take him to San Francisco. Unable to prove the disappearance of unrecorded cash funds through Metkin, he had set Metkin up in a sting with the one-million-dollar sale. The embezzlement of the high figure carried enough impact for Center to put Metkin away permanently and to convince the senior officers that he, Bachmann, was aligned with them.

In his communique to them, he allowed Center to save face by understating they had misplaced their concern regarding duty and loyalty and commitment and, in the future, had no necessity to spy on him. "The irony of Metkin speaks for itself," he had said.

At the controls of his Lear, he rose into the star-studded night sky and rocketed over the northern Sierra Nevada mountains to set down at the San Francisco International Airport.

A waiting private limousine whisked him to his second home across the bay in Marin. Feeling unusually weary, he slept in one of the extra guest bedrooms so as not to disturb his wife, Lili, who had taken a flight up from Los Angeles that evening. The following morning, they would attend their daughter's graduation at Stanford University, a short drive down the peninsula in Palo Alto.

She had written to them about her boyfriend, a business and economics major who was graduating with his master's degree. Later, she had told Bachmann on the phone, "Daddy, he's too proud to ask you for a job, but he's smart. You'll like him."

"Not too proud to ask you to ask me though."

"Dad, be fair. He didn't ask me. He doesn't know I mentioned it. I'm doing this on my own."

"If he wants a job, then he should just come right out and ask for it, or at least inquire."

"He's sharp. He's really sharp. Magna cum laude, Dad. Magna cum laude. You talk to him, okay? It doesn't have to be all business right away. Invite him to come down to Los Angeles for an interview in a week or so. All right? Do it for me, please."

"If you say he's that good, I'd be foolish to pass up the opportunity. You don't mind if I refer him to other companies, as well, do you? He may find a better situation than what I could offer."

"You're great, Dad. I love you. I won't have a chance to see you and Mom on Friday before the ceremony. Too busy."

"That's all right. We understand. We'll celebrate with you Saturday."

"Love you, Dad. Give my love to Mom. Bye for now."

"I love you, Dear." Almost wistfully he recounted the brief conversation. He wondered what kind of father he had been over the years. How did his son and daughter view him? What did they think of him? Certainly it seemed they loved him, or at least respected him, but he had never given them much of his time. There had never been enough time, not for them, or for his wife, Lili.

She had been and still was a perfect wife. He must think of a special way to show his appreciation. Perhaps a trip to Vienna, a walk through their old haunts where he had courted her twenty-four years ago. That would mean a lot to her.

There had been moments when he had wanted to share his secret with her, his real origins, the story of how as the ten-year-old youth, Boris Sergeevitch Pondoev, he had been smuggled across the Soviet border into East Germany and subsequently into West Berlin to become Helmut Bachmann, protégé of the KGB.

And now, here he was, one of the most powerful corporate figures in the world. The thought of it used to stagger him, but no longer. He took Tri Con's global influence in stride. Tri Con was his instrument. He was Tri Con.

"Five more years," he thought. "I'll be forty-eight and that's long enough in this game."

He had already purchased a 360 acre ranch in the Sierra Madre foothills overlooking Santa Barbara and Montecito. That was his and Lili's retreat, a California rancho hacienda with a large sculpted pool and spa, stable, and hundreds of avocado trees on the surrounding slopes.

After thirty years of international globetrotting and fighting Tri Con's corporate battles, he wondered if he could adjust to the sedate retirement life in Santa Barbara.

A few Hollywood movie stars had homes there, Michael Douglas, Jane Fonda, Kevin Costner, and John Travolta. And Robert Mitchum had an estate.

Michael Sloan and Kasia Kerenski had talked about buying a home there. His thoughts stopped for a moment on her. What a survivor. But she eventually would have to be terminated according to plan in a manner that was not traceable back to Tri Con and especially to himself.

The CIA and FBI would tear the Tri Con cell apart, and that would end his dreams of retirement. The South American plan was still intact. He and Kasia Kerenski would never be neighbors in Santa Barbara.

Arranging for his retirement, he knew one of the many things he must do was make certain his ass was covered. He had already chosen his successor, Nathaniel Hauser, and was grooming him through the position of executive vice president for overseas development. Hauser had been born and raised in Chicago too, just like Alex Pondoev, the banker, another Mid-western lad.

Hauser didn't know all the secrets yet. But he had been thoroughly trained and indoctrinated in Leningrad and at Vladivostock University in the Soviet Union. During that two-year period, he had supposedly been residing in West Germany on Tri Con business. The entire world was Tri Con business.

He glanced at the luminous digital numbers on the bedside clock radio. "Christ, it's five a.m.. It's a good thing Nancy's graduation isn't until tomorrow afternoon. I'd hate to embarrass her by falling asleep during the commencement ceremony."

"Better stay on the board of directors for a while after retirement. Keep a hand in the operation. Too risky to totally let go. Don't give up everything to Hauser when the time comes. Make him depend on me for a few years."

At this final thought, Bachmann let himself drift into a deep slumber.

CHAPTER THIRTY-TWO

The Guerrillas

Malcolm Karazississ disembarked from a Pan American jet in Buenos Aires. After processing through customs as a tourist under the alias of Thomas Trenton, he jumped aboard a *collectivo*, a small bus, just outside the terminal and rode to *La Boca*, an artists' colony near the waterfront.

Walking past the clustered bright hued apartments of reds, greens, yellows, and blues, he found the address he sought and knocked on the door. A pleasant looking dark-skinned dark-eyed young woman answered.

In Spanish, he said, "I'm looking for Juan Martinez."

"He is not home. May I ask who you are?"

"Malcolm Karazississ. He's expecting me, although he didn't know the exact date of my arrival."

"Si, he is expecting you, Senor Karazississ. Please come inside."

Smiling at the soft-spoken woman's tumbling black curls, he followed her into a small living room.

"*Por favor*, please, sit down. My name is Carla. Would you like *mate* or perhaps a *cerveza* or a cocktail."

"A *cerveza* would be nice, *gracias*." He dropped his suitcase and strolled briefly around the neat modest apartment, then took a chair facing an open-air window overlooking the *Rio de La Plata*. Boats of many shapes and sizes powered by wind and by fuel passed carrying trade goods and passengers.

Carla returned with a cold Argentine beer. "Juane is visiting a neighbor. They're watching a soccer match on television. Please make yourself comfortable. I'll go tell him you're here."

"*Gracias*." Malcolm appreciatively sipped his straw-colored beer.

Ten minutes later, Carla returned with her husband, who came forward with a strong handshake and a warm smile. "Welcome, Senor Karazississ. I am Juan Martinez."

Although Malcolm towered a good head and shoulders over the man, he realized that Martinez was rock hard with muscle and in excellent physical shape. He made up in compact strength and energy what he lacked in size.

"Did you have a good flight?"

"Excellent service, first class all the way."

"Well, prepare yourself for some rough going. Not immediately, however. We'll leave soon after dark. The journey will take us two days. Our people are anxious to meet you. Carla, I'll have a beer, as well." He turned back to Malcolm. "Now that you are here, let's discuss what is to happen in Chile."

Malcolm provided him with only the sketchiest information. He professed that many details had yet to be worked out once the guerillas had crossed the Andes and established their base camp.

He said nothing of the American film company being used as a front to bring in tanks and heavy artillery by sea. He was primarily interested in the physical condition of the men and the quality and sophistication of their training. He would supply them with the latest in automatic weaponry at the time of the crossing. They would continue their training under his command for a few weeks before the assault on the Chilean capital, *Santiago*.

Malcolm commented on the excellent taste and execution of the artwork displayed throughout the apartment.

"That's Carla," said Juan. "She is the artist. I am a businessman and, most recently, a military commander. Perhaps you would like to rest for a while. We will be moving on the road all night."

"Will you have dinner before you leave?" asked Carla.

"No, we'll stop in Rosario. Carla will show you your room. I have some paperwork to finish and phone calls to make."

Malcolm picked up his suitcase and followed Carla to the bedrooms in the back area, graciously thanked her, then closed the door.

The hours dragged as they drove through the hot sluggish night into the far northern sector of the country, the *Chaco*, covered by the great forests of the *quebracho* trees.

Every two hours, they spelled each other at the wheel of the military jeep. Late at night, Martinez slowed at a particularly deserted area and turned off the main highway onto a narrow rutted dirt and gravel road that led to a cluster of small earthen and stone huts set well back among the trees. No lights shone in the windows which were covered with blackout curtains.

Martinez cut the headlights, stepped out of the jeep and came around to Malcolm. Touching him on the shoulder, he said, "Some of these men are quick tempered. Be agreeable and listen to whatever they have to say. However, keep this ready." He placed a loaded .45 handgun in Malcolm's right hand. "You are more important to the cause than any given one of us here, except me. If you are threatened, do not hesitate to use this. All others will understand and they will respect your position as a compatriot and as a man."

Malcolm nodded and slipped the revolver into his belt, then followed Martinez toward the nearest hut. As they approached, his sharp eyes discerned the shapes of men huddled in the shadows of nearby trees and brush. They had been smoking and spoke in low voices. Malcolm noted the glint from the barrel of a submachine gun aimed at him and Martinez. His .45 would not be of much use in a firefight.

They stopped several yards from the crouched and semi-concealed men. Martinez exchanged greetings with *Jefe*, the commander, who came forward and listened to Martinez's explanation of who the tall, red-bearded man was who accompanied him.

Three others left their positions of concealment. Martinez and Malcolm followed Jefe toward a dim light that outlined a door. They went through into the hot claustrophobic hut. Malcolm heard shuffling footsteps and movement filling the area behind them with many others he had not heard nor seen who emerged from the surrounding darkness.

Malcolm sat on a rough wooden bench next to a brown-skinned *mestizo*, casually cradling a Czech submachine gun. Cigars were lit, filling the close room with smoke and discouraging hovering insects. As Martinez surveyed the crowd, the chatter of conversation ceased and all eyes turned to him.

"This man with me is Malcolm Karazississ," Martinez spoke in Spanish. "He is the one I told you about. He has come to recruit soldiers for a coup in Chile."

"I have a question," the *mestizo* seated next to Malcolm exhaled a cloud of smoke. "Who hired you and where do you come from?"

To the surprise of the group, Malcolm answered in Spanish. "I am a professional soldier, a mercenary. Suffice it to say that whoever hired me has an interest in removing the Chilean *junta* from power."

"Your answer does not satisfy me. How do we know you are not a spy? Perhaps you were hired by the *alianzo* and will lead us all into a trap." The man's reference was to an alliance among the secret police and governments of Brazil, Argentina, and Columbia to repress and eliminate insurgent activities in their countries.

"You have no need to worry. I am a friend of Bernardo Leighton."

"Leighton."

"Si," Martinez interrupted. "Senor Karazississ has come to us through Leighton."

The others nodded and muttered their approval, but the challenger still did not relax his suspicion. "How can you fight for a cause about which you know nothing?"

"I have fought for many causes such as yours and I know the cause of the MIR well. Leighton has briefed me." Malcolm's cool gaze traveled over the others, gauging their position and feelings toward him.

"What did Leighton tell you?"

The anger in Martinez's voice cut through the next moment of intense silence. "You have said enough," he verbally lashed out at the *mestizo*. "Senor Karazississ has come here to help us and he is our guest. No more questions."

Malcolm raised his hand, indicating his willingness to answer the question.

"I have met and talked with Bernardo Leighton. He is the spokesman for the MIR and other exiles in Caracas, Venezuela. I also attended their conference in 1975. In Leighton's words, the *junta* is under attack from within the government. Christian Democrats are now joining with the left to work actively against the *junta* and return Chile to constitutional rule. Leighton says this cannot happen swiftly, but that all opposition forces must be in alliance to overcome military rule. That is why I am here."

At the end of Karazississ' explanation, Martinez stated flatly. "We have soldiers waiting."

The group scraped back their chairs and benches and spilled out of the hut to waiting trucks and jeeps that had been hidden under camouflage nets.

Along the twin-rutted road, they navigated dry stream beds, rockslides, enormous potholes and chunks of gouged earth. They stopped an hour later. Martinez walked off into a dense thicket. Except for his bobbing flashlight, the darkness swallowed him. He scrambled up an embankment and down the other side until a security guard at the perimeter halted him.

He received access from the checkpoint, then he and the guard ducked their way through low hanging tree branches. The thicket opened suddenly. The beams of several flashlights and lanterns revealed a clearing and four ranks of troops of the MIR. A dark-bearded company commander wearing jungle fatigues and a green beret brought them to attention with a shouted command and presented arms as Martinez stepped forward into the hazy light.

He delivered a brief speech and ordered another formation to be held the following day. At that time, Karazississ would evaluate their training and competency and make his selections.

After the last of the guerilla troops had clambered into one of the battered convoy trucks and disappeared into the night, Malcolm and Martinez and his staff of bodyguards drove to a nearby village where a family who supported the MIR offered them food and a place to sleep.

The next morning, after a meager breakfast of beans, rice, and flatbread, they returned to the base camp and Malcolm reviewed the men. Their average age ranged from eighteen to thirty and they were all in excellent physical condition.

In observing them go through maneuvers, he noted their level of discipline, smooth handling of weapons, and unflagging spirit despite that many of them wore sandals and patched and tattered uniforms. Even under conditions of poverty and deprivation, they projected pride and dignity.

He selected five hundred men. At the end of one month, they would rendezvous on an isolated stretch of the *Rio de La Plata* where Karazississ would be waiting with transport aircraft to fly them over the Andes into Chile.

As Malcolm chatted with the three special combat instructors, a messenger ran up to Martinez, who listened, then quickly came over to Karazississ.

"Police agents have been spotted along the road. We must leave at once."

In the rush to depart, Karazississ took a few extra moments to shake hands with the nearest soldiers. Then he and Martinez climbed into a transport and, under heavily armed escort, began the long journey back to Buenos Aires by an alternate route.

Karazississ was booked on a Pan Am flight to Miami but left the country by private jet and landed in Cuba to finalize his plans for the movement in Chile.

CHAPTER THIRTY-THREE

The Counter Mission

Sipping a beer, Michael sat by the pool as he reworked a page of dialogue in his script. From time to time, he raised his eyes to watch Kasia laughing and playing with their daughter at the shallow end.

A year had gone by since the abduction. The slash on Danielle's face had healed, but she would bear a thin permanent scar unless, as a teenager or as an adult, she would be willing to undergo plastic surgery. For now, their child was content merely to be with her parents again. She was occasionally tormented by nightmares and the fear of being separated from them. Leaving the house to go to work at the studio each morning was even a major trauma for Michael. Kasia described how, for the first few months, Danielle had clung to her throughout the day and would not let her out of her sight, but that this behavior was becoming less frequent since she had recently made three friends at the preschool. At one point, Danielle had requested to be taken to preschool.

The situation concerned Michael, since in a few months, he and Kasia were scheduled to fly to South America with a film crew to begin production on their next project, *Borders*. They would be gone for three months. Danielle would not accompany them.

Following the kidnapping incident and the recovery of his wife and child, several events happened that caused Michael anxiety as to the future of his career in the motion picture industry.

The first was a national change from a liberal to a conservative political climate with Republicans coming into power under Ronald Reagan. Regarding foreign policy, the administration was steadfastly anti-communist, calling the Soviet Union an "evil empire". Reagan accelerated the massive buildup of the military started by the former

President, Jimmy Carter. The "Reagan Doctrine" also granted aid to paramilitary forces seeking to overthrow socialist governments in war-torn Central America and Afghanistan. Reagan also promoted missile defense systems to confront the Soviets and their allies.

The second was the apparent firing of Kurt Heinrich from Tri Con Pictures. Heinrich had gone back to Germany.

The third was the pulling of Michael's anti-CIA film, which had been favorably reviewed and was doing a brisk business at the box office. The television version was then so badly butchered and spotted with second rate commercials as to make the film incomprehensible with all references to the CIA removed.

Helmut Bachmann had deliberately pursued this handling of the film to discourage the FBI from covert spying on Tri Con Pictures. The discovery that several office phones had been tapped, including Michael's, had alerted Bachmann.

Heinrich had ended his affair and returned to Europe with his wife, Gerta, on Bachmann's orders. It was Bachmann's intention to clean house as quickly as possible.

Michael feared that the U.S. Government was undermining his career. To enter litigation would drain his own financial resources. So he struck back through a series of news stories about the incidents, after Bachmann refused to make waves and put Tri Con up against the federal government in a civil rights suit. The articles were written by Suzanne Kirkeby and published in every major newspaper in the country.

Because Kasia's acting career was so directly tied to that of her husband, if he should go under, she would likely go with him, unless she agreed to work with other directors in films of considerably less substance.

Bachmann assured Michael his South American film would be totally financed and would see distribution.

Michael's films and especially his next project, raised sensitive political questions and challenged the federal government in its responsibility to the American people and its relations with foreign governments in areas it did not wish to have brought to the attention of the general public, especially the intervention of the CIA.

In her analysis of what the films portrayed and their social impact, Suzanne had explained Michael's themes and concerns as an artist. The world was dissociated, like a neurotic, with the Iron Curtain marking the symbolic line of division.

The rising specter of "the will to power" in the eastern European countries threatened western man to the extent that he took extraordinary measures of defense while priding himself on his expressed virtue and promised intentions.

What western governments failed to acknowledge, especially the United States Government, was their own diplomatic lies and policies of deception, a mirror of what was done openly by the communist world. Western man viewed the communist world as his own evil shadow grinning back at him from the other side of the Iron Curtain.

Michael's films explored the shadow side of western culture, the dark side of its nature. The government didn't want the people to see or understand what it was they were doing under the guise of diplomacy.

Michael had pointed out that the myth of the communist world was also the same myth of western society, the dream of an unattainable utopia or a golden age where everything is provided in abundance for everyone, eliminating want. Everyone unconsciously cherished that hope and the prejudices and expectations that accompanied it.

Western society also believed in that utopian welfare state, in universal peace, in the equality of man, in his eternal human rights, in truth and justice, and in God. But the reality was a matrix of inexorable opposites – day and night, birth and death, happiness and misery, good and evil. Life was a virtual battleground. It always had been and always would be.

***

Roger Lakein watched Suzanne Kirkeby fill her plate with samplings of the various gourmet preparations offered at the Press Association buffet. Following her to a table, he sat within easy listening and conversational distance. He caught her glance that conveyed an initial physical attraction and interest in his air of warm sophistication and blonde youngish features that belied his real age.

They engaged in casual conversation. He complimented her on her Pulitzer Prize winning coverage of the Kasia Kerenski kidnapping and all its ramifications. He said it had been more like reading a serialized book than a group of news stories.

She responded graciously, never imagining the irony of his comments, since he had set that abduction in motion. He told her that he freelanced for magazines and newspapers and was developing a book about South American politics.

Bachmann had suggested to Lakein that he come to California and work his way into Michael's and Kasia's social circle with the objective of going with the film company to Chile as an advisor. Bachmann also wanted to ensure the right connections were made regarding the landing and disbursement of heavy artillery for the project. And most importantly, he was to be certain that Kasia Kerenski was accidentally killed while on location.

Lakein's presence in California raised some questions in the mind of Gordon Frasier at the CIA until Lakein explained he suspected a connection between Tri Con Pictures and the Tri Con operations in South America.

Since Frasier had begun a covert investigation of Tri Con, beginning with studio corporate personnel, he allowed Lakein to proceed and infiltrate. Frasier also began to wonder if he had been mistaken about Lakein in suspecting him as the mole when, in fact, he appeared to be digging into Tri Con.

After three hours of food, wine, conversation and listening to a humorous guest speaker, Suzanne decided to accept Roger's invitation to follow him home. Throughout his modest, but roomy house, the large number of paintings reminded her of a small gallery. His selections and décor reflected a discriminating taste. Noticing her linger before one of the expressionist oils, he called out from the west bar where he was pouring them each a snifter of Remy Martin cognac.

"Where do you think I came across that?"

"France maybe."

"A farmhouse attic in Oklahoma."

She stared at him in disbelief. "Yours?"

"My grandparents."

"How did they come by it?"

"My father was an artist. No one you ever would have heard of. When I was a small boy, I was told by my mother he was insane. I left home when I was thirteen."

"You must have known some hard times."

"I promised not to let myself starve, whatever the circumstances." He brought her cognac. "You seem a little tense? Anything wrong?"

"I am. I have a slight headache. The perennial journalist's pain from being hunched over a typewriter ten hours a day. Tends to settle in my shoulders and the back of my neck."

As he tentatively touched the back of her neck to see how she would respond, he was pleased that she did not move away at the gesture. He slowly and gently massaged her neck, then leaned over and placed a kiss on her left shoulder, enticingly bared by the cut and design of her evening dress. They rose from the couch. With an arm around each other, they carried their cognacs to the bedroom.

Although Michael and Kasia had met Lakein one stormy night in Puerto Montt in Southern Chile, Suzanne unknowingly now provided the social connection.

The details and forces at work concerning class warfare, about which Roger claimed to be highly knowledgeable, prompted Michael to accept his offer to become an advisor on the film production of *Borders*.

Kasia contacted Frasier at The Security Bank, wanting to know what Lakein was doing in California and why he was ordered to become involved with the film project. Frasier told her the CIA was using the movie production to discover who in Chile was plotting a coup to overthrow the junta. He would not elaborate for her and refused to reveal names and details.

Lakein had been instrumental in many agency operations providing training and support for government police and military forces, especially in areas of intelligence combined with United States military assistance missions that gave the ruling class even stronger means to retain their power and disproportionate share of the national income. Even now, his involvement as conceptualized by Frasier was part of the operation to penetrate the extreme leftists and eliminate a potential threat to the ruling officials in Chile.

Few knew better than Lakein how the interests of the ruling minority in a poor Latin American country were directly tied to the financial interests of the rich and powerful who controlled the United States economy.

The doctrine of counterinsurgency employed by the CIA attempted to camouflage that relationship by exploiting the surface emotions of patriotism and nationalism and then falsely explaining uprisings against the ruling capitalist minorities as Soviet intervention and expansionism. In some cases, Soviet intervention was directly involved.

Counterinsurgency functioned to protect capitalist interests in the United States. As propagandized to the American public, U.S. national security was the financial security of U.S. capitalists, not the majority rule of the American people.

Roger understood that the United States Government financed and supported corrupt dictators and unjust regimes to insure the rich and powerful corporate and Wall Street executives would be able to retain and expand those riches and influence foreign markets.

Whatever the cost, the film *Borders* and the production company were caught in the middle. Bachmann and the Soviet communists were using the production as the front for a major coup. The CIA could not allow the film to be made and expose the relationship of American foreign policy and counterinsurgency. Such a film would inform and influence the collective mind of the American public in a negative way and would likely foment political challenge and discord.

Roger was playing both sides. His position would allow him to expose the plot against the *junta* in order to retain his credibility with the CIA and cast suspicion away from himself that he was the mole.

CHAPTER THIRTY-FOUR

The Double Cross

Roger Lakein enjoyed dining at the Prince of Wales Country Club in Santiago's fashionable *Los Condes* district. He had a favorite table overlooking the golf links and would often dine alone, although he preferred the company of various women he dated. The elegant gourmet experience was incomplete unless shared with a companion.

Fresh oysters, seafood bisque, grilled lobster, and tender pepper steak in a wine reduction sauce were his favorite courses accompanied by vintage Chilean wines.

He knew that Manuel Contreras liked a good spread. He had suggested they meet at the Prince of Wales for lunch. At Contrera's arrival, Lakein detected a sudden unrest among the other diners in the proximity of his table. Boisterous conversations dropped to whispers and became silent. Even though the patrons were upper class entrepreneurs and managers of business and energy operations, they all feared the powerful man who headed DINA, *Direccion de Intelligencia Nacional*, the Chilean government's dreaded secret police.

Even Lakein himself held certain reservations about the man who carried out Pinochet's policies of institutionalized brutality, human torture, and mass killings. As a CIA field operations man during the coup in 1973 that culminated with President Allende's death and the installation of Pinochet in power, as an operative of the CIA, Lakein had worked with Contreras. He had witnessed countless arrests by Contreras and his sadistic inhumane torture with emotionless objectivity of political prisoners.

Following the coup, the plan had called for the military government to imprison thousands of people without charge or warrant. Thirty thousand Chilean citizens had been executed. The propaganda Lakein and others had circulated rationalized the actions "for the defense of democracy and political stability."

The American ITT Corporation had supported the coup with the sanction of the U.S. President's "Executive Order." ITT's holdings and mining operations had been among those seized by the Allende government.

Many political prisoners jailed by the secret police disappeared, executed by Contreras' death squads.

Pinochet used DINA to reach even beyond Chile with terrorist acts to eliminate exiles and expatriates who posed a threat of political opposition. He ordered his secret police to track down and attempt the assassination of Bernardo Leighton, leader of the exiles and insurgents, at the 1975 conference in Caracas, Venezuela.

In another instance, a bomb placed by a DINA agent had killed General Carlos Prat Gonzalez and his wife in Buenos Aires, Argentina. General Prat had been one of the few public figures capable of organizing a return to constitutional rule in Chile.

A Chilean who supported a return to constitutional rule was shot and killed in Rome after efforts to coordinate an alliance of exiles and the anti-*junta* wing of the Christian Democratic Party.

In response to the charges of brutality and mass murder, the Chilean government had labeled the campaigns as attempts by exiles and international communists to blacken the image of Chile and the *junta*.

The American Civil Liberties Union and Amnesty International were singled out and identified by the Chilean press as "arms of the communist party in the United States."

Contreras was a psychotic killer. But Lakein had dined with murderers many times in the past. He had even hired a few to kidnap and assassinate foreign government officials the CIA wanted removed from the political system in South America. Regime change was nothing new to him.

He had been centrally involved in plotting the kidnapping of General Rene Schneider under the Allende regime. Schneider had died of gunshot wounds inflicted while resisting the attempt by Chileans posing as "dissidents" to take him hostage.

As Commander-in-Chief of the Army, General Schneider had been considered an obstacle to the United States Government's move to block Allende, who had nationalized American Corporate holdings in Chile, ITT among others. Lakein' and his agents had supplied financial aid, machine guns and other arms and equipment to various military figures who opposed Allende. Later, Allende's death by machine gun fire was pronounced a suicide.

So Lakein was not altogether uncomfortable with Contreras, especially considering the information he was about to share with him. Contreras would be eternally grateful and Lakein never knew when he might need to call in his cards and ask a personal favor of the man. Contreras was not only politically well-connected in Chile, but in Brazil and Argentina, as well. If Lakein were discovered to be a double agent, he would be looking for a place to hide.

He rose from the table to greet him, as the *maître de* efficiently pulled out a chair for Contreras. He settled his blocky frame into place in a single quick motion. A hovering waiter placed the white linen napkin in his lap with a flourish. Contreras ordered a *pisco sour*, then peered intently at Lakein, who met the dark inscrutable gaze with a slight smile. "Hello, Manuel."

Contreras offered a steely grin in return. "I haven't seen you around for the past few months. Have you been out of the country?"

"Yes, the States, California, on related business. How are things in Santiago?"

"Business as usual. Never a day goes by."

"I see the demand for copper has increased on the world market."

"And production, as a consequence," said Contreras, fiddling with his fork.

"I've made a discovery that should interest you."

The waiter interrupted them bringing Contreras his *pisco sour.* He presented them with menus and a wine list, announced the specialty of the day, then departed. Ignoring his *pisco sour,* Contreras motioned for Lakein to continue.

"I received a report from Argentina that there's unusual activity with the MIR."

Contreras leaned forward. His dark pencil thin mustache twitched like a cat's whiskers. "Is it confined to Argentina?"

"This time, no, which is the reason for this meeting."

"Have they moved into Chile?"

"We don't know yet. I understand the regime has granted permission for an American motion picture company to film here on location."

"That is correct."

"I've managed to become a cultural adviser on the film."

"Interesting. Two of my DINA agents will always be with the company."

"You're allowing arms and heavy artillery to be brought into the country for the production, as I understand the arrangement."

"The agreement is that they will be turned over to the army at the conclusion of the production."

"May I discreetly recommend that you confiscate them at the port upon arrival and arrest the entire film production company, excluding myself, of course. The movie star, Kasia Kerenski, and her husband, the film's director, Michael Sloan, are communist agents working under cover."

Contreras raised an eyebrow.

"The film company is connected with the MIR action."

"Who is behind this?"

"I don't know yet," said Lakein. "I'm working on finding out. We probably won't know until we get the leaders. My concern about the artillery is the distinct possibility it is to be used by the MIR guerrillas"

"At what point will they enter the country?"

"We don't have a fix on it yet, but most likely somewhere south of Puerto Montt."

The waiter returned. "Are you gentlemen prepared to order?"

A few more minutes, *por favor*, said Lakein.

Noticing Contreras's untouched pisco sour, the waiter asked, "*Cuelo es problema?*"

"No, no it's fine," Contreras replied in Spanish and the waiter retired to wait until they signaled to him to return.

"Is the Tri Con Corporation itself involved with this movie company?" asked Contreras.

"To my knowledge, the corporation is not aware of what is taking place. The CIA is not yet prepared to reveal to Tri Con any of our findings in the event there is a cell operating within the company. We want the leaders of the MIR action to show us who is pulling the strings with Tri Con. So you understand the need for absolute secrecy in this matter." Lakein was satisfied by Contreras's expression that he had swallowed the lie.

"What is the source of your information?"

"Messages in code that we managed to decipher. That was what I was doing in California. What we have found is not definite, so we must move forward carefully. But I do know for a fact that the star of the film, Kasia Kerenski, is a Soviet spy."

"It will be my pleasure to interrogate her."

"I believe that what we have uncovered is only the tip of the iceberg that floats under Argentina, Brazil, and Venezuela, as well."

"The film company arrives in one month," said Contreras. "That means the MIR activity may be happening in the south as we speak. If you will excuse me, lunch is no longer important." He rose to leave. "Other matters have become a priority."

***

On June 3rd, 1981, the West German military transport, Guttenberg, set out from the Soviet port of Vladivostock on the southeastern Russia seaboard. Several Russians, including two agents of the KGB had joined the crew. The Guttenberg had just taken on a several thousand ton cargo of the latest armored Soviet tanks, supply trucks, and heavy artillery. In addition, the freighter carried a formidable arsenal in her hold. Her escort was the Petrov, a nuclear powered submarine.

Together, they made the Pacific crossing to the west coast of South America in thirty days. While still in international waters, the Petrov swung south two hundred miles beyond Concepcion and established a radio communications network between the MIR guerilla base camp in the southern forests of Chile and a Soviet satellite which beamed the Petrov's coded messages directly into a Tri Con satellite communications center in San Bernardino, California. Helmut Bachmann would be kept informed by the commander of the Petrov as to the progress of the coup and if anything should go wrong. The Petrov maintained direct radio contact with the KGB agents on the Guttenberg, as well.

Disguised as West German sailors, the Russian crew members and KGB field operatives supervised the unloading of the artillery and armor at the Chilean port of Valparaiso, north of Santiago.

Thirty minutes after the last vehicle was lowered by a boom crane to the dock and all pieces secured, Manuel Contreras secret police descended on the dock to cordon off the weaponry. More secret police and a squad of Chilean soldiers suddenly materialized from the warehouses and nearby streets where they had been sequestered. Bristling with firepower, The troops swarmed along the dock and held the Russians at gunpoint. The two KGB agents realized at once that the mission had been compromised.

They transmitted a coded message to the Petrov commander advising of the seizure. The message, in turn was relayed to Bachmann through his communication center in Southern California.

He wasted no time in sending a return coded message to the Petrov, an order for transmission to Malcolm Karazississ bringing his guerilla insurgents into Chile from Argentina.

Terminate Roger Lakein at the earliest opportunity. Mission compromised. Proceed as planned.

***

The film production crew had been on location for five weeks. The script was one third shot with the production on schedule. For the twentieth time that day, Michael put Kasia and part of his ensemble cast through a difficult scene in a country setting a few miles outside of Santiago.

As the cultural consultant for the duration of the film project, Roger Lakein hovered about behind the cameras, offering an occasional point of authenticity to Michael between set-ups and helping interpret to the native *campesinos* what was requested of them. They were making more money in a single day as extras than they made during months of back-breaking labor. However, Lakein experienced some difficulty in convincing them to forego their customary afternoon siesta, since the availability of sunlight was so necessary to the filming.

Finally satisfied with the take, Michael called, "Print. Wrap it up." He addressed the cast and crew. "Thank you all for your patience and excellent work." Then he discussed the next day's shooting schedule with Kasia and other principles of the cast while the crew stored the shot film and broke down cameras, sound and lighting equipment. They all caravanned back to Santiago where they left the trucks and vans parked in a local studio warehouse.

A message was waiting for Michael at the hotel advising him that the shipment of tanks, trucks, jeeps and artillery for the production had arrived that afternoon at the port of Valparaiso. He immediately called Bill Thomas, his property manager, and asked him to oversee the deployment and delivery of the vehicles to the set the following week while he continued with the shooting schedule.

Michael, Kasia, and Lakein had gone out for their usual ten o'clock dinner at one of Lakein's favorite restaurants in the heart of downtown Santiago. Between the three of them, they had gorged on seafood and put away two bottles of the delicious wine that was second in the world only to the finest French wines.

Returning in a taxi to their hotel, they saw three military jeeps and a large convoy truck parked outside and blocking the front entrance. Lakein ordered the driver to stop a black away from what was happening. Members of Michael's production crew were being marched at gunpoint out of the hotel and loaded onto the truck.

Michael started to climb out of the taxi to intervene. "What the fuck is going on?" But Lakein pulled him back in.

"No, don't go out there. They'll take you too."

"For God's sake, we haven't done anything."

"It's the artillery that arrived today. Must be." Roger glanced over at Kasia. "It's got to be that. And there's other political activity brewing. I spoke to someone at the embassy this morning," he lied. "It's known that mercenaries and guerillas from Argentina have infiltrated the country and are hidden somewhere in the north. The junta believes the film production is linked to the planned guerilla action against the government."

"What? We're just shooting a goddamn movie. Nothing else. How come you waited 'til now to tell me this? Who the fuck are you anyway? You're with the CIA, aren't you? Shit, you have to be to know all that. You set us up, didn't you?"

"Lakein," Kasia's voice cut through the tense silence that followed. "You're dead unless you get us out of the country. Gordon Frasier, the CIA, has penetrated Tri Con. He knows you're the mole. So does Contreras. And obviously, so do I."

Lakein stared hard at her, uncertain if she were bluffing or telling the truth, but he had no way nor the time to check out her information.

Her expression told him what she said was true. If he were taken in this sweep by Contreras and the DINA, he could be executed along with Kasia and Michael.

Michael was staring at Kasia and now looked back and forth between them. What he suddenly realized sent a chill up his spine. His wife was also an agent for the CIA.

"Well," said Lakein coolly. "We're all in this together."

"Hell, I'm going to stop this." Michael was still determined to leave the taxi and attempt interference.

"They're not going to believe anything you tell them," said Lakein. "We have to leave the country."

"I can't cut out and leave all my people stuck down here in a stinking prison for no reason."

"The police won't do anything to the crew. They'll just send them back home to the states. It's a different story for you and Kasia."

"What the hell is that supposed to mean?"

"I'm telling you, don't go out there."

"Let go of me." Michael kicked open the door. He saw three armed police running toward them. He froze at the clatter of their jackboots on the spiny cobblestones and Uzi submachine guns swinging at each stride.

Lakein shouted an order in Spanish to the driver. The taxi dragged away with screaming tires that left a swatch of burning rubber. Michael fell back onto the seat as the police opened fire and strafed the departing auto, shattering the rear windshield just before the vehicle careened sharply around a street corner out of range. He reached out and pulled the wildly swinging door shut.

Lakein barked terse instructions to the frantic driver whose dark curly hair had become the repository of tiny shards of glass. Lakein gave him a destination somewhere in the western sector of the city. Glancing back once, he quietly announced, "They're coming after us," and urged the driver to increase his speed.

Michael and Kasia looked behind to see two military jeeps maneuver recklessly through the traffic to catch up.

"How could this happen?" Michael blurted causing the cab driver to glance at him sharply in the rearview mirror.

"That's something about Latin America you have to learn to live with," said Lakein grimly. "You never know from one day to the next what side you should say you're on."

"Why don't you ask the driver to perform a miracle?"

Roger thrust a handful of cash forward past the driver's right shoulder and told him to lose the jeeps. The additional incentive was not necessary since the driver feared for his life.

Making an abrupt cut to the right, he nearly ran down a donkey cart which crashed over spilling its load of fruit and vegetables in baskets and blocking the entrance to an alley. The cab roared on between the double story stone buildings pressing them on either side.

The nightmare horror of being pursued again and running for her life gripped Kasia, the dreamlike unreality of moonlight stabbing across the shadowed passages between narrow breaks in the houses bled her memory with the cutting force of lasers. She clutched Michael and fought to contain the scream and choking nausea of fear rising from the churning pit of her stomach as she thought of their child, Danielle. Kasia had realized her worst suspicion. She cursed herself that she had not left the production before it had progressed this far.

The car nearly spun out turning another corner to the left, crunching the passengers hard against each other to the right. After three more such gut-wrenching maneuvers, the driver informed Lakein that he had lost their pursuers.

Lakein gave him another generous handful of cash and asked him to proceed quickly to another section of the city, a shanty town that clung like an infestation to the urban center.

Michael and Kasia exchanged glances of alarm when the driver finally stopped in the heart of this squalid ghetto bordering on the eroded hillside that reeked of filth and excrement.

As Roger led them from the cab along the dirt streets, they saw the keen edge of hunger and deprivation all about them in the night shadows, the shoeless beggars and gangs of shirtless young men wearing knives stuck in their belts and watching them with lethal intent.

Roger warned them to keep moving. Michael and Kasia resigned themselves to the tension of whatever lay ahead. Now, there was no going back. They needed to concentrate totally on survival and, in so doing, entrust themselves to a man they suspected would kill them, once he had used them to his advantage.

"This way. Stay close together." Lakein gripped Kasia's hand, towing her after him to Michael's surge of resentment at Lakein playing the hero, a feeling Michael thought he would not have the time nor energy to engage, considering the circumstances. He figured Lakein's gesture was an attempt to reconnect with Kasia and communicate that he was genuinely concerned for her well-being, not just his own ass. Lakein could have left them at any time to the mercy of the secret police and gone on alone.

The stench of open garbage and smoke from charcoal cooking fires swarmed into their nasal passages like toxic gas stinging their eyes and lungs.

Lakein suddenly stopped. He knocked three times, paused, then twice, paused, then once sharply on the side door of a storage warehouse with a corrugated tin roof. After a few moments, they heard the click of a lock, and the door squealed open on rusty hinges. A compact swarthy *mestizo* with a dark drooping mustache warily peered out at them. Upon recognizing Lakein in the dim light, he motioned for them all to enter, then closed and relocked the door.

Several moments were needed for their eyes to adjust to the dusty gloom penetrated by scattered pencil-thin rays of moonlight and a single bare bulb in a junk cluttered alcove near the garage door entrance.

Nearly surrounded on three sides by unmarked crates and cartons, a two and a half ton military convoy truck with a high canvas covered bed loomed like an ancient sleeping tortoise on its tractor tread tires.

Lakein conferred briefly in Spanish with the man, whom he introduced as Petra. They would wait there hidden in the warehouse until nightfall. Then Petra would drive them in the truck to the coast where they would be met by a fishing trawler.

"So just make yourselves as comfortable as you can," said Roger. "We'll be safe here, at least for a while."

"What is all this?" Michael asked in reference to the truck and supplies. "And who is he?"

"As a journalist, I have connections and information sources with the underground, as well as the privilege of moving in embassy and government press circles. At least I used to." He looked at Kasia. "Of course, these are carefully guarded secret contacts for such emergencies as this when we need them to assist us in getting out of the country."

"Is there someplace we can sit down?" asked Kasia.

"Yes, an area at the back of the warehouse. And there's a toilet of sorts."

While Roger stayed behind to talk with Petra, Michael and Kasia made their way further to a rough bench jammed among the crates and boxes.

"How long as this been going on?" he asked her when they were alone out of earshot.

"It started just before I graduated from college. I had to or my parents would have been deported."

"Because they're Russian?"

"Because they're Russian. The KGB sent them to America so I could be born a naturalized citizen and they could use me as a spy."

"Here I'm married to you and you represent everything I hate."

"Don't say that."

"Did you spy on me? I'll bet that was easy."

"Michael, stop this. You have nothing to do with what went before and what is happening now."

"Then what the hell am I doing standing here talking to you? Why didn't you tell me?"

"I was ordered not to."

"By whom?"

"The U.S. State Department, the CIA."

"Do they control your life?"

"Yes. This was unforeseen."

"Unforeseen. Who didn't foresee it?"

"We're both caught in the middle. I've been trying for a long time to get out from under them, Michael. But they won't let me. They'll even hurt you and Danielle if I try."

"Who are they? Who are you talking about?"

"I'm with the CIA, but I work as a courier, a double agent. The KGB thinks I work for them."

"I feel like I'm in the middle of a movie, but you're for real."

"Yes, I'm for real. This assignment is the last. It was to discover who Lakein is working for. He's a CIA operative but he cut a deal with the KGB. Once this is over, I'll be free. They'll let me get on with a normal life."

"Only if we get out alive. Can't you go to the U.S. Embassy?"

"Lakein has poisoned everything for me, for us, especially for me here. The police will arrest us or shoot us on sight. We can't risk going back out into the streets. We must escape another way."

"Can Lakein really get us out or is he just setting us up?"

"He's our only chance."

"Some chance. I'd like to kill him."

"You'd have to get in line."

They stopped talking at hearing the scrapes and bumps of Lakein making his way through the containers to join them.

"Will we be able to get something to eat tomorrow?" Michael lowered himself to the bench.

"There's food all around us," Lakein's gesture took in the stacks of boxes.

"We just help ourselves whenever we get hungry. Is that it? Lucky Lakein's halfway house."

At Michael's sarcastic tone, Roger leveled a cold stare. "I know how bitter you must feel. But believe me, you are lucky to be here instead of where they will put you if they get their hands on you. Your next stop was *Tres Alamos*. Once you're inside that prison, you never come out, except to be buried."

"What about my film crew? Can the embassy get them out of the country? They're totally innocent of all this shit you CIA play with."

"Yes, your crew knows nothing about this. They'll be put on a plane and sent back to the States within a day or two."

Kasia glanced down the length of the warehouse in the direction of the alcove. "Can Petra bring us some potable drinking water or at least something that won't give us dysentery?"

"I asked him to bring us beer. It's best not to take a chance on the local water, especially in this part of town. Typhoid, and malaria, dysentery." Lakein shrugged. "You drink the water to live and eventually it kills you."

Michael stood from the bench. "I'm going to walk around. I'm having a hard time accepting this. There must be something we can do to turn it around."

"This is not a movie, Sloan. You can't edit or change the script. Just don't look out any windows."

Michael hesitated and glanced back at Lakein. "Can Petra bring us a gun?" Now that they had become victims, not only did Michael want to make a clean escape, he wanted to do damage in return.

"Later, we'll all have guns."

"That's encouraging." Feeling like a caged lion, Michael stalked away, brushed past the giant truck and noted for future reference the location of both the heavily locked and bolted side doors, that the windows were barred and too high to allow for any manner of escape.

He stopped at the realization that suddenly his whole life, within a matter of hours, was oriented to survival and escape. He had difficulty accepting and believing what was happening, especially the revelation that he had married a CIA agent and she had never told him of the fact. He wondered if it would have made any difference in the beginning of their relationship. She had used him. Would he have loved her any less?

As he passed the alcove, Michael sensed the hostile wariness of Petra, who watched him establish a pacing routine, slowly steadily around and around the truck as though he were inspecting it for some exterior defect.

This was the second major crisis associated with Michael's career and personal life in which he had fallen prey to the forces of circumstances beyond his control. He could barely contain his rage.

For all of Roger Lakein's seemingly good intentions at this eleventh hour, Michael still believed that he and Kasia were somehow being manipulated for political reasons about which they were unaware.

He and Kasia were accustomed to long periods of waiting on movie sets while technicians arranged the lights and camera angles were established. Enduring the slow hours until their departure was not in and of itself a difficult ordeal.

Left alone with Kasia, Lakein studied her beautiful face for several moments, then asked, "How did they determine I'm the mole?"

"Things you said, assumptions you made. You were careless."

"Were you involved?"

"No, how could I be? Even if I were, why would I tell you? You set yourself up and caught yourself in your own trap." She looked unflinchingly at him.

"Charley and Maggie – do they know about me?"

Kasia shook her head.

"Let's keep things that way if you want to get out of the country alive and them too. They're the ones who will get us out. They have the escape route. You say anything about me, anything at all, then I give the word to the MIR that you, your husband, Charley, and Maggie all work for the CIA. They'll kill you up on the mountain."

"It's a deal, Lakein. You keep your part of it, I'll keep mine."

Returning to them, Michael assertively suggested to Lakein that since, in Lakein's words, he had a kind of diplomatic immunity, why couldn't he sneak out of there and go to the American Embassy. He could arrange for a special escort to rescue them all from this situation and put them on a plane back home.

Lakein shook his head and recapitulated that from the viewpoint of the secret police, he had violated that immunity by aiding them in making an escape. To himself, he speculated, if they really knew he was the mole, it was not any safer for him to be seen out on the streets than it was for them. The other factor that concerned him was that, according to Petra, one of the supply drivers had turned informer and he feared the secret police knew of this warehouse and its operation in support of the guerillas. The informer was subsequently murdered.

"The truth of the matter is," Kasia cut in, "Lakein is a double agent, what is known in the trade as a mole. He's on the Soviet payroll, but he double-crossed them, as well. He can't move around out there anymore than we can. You've got to run and hide now for the rest of your life, don't you?"

Lakein did not respond.

"What I just told you is between us, Michael. If you mention it to anyone, Lakein can have us murdered."

Toward midnight, Petra brought them hot food and more beer. The warm beer and oppressive heat of the warehouse tired them along with the uncertainty of waiting. Grimy and unshaven, Michael disliked the smell of himself and the foul spicy after taste of whatever it was Petra had brought them to eat.

He watched the fading moon diminish from the high warehouse windows as shadows consumed the pale light and crept in across the rafters, then descended like creatures sliding down over the truck and boxes until they had consumed the interior in darkness.

Roger lit the dirty stub of a candle protruding from a puddle of melted wax on a small tin plate. The wavering light only heightened the threatening aspect of the shadows, investing them with a life they did not otherwise possess. The three of them were snared in an irreversible nightmare in which the monsters that lurked out there in the darkness were not creations of their own imaginations, but the cold impersonal agents of bureaucratic paranoia and death.

Petra had been gone now for over an hour. Michael noticed Lakein's nervousness in lighting up a second cigarette before even finishing the first one. From time to time, Lakein left them alone and walked forward to the alcove and listened at the large garage door for any unusual noise outside.

Kasia and Michael dozed off at 1:00 a.m. Petra had still not returned and Lakein began to suspect a double-cross. He decided to wait only ten more minutes. If Petra didn't show, he would drive the truck himself. He was familiar enough with the route and the pickup point.

Five minutes later, to Lakein's relief, a breathless Petra slipped in at the side door and hastily warned him that they had no more time to wait. The police had begun making a sweep of the area and within a short time would discover them.

Lakein rushed to the back of the warehouse and woke Kasia and Michael. "We're leaving now. Have to move fast."

They ran for the truck and climbed into the rear, which was partially filled with traditional canvas and supplies behind which they could lie or crouch down and hide. By the beam of a flashlight he found, Lakein revealed two submachine guns and a carton of ammunition clips. Michael instantly grabbed and loaded one of the models.

They heard the rattle of the heavy garage chain cranking up the corrugated aluminum door. It finally reached the top with a booming shudder and was still, its echoes fading away in the warehouse cavern.

Petra clambered into the cab and slammed the door as he started the engine. It roared to life, sending vibrations back through the truck and filling the warehouse with choking exhaust fumes.

After a few minutes warm-up, they lumbered out of the warehouse and the gargantuan truck moved ponderously through the narrow streets of the sleeping ghetto. Petra did not risk going back through the city, but took a circuitous route near the perimeter until the smooth hum of the massive calked tire treads told Lakein in the rear that they were finally headed south on the coastal highway.

"We might as well get some sleep," Lakein said to Michael and Kasia out of the dark. "It's a couple of hours away."

As they settled down into the canvas, Michael quietly asked, "How long is this going to take – getting out of the country?"

"I can't tell you in numbers of days."

Kasia sat upright. "What about the fishing trawler. Doesn't it take us north?"

"No, south, Down the coast – only for a few hundred miles. After that, there will be a long trip upriver into the forest country where we contact Charley and Maggie. I can't be sure of what will happen once we're in there. They'll have to arrange with the MIR to fly us out, if possible, from one of the high country lakes. But the weather's bad down there this time of year, violent storms. We have to make it into Argentina, but if we can't fly over the mountains, then we'll have to go another way."

"How, by llama?" Michael snorted with derision.

"Mining train, out of Antofagasta."

"That's way the hell up north."

"If the weather doesn't hold, that's where we'll have to go. DINA intelligence will never suspect us of doubling back. The trains make day and night runs back and forth from the copper mines. Only, there are guards and checkpoints."

"Shit, Lakein, I already did a tour in Viet Nam," said Michael. "Isn't there a more reasonable way out of this fuckin' mess? Some way a little less risky?"

"If there were, we'd be taking it. I'm not any happier about this than you are. I don't care for surprises either."

"You're in a lousy business."

"We'd all better get some sleep. We're going to need it."

As tired as he was, sleep did not come easily for Michael. He sensed Kasia thrashing with nervous tension, her twitches of anxiety barely subsiding as she succumbed to an overwhelming fatigue. The gun metal smells and sounds and hot coastal dampness placed him back in time to other such truck convoys in which he had traveled across rice paddies and deltas in Viet Nam.

Now, here he was again, reliving the sweat, stench and expectancy of fear in a foreign country where death struck out of the darkness. Struggling with his dilemma, he finally slept.

***

The three of them were so exhausted, they did not realize when the truck left the paved highway and slowed its progress over a semi-rough dirt road. Petra pulled the cumbersome vehicle off into a cleared section of tropical undergrowth that butted on a beach of enormous sand dunes.

Trying to screen out the distant pounding of surf beyond the dunes, Petra climbed down from the truck cab. With rifle in hand, he scanned the clearing, then scrambled to the top of the nearest dune and peered over.

Running without lights, a trawler materialized moving in on the dark undulating swells. A bank of distant fog concealed the moon hanging low in the sky. Amid the occasional white flashes of foam out beyond the swish, crackle and boom of surf, Petra spotted a dinghy making slow steady headway coming in toward the beach.

With a sniff of satisfaction, he slid back down the dune and returned to the truck whose engine threw metallic heat and fumes that vied with the smell of the sea.

He pushed open the rear canvas flaps and flashed his battery-powered lantern inside. He said the trawler was waiting offshore. Lakein answered in Spanish, then shook Kasia and Michael awake. One after another they moved to the tail gate and jumped to the ground.

Suddenly they heard two jeeps coming along the road at a nearly idling pace, a patrol.

"Let's go," Lakein took the lead with Kasia and Michael following him up the side of the dune. They saw the dinghy break through the surf and slide in on the spreading foam.

As the jeeps broke into the clearing, their headlights and spotlights nailed Petra clawing his way up the dune after the others. A burst of automatic fire killed him instantly.

Dropping prone at the ridge on the opposite side of the dune, Michael and Lakein returned the fire, blasting out the lights and wounding two soldiers who were running past the truck toward the dune. A machine gunner raked the top of the dune with tracer fire kicking up sand in their faces.

Ankles deep in soft clinging sand, they plunged down the hill and sprinted out after Kasia, who had reached the small boat bobbing and swerving in the shallows. Pushing the dinghy back out through the surf, Michael and Lakein fell in nearly upsetting it as the oarsman pulled furiously to place them out of range.

Michael pushed Kasia down low beside him. A few minutes later, a scatter of automatic rifle fire spat inaccurately from the beach.

As the dinghy came alongside the trawler, a flare fired from the dunes illuminated them, but they were out of range. A second crew member assisted Kasia aboard first, then Michael.

The man who had rowed them out steadied the smaller craft while Roger went aboard, then followed, allowing the dinghy to drift out astern to the end of the tow rope.

Michael, Kasia, and Lakein hunkered down among a pile of ropes and fishing net and watched the dark shapes of the crewmen as one pulled up anchor and the other started the engines sputtering below deck.

Michael's arms went protectively around Kasia's shoulders as the trawler's high prow swung about knifing and splitting through the black glossy swells. It moved steadily out to sea for another mile, than angled south paralleling the dark coastal landmass to which they eventually had to return.

CHAPTER THIRTY-FIVE

The Running

At dawn, the sun became a presence on the sea, more felt than seen in the morning haze until it transformed the foam-flecked gray swells into a deep intense blue as thick as paint.

The heat on the grimy faces of the two men and one woman irritated them awake. They rose from rigid bunks and stretched the stiffness and discomfort from their joints. They desired first and foremost fresh drinking water to assuage the salty dryness in their throats.

Balancing unsteadily against the shift and toss of the trawler, Lakein went up on deck and forward to the steerage cabin. He returned with a canteen, which he shared with Kasia and Michael.

"There's a toilet in there," he incidentally informed them.

A sharp hunger speared them from the wafting smell of coffee, and fish frying in tomato sauce. They each made use of the toilet, then walked to an area on the stern deck to wait for breakfast to be served.

"The cook told me it will be ready shortly," said Lakein.

The nausea in Michael's gut rose and fell in unison with the rising falling rock and sway of the boat as it slipped from crest to trough in the long lazy rolling swells. Looking out across the water, he could no longer discern the shore line, only the purple mass of the continent in the dawn mist.

A few minutes later, a crew member, the first mate, who was doubling as cook, called to them in Spanish from the open galley. Lakein assisted Kasia to her feet as she stumbled.

Michael hesitated a moment clutching the rail trying to decide if he were about to retch or should go eat. Determined to overcome his motion sickness and keep down whatever was creating the hunger-inducing aromas, he turned and followed the others.

The distant drone of an approaching engine stopped them. They scanned the surrounding sea and sky. Not a boat or a plane was in sight. The sound continued to come steadily closer and closer.

Moments later, a small reconnaissance plane containing a pilot and a passenger with binoculars appeared winging toward them out of the rising sun directly in their eyes.

Michael brought up his rifle prepared to shoot, but Lakein warned him, "Don't do it. We're just fishermen unless you fire at them. We don't want the navy or the coast guard coming after us."

The plane made a high pass, then angled back to the north. Standing on the stern deck munching fish and *tampanados* and gulping strong black coffee, they watched the slim birdlike shape recede up the coast.

Later that morning, one of the crew noticed a second craft, a naval gunboat barely visible from the cabin. It was following them ten miles back. He nudged the boat captain's shoulder and pointed.

Lakein noticed the gesture and climbed up the ladder to the cabin so he could see above the cresting waves. After a few moments, he, the captain and the first mate, climbed back down the ladder and conferred on the lower deck.

"They have radar," said Lakein. "How can we lose them?"

They told him the trawler would soon be approaching the southern archipelago, a long chain of rugged deserted islands. They would reach them in less than an hour. There they could lose the gunboat and hide the trawler until nightfall. The gunboat would not catch up to them for at least another hour at the speed they were traveling.

Lakein wondered at that, why the gunboat just hung back there pressing when it could have closed rather quickly if it wanted to. The trawler could not hope to outrun it in the open sea. Yet, the gunboat was unmistakably following them. They had another one hundred miles to go before they reached the river that would take them to the interior of the continent.

As the captain had promised, the tip of the island chain appeared through the swells disturbing the perfect continuity of the endless sea greening out with the first signs of a reef.

The first mate ran to the bow and directed the pilot using hand and arm signals as the trawler followed a familiar channel that carried it into quiet water inside the reef. For the next hour, they zig-zagged through a maze of treacherous reefs and shallow lagoons and soon were well out of sight of the pursuing gunboat by the time it reached the southernmost tip of the archipelago.

The captain finally jockeyed the trawler in among several tall, wooded pinnacles of rock that were pocked with coves and fenced off a narrow channel between the rocks and the small central island.

After they had dropped anchor, the three fishermen brought out submachine guns and ammunition from below. The mate set about preparing a cold supper and they waited while Roger and the captain went ashore in a dinghy. They climbed a bluff three hundred yards to the south to watch the progress of the gunboat.

Toward sunset, it came into view. The shallow keeled gunboat had considerably less difficulty navigating the reefs and sand bars and was able to make good time. It passed to the opposite western side of the island where the captain knew of a cove where they would most likely anchor for the night. Navigation of these waters in the dark would be hazardous.

Roger questioned him about the terrain of the island. After some discussion, they settled on a plan they hoped would permanently throw the marines off their track.

Kasia sensed a change among the four men, a tension in their manner and behavior. They were grimly silent as they cleaned and oiled their automatic weapons and stocked ammunition clips with extra loads.

When the time came, she hugged Michael while the other three climbed down the boarding ladder to the dinghy. "Be careful. Don't take any chances," she whispered. "They are more than fishermen."

He kissed her raised lips, then released her and went over the side.

The small boat crunched ashore. The four men leaped out. The captain and mate secured it up on the beach. Lakein and Michael moved on and waited in the shadows of the rough undergrowth. They slung their submachine guns and pushed their way toward the center of the island.

Slivers of pale moonlight filtered erratic patterns through the canopy of towering spruce. Thickets of nearly impenetrable undergrowth hampered the men's progress. They stumbled and maneuvered along in single file, fighting hordes of blood-thirsty mosquitoes swarming out of the fetid night. Leaking sweat soaked their clothes and stung their eyes. The strong dank odor of the sea mingled with the living plants filling their nostrils with herbal pungency that forced them to swallow sneezes to avoid giving away their position.

The captain led the way, angling about, seeking a trail. The others followed his progress more by sound and subliminal primitive senses than by sight.

After two hundred yards, the terrain rose at a sudden angle. The dense undergrowth thinned out to be replaced by rocky soil studded with uprooted granite spires.

Breathing heavily from their exertions, the column made better time in a strenuous scrambling climb to a high ridge that created the peak at the center of the island. On a patch of open ground illuminated by the astral sky, they paused to rest.

From their vantage point, they looked down the other side over the top of the mushrooming dark forest to the moon-rippled lagoon where the gunboat rode at anchor. Tendrils of grayish smoke rose in acrid wisps from a cooking fire on the strand of beach below.

The captain led off and they began the descent. Negotiating the terrain was less severe and challenging than the previous ascending slope. They traversed gradually down into the thickets and advanced slowly, cautiously with controlled movements and bitter stealth through the curtain of foliage.

Within a half hour, they came to a break among the trees. The caress of a fresh cooling breeze blowing in off the lagoon touched their faces drenched in salt sweat. The draft carried the fresh scent of the sea mingled with woodsmoke.

As they moved in closer, they could see the tentative flickering firelight and hear men's voices in low unintelligible conversation punctuated with an occasional bark of laughter. Then, although still some distance, they clearly discerned four Chilean navy marines seated around the fire. One rose and left to return to the gunboat where the shadow of a fifth man passed across the cabin light.

Michael heard the captain next to him flip off the safety, work the bolt and ram a shell home. The weapons of Lakein and the mate spoke with a simultaneous metallic clack, then spurt a sudden rapid-fire of white flame and lethal slugs that raked the sand and fire and toppled the remaining three soldiers where they sat sharing a bottle of brandy with their coffee.

Roger, Michael, the captain, and the mate took their time climbing back over the ridge the way they had come. Michael had not fired a single shot. At the last moment, his zeal to strike back and kill, especially the unsuspecting men, had deserted him.

Far out in the distance, they could see and hear the booming white surf rising from the black sea and exploding over the reef pearling with bioluminescence. For all the trouble they had taken, the incident had happened so quickly and at such a deceiving distance, he doubted his ability to clearly witness what he had heard and seen. The captain assured them that the gunboat would not discover and overtake them the following morning.

A pale predawn light hung over the trawler leaving the island behind. They moved southward deeper into the maze of the archipelago. The cloud cover did not abate, but dropped lower and lower, catching them in a rough squall.

Michael, Kasia, and Lakein moved quickly into the shelter afford by the cabin as large raindrops pelted the open deck. The trawler dipped and rocked surging steadily through the heavy leaden swells.

By late morning, they were free of the storm's ragged clouds. Kasia and Michael noticed that the trawler had been gradually angling in landward and the water in their vicinity was an ochre color, mud from the delta where the river flowed into the sea.

Thousands of feeding birds rose at their approach filling the sky with frantic winged bodies and deafening cries warning of this invasion of their estuary. The trawler churned past the mud flats and followed the main channel upriver where it cut through a hardwood forest so green with dense foliage that it appeared black and dripped with steam.

They forged on farther and farther, wending their way into a primeval grotto of cavernous silence broken only by the muttering drone of the trawler's engine and the occasional eerie shattering cry of a lone bird. The humid odor of rotting undergrowth and the sharp spicy smells of the river seeped up around them, saturating their senses. The heat became a living force that enclosed them with its oppressive weight, drawing perspiration from their bodies until their rancid clothes and hair clung to their skin.

After two more hours of meandering monotony during which Kasia and Michael's spirits sank lower and lower as they moved deep into the wilderness, they finally saw a break in the evergreen forest that appeared to have recently been cleared.

The river widened rounding a bend presenting them with a wooden dock and a small crude village, like an apparition projected against the forest wall. The crow of a rooster and barking of dogs brought the jungle frontier reality to life.

Pulling in to the dock, they saw several native men and women squatting under an open shed with produce and baggage as they waited for the mail boat from upriver to arrive. Two dozed. Others talked quietly or watched their half-naked children run out to greet the trawler and chatter at the first mate who jumped onto the dock to moor the boat.

"This is as far as we go," said the captain.

"What happens now?" Michael asked.

"We wait for the mail boat," said Lakein.

"Here?"

"In the village. Let's go."

They stepped onto the dock and, followed by the small group of curious children, walked along the rutted main street.

Two soldiers in a military jeep with a machine gun mount careened into sight at the other end of the village. Grinding and sliding it roared directly toward them. The children nimbly scattered like chickens and Kasia, Michael, and Lakein scrambled aside as it passed, spraying them with chunks of black mud. It slammed to a precarious halt in front of the cantina that the three had just passed near the dock. An officer stepped out of the jeep, then reached back in for a small haversack. His intense dark eyes swept over them with suspicion as he entered the cantina.

The jeep's driver executed a turn and sped back toward them.

"Watch out," warned Lakein. "He's coming again."

They moved into the shelter of the nearest doorway as the vehicle roared past and disappeared along the forest road at the end of town.

"I need a change of clothes," said Kasia. "Can we buy anything here?"

"There's a store. Let's find out." Michael sloughed off a glob of mud that had struck him in the face. He felt uneasy about leaving the submachine guns on the trawler. To do otherwise would have only drawn unwanted attention. Lakein had explained that carrying weapons, they might be mistaken for mercenaries and shot on sight. He suspected that word of their escape had not yet been received at the military outpost.

In the cantina, the few local patrons and three men sitting at a table and another standing at the bar dropped their casual manner and eyed the officer with wariness and suspicion. He ordered a beer, then, uninvited, approached three villagers and took the empty fourth chair at their table. They avoided his greeting nod and smile with silent hostility at his rude intrusion, but respectfully deferred to him. He raised his glass in salute to them and drank. Suddenly anxious to get away, they rose awkwardly and with uncertainty as to their manner and reason for leaving, and crowded out of the cantina.

The satisfied officer removed his cap and dropped it at the center of the table, propped his boots up on one of the vacated chairs and leaned back with a belch and a sigh.

He lit a cigar, shook out the match and dropped it in a thin spiral of smoke to the floor. Blowing copious clouds of smoke, he hummed a tune to himself.

Kasia, Michael, and Lakein came from the village store and walked slowly back in the direction of the river. Kasia now wore functional men's clothing and had tied back her hair with a green scarf. Her other clothes and a few personal items rode in a rucksack slung over one shoulder.

As they approached the cantina, Lakein suggested, "It could be a while before the boat arrives."

"What about the officer in there?" Michael was visibly tense and nervous.

"He doesn't know who we are."

After a moment's hesitation, Michael and Kasia followed him inside. They stood clustered at the door, getting oriented to the location of the bar and several tables and assessing who might be seated at them. Sudden low laughter from the officer drew their attention.

They stared at him. He watched with an expression of amusement as they walked to the bar to avoid him. He abruptly rose and pulled out a chair, inviting Kasia to join him. She hesitated, searching her mind wildly for a way to react until he indicated they should all join him. To their surprise, he spoke perfect English.

Lakein cocked his head in a half-nod, half-smile. Kasia cautiously sat down while Roger and Michael went to order beers. They returned, suspicious, offering a reserved front until they could be certain of the officer's intent and what he knew or might choose to reveal he knew about them.

He warmly introduced himself, "I'm Capitan Carlos Baravalle. Am I correct that you are Norte Americanos?"

Lakein responded in Spanish that they were tourists.

"If you will pardon me, but it is most unusual to see American tourists in these parts. Your baggage?"

"It was sent ahead of us."

"Ah, then you trust to the gods. It allows you to move quickly and more freely." He took a swallow of beer. His wet mustached lips parted in a good-natured grin. "If you will permit me to advise you, you must take especial care in traveling up this river beyond the village. There is insurgent activity, and we have recently encountered mercenary and guerilla forces." He smiled again. "You don't look like mercenaries. They have been known to fire even on the mail boat. Fortunately, we have been able to contain their movement, but a few slip past our patrols. Of course, my commandos are highly trained by your own United States special advisors to our country." A sardonic grin replaced the smile. "So you are all three on vacation," an inquiry stated as fact.

"We're traveling throughout the South American continent," explained Roger, "doing research for a collaborative book. This is Kasia Kerenski, Michael Sloan, and I'm Roger Lakein.

"Then I take it you don't plan to stay here in the village."

"We're only waiting for the mail boat," said Lakein.

"Ah, as I thought. You must have accommodations at Charley's and Maggie's hotel. Well, for you, that should be an experience to write home about."

Lakein smiled with casual interest. "What can you tell us about the hotel."

Carlos laughed. "It's not modern. Primitive. As for Charley and Maggie, you will have to see for yourselves. My description would not do them justice. There are some who love them and others who would like to see them dead. They are Norte Americanos like you. Only deep down, I suspect they are exiles, not retired expatriates like they claim.

"Charley also runs the mail boat service between this village and the hotel. The mail is brought in by air to a landing strip just outside the village near the camp. We also have a small military outpost here and a compound upriver near the hotel. Their little hotel is called Charley's Roost. Charley and Maggie came here about five years ago and have managed to keep their business alive. Hard to do here."

Michael leaned in slightly. "When does the boat arrive?"

"Every one or two weeks, depending on Charley's mood. He is not what you call reliable and he doesn't live according to the schedules of other people. One time when he came in here to town, he stayed drunk for a week, sleeping here on the floor and refused to take any passengers or mail upriver. Maggie worries when he does not return and then things get very ugly between them. She is Charley's wife, or so he says. Sometimes he calls her his mistress. I believe they are married. Would you like another beer? Allow me."

He quickly stood from the table. "The boat ride is long and very hot and dull. It is better to sleep or be drunk." He went to the bar and bought a bottle of whiskey and brought more beers and several limes in a wooden bowl.

As the next few hours passed, Carlos grew progressively louder and drunker talking about his wife, children, and mistress, politics, the Catholic church and his career as a military officer, Michael and Kasia finally excused themselves and walked outside to the dock.

Lakein stayed behind and allowed Baravalle to save face. He listened and encourage him to talk so the man would not become miffed and ornery and start asking inappropriate questions about them. For the moment, Lakein felt confident that Carlos did not know they were fugitives, but the officer possessed a certain slyness of behavior that Lakein had not yet been able to decipher.

Kasia and Michael walked self-consciously out onto the dock under the rain shed and took seats on a side bench among the other waiting native passengers who stared at them with bold curiosity.

Expressing a shy interest in these white-skinned strangers, a small, brown, dark-haired mestizo girl wandered over to them in an oblique manner. Kasia smiled at the charming innocence in the luminous black eyes. A sharp lump rose in her throat at the thought of her daughter, Danielle.

The girl's mother called her back and when the child returned, gently admonished her to not bother strangers, especially Anglos. The girl pouted, then smiled and looked back at them, hoping for a gesture of invitation.

Four sudden deep blasts of the mail boat horn sounded from upriver like some monster warning of its approach. The waiting passengers stood and looked expectantly in that direction, grabbed up their baggage and other belongings and crowded further out onto the dock.

Michael glanced back toward the village street in search of Lakein, who would certainly have heard the boat horn. Then he turned again to watch.

The old steamer appeared around the bend, approached with a ponderous chugging of its engine and slid alongside with a sickening crunch that knocked wood slivers into the water and caused the dock to sway.

Two native deck hands leaped off and secured the boat to pilings fore and aft. A few passengers and soldiers disembarked and headed for the village as the new passengers clambered aboard and claimed small territories about the cabin and open deck.

Kasia and Michael remained on the dock watching the boat captain, Charley MacIntosh, now a crusty graying unshaven man with a caustic temper and feverish alcoholic gleam in his steely blue eyes, blasting one of his Spanish crew for not warning him to make a wider swing at the dock.

Stepping off the boat, he stopped to light a limpid cigarette and stared at Kasia with a crude directness. They had never met nor seen each other before in California and Charley had never known about her role as a courier or her identity as an operations agent.

"Well," he snorted with a mixture of derision and pleasure. "Well, well, well, never thought I'd lay eyes on another one of the breed. Gringo and gringa, Norte Americano, if I'm not a day over fifty or out of my mind, both bein' possible. I've been known to have spells and see visions."

Kasia grinned, liking him immediately despite or because of his garrulous manner. He reminded her of her Russian father.

"We're for real."

"A voice, a sweet live voice. Haven't heard one like that in years, years I tell you. So you are for real. So you are. Long way from home here, ain't it? Word of advice – don't stay too damn long. You kin lose your faculties livin' out here in the boonies." He tapped the side of his white head.

"We were told you can help us," said Kasia.

"Help you? Who's gonna help me? We all need help one way or another, don't you know? There's a cozy little cocktail lounge up the street a way, if you haven't already discovered it. Finest Cantina in this part of the country, and the only one, except for mine at the hotel. You heard about the hotel, I take it."

Kasia and Michael nodded.

"Let's go raise a glass and talk about what you need while we're at it. This tub ain't goin' nowheres 'til I tell it to, though sometimes it has a mind of its own."

"I think we'd prefer to wait here," said Michael.

"Ah, then you've been in the pub. The décor must not agree with you or something. Suit yourselves. This rust bucket don't leave for at least an hour, maybe two. Better count on two."

"Two hours?" Michael glanced downriver aghast. The marine gunboat chasing after them could appear at any moment.

"You heard me, son. Sheets ain't been washed yet back at the hotel and Emilio, my chef, got the clap from one of my girls. I brought her down here for a treatment at the base hospital and to get some penicillin for poor Emilio." He started away, then suddenly turned back. "By the way, you two in trouble with the police or on vacation?"

Michael nudged Kasia to not say anything. Charley missed nothing. "I see. We'll have to get to know each other a little better, won't we? I get to know everything I can about my guests. It's good business if you expect to stay alive out here. Know who you're talkin' to. I could say healthy, but ain't nobody healthy in this neck of the woods. Either they've got a brain full booze or cocaine. Believe me. I speak from experience. Pardon me while I go and sterilize my blood." With an erratic wave, he walked off vigorously scratching his ass.

"Is he for real?" Michael stared after him. "It's almost like he stepped out of a movie."

"He's for real," said Kasia. "At least I'm beginning to feel like we're halfway to someplace.

"Shit, except that we stink, I'm beginning to wonder if anything's for real anymore."

As Charley entered the cantina, he clicked his heels and rendered Captain Baravalle a snappy mock salute, then swaggered up to the bar and brought his hand down on the counter with a resounding slap.

The grinning native bartender took the mail sack he was carrying and pushed him a small glass and a bottle of gin. Charley poured one and tossed it off with a gasp. Snatching up the bottle, he buoyantly carried it to the table and straddled a chair across from Carlos and at an angle to Roger Lakein. Resting his chin on the back of the chair, he concentrated on pouring another glass, then firmly set the bottle down.

"Cheers, mates," he sipped this one slowly. "Well, Capitan, how was furlough, huh? Wife and kids happy to see you or did they tell you to get the hell back to the jungle and leave 'em in peace?"

"It is always difficult to come back here where Charley MacIntosh is the height of refinement."

"He sure knows how to pay a man a compliment in a backhanded sort of way, don't he?" Charley grinned at Lakein, who intently watched the act so he could match himself to what was happening. But he conveyed only a mild cordiality. "You with them other two birds down at the dock?" asked Charley.

Lakein nodded with a slight smile. "We're friends."

"Well, Capitan, you can always come over to the Roost and engage in some enlightening thunderbolt conversation with my three gringo guests. Ain't it a shame how important affairs interfere with a man's life?"

"The life of a soldier is duty."

"Knowing you, it can't be by choice. You must have other ambitions."

"Perhaps."

"Your compadres out at the dock seem pretty damn anxious to get started," he said to Lakein, who nodded. "I like enthusiasm and Maggie and I do our damndest up at the Roost. But life moves real slowly around here. I don't recall your name on the advance reservation list."

"Roger Lakein."

Charley extended his right hand across the table. "A pleasure, Roger, a real pleasure. What is it you do for a living that brings the three of you upriver?"

"I'm a travel writer. I write articles for a magazine on foreign travel."

"I guess business has picked up while I've been gone," said Carlos. "My second in command can be lax in such matters."

"When there's – "Charley belched loudly. "When there's no skirmishing, my business tends to pick up. But you send your troops out lookin' for that new big game and they get their ass shot up, business drops in every sense of the word. That's how I read my own local stock market. A basic principal of economics I learned at Harvard Business School. Of course, without a war, we have no solid business. You'd all pack up and go back home, leave Maggie and me and my girls jerkin' off all alone out there on the wild frontier. War stimulates the economy, right? And other important parts."

"When were you at Harvard?" Lakein asked.

"In my salad days, just after War Two. Majored in business administration and hotel management. Look at what it got me."

"You will discover that Charley's life is structured on lies, Senor Lakein, if you stay at the Roost long enough. I'm not certain the real Charley MacIntosh can risk revealing who he is. But he provides a necessary service, and we get along well together, most of the time. So, when does the boat leave? Today? Tonight? Tomorrow?"

"As soon as I pick up the mail and my girl returns with her butt full of penicillin."

"I don't believe what I'm hearing. I expected to be sitting here for at least another twenty-four hours."

"I didn't say when I'd pick up the mail, did I? Ten or fifteen minutes. Don't want to keep our guests waiting. Get them checked in before dark. Besides, I might have new patrons who want to do business by the time we arrive. The compound was hit last night."

Carlos suddenly straightened. "How bad?"

"Don't know for sure. Didn't think it was healthy for me to go pokin' my nose around over there. Might get it shot off by some nervous type. It's red enough and finds plenty of trouble to get into as it is. Intense firefight, old man. Lasted for most of the night. Damn near kept me awake. You'll have to start doin' something about all that noise and outburst. We're civilized folk."

"No wonder the radio contact was out this morning." Carlos picked up his cap and bag and walked out of the cantina.

"That sure sobered him up fast," said Charley. "Before we get on that tub, Mr. Lakein, maybe you'll answer me a few questions."

Lakein waited.

"We ain't on the travel map. Who recommended us?"

"We're here to do a story on the insurgents." Lakein dropped his voice. "The coup is off. Someone informed the *junta*. They confiscated the tanks and artillery and arrested the film crew. It's time for all of us to leave the country, including you and Maggie."

"Thought we knew each other."

"We need a guide and escort and a plane out of the country to Argentina. Will Karazississ give us safe passage?"

"Escort I can provide. Safe passage – that's another story. No guarantee. Ain't nothin' safe in this God forsaken hole. Not even a condom. Everything here rots, especially people and politics. I hope you've got something more than traveler's checks. I want five hundred a piece U.S., if you've got it, up front when you're ready to leave. Call it a nonrefundable retainer. Harvard business."

Lakein took out a money clip and handed him the cash in local currency. Charley quickly pocketed the bills without counting. The entire exchange was done for the benefit of the bartender and any others who might be spies watching and listening.

"Does that cover room and board?" asked Lakein.

"It'll do. How long you plan to stay?"

"Only a short time."

Charley finished his glass of gin. "Let's get started." He rose, then in an undertone said, "Police hot on your ass?"

Lakein nodded. "Navy gunboat. Stopped for a while. Took a break."

Charley went over to the bartender for the return mail sack, then left the cantina. Lakein waited a moment longer to finish his beer, raised a hand in farewell to the trawler captain and first mate and followed after Charley waiting in the street.

"By the way," said Charley as they walked along shoulder to shoulder, "seein' as you didn't answer my question back in there, I'll give you fair warning. If you and your friends ain't who you claim to be, the only passage you'll get from Karazississ is a bullet through the head."

The passengers and crew were all on board waiting for Charley. As Lakein came over to them, Kasia and Michael stepped on, avoiding Carlos, who sat on a crate in the foredeck area smoking what remained of his cigar.

Charley climbed up to the pilot house and started the engine. At a blast of the horn, the screeching girl he had brought for medical treatment came running down the street and around the corner along the dock. Cursing at Charley in Spanish on the chance he was going to leave her stranded in the village, she leaped aboard and scrambled up the pilot house ladder with the penicillin for Emilio.

The crystal-clear mountain water churned as the steamer backed off from the dock and swung around in a sweeping arc until her wide bow aligned with the central channel. Charley thrust the control forward to give her more power. She strained against the frothing current and slowly pulled away upriver deeper into the heart of the forest.

CHAPTER THIRTY-SIX

The Roost

The steamer crawled along the surface of the river like a sluggish beetle between the imposing green walls of alpine rain forest growth.

As Kasia slept, Michael observed the passengers and chugging movement of the mail boat, implanting the impressions in his mind, the hazy surreal timelessness that enshrouded them all.

Lulled by the incessant throb of the engine below the deck, most of the passengers dozed, sweating and reflexively brushing away flies in the oppressive heat. Only the small girl who had walked over to them back at the dock seemed to have any energy as she wandered about fascinated with looking over the side rail at the steamer's pearling wake and watching the gliding movement of the passing river.

Carlos stood, yawning and stretching the stiffness from his arms and legs. After a few minutes of studying the riverbank, he ascended the ladder to the pilot house.

Charley removed his cap and wiped the grime from his forehead. He glanced at Carlos coming up the ladder and through the narrow door, then concentrated on the river channel where it began to narrow up ahead.

"How many times have you made this trip?" asked Carlos.

Charley adjusted the helm to avoid a sandbar evidenced by an innocuous spreading surface ripple a few points off to starboard. "More than I can count or care to remember."

"You sound discouraged, or is discontent a better word?"

"Both Capitan, both."

"Well, we're friends and I feel I can confide in you. I'm sick of the way things are, as well. It is time for a change. The *junta* is not good for this country and its people."

Charley gave him a sharp questioning look, speculating if the comment were an attempt to draw him into a trap. Carlos had no knowledge of Charley's association with Karazississ and the MIR guerillas and mercenaries who were gathering in the mountains and leveling attacks against the smaller remote military installations. Charley had never entirely trusted Carlos and did not commit himself now.

"While I was home on furlough," Carlos continued, "my wife asked me to consider resigning my commission. I wouldn't admit it to her, but the thought has been at the back of my mind."

"And it's just a matter of time before it moves forward."

"With conviction. I don't see any promotion beyond Capitan. I've been out here now for three years. If I'm not assigned duty in Santiago among the politicos, I'm told I'm not likely to advance anywhere. But that society is not for me. I'm not self-serving and brutal enough. They are all opportunists and sadists. To see Pinochet deposed would not move me to tears, although I never made that statement, you understand."

"I understand you perfectly, Carlos. You speaks da English real good, justa like an Italiano."

"You have an abrupt and unusual way of expressing matters that are personal and sensitive."

"Maybe you're being oversensitive."

"It's a strange coincidence that suddenly those three Americans are here. Of course they are not tourists as they claim to be."

"No stranger than you or I, my friend, me *amigo*, and what we do for a living. This is a strange land."

"They do intrigue me," said Carlos. "Especially the woman. She is quite beautiful."

"I'm sure that woman intrigues every man who lays eyes on her."

"Did you know she's an American movie star?" Carlos stared down at her on the lower deck.

"No, where did you hear that? Although I can believe it."

While I was in Santiago on leave, she and her husband were shooting a film. News of it was in the papers and once I saw them on the street."

"Makes no difference to me. They probably finished shooting and are taking a tour. Lakein tells me he was an advisor on the film. He knows South American culture, especially Chile. After all, he's a travel writer. Now me, I wouldn't recognize her on the street. That's not to say I wouldn't look at her. She is something, eh?"

"I would like to know what they're really doing here. Lakein a travel writer," Carlos sputtered.

"What makes you think I can find out more about her than you can?"

"Out here, in this place, Charley, you are a man in the middle. Information seems to find its way to you. I'm not unaware of that."

Charley coughed. "But it's not acquired nor given freely."

"I know. One always pays for the service, but it can be repaid in kind, like political immunity."

Charley shot him a rapid sideways glance. "What you getting at, Carlos?"

"We are friends." Carlos placed an arm lightly across the back of Charley's shoulders. "I know I can tell you things, my opinion about the junta I wouldn't share with another man. We can trust each other and share political secrets. If you only knew how much I despise Contreras and Pinochet. They are inhuman, monsters who should be sent straight to hell."

Carlos paused, his eyes straying below again to the woman sleeping on the deck.

"The appearance of mercenaries and the MIR in the outlands is the first sign of unrest and resistance in five years. Either someone inside is calling the shots or a power struggle is about to take place with assistance from outside the country. I hope you realize, Charley, that you have not gone unnoticed by Contreras and his secret police. His informers and spy network extend even out into these forests, perhaps even one of your whores, or Emilio."

"Ha! Emilio a spy, an informer? Never. He is without politics. Doesn't know the meaning of the word."

"I can tell you there is an active file on you and Maggie at police headquarters in Santiago."

"I have nothing to do with communist insurgents or the Christian Democrats. You know that. I run the hotel, manage my girls, deliver the mail, and mind my own business."

"But considering why you came here in the first place; you would have difficulty persuading Contreras to believe you. Selling defense secrets is clearly espionage and conspiracy."

"Are you fishing, Carlos? You must be fishing. I have nothing to do with defense secrets."

"If you did it in one country, who is to say you would not do it again in another."

Showing no outward sign that what he had just heard had alarmed him, Charley concentrated his focus on the river ahead, knowing that Carlos was watching him closely for some reaction. He and Maggie had entered the country from Brazil under the pretext they were retiring and wanted to manage a hotel they had purchased in the back country of Chile. They had done their research. Their story had been that after studying about and visiting various countries in South America, they had settled on Chile for its climate and the hotel's remote location. Adventuresome vacationers would come there.

The information that Carlos had just revealed could have come from no other source than Roger Lakein. There was no doubt in Charley's mind that Lakein was the mole and had given the information to the police to cover his own ass. But he had made Charley and Maggie out to be Soviet spies, the total opposite of what and who they were. Charley knew that belief could never be altered in the inflexible minds of Contreras and the secret police. Carlos held Charley's and Maggie's lives in his hands.

"The only things I ever sold in my life were a 1956 Dodge convertible with eighty thousand miles on it, a few war bonds, and my soul to the devil."

"Secrets."

"What?"

"That's the problem with you, Charley. You keep too many secrets to yourself. You would be better off without them I guessed long ago you're a communist spy."

"If you only knew how far from the truth you are. But it wouldn't make any difference. I can see your mind is set."

"At heart, Charley, you are a good man and an idealist."

"Don't worry. Idealism isn't contagious in this country."

"Don't mistake me, my friend. I am sympathetic to your cause despite my uniform."

"Maggie and me will be having dinner with our gringos tonight. You're welcome to join us."

A sudden high-pitched whistling "WHOOOSH" rushed toward the mail boat. They looked up in alarm, then fell to the cabin deck as an explosion several yards to the left of the boat sent a geyser of spray over the exposed passengers.

Shouting and screaming, they scrambled for the nearest available cover as a second mortar shell lobbed toward them arcing with an ominous rush of air and exploded slightly astern, raising another shower that drenched all the passengers.

"Keep your head down," Lakein shouted.

Charley leaped to his feet and gave the old steamer full power to surge ahead.

Two of the passengers, soldiers who traveled with the steamer on assigned patrol, pulled a tarpaulin off a mounted machine gun at the bow, lined up on the bank and riddled the undergrowth with automatic fire.

The concussion from the third mortar shell rocked the steamer, throwing the passengers violently against each other.

Within minutes, the boat pulled out of range and the forest again grew silent.

Among the moans of two wounded, a sense of relief swept through the passengers, then a wail of despair from the mother of the little girl drew the attention of the others. As the passengers reassorted themselves and returned to their places, she wept with great heaving sighs over the dead child.

"Oh, Christ," Kasia's heart went out to the grieving woman. "Not her. Not the little girl."

The two native crewmen rushed about inspecting the surface hull for damage. Carlos climbed down from the pilot house and checked with the artillery gunners, then went to speak with the wounded. The sight of the weeping mother cradling her dead child saddened him.

The crewmen reported to Charley that there was no visible damage.

Kasia could not tear her eyes from the trickle of blood that streamed from the child's head down the side of her face.

"We never should have come here," she said to Michael. We never should have come. They're going to kill us. Think of Danielle."

He placed an arm around her shoulders. "We'll get back," he said quietly. "We'll get back."

An hour later, Charley sounded two long blasts on the steamer's horn as the boat approached another military outpost and the adjacent hotel. A small sign lettered 'Charley's Roost' hung out at the end of the dock.

The hotel made a few pretensions to rustic elegance. A small cluster of crude cabins crowded the base of the hill below the hotel. A barbed wire compound containing Quonset huts housing the military unit stretched beyond.

As the steamer coasted in, Charley cut the power, and the engine sputtered to silence. The boat scraped the dock and bumped to a stop rocking slightly at the recoil and the slight chop of the river surface. The crewmen jumped off and secured the boat.

The passengers and two artillery soldiers disembarked. The tearful mother carried her dead child like a small infant and the two wounded men stumbled along assisted by other passengers.

In parting at the end of the dock, Carlos invited Lakein, Kasia, and Michael to dine with him that evening at the hotel. He trudged off through the village to the military compound while they climbed a pathway of stone steps up the hill to the hotel. Shortly, Charley slung the mail sack over his shoulder and left the boat to follow them.

At the veranda entrance, they were met by Emilio, a tall lean Chilean native, a mestizo, with a world weary, patient suffering expression. Shuffling about in worn, backless slippers and old clothes that hung on his bony frame, he assumed the role of desk clerk, bellhop, concierge, bartender, chef, and housekeeper. Ambling over behind the registration counter, he waited for the arrival of Charley and his guests.

Dropping the mail sack on the floor, Charley made short work of the introductions. "Emilio, put them up in the cottage. Here are your newspapers and penicillin." He dropped them on the counter.

"There is a problem," said Emilio in a doleful bass monotone. "The cottage is already occupied."

"Who the hell's in it?"

Emilio looked askance, concerned that it was not appropriate public relations for the hotel to explain in front of legitimate guests the reason. But Charley understood the situation.

"Is it Consuelo? Get that bitch out of there. She doesn't need two rooms for what she does."

"I'm afraid that will be a delicate matter, Senor Charley. You see, she is entertaining a visitor."

"Delicate my ass. Kick 'em both out. These three are a different class of clientele, as you can see. Where's Maggie? Tell her to take care of it. Not even Consuelo dares talk back to her. I'd handle it myself, but I must take this mail down to the village and the compound." He picked up the mail sack and started away. "Give these people anything they want, as long as we have it. It's all paid for." Charley stepped off the end of the veranda and disappeared down the trail through the brush.

Emilio held out a long dip pen to Michael and graciously inquired, "Would you care to sign the guest ledger please, sir."

Michael shrugged at what struck him as an absurd formality and signed for himself and Kasia, then stepped aside and handed the pen to Lakein, who signed with feigned seriousness while Emilio intently studied the signatures in a snobbish manner intended to impress them with his official position. He nodded his approval.

Moving around from behind the counter, he said, "I will have the keys for you shortly. In the meantime, would you care to take some refreshment in the cocktail lounge?" There will be a brief wait until the room is ready. Is your luggage still on the boat? I will see that it is brought up."

"Unfortunately, it was lost," said Lakein.

"Oh, that's indeed a shame, Senor Lakein. Well, if you will please follow me." He bowed slightly and gestured the direction as he then escorted them to a table. After assisting Kasia with her chair, he asked them at large, "Now, what is your pleasure?"

They all ordered *pisco sours*. Emilio nodded solemnly and shuffled off behind the bar. He put a record on an ancient stereo turntable. A scratchy rendition of a Latin tango suddenly blurted from two speakers, startling them. They looked over at Emilio, who returned their expressions of surprise with a flat energy-less grin and went about preparing the cocktails.

Kasia casually scanned the screened open air lounge and dining room protected from the elements by a high pitched log roof and thick wooden shutters propped open just below the overhang.

Emilio brought the drinks, each with an artistic twisted curl of lime. They thanked him for his gracious service. He acknowledged their compliments with a bow, then went off to see about their rooms.

Behind his back, Lakein, Kasia, and Michael grinned at each other.

***

Lately, Maggie MacIntosh had been having dreams that disturbed her, nightmares when she would awaken screaming at something or someone about to come slinking through the door.

Charley told her it was just the booze working on her brain. But she had not been drinking nearly half as much as she used to, mainly because she was just getting too damn tired of it. As it were, they drank now just to endure their lives. She sensed a change burgeoning up from the dark recesses of her mind and that was the spirit coming through the nightmare door.

Now, here she lay on a cot, stinking of sweat and gin in a remote forest region in South America. The possibility she was losing her sanity did concern her. She had just turned forty-eight two days ago and Charley's birthday was also coming up in a few months. He would be fifty-one.

They had fulfilled their end of the agreement. It was time for the CIA to bring the curtain down on their act so they could retire and live out their days in peace.

Lakein had been their Russian contact in Santiago. Acting as informers had exposed them to relatively little risk until the recent encroachment of terrorist mercenaries and MIR guerillas who had been flown in over the Andes from Argentina. The mercenaries came from Libya, the terrorist headquarters of Malcolm Karazississ in the Middle East.

The quiet invasion had occurred within the span of a week. The flying boats carrying troops and supplies had landed on an isolated Andean Lake. Artillery and supplies had then been packed down to the lowland forests by mule and llama to where the mercenaries had established their base camp.

Within another month, using the mail boat on the river, the guerrillas infiltrated to the southern coast at Puerto Montt where the tanks, trucks, and heavy artillery brought in for the motion picture production were expected to be staged along with a supply ship carrying a full munitions arsenal from North Africa.

The plan called for an advanced terrorist force to assassinate Pinochet and his advisors. Troops would move steadily north, take out the naval base at Concepcion, and continue to Santiago.

The mercenaries did not know the plan had been compromised until Karazississ had received the warning message from the Soviet submarine, *Petrov*. A fully armed military strength was tracking and following Lakein, Kasia, and Michael up the river into the forests.

Although Charley's Roost had originally been a CIA code name, Charley and Maggie were suspected by the Chilean secret police as communist agents. They were pushing them now to lead the Chilean army commandos to the MIR camp. The junta had been moving forces up the river to the isolated village outpost for the past few weeks in preparation for the maneuver.

Charley was the only one who knew the hidden location of the MIR base camp. He had chosen to withhold that information even from Lakein, stressing that he was under orders from a KGB agent, which was how Malcolm Karazississ presented himself to Charley.

Charley's original intention had been to put both Lakein and the mercenaries and guerillas in a trap from which there would be no escape. Then, as a prisoner, Lakein would be made to talk.

In Santiago, Contreras, resenting he had not been told from the beginning of Operation Inca, was informed by the CIA that Lakein was suspected of being a mole, but that the CIA wanted to use him to discover a higher KGB source known to be functioning somewhere within the vast American Tri Con Corporation.

They did not inform him, however, or give away Charley's cover that he worked for the CIA. So now Charley and Maggie were suspected by Contreras of being linked to the insurgent MIR campaign.

The ingenious operation Charley had organized and managed appealed to both sides, a brothel for the local government troops and military strategic intelligence for the MIR rebels hidden back up in the mountain forests.

A sharp rap at the flimsy door jolted Maggie's meandering thoughts back to her present reality. "What the hell is it?"

"We have guests, Senora," Emilio's simpering tone penetrated her edgy nervousness. God, with a voice like that, he deserved to get the clap once in a while. Although she had to admit, were it not for Emilio, the Roost probably would have succumbed to apathy and wood rot long ago.

Emilio held the business together and he personally knew many of the government soldiers stationed at the neighboring outpost. They regarded him highly for his ability to turn a filthy backwoods brothel into a crude sort of nightclub where they could dance the tango with the whores.

Emilio watched with a resigned expression at the sounds of thrashing and thumping from within the room. A loud curse preceded the appearance of Maggie as she flung open the door and confronted him in all her sagging naked glory.

Lines of weariness and dissipation weighted her body. With ashes crumbling and falling from her cigarette, she pushed back her greasy tousled reddish mane and scratched and pushed at her drooping breasts as she pulled on a loose flowing green cotton shift. One dirty calloused bare foot scraped an itch on the big toe of its partner.

"Guests? What do you mean, guests? Soldiers aren't guests. They're shit.."

"No, Senora, these are real guests, Norte Americanos like you."

Maggie's interest suddenly sharpened into focus. If they were truly Norte Americanos, then they had to have come from the CIA and were finally going to take her and Charley out of their shit-hole existence.

"Norte Americanos, are you sure?"

She could not handle and endure disappointment, not at that moment. They had to be field agents, but what if they were not?

"Si, they are Norte Americanos."

"How do you know? Except for Charley and me, have you ever seen one before?"

Emilio gave her a withering glance. He refused to be intimidated by her bitchiness. "Senor Charley says they are to stay in The Cottage," he referred to a large duplex cabin a short distance down the hill.

"Where is the son-of-a-bitch?"

"The son-of-a-bitch took the mail to the village and the compound."

"Don't get smart-ass with me, Emilio. Keep your place. You work for me, for us."

He shrugged with disrespectful indifference. "He said to tell you to remove Consuelo and her visitor. They are in The Cottage."

"Where are the Norte Americanos now?"

"They are waiting in the lounge for clean sheets."

"Go tell Consuelo I said to move her ass and her friend's ass into another unit, pronto. Then change the beds. Find some sheets that don't have any piss or blood stains, if we even have any. Whatever, make damn sure they're clean. Nothing is too good for my Norte Americanos."

"*Por Favor,* you know I cannot perform miracles, and I will not be the one to tell that bitch Consuelo. I value my life as well as my balls. She will not hesitate to use the knife."

"Gutless bastard. That means I'll have to do it. How long did the Norte Americanos say they are staying?"

Emilio shrugged again.

"Did they say?"

Emilio shook his head. If they did, I would tell you."

"God, you're conversational. Don't you ask questions? Why the hell didn't you ask them? Shit, Emilio, what kind of hotel clerk are you?"

"Senora, please, I am not a mere clerk, if you don't mind. I am a *concierge*."

Shaking her ragged head, Maggie set herself in a firm frame of mind to confront the vicious Consuelo, the brothel terror. Her bare feet thumping along the boardwalk, she went to The Cottage.

CHAPTER THIRTY-SEVEN

The Charade

Anger festered in Carlos as he followed his lieutenant about inspecting the damage to the military compound caused by the guerilla attack during his absence.

His men were supposed to be commandos, the cream of the crop, as the American special advisors had aptly described them at the time they were recruited and trained. How could they have allowed themselves to be taken so completely by surprise.

The compound showed signs of devastation that demonstrated an enemy firepower of far greater magnitude than Carlos would have imagined possible, especially under such conditions which the guerrillas must have to function.

That only one of his men had been killed and five wounded struck him as a phenomenal stroke of luck. All the others must have either been hiding their heads in the trenches or under the beds or shacked up with the whores at the Roost.

Recognizing that the Capitan was recovering from a serious hangover, irritation that his furlough had ended, and the disgust of having to endure the monotony of the mail boat trip, the lieutenant let the Capitan's tirade and verbal abuse slide over him like a deluge.

Of course, the forceful attack had to occur when the Capitan went on furlough. And the Capitan would have to return incensed in a drunken state of mind and body and blame his poor lieutenant, who had done everything that could be asked of a soldier short of sacrificing his own life, which, Christos forbid, he would resign his commission before even considering as an option.

His professional estimation of the physical layout of the compound was that it had not been either well-planned nor designed to repel sneak attacks from the surrounding forest perimeter. The arsenal should have been bunkered back toward the river, rather than near the forest wall, or even located closer to the village. Instead, the officers' quarters claimed that safety spot and the troop barracks extended only yards from the barbed wire fence.

As a matter of fact, a Private who was a member of the fence repair detail had taken a sniper bullet in the head when the attack hit. The lieutenant determined he would solicit his uncle, a highly placed bureaucrat in the government, to have him reassigned to a desk job in Santiago.

Charley had finished delivering the sparse pieces of mail to a few local villagers and was admitted by a guard into the compound. He carried the bulk of the mail to the post headquarters.

From the standpoint of his lieutenant, the Capitan seemed more intent on planning his evening entertainment at the Roost with Charley MacIntosh than he did about discussing the retaliatory strategy against the guerrillas for their brazen assault. Yes, he would write a letter to his uncle that very night.

Consuelo roused herself and finally rolled her plain-featured ample body out of bed to answer Maggie's insistent loud knock at the door. In an abrasive verbal exchange in Spanish, Maggie ordered her to relinquish The Cottage for important *Norte Americano* guests. She ordered Consuelo to move in with Rosa for a few days.

Consuelo blasted Maggie and her message. Her soldier's erection had fallen just at the moment of Maggie's interruptive knock, to which Maggie replied, "I probably just saved him from a case of the clap."

"Have I no privacy, no rights?"

"Not in this business, baby. Our guests are dignitaries of the highest rank," Maggie smirked. "They must have only the finest we can offer."

"Go fuck a peeg, lady!"

"Listen, you whore bitch, if you and your soldier ain't gone in ten minutes, I'll send you packing down the river on the goddamn mail boat. You take orders from me and don't you forget it. You got any ideas of running, then you better be able to swim real good."

The disgusted, embarrassed soldier climbed out of bed and quickly dressed while Consuelo continued to rant naked about the room waving her hands and shouting with high-pitched squeaks of profanity.

As the half-dressed soldier attempted to leave, Consuelo grabbed his arm and fought him howling back into the room. Shouting in Spanish, ordering each other with contradictory commands, they engaged in a slapping brawl. The soldier finally thrust her away and ran out down the boardwalk past Emilio, who patiently stepped aside as Consuelo roared epithets and shook her fist and flailing tits after the departing soldier, calling him a coward and a pig fucker and to never ask for her again.

Maggie grabbed a bucket of stagnant water from a rain barrel and dashed it in the other woman's face and drove her sputtering back into the room for her clothes.

Pulling on his tunic, the soldier passed on through the veranda and hurried down the trail to the village and military compound.

Maggie decided attempting to improve her appearance before meeting the guests wouldn't make an appreciable difference. She lit a cigarette and walked to the lounge. Her bare feet slapping the wooden floor, she joined the *Norte Americanos.*

"Good afternoon, gentlemen and madam," she extended her hand. "My apologies for the delay. We encountered a slight problem over room priorities that has been resolved."

Michael and Kasia couldn't be sure at first whether this display of poise and the apologies were sincere or not and wondered where the strange behavior originated. The contrast between her haggard dissipated appearance and gracious manner startled them all. They had the distinct impression of witnessing a performance.

"I see Emilio hasn't overlooked your comfort," she said. "Would anyone care for a second?"

They shook their heads. She pulled up a chair and joined them. "I'm sure you can imagine what it's been like living out here for the past five years. It's a relief to finally see you."

Silently questioning the woman's sense of reality, Michael and Kasia exchanged a surreptitious glance.

Maggie flicked a steadily growing length of cigarette ash to the floor. "So what sort of plans does Uncle Sam have for Charley and me?"

Michael straightened in his chair.

"You are all CIA, aren't you?" Suddenly on guard, Maggie stared at Michael, then Lakein, who was working too hard at not seeming to react to what they had just heard while his thoughts made several startling connections through this inadvertent discovery. Charley and Maggie had not come to South America as part of the KGB's deal to hide them in exile. They were double agents working for the CIA.

"Excuse me," said Maggie rising. "I'm going to pour me a drink and change the record. She went behind the bar. Reaching under the counter presumably for a glass, she came up with a submachine gun which she rested on the counter top so that it was aimed directly at them. They froze at the apparent possibility she was mentally deranged and might pull the trigger.

"NOOO!" Kasia stood violently toppling her chair. "Enough! That's enough! When is it going to stop? When is this insanity going to stop?" Her act was calculated to distract Maggie.

Keeping the lethal weapon leveled at them, Maggie walked out from behind the bar.

"What's the matter with you?" Kasia hissed at her. "Who the hell do you think we are anyway? We're not here to get you. We don't know anything about the CIA. We came here because we need your help."

Maggie's bloodshot eyes bulged. "You need my help?"

"All we want is to get out of the country."

Throwing back her head, Maggie laughed uproariously.

Charley was just walking up the hill with his empty mailbag. Reaching the veranda steps, he stopped at the sight of Maggie howling with laughter and threatening their guests with an automatic rifle. He rushed forward, "Maggie, what the hell are you doing? Give me that, for Christ's sake."

"Doing? What am I doing? I'm just getting acquainted." She broke out laughing again.

In seizing the weapon from her, Charley jerked the barrel upward at which moment Maggie's finger pressed the trigger and drilled several rounds into the roof.

Charley ferreted the gun behind the bar. "It's not them we have to worry about. It's who's coming after them."

"And who the hell's that?"

"Contreras's police. We're helping them get out of the country."

"To Argentina?"

"Yes, and we're going with them. So be nice."

"And what happens after that?"

"We'll talk about that later. First things first. Tonight, we're throwing a farewell party, for them and for us, only we won't call it that. These people are guests of honor. Carlos and some of his men are coming over to help us celebrate. They don't know we're leaving, so don't make a slip and say anything."

"Carlos?"

"Capitan Baravalle. He came up with us on the mail boat."

"Five years. We've been here five fucking years. Were they just going to let us rot here?"

Maggie's second reference confirmed for Lakein that he had been sucked into a trap. He must continue to let Kasia and Michael think he didn't know. But when they reached the MIR guerrilla camp, he would turn the tables on them and have them executed as agents of the CIA.

"You kick Consuelo out of The Cottage?" Charley asked.

"You mean you didn't hear her? Emilio is changing the linen right now. I'll get him started in the kitchen. How many do we expect? Thirty? Forty?"

"Better figure on forty."

As Maggie clumped away, Charley poured a straight gin while watching Kasia, Michael, and Lakein, who had not moved from the table. He raised his glass and grinned, "Cheers."

Maggie returned a few minutes later. "It's ready."

They rose and followed her outside to the boardwalk where she directed them to The Cottage. "That's it up there. Supper's at eight. You can drink any time. It's a custom here." She hesitated. "I'm sorry about that upset in the lounge. I guess I was more than a little disappointed." She patted Kasia on the arm reassuringly. "Don't worry, honey. I'm only half crazy and the other half is trying to make up its mind." She watched them walk away and up the incline to The Cottage, then she returned to the lounge to talk with Charley.

"So it's finally farewell to the Roost. You know somebody in Argentina I don't?"

"We're friendly people. We'll manage all right. My concern now is that we don't get caught making the break."

"What are you talking about?"

"Watch what you say to Roger Lakein. If he knew for a minute that we work for the CIA, our lives wouldn't be worth a penny post card home." He saw Maggie's expression fall. "What is it? What did you tell him?"

"I thought – Oh, Jesus Christ, Charley. I thought they were all together and they'd finally come to take us out of here. I'm sorry, Charley. I'm sorry for shooting off my big mouth."

"Damn it, Maggie," he said quietly. "You blew the lid."

He thought desperately. He was sure Lakein wouldn't say anything until they reached the MIR camp. "We can't go back down the river. The way things stand now, the police think we're Soviet spies. Carlos told me they have a file on us."

"And we thought we were so safe and secure up here."

"Not anymore. Lucky for us Carlos is *simpatico* or he would have arrested us long ago. The police think we're helping the MIR."

Shaking her head, Maggie wandered off to the kitchen where she found Emilio banging pots and pans around and grumbling testily under his breath. She asked, "Do you need or want some help? It's going to be forty plus the girls."

"No, am I or am I not a chef? Yes. Do I need help? No, unless you are a sous chef. If I need help, I will command it. Girls? They aren't girls. They're pigs, sluts, whores."

"If you change your mind, call me. Charley's at the bar."

"Charley's at the bar - something I can always count on."

"Emilio, what did I say about smarting off with me? Let's be civilized now, shall we?"

He blasted such an intense snort of derision; the nasal vibration stung the walls of his nose. "I don't want Charley in my kitchen."

"Just make whatever it is you're making good, Emilio. Make it nice – the presentation."

"Do you need to remind a gourmet chef to make it nice – the presentation? No, you do not. Am I a gourmet chef? Yes. Leave my kitchen."

Returning to the dining room, Maggie passed near one of the lower-level units and was stopped by a loud sharp hiss from an open window. Nina, a young, owlish-looking prostitute, motioned for her to come close. In half intelligible Spanish, she warned Maggie to beware of Consuelo, that Consuelo had threatened to kill her in her sleep.

Maggie grinned, patted the fourteen-year-old on the head and continued to her own unit.

In The Cottage, Michael turned from staring out the window and looked across the room at Kasia sitting on a wooden chair.

"Why don't you try to relax," she said.

"I can't." He rubbed his unshaven face. "I don't feel right about them."

"Charley and Maggie?"

Michael nodded. "I'm not sure I trust them to help us."

"Without stretching the point, we don't have any other option."

"Maybe it's because they're tied in with the CIA. That's what's so strange about all this – this hotel. Does Charley know you're an agent?"

Kasia shook her head.

"So you're involved in exposing Lakein."

Kasia quickly signaled to him not to continue as they heard Lakein moving about in the neighboring cottage.

Michael absently shambled around and sat on the other bed facing her, then slowly lay back with a sigh of utter physical and emotional exhaustion. He could not remember closing his eyes.

After cleaning up and resting briefly, Lakein walked down to the dining room where Emilio was pushing a hand cart around and setting tables.

"Mind if I help myself?"

Emilio waved him to the bar. Fixing a strong whiskey and soda, Lakein strolled out to the edge of the veranda and looked down the hill at the river and steamer snugged against the dock. Both appeared sluggish in the muddy orange twilight.

He turned defensively at a slight scuffing noise close behind him. Wearing a provocative chemise, the young prostitute, Nina, smiled a shy disarming invitation. She did not speak any English, but her intent rendered spoken language unnecessary. Her message was unmistakable. He smiled in return and held out his drink to her which she eagerly accepted and took a full swallow, coughing at its unexpected strength.

Emilio took a cigarette break from his hectic preparations and watched the couple walk back through the dining area to Nina's unit.

In her spare primitive room, Nina raised up on her small bare feet and put her arms around Lakein. She pressed her groin against his and rotated her hips according to what the other girls had instructed her a man likes.

Charley rummaged about in his supply warehouse for thirty minutes and emerged with an armload of military combat fatigues, socks, and boots of various sizes. Hefting and readjusting them, he stumbled along the boardwalk and carried them up the incline to The Cottage.

Michael snored loudly on one of the beds and Kasia was just stepping out of the shower when she heard a single knock at the door. She pulled on a clean shift she had discovered hanging in the closet and went to the door.

"Yes? What is all this?"

"All this is for both of you. I could only guess at the sizes." Charley pushed past her into the room and dropped the bundle onto the floor. The dull clunk of the boots caused Michael only to alter the rhythm of his snores.

"Like a babe," said Charley. "So if they don't fit, you can come down to the warehouse in the morning and take something else. We'll be traveling light so we can move fast. Be going through some dense forest for a few days. Can't stop for nothing. When those police finally get upriver to this place, we'll have soldiers on our tail right along with 'em."

"Bachmann is the Tri Con mole. He set us up, all of us."

"I've got the picture. Doesn't matter anymore. There's still soldiers to get past out there in the woods. Well," He slapped his thigh, jerked his thumb at Michael's sleeping form and gave Kasia a good natured wink. "He gonna be on his feet soon, you think?"

Kasia nodded.

"Don't be so down in the mouth, Ma'am. Think of this as an adventure."

"We both know it's not an adventure. I've been trying to get out of The Company for a long time. Thanks for the boots."

Charley walked to the door, paused a moment, then looked back at her. "Once you're in, it's hard to impossible to get free of them, especially when you're in so deep. They're afraid of what you'll do with what you know."

"All I want is to get back to my child and put them out of my life forever."

"Maybe you'll make it." He left, quietly closing the door.

Charley found Emilio down in the kitchen hovering over large steaming pots of food and steamy aromas rising from iron skillets on the stove burners. He glanced briefly at Charley, who seemed to be watching him affectionately for several moments before he spoke.

"Maggie and me are leaving tomorrow – for good."

Emilio nodded slowly in rhythm with his stirring of a thick pasty yellow broth.

"Yeah," Charley popped a slice of goat cheese into his mouth. "We're pulling out with them. So, old man, you've inherited yourself a whorehouse and a pleasure yacht. What more can you ask out of life? How does that make you feel?"

"Blessed, Senor Charley, blessed."

Grinning, Charley placed a hand on Emilio's shoulder. "You're quite a fellow. I'm going to miss you. Did you take your medication?"

Emilio nodded unemotionally and continued to stir the chicken soup, then suddenly held up a sample on the large flat wooden spoon for Charley to taste. "Look out for yourselves – both of you."

"Anybody who can brew up soup like that could make it big in the city."

"As you said, what more can I ask for. I have it all here."

Charley clapped him on the back and walked out through the dining room. He found it a difficult, although finally welcome thought that this would be the last night of his life he would spend at the Roost. He experienced the sensation of a long overseas military tour coming to a conclusion. He continued outside along the boardwalk to his and Maggie's unit.

She sat naked before a wicker vanity and tall mirror while she concentrated on the diligent application of green mascara. She glanced briefly at him as he sank into a chair near two M-16 rifles stacked in the corner. Leaning back, he kicked off his sandals and watched her.

"If there was some way we could go back to the beginning, I'd do it. Only not like this – espionage. That young woman, Kasia, she's a double agent. Wanted out for a long time, she said." He shrugged. "Guess we outgrow the reasons we got involved in the first place."

"Sounds like me. Let's face it, Charley. The way things are happening, we might never see California again. We would have been written up in the newspapers back then. That's what."

"Simple change of identity, pet. Simple change."

"I'll be happy just to get back to civilization somewhere and not be caught in the middle of their goddam politics."

Charley yawned. "Me, just get me clear of South America."

"We'll be all right. We'll make it." He stripped off his shirt, reached into the stall and turned on the shower.

As the thick forest night closed in, Charley flipped a switch behind the bar and transformed the lounge into a night club atmosphere of rustic design that was further carried out by candles Emilio was lighting at each of the tables. Latinized renditions of 40's popular dance tunes competed with an incessant chorus of tree frogs and insects.

Maggie came from the kitchen, pointed here and there giving a last few minute instructions to Emilio, who assisted her in placing cut orchids in slim vases on each dining room table.

At the bar, Charley served drinks to Consuelo, Nina, and ten other girls chattering animatedly in Spanish in anticipation of the soldiers' arrival. Another girl, a singer and dancer, watching at the outer edge of the veranda, saw the dark cluster of soldiers against the lights reflected in the shimmering river below as they trudged up the steps along the forest path. She turned and announced to the others that the men were coming and the girls fluttered from the bar to greet them.

Maggie looked up at the soldiers' entrance, quickly finished with the flowers and went to join everyone in the lounge where they talkatively flocked to the tables and bar.

Up in The Cottage, Kasia finished her letter to Gordon Frasier. She planned to send it through Suzanne Kirkeby advising what had happened to them. If they were caught by Contreras's police, media exposure might help extricate them should they encounter further bureaucratic obstacles after they escaped over the border into Argentina.

If they didn't get out, contact would be essential. Although she was a CIA field operative, that fact was unknown to the *junta*. As far as they were concerned, she and Michael and Lakein were members of a communist plot to overthrow the regime.

Buckling up his trousers, Michael came from the bathroom. "Even if your letter goes down by mail boat, do you really think it will make it out of the country?"

"It's better than doing nothing about trying to establish contact with home. We could just disappear down here, you know that. I really don't want to think about it."

"What if the letter is intercepted. Won't it give away our position?"

"No, it is not likely it will be intercepted. It's coded in Spanish to our housekeeper. But it will go to my CIA boss."

"Who's that?"

"I can't tell you. Anyway, it's better that you don't know."

"When?"

"Someday, when we get back."

"You owe it to me."

A few minutes later, as they entered the lounge, Charley waved them over and set them up with tall gin and tonics. Kasia handed him the letter which he tucked into his shirt pocket and assured her that

Emilio would take it down river on the mail boat within the next few days.

Scanning about, they saw Lakein sitting at a table with Maggie, Carlos, and two of the girls. In the dining room, Emilio began to serve the first course of his gourmet meal to the most hungry trickling in from the lounge.

The level of conversation and the music grew louder toward the end of the meal, the laughter more boisterous. A few of the soldiers had girls seated on their laps. Hands groped up under their tight skirts.

Lakein departed upon finishing his dessert and left Maggie and Carlos alone together at one of the tables. Michael glanced across the dining room to the lounge and noticed that Charley had vacated the bar, as well. He nudged Kasia. The time had come to leave.

Out of sight in the kitchen, Charley opened and quickly read Kasia's letter. He didn't understand the code written in Spanish, but easily understood the reference to travel arrangements and domestic concerns. He touched a match to the paper and watched it flame into crumbling ash.

He and Maggie could not risk any CIA affiliation with Kasia and Michael, especially if the information contained in the letter ever appeared in the American press.

He left unobserved and went directly to his unit to sleep. They would have to get an early start in the morning. He wanted to be miles from the Roost before those SS agents and government troops arrived to place them all under arrest.

CHAPTER THIRTY-EIGHT

The Chase

Maggie sank her teeth into the juicy melon, savoring its sweet pale orange flavor accented with a squeeze of fresh lime.

For the first morning in months, she felt alive and alert to the aromatic smells in the air, the peppery taste of her eggs and the strong black coffee, the excitement of a new beginning. She brushed her hand lightly over the fabric of her khakis and nudged one combat boot solidly against the other.

She paused in mid-bite at the sound of a distant low-pitched hum she was unable to place immediately among the cries of forest birds. Moments passed and the sound registered. She leaped up, spilling her coffee and knocking over the chair and ran madly back through the dining room to her unit.

She startled Charley lacing his boots, as she slammed through the door. Maggie's tense expression told him what he feared. He gave the laces a final tug, snatched up his M-16 rifle and rushed out after her. They jammed in ammunition clips as they ran.

Seeing and hearing the activity from his window, Lakein shouted next door to Kasia and Michael. "They're coming. We have to go, now!"

They rushed outside and met Maggie and Charley on the boardwalk. The still distant sound of the motor drew steadily nearer. Charley warned, "We must keep moving. No stops. No breaks. One long push. We have only twenty minutes on them at best."

Charley took the lead as they clattered off the boardwalk, plunged into the forest behind the hotel, and ran through the undergrowth at a hard relentless pace.

Carlos and his lieutenant stood attentively waiting at the dock. The military launch containing six marines and two agents of the secret police wearing civilian fatigues cruised into sight at a moderate speed. The boat came in cleanly to the dock. Following a brief exchange, the two agents accompanied Carlos to the compound while the lieutenant led the six marines off into the forest along another trail.

As Charley, Maggie, Kasia, Lakein, and Michael pounded along, they did not realize that at quarter mile intervals their direction and progress were being tracked by hidden soldiers with two-way radios who relayed the information back to the compound headquarters. Ten minutes passed before the soldier at the first relay position met Carlos, the two agents and a small patrol moving along the trail at a rapid walk. He joined them.

Charley did not let up on the grueling pace for over an hour until Maggie gasped on the verge of collapse.

"A little further," he encouraged, short of breath himself. "Stream up ahead."

A few minutes later, they broke clear of the woods along a game trail and dropped down at the edge of the stream bank to soak their faces and to drink.

"We can't stay here long," Charley warned. He looked over at Maggie, heaving like a beached whale on the ground, and Kasia, who crawled off into a patch of shade and sponged her face and neck with a wet handkerchief.

Shortly, Charley urged them all scrambling to their feet with the admonition that every minute they spent resting, their pursuers were drawing closer, and they would have to run that much harder to stay ahead.

"We should have started yesterday," Michael retorted, wondering where Charley got his stamina. "What was the point of waiting? We knew it was just a matter of time. We should have traveled at night."

"There's more involved here than you think," said Charley. Only he knew they must reveal the MIR base camp to the agents and commandos and still make their escape.

Crossing the stream, Kasia slipped on the wet mossy stones and plunged hard into the racing waters. Michael waded in and pulled her upright. "You okay? Nothing broken?"

She nodded. "I'm sorry. Should have been more careful."

"They're going on ahead. We must move fast before we lose them. Charley's the only one who knows the way." He supported her as they clambered up the opposite bank and double-timed after the others who had already disappeared around a turn in the trail.

By sunset, they sensed the slow drag of a gradual climb, an indication they were advancing into the highlands. Charley called the fifth brief halt of the day and informed them they would continue until after dark. Weighted by such extreme exhaustion they could not even think coherently, they all shuddered and trembled to the ground.

They walked on at a slower pace until they could no longer see the trail ahead of them. Charley finally stopped and told them to find a place and make themselves as comfortable as they could. From a small pack, he rationed sealed packages of dried food which they opened by the glare of his flashlight.

Lakein was the first to wake just before dawn. He stretched his limbs, cramped from sleeping on the open ground, then stepped off to the side of the trail. The rattle of his piss in the leaves woke Charley, who struggled to his feet and went to do the same.

Kasia, Michael, and Maggie seemed frozen in their semi-curled positions. Charley nudged them awake. Everyone's features looked haggard and swollen, pale in the chill air.

When they were up and moving, he said they would travel for one hour, then stop to rest and eat. Kasia and Maggie grunted from fatigue and stiffness of their bodies as they limped out after Michael and Charley with Lakein bringing up the rear.

Eventually, as they climbed, the forest growth thinned out, offering clearings and meadows and finally as they topped a promontory ridge, the grand splendor of the Andes Mountains reared up its snowcapped peaks in a mammoth panorama that they could not take in at a single glance.

Traversing the steep downside of the promontory slope, they arrived at the encampment of the MIR guerilla forces.

The untrained eye could not readily perceive the hidden camp. Memories of Viet Nam returned vividly to Michael at the camouflaged tents and other structural shelters housing ammunition, food, and supplies. He estimated that what existed at this site could support no more than a few hundred troops. He did not see any trucks or jeeps. A herd of thirty mules provided transportation of supplies.

A guard intercepted them beyond the perimeter. They had been under observation during the last few miles of their approach.

Unless a traveler were aware of the camp's precise location, it would be difficult to find, even from the air. Movement within the camp was minimal and efficient. A patrol passed them headed out quickly back in the direction from which the four had come. Michael recognized the uniforms, berets, and tough professionalism of three mercenaries among their ranks. Several others looked like they had come from Africa and Latin American countries.

The guard led them to an underground bunker which served as command headquarters. Michael felt he had seen the powerful, red-bearded grizzly of a man before. Karazississ scanned the weary fugitives with penetrating fascinating eyes that reminded Michael of a lethal predatory animal.

"Hello, Charley, what brings you here? And who are your friends?"

"My wife, Maggie, and these three just happened to come my way. Police jumped them in Santiago."

Lakein was anxious to have a conversation alone with the leader of the mercenaries and wondered how he could create that opportunity. He wanted to set-up Kasia, Michael, Charley, and Maggie as the ones responsible for the confiscation of the vehicles and artillery by the secret police at the time they were unloaded from the freighter.

"We're leaving the country," Charley continued. "We need a light plane out of here over the big hill."

"Introduce your friends."

"Michael Sloane and Kasia Kerenski. Roger Lakein, he's a journalist."

"I'm Malcolm Karazississ." He walked around from behind his crudely constructed desk as if to personally shake hands with each of them.

Grinning at Charley and Maggie, he exploded a sudden brutal karate punch that slammed Lakein in the face, putting him down hard and out immediately unconscious.

The others stared in shock, wondering if they were next.

"CIA," Malcolm sneered. "He's a double agent." He ordered the guard in Spanish to drag Lakein away and put him in the stockade."

As the guard took Lakein out of the room, Malcolm noticed Kasia closely watching. "You should be glad to see him go. The only reason the two of you are here instead of making your movie is because of him."

"What are you planning to do to him?"

"I don't think you have the stomach for it. It's not that I'm uncivilized, but this is business. You will all join me for dinner tonight. When the guard returns, he will show you the sleeping quarters so you can clean up and get some rest. You look tired," he grinned.

Charley could not understand the turn of events, how Karazississ either knew or had been informed about Lakein. Obviously he didn't suspect him, Maggie, and Kasia. He was pinning all the blame on Lakein, who would die brutally for it.

That night, with moths and insects slamming against the screen, they finished a heavy meal of Llama steaks that added to the soporific effect of scotch and wine. Nodding over their food served in aluminum field kitchen plates, they relaxed and their initial reserve faded.

"I was a small child during the Second World War," said Malcolm. "After my homeland, Greece, was devastated, my family immigrated to America," he fabricated a false history. "We wanted to escape war, the horror, the nightmare, the agony."

He refilled their glasses with wine. "And yet, my life has come full cycle and I am a creator of war. My papa opened a small restaurant in New Jersey. Life was not so bad, until one day a man with a gun forced his way into the kitchen as he and my mother were closing for the night. My papa did not know he had a gun. The man appeared to be hungry. After he had eaten the free meal they provided him, he robbed them, tied them to chairs back-to-back, and shot them each in the head.

"So all my life, I have known war of one kind or another. It is the natural condition of man and society. I learned to accept and profit from it. Would anyone care for more meat?" He lifted the serving platter toward Michael, who shook his head.

Charley's gurgling snore interrupted the monologue. Malcolm glanced at him with a weary smile. "The conversation must be dull."

Maggie stood and shook her husband awake. "Come on. Time for bed."

Charley staggered to his feet and followed her out into the night.

As Michael and Kasia rose to leave, Malcolm called after them, "Sleep well."

The explosion of a mortar shell at the center of the compound woke the entire camp at dawn. The rattle of machine gun fire and crackling spurts from assault rifles punctuated by the shrill metallic rip of grenade launchers sent Michael, Kasia, Charley, and Maggie diving into a bunker a few yards from the tent.

Malcolm was surprised. He had assumed that the patrol sent out on the back trail of his visitors would have ambushed and eliminated anyone following.

Out in the surrounding brush and boulders, Carlos had strategically deployed his troops. His own men were not taking any punishment as far as he could determine and they had the advantage.

By the sounds and firepower of the attack, Malcolm could tell the camp would be taken. He executed one final act before making a run for it. Keeping low to the ground, he crab-walked to the stockade, jammed the muzzle of his UZI submachine gun through the bars and terminated Lakein with a rapid-fire spray of bullets that nearly cut the man in half.

Malcolm then ran in a half-crouch to the mule pen at the rear of the camp, a short distance from the main clearing. Charley spotted him and shouted to the others, "He's making a run for it. Let's go."

Multiple explosions of gunfire rattled at their heels, chasing them in their mad sprint across the compound into the shelter of trees and boulders. The frenzied mules leaped and surged against each other in the corral. Using only ropes and halters, Charley and Maggie waded in, following Malcolm among the rearing frothing animals and snagged two, then led them out the gate.

Michael came into the corral after them with two additional lead ropes, snapped them to the halters of the mules and led them out to Kasia. She snatched one of the lead lines and she and Michael ran after the others on foot. They took the animals in single file among rocks and boulders away from the camp until the explosions and spat of rifle fire faded behind them. Pausing only a few moments, they mounted the snorting skittish mules bareback and rode at a jarring trot after Charley, Maggie, and, further on, Malcolm, in the direction of the rising mountain peaks.

The return fire from the mercenaries and guerillas subsided as they separately and in small groups melted away into the surrounding landscape of scrub brush and boulders. They would survive and either regroup or get out of the country as best they could.

An evacuation plan called for the return of the transport flying boats upon orders from Malcolm to airlift them out. The plan could not go into effect until Malcolm had escaped to a safe position with a radio to contact the flight leader.

Carlos and his men ceased firing. Wary of booby traps, they moved forward cautiously into the compound. The commandos first dropped into the perimeter bunkers, then fanned out to enclose the area on three sides as they made their sweep. They discovered several wounded and dead, including Roger Lakein.

The open corral with the remaining herd of mules foraging about told Carlos the story of the escape. A quick search of the ground gave him the rest of the information, fresh hoof prints in the morning mud along the trail headed off into the mountains.

Carlos's men discovered the headquarters bunker and called him over. Carlos ordered that certain documents be confiscated. He went back outside to where another group of his men waited, sitting and standing in attitudes of watchful repose, weapons at the ready. Three guerilla dead and two wounded lay nearby.

He selected eight marines to accompany him, and they set out along the trail taken by the fugitives on their mules. No more visible than a spider web, a trip-wire made of thin monofilament stretched just a few inches off the ground across the path.

Carlos and the first four soldiers stepped over and missed the wire. The fifth triggered the grenade. Shrapnel passed through the soldier's neck, raked open the back of the man in front of him and gutted the man behind him.

When the air cleared, the forward party rose from the ground and returned to inspect the casualties.

After progressing two miles on the mules, Malcolm, Charley, Maggie, Michael and Kasia gained considerable distance and valuable time which they needed as the trail ascended into a high mountain valley.

CHAPTER THIRTY-NINE

The Mountain

By early nightfall, the moon rode high, reflecting off the sheer rock spirals of the still distant peaks.

Managing with only a cold camp in a small meadow near a stream, the fugitives settled down to wait out the hours.

The mules' ears flagged, and their nostrils quivered with nervousness at the smells and tension on the chill air. Sensing a threat and fearing what they could not see, they ranged at the ends of their rope tethers and shied jostling each other at any noise from the surrounding darkness.

The lethal rush of a mountain jaguar through the camp sent the mules stampeding. Their ropes popped like gunshots snapping from the strain. Malcolm and Charley woke just in time to snatch up trailing ropes of two and hauled them around to a standstill with loud commands of "Whoa" in attempting to calm them.

They heard a roar, followed by a violent thrashing in the brush, then silence.

The death of one of the animals and disappearance of another forced the riders to double up. The additional weight slowed down the mules.

By mid-afternoon of the second day since they had escaped the attack on the guerilla encampment, the diminished caravan ascended a rock cluttered switchback trail that traversed a steep slope.

Malcolm felt secure enough about the distance they had put between themselves and their pursuers that he shot three game birds, which he roasted over an open fire partially concealed by large boulders.

A thunderstorm moved in the following morning, and they watched the massive black clouds festering with lightning slam into the mountainside. Chilling rain fell in a torrent with a clatter and roar soaking them and terrifying the mules so that they plunged about and became hard to manage.

Kasia clutched Michael around the waist and gripped the mule's flanks hard with her legs. Michael held the animal short on the rope as it see-sawed its head, fighting the restraint. Michael shouted and cursed at the mule to keep its attention on him as its hoofs slipped and skittered at the edge of a steep slope.

"If you feel him start to go over, jump clear," he called back to Kasia.

He finally brought the mule into line, and they continued after the others. More than he wanted to get rid of the riders on his back, the mule did not want to be left behind.

Their muscles ached with soreness and fatigue at having to fight the mule and the rain's icy chill cramped them with pain.

The small group had now begun to leave the endless expanse of forest below and had progressed up the gradual face of the slope for five miles when they encountered a slide where the driving rain had loosened the embankment, pouring tons of mud and rock across the trail.

Cursing and wiping streaming water from his eyes, Malcolm dismounted from his mule to assess the density of the slide and if it were passable. The mules could not scale it or traverse around the outer slope without plunging into the deep canyon off to the left. Slipping in the creamy mud, he scrambled up over the boulders, surveyed the blockage, then looked back down at the others.

"Leave the mules," he shouted and turning away, continued on across the uppermost section of the slide.

The others dismounted from their sagging animals. Drenched, slipping and falling in the rocks and mud, they climbed to the point where Malcolm had disappeared. The mules watched them go.

Realizing they had been abandoned, they crowded nose to rump back down the trail seeking shelter.

Swollen by the rain, the wide creek rose not in inches at a time, but feet. Its swift current halted Carlos and his marines as they studied its sudden dangerous increase in width and depth. They decided discovering a better crossing either up or downstream was not likely. After a brief consultation on how to best proceed, one of them volunteered to go first.

A commando lashed one end of a long stout rope to a boulder. A second man held the rifle of the first while he fashioned a loop about his waist. Slowly paying out the rope behind him, he began to wade across. At the center, the chest deep water swept him off his feet. He thrashed to reach the opposite bank and pulled himself out onto a gravel bar with some difficulty several yards downstream from where he had begun the crossing.

Climbing through rocks and brush back upstream, he then securely fastened the other end of the rope around a boulder and waved and motioned to the others to come across.

One soldier slipped, lost his grip on the rope and with a sharp cry was swept away. Minutes later, responding to his shouts, two of his comrades discovered him one hundred yards downstream clinging to a log jammed among rocks at the base of an embankment impossible to scale without a rope. To worsen his condition, his left wrist was broken, so a man would have to go down after him and bring him up.

Carlos was hoping that the storm and the openness of the mountain slope was also hampering the fugitives in some manner and forcing them to stop and seek shelter.

By then Malcolm had led the group into a cave. Wet and shaking violently with chills, they sank to the hard ground and stared in misery at the wall of pounding rain.

With no fuel for a fire and no means of drying out, they clustered together and managed to survive the cold through the sharing of their limited body heat. Malcolm ordered them all into a circular huddle in which they hugged each other and read the mutual suffering in their eyes. Of the five of them, Maggie carried the most fat like a she bear and bore up under the strain better than the others.

"We're going to freeze to death," said Michael.

"This will work," said Malcolm with a hoarse cough. "Just stay together and keep the circle tight."

"This is what's called an Alaskan orgy," Charley's attempt at humor hissed through his rattling teeth. No one laughed.

"Wait a minute," said Malcolm. "Forgot I was carrying this." He pulled some dampened cocoa leaves from his fatigue jacket pocket. "It'll get you high and keep you warm at the same time. Cocoa leaves, make cocaine from it. Indians chew it so they won't get *soroche*, altitude sickness." He passed portions around and everyone took some to chew. They had begun to experience nausea, dizziness, and nose bleeds. The cocoa leaves helped and sent the blood racing through their bodies.

At mid-afternoon, the storm gained in strength, bringing with it hail and stinging sleet. Malcolm worried that the violent weather would prevent them from flying out when they reached the lake where the light escape plane waited.

The hard driving rain lashed them mercilessly as they trudged and climbed the last ten miles to the lake where a docked twin engine seaplane sloshed on its pontoons in the shallows.

Sleet and hail bombarded them like tiny comets. They walked with heads bowed and arms up to shield their exposed faces red and raw from the bone cutting wind.

Malcolm forced open the door and climbed inside to the pilot's seat and control panel. Charley was the last to enter the five-passenger aircraft and disengaged the ropes that moored them to the dock and the shore.

Malcolm looked out at the ice forming on the wings. With some difficulty, he started the cold twin engines. The windows fogged over from their hot breath that steamed in the enclosed space.

"We'll never get over the mountain in this storm," Malcolm shouted back to the others. "We have to go to the coast and head north."

"What about fuel?" asked Charley. "How far will it get us?"

"About six hundred miles."

"Where will that put us?"

"In the desert. There's a railhead at Antofagasta. We'll have to hijack an ore train."

He let the engines warm up for a full twenty minutes while they all crouched shivering in the tiny plane dwarfed by the Andean peaks towering thousands of feet above them.

With the wipers slashing in a feeble effort to clear the windshield of slush and ice, the aircraft moved out from the shore, taxied and lifted bucking into the howling wind whose force set it rocking and shimmying.

Fighting for control, Malcolm immediately pulled away from the peaks and out over the forest headed toward the coast to escape the grip of the storm. Then he gradually angled northward veering toward the sea.

Three hours later, they finally left the gale behind. He remembered there was food on board, not appetizing, but nutritional, cured dried Argentine beef and several pounds of dried cocoa leaves stored in canvas sacks at the rear of cabin.

While the others slept, Malcolm chewed cocoa leaves to ward off fatigue. Flying at only five thousand feet, he kept a watchful eye on the fuel gauge.

They passed several towns and seaports which Malcolm identified from his aviator map, Valparaiso, Coquimbo, and La Serena. Looking down, he noticed how the terrain had gradually changed from cultivated fields to a semi-arid landscape. North of Copiapó, the land transformed into a stark desert, one of the driest regions in the world containing rich nitrate deposits and the location of Chile's major copper mines.

Within another two hours, the fuel indicator needle dipped toward empty. Malcolm could not yet see the port of Antofagasta. He mentally estimated how much longer they could remain in the air and dropped to an altitude of one thousand feet.

The other passengers were awake now, looking expectantly out their windows as the Pacific Ocean and shoreline loomed up at them. Malcolm brought the aircraft down to five hundred feet. He hoped to find an inlet or quiet back water bay on which they could land. Otherwise, they would take a beating and risk capsizing in the surf.

The analog fuel gauge needle eased toward empty. The plane remained flying two hundred feet aloft on reserve fuel. Malcolm spotted an abandoned dredging operation where the tide had created a small lake protected from the pounding surf. He landed quickly and smoothly.

One by one they stepped down onto the pontoons lightly bobbing on the surface. After wading ashore, they sat for a while on the rocks and sand and let the sun rejuvenate them.

Antofagasta was still another ten miles up the rough coastline.

They watched the sun drop imperceptibly to the sea. As it disappeared below the shimmering blue horizon, they began working north along the shoreline and discovered a rutted unused road. An evening breeze sprang up and cooled the scorched land, but the group did not mind the heat after the extreme cold of the mountains.

Toward midnight, they saw the port lights of Antofagasta. The distant deep blast of a whistle came to them on the night wind as an ore train approached the loading terminal. The mines and the port facility ran on a twenty-four-hour operation.

Skirting the port and town itself, Malcolm led his followers inland a few miles until they stumbled on the tracks that ran to the mountain range in this northern sector of the country. They crept in near the vicinity of an intermediate rail switch yard containing lines of hundreds of ore cars, some full, some empty.

Malcolm studied the terrain and observed how the flat gradually rose for about two miles as it left the yard. They quickly followed out the main track to the highest point along the grade and settled down to wait.

Kasia rubbed her hands through the dirt and sand, then slowly wiped the small grains that clung to her fingers off onto her fatigues. She looked over at Michael who sat with his back leaning against a boulder as he stared down and across the sweeping stretch of desert from where they had come.

Her eyes traveled to the faces of the others barely illuminated by the starlight and pale night-shine off the desert. They had all stopped talking to each other long ago, saving their energy for the moment, as though thinking and expressing their thoughts, numb from exhaustion, were a wasted effort. But she felt strongly the emotional connection that they were inextricably bound together, dependent upon each other, a kind of fugitive *esprit de corps.* Together they were overcoming incredible odds in the thick of war and danger to achieve a goal, to escape and to live.

She felt her energy running out of her veins into the earth and she was so weighted with weariness and muscle cramps that she could no longer move. She dreamed her blood was flowing out of her into the earth until a distant sound awakened her.

They heard the train engine and saw only its beacon light for a long period of time before they could discern its black blocky metal frame and string of ore cars as it chugged across the desert flat.

At Malcolm's direction, the group crouched out of sight near the roadbed where they could watch the progress of the train, yet not be caught in the probing glare of its Cyclops eye.

Two uniformed armed guards were stationed at a small wood and metal shack back near the loading platform. One had just stepped outside to smoke a cigarette. He looked up at the whistle of the train as it drew near. The second guard left the shack and crossed to the barracks housing the Indian labor crews and entered the manager's office. Malcolm noted that twenty-five ore cars stood loaded at the side.

The ore train pulled up to the final grade and into the loading area. Carrying a clipboard, the manager, accompanied by the second guard, came from the office and walked to the siding under the yard lights. The train steamed to a halt. There was a brief exchange between the manager and the engineer. The brakeman stepped off as the train then moved onto the track siding and stopped again.

The brakeman uncoupled the last twenty empty cars of the one-hundred-yard train, returned to the engine and climbed aboard. The first guard also boarded the engine to escort the train which slowly pulled away towing the remaining fifty empty cars toward the distant mountains.

Malcolm, Charley, Maggie, Kasia, and Michael watched the train leave the vicinity of the yard and creep in their direction.

"I'll take out one guard and the brakeman," said Malcolm. "You get the other guard and the engineer."

Charley nodded and prepared for automatic fire as the train made its laborious climb. When the engine was within easy range, they opened up, blasting the windshield which shattered as the cab occupants went down with faces streaming blood.

Kasia crouched and turned away, not wanting to witness the horror, the death that happened so suddenly out of the serene night. She was there, a part of it, a bringer of death. Those men were just innocent people doing their job and now they had died for it.

Violence and death pervaded her world, her thoughts, her dreams. Not only must she escape the power of the *junta*, but the acts of death that scarred her memory and her view of life. She saw clearly now that from the beginning she had been a courier of death that happened far beyond the realm of her knowledge, arranged by others, but she was part of the system, to kill and maim, to conquer rather than co-exist.

Remorse filled her that she had not the strength to escape the real murderers and manipulators who exploited so many. She had never been fully aware of that other side, that dark side, only that she had become its victim.

Back at the loading platform, a third guard ran outside at the crackle of gunfire and looked up the track at the train, which was a good mile along. The train did not lose its slow consistent footage. Then just as suddenly as it had started, the gunfire ceased.

Malcolm ran alongside the engine and swung up aboard the cab. Stepping over the bodies, he simultaneously cut the throttle and braked the train. The attached cars strained and clanged to a jarring halt.

Charley and the others raced up to the front of the train. He and Michael uncoupled the car nearest the engine and the entire line of eighty ore cars began to roll back down the grade toward the switch yard.

Malcolm heaved the dead guards, brakeman, and engineer slick with blood to the ground and shouted to the others to climb on as he immediately started the engine forward.

The speed of the rushing ore cars increased as they clanged and slammed rolling loose down the track to the yard. The manager and guard who had remained behind watched in disbelief, helpless to do anything but sprint to safety. At high speed the ore cars rammed and smashed into the others at the siding with a crashing impact that derailed the following cars in a series of resounding metallic explosions.

Free of its tonnage load, the lone engine pulled away upward into the foothills and shortly passed from sight around a switchback curve.

The guard, manager, and a handful of mine workers emerged from behind their shelters and ran along the track to the site of the ambush.

Thirty minutes farther up the track, the night foreman of the strip-mining site hung up his phone after receiving the message and warning from the first manager down the grade. He and an assistant rushed out of their shed to a work crew at their siding where forty heavily loaded ore cars were staged waiting for a pickup. They called over an armed guard and together they looked back down the empty track that approached the loading area. The manager pointed at the single engine pressing relentlessly along the curves and switchback straight-aways to the higher elevation.

Slinging his rifle over his shoulder, the guard ran down along the siding under the yard lights to the point where it connected with the main track at the lower end. He threw the switch so that the hijacked engine would travel off the main track onto the siding when it arrived. Then he posted himself in hiding back in among a cluster of boulders nearby, readied his rifle and waited. Its motors laboring, the engine pulled into view. The guard slammed home a round.

Bristling with weapons from the cab, the engine slowed. Malcolm realized the main track switch had been thrown and would carry them off onto the siding. He cut power and braked the engine.

"We must throw the switch. The bastard put us on the siding."

The hidden guard trained his gun sight on the cab windows. Blowing clouds of hissing steam, the engine halted with a squeal of metal. Charley descended the steps to the ground. Crouching low, he ran to the switch. The guard cut him down with one clean shot, then swung up and sprayed the cab with automatic fire.

A slug slammed into Kasia's left shoulder. The shock and impact immobilized her in a gasping slide down the opposite wall of the cab.

"Kasia," Michael shouted in fear. His eyes flashed away and he caught a glimpse of the guard. He and Maggie returned the fire and saw him fall.

Maggie scrambled down the iron ladder and rushed to Charley's inert form crumpled over the base of the switch. Blood poured from a black hole in his neck.

With a savage cry, Maggie threw the switch. She stood over the body of her dead husband and stared at the small dark ghoulish figures of the mining crew looking down at them. She turned and climbed aboard the waiting engine.

Malcolm opened the throttle. The snorting puffing black monster built power heading up the main track past the siding. As it approached the guard house, Michael and Maggie opened fire. She could not see where she aimed. Her eyes were blurred with tears. The gawking crew scrambled and dove for cover, but two fell dead in mid-stride and three doubled over wounded.

The engine plowed on ascending the grade past the mine.

Blood leaked from Kasia's wound. Gasping and whimpering, she fought against succumbing to unconsciousness from the shock and impact of the bullet. She coughed and choked on the dryness in her throat and wanted to vomit with fear, but could not as a strange weakness she had never known took over her body.

Michael knelt and applied hand pressure to stem the flow of blood that slicked the already slippery floor of the cab. The raw meat smell filled their nostrils.

"Kasia, can you hear me?"

She could barely nod. "I'm sick," she whispered. "Help me. Help me. It hurts so much. It hurts."

Michael was out of his mind with anger and that he could do nothing to take away the hurt and comfort her. He shouted up at Malcolm, "You got us into this mess. Now get us out."

Malcolm opened the throttle all the way, straining the pistons as the engine finally topped a rise onto a rock-strewn plateau.

Kasia's body took over, allowing her to endure the foreign piece of metal imbedded in her shoulder. She dozed in a half faint. Her arm, hands and clothing were soaked with blood. Michael had managed to stem the flow by tearing off a section of his own shirt and creating a pressure bandage over which he kept his hand. He was concerned at the loss of blood. This wasn't like in Nam where he could call for a medic and hook up a pint.

Maggie's expression had gone blank as though leaving Charley dead back there she had left her life alongside the tracks. She stared at the passing landscape without seeing it.

Sixty miles further up the mountain, they drew in sight of a small Araucanian Indian village at the end of the line. The local dwellers gathered in the predawn light to watch as Malcolm and Michael carried the pale wounded woman from the engine and gently lay her on the ground. From the cab, Maggie watched in despair and contemplated putting her rifle to her head.

"Doctor! Doctor!" Malcolm shouted at the curious villagers. "Brujo! Brujo!"

A man ran off in response to the request to bring the village practitioner. He came quickly and led them carrying Kasia to his clinic.

Bare of hygienic and medical necessities, it afforded them only a low wooden bunk on a hard packed dirt floor, a few shelves and two wooden chairs.

Assisted by Malcolm, Michael settled Kasia on the bunk and watched while the local *brujo* and his assistant examined the wound. Maggie looked in sympathetically from the doorway.

Finally, Malcolm said, "We're going on. You with us?"

Michael looked at him in disbelief. "Are you out of your mind? She's my wife."

Malcolm smiled, a small play of his facial muscles, but his eyes gone lethal and cold. He shook his head. "When they get here, you know what will happen. If you're lucky, in the end they will kill you quickly, both of you. To be merciful is not Contreras's style. His torture is slow and goes on for a long time. Pray for a firing squad. If you change your mind, the border is only fifty kilometers from here."

Michael turned his back.

Malcolm hesitated. "You do have one other option. There's an airstrip here. We destroyed the track down at the mine. They won't be able to get another train past until they make repairs. You can get down the other side of the mountain on the mail plane. Maybe you can bribe the pilot to take you into Argentina. If you do reach Santiago, try for the embassy. But if you're caught, once they lock you away in *Tres Alamos*, no one will ever see you or hear from you again."

Minutes later, Michael watched Malcolm and Maggie leave, as they began their climb up the slope above the village.

***

Several villagers had come to the clinic to see the white man and the white woman. Michael noted how different they were from Kasia and himself, their specialized physique. They tended to have deep broad chests to allow for a greater intake of the thin air at that extremely high altitude.

Michael recalled reading about the modified circulatory system of these highland Indians, that their lung sacs were permanently dilated to provide a maximum surface for the transference of oxygen into the blood. They also possessed a greater volume of blood than lowlanders and larger red blood corpuscles to carry the oxygen. Even their heart size was larger than normal. Their arms and legs were short and hands and feet small to accommodate the pumping of blood from the heart and also reduction of the surface exposed to freezing temperatures. Mountain natives were known to walk barefoot in the snow with no discomfort.

Michael watched the stolid, brown-skinned little man with his quick intense dark eyes as he made the incision at the bullet's point of entry. Holding Kasia's hand, Michael marveled at the consummate skill and deftness that accomplished the fete of lessening the pain, for Kasia flinched only slightly as the *brujo* probed for the slug without benefit of an anesthetic, although by then, Kasia had fainted.

His assistant swabbed the blood flow, which he encouraged as a natural means of cleansing the wound. At the point of removal, Kasia suddenly woke and a weak cry broke from her. The *brujo* stopped and she slipped back in unconsciousness, more from shock and fatigue and loss of blood than from the minimal pain.

The *brujo* did not suture the wound but applied a kind of herbal paste which immediately cauterized it. Then he neatly bandaged Kasia's entire shoulder and upper portion of her arm.

That night, Michael purchased fuel from a local villager to maintain a barely adequate charcoal fire glowing, their only source of heat against the pressing mountain cold. He also wrapped her thoroughly in quilts and blankets borrowed from the *brujo* and spoon-fed her a hot broth consisting of herbs and chicken stock.

From time to time, he went to the door to stare up at the forbidding mountain peaks and infinite rich black sky brilliant with stars. He was finding it difficult to bridge the reality between where he and his wife had come from and what had happened in between. The perception was as if he had stepped into one of his own films and was living out its reality rather than creating its fantasy.

By the following morning, Kasia tossed and moaned and was sweating delirious with a high fever. Michael ran to the *brujo's* house, woke him and brought him quickly to the clinic. The *brujo* touched Kasia's pale emaciated face and uttered a single word, "*Veneno.*" He pointed to the swelling redness radiating outward from the vicinity of the wound and Michael understood at once, blood poisoning.

They watched the mail plane climbing out over the valley, gaining enough height to make a landing on the cleared field near the village. Supporting Kasia, Michael walked out accompanied by the village magistrate to meet the plane as it made a brief taxi in. Its World War II vintage double props sputtered and backfired as it finally swayed to a halt on the uneven strip.

The side door was kicked open and the co-pilot handed down the canvas mail sack and took the return mail aboard. Then while Michael and the magistrate talked with the pilot, who had stepped out to stretch his legs and enjoy a quick smoke, the co-pilot walked away several yards and pissed into the rocks near the tail of the battered aircraft.

The flight down the mountain subjected them to a rapid series of stomach lurching drops while unyielding heavy winds slammed and buffeted them from side to side. Through one of the porthole windows, Kasia watched the wing flaps adjusting up and down against the cold violent turbulence.

After several hours and three heart-wrenching landings at the three other villages enroute down the wild slopes, the terrain leveled out onto the desert flats. They came skimming in low over the wasteland that dwarfed a small airstrip, boasting an asphalt landing pad and a few additional commuter prop aircraft of a similar age and condition to the mail plane.

The adjoining village was not much larger than those they had left behind at the higher altitudes, only now the air was hot, dry, and oppressive.

Since there were no boarding houses or inns, they had to spend the night in the mechanics shed, which doubled as a terminal office. The pilot provided them with cots and a small amount of unappetizing food and tepid water, as well as several beers.

In the middle of the night, Michael woke at a sharp metallic click and stared into the barrel of a rifle held by a government soldier. His eyes were drawn to the surrounding shapes and shadows of ten others and an officer barely illuminated in the greenish half-light of the hangar.

Kasia could no longer even sit upright and had to be carried to the waiting truck. With hands tied, Michael was kicked and prodded into the truck and forced to lie on the floor while the soldiers rested their boots on his back.

Michael knew that if Kasia did not receive adequate medical attention soon, she would not survive. Yet, he had no way to convey this fact or to gain the cooperation of their captors. Had he known where they were being taken, he would have attempted to at least say something, to make a final try before they were thrust within the terrifying walls of *Tres Alamos*.

CHAPTER FORTY

The Prison

Michael's sense of helplessness outraged him, that he could do nothing for Kasia and himself. That they were at the total mercy and control of a brutal political force that did not account for human need or emotion terrified him.

Heavily armed guards roughed him along drafty stone passages behind the impenetrable high gray walls of *Tres Alamos*, the Santiago prison facility feared by everyone for its medieval tortures, squalid primitive conditions, and sadistic guards.

As his three guards marched him into an empty cell, two grabbed him by the arms and forcefully hurled him against the far wall. He twisted at the last moment to absorb the impact against his right shoulder, but the momentum of the savage thrust was so great and sudden, the side of his head cracked against the damp, lichen-covered stone. Stunned he slumped to his knees. He remained leaning back against the wall as a ribbon of blood trickled from his scalp past his ear and down his neck.

He gave no sign of resistance, steeling himself and absorbing the incredible pain that weakened him. His body recoiled reflexively at the brutal kick to his ribs that left a searing burn somewhere deep inside. Curled on the floor, he knew instinctively that one or two ribs had been broken. For the moment, he couldn't move and did not dare for fear of puncturing an organ. Protecting himself with his arms and knees, he tucked in his face and prayed they would not rain him with any more injuring blows. To his relief, he heard their footsteps move away and the resounding clang of the solid metal door followed by the thunk of the heavy iron lock.

He stayed in his curled position for several minutes, then slowly unfolded his limbs one by one, cursing the fact that he was now so incapacitated by pain. His blurred vision moved from the rusted slop bucket in one corner to the hard spare cot in the other.

As he extended his left arm for the blanket, he hesitated, quickly drawing it back at the sharp jab of pain from the lift of his broken ribs. Holding his bruised right side with his right hand, he slowly stood, supporting himself against the wall with his left. He shuffled slightly bent to the cot. He listened for a moment to footsteps and voices outside his cell door before lowering himself to a seated position.

His thoughts went out to Kasia. Had they just thrown her wounded into a cell such as this? He thought about the letter she had given to Charley to have been sent down the river on the mail boat. That was their only chance to make contact outside the country, provided the letter had made it through to the states. Even then, the content of the letter had indicated they would be crossing the border into Argentina.

They had not been gone from home long, a little over one month. So there was no reason for anyone in California to be searching for them, with one exception. Roger Lakein had said the film production crew would be sent back to the United States. They would not be detained. Surely someone, at least his production manager, would seek the help of the U.S. Embassy in Los Angeles to arrange for his and Kasia's extraction and safe return.

Now, there wasn't even a remote possibility that anyone would know they were locked away in *Tres Alamos*.

The more he thought about their irreconcilable situation, the more depressed he became. He needed to see a way out for them. Help must somehow come through those massive concrete walls from the outside or else they would have to resign themselves to whatever misery and torture was in store for them. They had no strength or means to fight back.

Kasia's guards had locked her in an isolated cell. Barely conscious from her fever, she sat on her cot with her back reclining against the cold stone wall.

She could not fathom from where her body pulled its strength and resiliency to stave off the infection. She experienced moments of absolute lucidity followed by a despair that plunged her into blackness.

Later, when a guard returned with food and water, he thought she was on the verge of death and went to consult with the prison warden. The guards had been ordered by Contreras to keep the two prisoners alive and able to be used for purposes of propaganda against communist sympathizers. His intent was to illustrate how far the communists would go to infiltrate Chile, which fully supported and cooperated with the CIA, the United States Government and its corporate interests in Chile.

A nun came from the infirmary to examine Kasia. She stated that if the prisoner did not receive immediate treatment, she would die in twenty-four hours. The warden ordered that Kasia be taken immediately to the crude medical center.

During the next week, Kasia was dosed heavily with sulfa and penicillin. Her fever abated and she began to question what had become of her husband. The nuns consistently responded that no information was available from the warden.

Following her recovery, she was transferred to a communal cell overcrowded with women of all ages. Haggard and unwashed, they assessed her strength and saw that she was thin, pale and weak and posed no threat to the leaders among their subgroups.

Gabriele Montalva instantly recognized Kasia and brought her through the cell to a small cluster of women in a corner. These were wives of men who had been in the communist party when Pinochet had seized control of the government.

After explaining her situation, Kasia asked, "What are my chances of getting out of here alive?"

"I've been living in this cell for three years and never had a trial. It would just be a circus anyway. In the beginning they tortured me."

"Three years, like this?"

"I was arrested shortly after you and your husband came on your location tour. Some prisoners have been in here for eight and nine years. After a while you forget what it's like outside and accept and adjust to it. If you resist too much, you can die quickly. The longer you fight it, the more they will torture you. Some here have lost their sanity, as you can see. But once you're in here, you either become one of us or you're an outcast. And then you become fair game."

"Meaning?"

"We live by a whole different code in here. Did you notice how the others looked you over when you came in? I can point out two leaders who will be fighting tonight for the right to claim you. A woman as fair and as beautiful as you are, unless you're strong enough to fight back. If they decide they want you and you fight back, they will gang rape you. My advice is don't fight it when the time comes. I did and regret it to this day. Now, instead of being a bitch to one of the dykes, I get passed around. I'm considered community property.

"We have a whole society in here," Gabriele continued. "Everybody has a specific level and function. There's a pecking order, something like in a hen house all the way up to the cocks, the bull dykes. Depending on how strong and smart you are, you can work your way up the pecking order. But each time it will mean a challenge and a fight. It's not pretty to watch."

She motioned to two of the strongest dykes, each surrounded by their "ladies in waiting." "The dykes see you as some golden virgin princess from the outside world. Because of your beauty, one of them will make you her queen, the queen of her harem, provided you do not fight her. But others will be jealous of you. Once you are a queen, you will not have to fight though. Your dyke will fight for you."

After the guard had come by on his final rounds for the night, the women in the large cell silently rose and formed a circle, creating an arena for the combatants. The guard had been informed and bets were taken among the others as to the outcome.

Stripped totally naked, the two women entered the circle, snarling epithets at each other in Spanish which were chorused by their harems.

With bare feet slapping the concrete floor, they stalked each other, feinting with their hands and oil glistened arms. Bernarda, the thin one, occasionally flashed up a martial arts kick. In spite of her bulk, Bernarda's opponent, Lupe, moved with short bursts of amazing speed. It was she who landed the first effective blow to the side of Bernarda's head amid a scuffle and flurry of strikes and parries.

Bernarda fell stunned, rolled away reflexively and barely escaped Lupe's great ham feet crushing her ribs. Lupe leaped onto her and the two sweating bodies interlocked. Bernarda's thumb found Lupe's eye and dug in. With a howl of rage and pain, Lupe released her and rose to her knees, clutching at the gouged eye, as Bernarda's supporters screamed in triumph.

Bernarda's foot suddenly smashed into Lupe's face with such force it flipped the heavy-set woman over onto her back. The tall woman's hard heel rammed down against Lupe's pubic bone. Clutching her eye and groin, Lupe rolled away, and the fight ended among cheers for Bernarda and boo's and coarse profanity for Lupe, who was assisted off to another area of the large cell by her faithful seconds. They caressed her and crooned to her until she savagely shrugged them off and ordered them to call the guard. When he came, she told him she needed to go to the infirmary to have her eye treated and her pubic bone examined.

At the opposite end of the cell, the crowd parted to allow Bernarda to approach Kasia, who stood straight and rigid against the wall. Her eyes never left those of the sinewy nude woman, whose lean, sweat-streaming brown body confronted her.

In halting Spanish, Kasia said she would not resist her, but that she, Kasia, was diseased with syphilis and had only recently been treated.

Angered, Bernarda said, "I'll have you taken to the infirmary and checked. They will tell me if you are lying. If you lie, you will pay. You are going to be my lover and I will protect you and do everything for you and you will do everything I command."

Bernarda rose on long flexing legs.

Kasia had heard the words she needed to hear. Once she was admitted again to the infirmary, she would carry out her plan.

The next morning, at Bernarda's request, the guard escorted Kasia to the infirmary. She was ordered to wait in the clinic until one of the convent nurses could give her a preliminary examination. Only in progressive or emergency cases were medical doctors involved. These, by and large, were interns from local hospitals seeking experience and a few extra dollars.

As she sat waiting, Kasia saw Sister Terracina, a young nun who had cared for her during her treatment for blood poisoning, pass through the holding area. Kasia called her name and the sister turned and smiled in instant recognition. She rose and taking the nun by the arm, maneuvered her into a corridor where they had some temporary privacy.

Sister Terracina was different than the older traditional nuns. Kasia had detected this from the beginning. During the period while her fever was at its height, Kasia had recalled Sister Terracina sitting at her bedside consoling her and listening to her babble through her delirium.

Kasia hurriedly related her current problem to the young sister and asked for help in getting an infirmary bed. Kasia then discreetly asked Terracina to help her escape. She promised that upon her return to the United States, she would send a large sum of money to the convent.

Being simple and affectionate as opposed to complying with the accepted code of silence except when communication was necessary,

Sister Terracina did manage to get a temperature reading entered on Kasia's chart that established the possible recurrence of her infection.

Later that night, the compassionate sister returned with a nun's habit of her order concealed under her own cloak. Kasia changed hastily in the commode, accompanied Terracina on her rounds, then left the infirmary and returned with her to the convent.

Terracina had shared her confidence about Kasia's escape with one of the other sisters whom she trusted not to reveal the plan. She cautioned that they be extremely careful, because even among the sisters, there were those who would turn informer in deference to the Mother Superior, who coveted and harshly applied her authoritarian powers.

Kasia offered to take Terracina back to the United States with her, rather than risk discovery and retribution. She detected the young nun's fear and wavering uncertainty.

Terracina had entered the convent at the insistence of her parents, who had already married off seven other daughters. They had wanted a member of their family in the church and, since all four sons had declined studying for the priesthood, Terracina had been programmed from early childhood for her destiny as a nun. She asked that Kasia return the kindness and help her to escape from a life that she did not wish to live and to take her to America.

They rose early and walked side by side through the dawn light to the gates of the American Embassy. A guard admitted them when the doors were opened. Kasia identified herself to the secretary clerk, who disappeared into an adjoining office for a long period. When the man returned, he said that Kasia and Terracina would have to wait, but that a field diplomat would consult with them.

As the time ticked by, Kasia grew increasingly nervous that nothing was going to be done to help her and her husband, as well as Terracina. Thirty minutes later, a man with chilling blue eyes opened the office door and asked only Kasia to enter.

She sat across the desk from him and gave a detailed account of all that had happened to her and Michael since they had entered the country more than a month ago. She realized he was taping the interrogation by his leading questions. She did not admit to discovering that Roger Lakein was an operations agent for the CIA, but she did say he had been killed. The man did not express surprise.

Two hours later, he left the office briefly, then returned and informed her that he would arrange for her and her husband to leave the country that night, but that Terracina had decided to return to the convent. He explained that Terracina had already departed. "She asked me to tell you that she had a change of heart and felt she needed to give care and comfort to the prisoners. She couldn't leave them behind. She's safe. She's being escorted in an embassy staff car."

Knowing that the embassy staff member had railroaded Terracina, Kasia repressed her anger.

"The local authorities will resist once they learn you have escaped," he said. "Certain concessions have to be made to allow them to save face."

Kasia understood that turning in Terracina had been the concession. After she was tortured, Sister Terracina would likely take Kasia's place in the communal prison cell. The arrangement was another factor in the long list of international diplomatic intrigue that sickened her.

At one o'clock the next morning, she was accompanied by two agents in a staff car to the air terminal. When she asked why her husband had not been released to go with her, she was told he would be returned under a different arrangement. The news terrified her, but she was in no position to argue with them, let alone question what that arrangement would be.

She boarded a special U.S. military flight that stopped to refuel in Panama, then continued on to an air base in Texas. There, she was further debriefed by a CIA staff member as to what she could and could not say to the press and broadcast media about her experiences, if she ever expected to gain the release of her husband from the Chilean authorities.

Gordon Frasier had flown in from California to observe her in the interrogation room during the entire debriefing. All evidence indicated that Roger Lakein had been in collusion with someone high up in Tri Con. Along with several others, Helmut Bachmann was a prime suspect. The FBI would investigate, freeze the assets, and shut down the Tri Con Corporation for alleged conspiracy. In the meantime, the state department would negotiate the release of Michael Sloan and bring him back to the United States.

Kasia slept the full three hours on the military flight to Los Angeles. She was holding her child, Danielle, by four o'clock that evening.

EPILOGUE

The Termination

Helmut Bachmann finished his breakfast of fresh trout and poached eggs, then moved sluggishly into the bathroom to shower and shave. He had hoped to get away early the previous evening, but his hosts at the private dinner party at the Russian Embassy would have called him on protocol. Drinking endless shots of vodka did not appeal to him.

He believed the agents at the embassy drank so much to endure their assignment. Mexico was not considered one of the more desirable missions. They had not concealed their envy of his arrangement in the United States.

A little over four years had passed since he had seen or personally spoken with Malcolm Karazississ. Malcolm's principal contact had been through the Russian Embassy in Mexico City.

The phone rang. He answered quickly, then recognized the caller.

"Hello, Bachmann," the full bass voice sounded in his ear. "I'm down in the lobby."

"Come on up." Bachmann slipped the receiver back onto the cradle. He buttoned his shirt. Before answering the knock at the door of his suite, he turned on a tape recorder built into his attaché case with hidden condenser microphones in the handle.

"Hello, Malcolm," he greeted him with a smile and firm handclasp. "It's good to see you. Have you had breakfast?"

"Yes, before I came over."

"How about a cup of coffee or perhaps something heavier, a bloody Mary?"

Malcolm shook his close-cropped red head. The beard and long hair were now gone. Only a trim mustache remained.

"Sit down. You look in great shape. So things fell apart down there. How unfortunate. I'm interested in hearing the details. But first you mentioned you have some special information."

"It relates to the aborted MIR mission. It also raises an important question that needs to be clarified."

"Go ahead."

"Charley MacIntosh and his wife came to my camp on the run from police agents and government troops. Roger Lakein, that film director, Michael Sloane, and his wife, Kasia Kerenski, were with him."

"What?"

Malcolm nodded solemnly. "Lakein was a double agent with the CIA. I terminated him."

"Did the others escape with you?"

"The woman, the movie star, was shot."

"Killed?"

"No, badly wounded. I left her and her husband in a mountain village. They were going to take the mail plane to Santiago and try to reach the American Embassy. I imagine they were caught and arrested."

"We can salvage that situation, maybe even get some mileage out of it. What about Charley and Maggie?"

"Charley was killed in a firefight. I left Maggie in Argentina. You can contact her at this address." He handed Bachmann a slip of paper.

"I'll see that she's taken care of." Bachmann studied the Greek. "It was a good effort all the same. I have another mission for you."

"Do I get a preview?"

"If you like."

"Of course."

"On the way to the airport then, in some detail. The logistics will not be as complicated as this last time. I need a few minutes to finish packing."

"I'm in no rush."

Bachmann called down to the desk to ensure a limousine would be waiting, then arranged and closed his suitcase and suit carrier. A few minutes later, the bell captain came for the luggage and Bachmann and Karazississ followed him down the elevator to the lobby.

While the bell captain placed the luggage in the trunk, the driver held open the passenger door for them to enter. Bachmann went in first. The door was closed, the driver took the wheel and the limousine pulled smoothly and quietly away from the hotel.

"It's a beautiful city," said Karazississ.

"I especially like the architecture," said Bachmann.

"Yes, it has an elegant old-world style."

Bachmann craned his head slightly to view a cathedral they were passing. He froze at the hard blunt end of a silencer pressed into his ribs. Slowly he turned back and stared at Karazississ.

"Here?"

"No, I'm taking you to Moscow."

"Five million in a Swiss account for a different destination."

Karazississ shook his head. "You've taken too many liberties, Boris Sergeivitch Karavslosky. Mother Russia wants you home."

"There is only one other person who knows my real name."

"Now there are two."

Bachmann looked at the driver who was watching him in the rearview mirror.

Karazississ smiled. "Three."

ABOUT THE AUTHOR

Author and retired business and management consultant in a wide range of industries throughout the country, Rob resides with his wife in Southern California.

He is a graduate of the University of California, Santa Barbara and of the University of California, Los Angeles with Bachelor's and Master of Fine Arts Degrees. He is a recipient of the Samuel Goldwyn and

Donald Davis Literary Awards and has also worked in advertising, corporate communications, and media production.

An affinity for family and generations pervades his novels. His works are literary and genre fiction that address the nature and importance of personal integrity. Keep up with Rob on his website:

www.rmtauthor.com